Once Upon a Time: A True Story
Black Knight, White Knight
Never Say Good-bye

The Memory Book of
Starr Faithfull

THE
Memory Book
OF
Starr Faithfull

A NOVEL

Gloria Vanderbilt

ALFRED A. KNOPF

NEW YORK

1994

My thanks are due to Anderson Cooper, who first put the manuscript on disk—through many rewrites his faith and kindness never faltered. To Corona Machemer for her editorial inspiration, her patience and perseverance. To Sonny Mehta for his guiding spirit. To all those at Alfred A. Knopf who worked so hard to produce this book. And as ever to Bob Gottlieb.

THIS IS A BORZOI BOOK PUBLISHED BY ALFRED A. KNOPF, INC.

Grateful acknowledgment is made to the following for permission to reprint previously published material:
Donaldson Publishing Co., George Whiting Publishing Co., and CPP/Belwin, Inc.: Excerpt from "My Blue Heaven" by Walter Donaldson and George Whiting, copyright © 1925, 1927 (copyright renewed 1953, 1955) by Donaldson Publishing Co. and George Whiting Publishing Co. Rights for George Whiting Publishing Co. for Canada controlled and administered by EMI Feist Catalog, Inc. International copyright secured. All rights reserved. Used by permission.
Edward B. Marks Music Company: Excerpt from "Manhattan" by Lorenz Hart and Richard Rodgers, copyright © 1925 by Edward B. Marks Music Company, copyright renewed. All rights reserved. Used by permission.
Harold Ober Associates Inc.: Excerpt from F. Scott Fitzgerald letter to his sister, copyright © 1974 by Frances Scott Fitzgerald Smith. Reprinted by permission of Harold Ober Associates Inc.

Library of Congress Cataloging-in-Publication Data
Vanderbilt, Gloria, [date]
The memory book of Starr Faithfull : a novel / Gloria Vanderbilt.—1st ed.
p. cm.
ISBN 0-394-58775-8
1. Girls—New York (N.Y.)—Sexual behavior—Fiction.
2. Young women—New York (N.Y.)—Fiction. I. Title.
813'.54—dc20 94-271 CIP

Manufactured in the United States of America
First Edition

To Wyatt Cooper

"Treasure all love."

Author's Note

In 1939 I came upon an article in a magazine about unsolved mysteries. There, as I turned the page, was a photograph of a girl who was very beautiful, with a face soft as a flower, tender and vulnerable. She was someone I wanted to know. Her name was Starr Faithfull, a magical name . . . but who was she really, and what had set her upon the dark journey suggested by the headlines surrounding her?

I wanted to keep her picture and I cut it out of the magazine, and over the years I thought about Starr Faithfull and from time to time read about her. In 1949, *The Aspirin Age*, edited by Isabel Leighton, included a piece about her by Morris Markey, originally published in *The New Yorker* in 1931. John O'Hara is said to have based his Gloria Wandrous of *Butterfield 8* on Starr. In 1977 Sandra Scoppetone's novel *Some Unknown Woman* presented her version of Starr and the circumstances leading to her violent death.

I knew that someday I too would write about Starr, and began collecting everything I could find about her. I combed through the back issues of newspapers; one article in particular, from the New York *Evening Journal* of Wednesday, June 10, 1931, struck me:

KIN AMAZED AT JEKYLL-HYDE LIFE OF GIRL. To adoring members of her family, Starr Faithfull appeared as a quiet, reticent, undemonstrative girl, preoccupied with her studies, remote from all the sordidness that lay in the great world outside their cozy apartment at 12 St. Luke's Place.

Her attractive, brown-haired mother, Mrs. Helen Faithfull, was the first to cry out in swift protest at rumors that the seemingly shy girl had been involved in cocktail parties and flirtations with strange men at the Cunard Line pier shortly before she was murdered.

"Our Starr," she murmured, despairingly. "It can't be true. She wasn't interested in boys or young men. Of course, she knew some officers on the Cunard Line, for we made trips to Europe, every one of them on boats of that line. But she didn't know them intimately—as friends!"

What was Starr Faithfull *really* like? All of her own that remained was a few letters printed in the tabloids. Even the diary she kept, which she called her Memory Book, had disappeared.

It was this, Starr's Memory Book, that kept filtering through my imagination over the years. Diaries fascinate. Do we confide to them our secrets only for ourselves—or for others to see and know us as we really are? Surely we intend them to reveal the truth of ourselves. But what is truth? We all have our own realities, our own truths. This book is mine, about the lovely, elusive girl whose fairy-tale name, foretelling a happy ending, belied the destiny that awaited her.

G.V.

The Memory Book of Starr Faithfull

1917

*D*ear Diary,

My name is Starr Wyman. Before I was born a fortune teller told my mother that she would bring a star child into the world and that it would be a special gift from God — and guess who arrived? Me. Today is my birthday. I am eleven years old. On the way home from school I spent all the allowance I had saved on you, dear Diary. From now on I'm going to tell you everything. I live on Davis Street in Evanston, Illinois, and my mother's name is Helen and my father's name is Frank W. Wyman II. My sister's name is Tucker but we call her Tooka. She will be six on January 28th. Her birthday is so close to mine that we always have her party on my birthday. I am in the fifth grade at the John Dewey School. Tooka does not go to school yet. We have two cocker spaniels called Puddin and Pie. My Daddy was born in Natchez, Mississippi, and my mother was born in Boston. We never see our relatives in Natchez because Ma doesn't get along with them. All she talks about is Boston and her relatives there. When I grow up I will do something important and be famous and have lots of children. My husband will be handsome and famous and very rich. We will go out dancing and have horses. That is what I would like most, yes — dozens of horses. I wish we lived on a farm instead of in this old house. I wish I didn't have to go to school. I wish Daddy would not be away so much and I wish Ma would stop fighting with him about moving to Boston. Daddy wasn't home for my birthday, but he sent me a complete set of the Elsie Dinsmore books. My mother gave me a white neckerchief. It has "To Starr Love from Mamacita" stitched in red in the corner. It is the prettiest one I have and I will never ever give it up when Camilla Foldes and I play Let's Trade. I want to tell you

3

more about Camilla, but not now. Now I want to tell you about the birthday party. All my friends from school came except Camilla. She had a cold and had to stay in bed. Ma was in a good mood. She always is when Daddy is away. She made an Angel Cake for me and another one for Tooka. Mine had pink icing with candy silver stars all over it and eleven silver candles around one tall one in the middle to grow on. There were only six candles on Tooka's cake and no stars and she made a fuss. When I blew out the candles I made a wish. I am not supposed to tell anyone what the wish was, but that means people. Besides, I said I would tell you everything! I wished for a white horse with a black star on his forehead. I will call him Black Starr and ride him all over Evanston. Everyone had a good time until Tooka started throwing cake at me. It missed and got all over the rug and was Ma mad! She took Tooka upstairs and locked her in her room. We could hear her banging on the door to get out. She just would not stop. I'd better go to bed now. Bye.

I have just finished reading the first Elsie Dinsmore book. I will tell you about it. Elsie has brown curls and hazel eyes and she is very beautiful and very rich. In the book it says her mother died when she was born and her father blamed Elsie, so he left her with his relatives on a plantation in the South and went to live in Europe. Elsie's cousins are mean to her and she has a very horrible governess, who is mean too. She wears a locket with a picture of her dead mother and prays most of the time. She tries to obey Jesus and be patient through her trials. Her favorite book is the Bible and her next favorite is *The Pilgrim's Progress*. Elsie believes she will meet her ma in heaven. Then, one day, her father comes. He is very stern. He tells her, "All you ever have to do is obey and you need never ask me why, when I give you an order." "I don't want my own way," she tells him. "I know it wouldn't always be a good way." Then he forbids her to do anything fun so her character will develop. After a long time she wins his love by obeying him every minute, so her fondest hope comes true, which is to sit in his lap and hear him whisper, "My darling, you're lovely as an angel, and you're mine, mine only, mine own precious one." Elsie is so happy. But she is still devoted to Jesus and one Sunday when her father asks her to sing for some friends at a party, she refuses because it is the Sabbath. Her father is furious and commands her to obey him, but Elsie stands firm. Mr. Travilla tries to persuade her. He says, "It's such a little thing, God wouldn't be angry." Elsie says, "O Mr. Travilla, surely you know that there is no such thing as a *little* sin . . ." After a while Elsie's father meets a lady called Miss Stevens. This lady tells Elsie how dearly she loves her. She gives Elsie a large bag of candy for Christmas. Elsie has a great fondness for such things and has to pray for the strength to resist temptation. Miss Stevens tells Elsie she can take them and her papa need never know. Elsie gives her a look of grieved surprise. "Oh!" she says, "could you think I would do that—but God would know, Miss Stevens, and I should know it myself and how could I ever look my papa in the face again after deceiving him so?" The darkies on the plantation keep saying "Massa Horace gwine marry dat bit of paint and finery!" Elsie is spellbound with astonishment when she hears this. It had never entered her mind that her father would marry again. Anyway, Diary, as you see, no one likes Miss Stevens except Elsie's papa. Everyone knows she is setting her cap for him but in the end she still has not caught him. Poor Elsie falls asleep and her papa kisses away a tear on her eyelash. He longs to tell her that all her fears are groundless and no other could ever fill her place in his heart, but he does not like to wake her up to tell her this. He kisses her again and presses another kiss on her cheek. Then he leaves her to dream on. That is the end of the story. What do you think, Diary? What will happen next, I wonder.

I had a dream about Daddy last night. I was in a dark place where I could not see. I was on some stairs, but it was so dark I did not know whether I was on my way up or down. I called "Help, Help," but no sound came out. I could not breathe. I started going up the stairs, but instead I was going down. I was falling. Then I heard my father's voice and I was not falling anymore. He caught me and rocked me in his arms. "My darling, you're lovely as an angel," he said. "My own precious little girl." Then we were in a boat. We rocked back and forth over the waves. But when I opened my eyes I saw it wasn't a boat at all. It was the rocking chair by my bed and Daddy was holding me. He said, "It was only a silly scrambled egg dream." He brushed my hair back and held me close. We were rocking back and forth. The next thing I knew it was morning and I was in my bed. The room was empty. The rocking chair was not there. Then I remembered. Ma took it away a long time ago. She said I was not a baby anymore. She put it in Tooka's room. So none of it was true after all.

School was closed today because of the snowstorm. Ma and Tooka and I were making Divinity Fudge in the kitchen when the door flew open and Daddy came in. He looked like a snowman all covered with snow. We had not seen him since Christmas. Even Ma laughed to see him. He gave us big hugs. Then he took off his coat and helped stir the fudge. It was so much fun, except Puddin got into it and we had to make some more.

Sometimes my Mamacita is pretty and calls me her Favorita. But that is when she is not being mean. Mostly she is mean to Daddy. When she starts he goes into the cellar where his tools are. He is making a surprise for me. I can hardly wait to see what it is going to be. Ma gets very angry when he goes into the cellar. She tries to follow him down but he locks the workroom door. Ma wants him to get a job in Boston so we can go there. She talks all the time about her cousin Martha Phillips. Cousin Martha is an heiress. She is married to Andrew James Peters. They live in a big house in the best part of Boston, which is called Jamaica Plain. They also have a farm near Boston in a place called Dover and a cottage in Maine. The Maine house is on an island. The cousins are in the Social Register. That is a very important book and no one can get in it unless a secret committee of very important people lets him in. I asked Ma if we would be in it if we move to Boston. "Absolutely," she said. "We will be in everything." Cousin Andrew went to Harvard. My daddy is Harvard Class of 1895, the same as Cousin Andrew. They both belonged to something called the Hasty Pudding Club. I asked Ma what that was but she said it would take too long to explain. I looked hasty pudding up in the dictionary. It is made of oatmeal. The Oatmeal Club. This is weird, don't you think so? Ma says Daddy had the same advantages as Cousin Andrew so why couldn't he be a big lawyer with lots of important connections in Boston and Washington like Cousin Andrew instead of being out of a job most of the time? Daddy never answers when she starts on all this and it makes Ma even screamier.

We are reading stories from *The Pilgrim's Progress* in Sunday School. Did I tell you it is Elsie Dinsmore's second favorite book? Our teacher says it is a very important book because it will teach us to know the difference between good and bad. It starts out with a dream and a man in rags carrying a great burden of sin on his back. He cries all the time while he is reading his Bible and calls out "What shall I do?" Then he meets an Evangelist who asks him "Wherefore dost thou cry?" The man says he is scared of death and judgment because the load of sin he carries on his back will sink him into Hell. So the Evangelist gives him a parchment roll which has "Fly from the wrath to come" written on it and points across the field to a Wicket Gate. He tells him to follow the shining light. The Evangelist calls the man Christian. So Christian shouts "Life, life, Eternal life," and departs from his wife and family. He has his fingers in his ears and the neighbors are all making fun of him, but that is only the beginning, Diary, because Christian is going on a long journey. He takes many false paths trying to find the straight and narrow one that leads to the Celestial City. He sees the Delectable Mountains from the House of the Virgins who are named Discretion, Piety, Prudence, and Charity, but first he must pass through the Valley of Humiliation and do battle with the foul fiend Apollyon. He has to go to Vanity Fair and the Slough of Despond and the Iron Cage, and lots of other places and he meets people called Faithful and Ignorance and Mr. Worldly Wiseman. I have to go now. Ma is calling me. Besides, I am getting tired with all this going around in my head.

I hate arithmetic. Today I got only 4 out of 10 right on my test. If we move to Boston I will get good grades and be at the head of my class. Daddy will have a better job and he will not have to travel. Tooka will stop being so whiny and we will all be happy.

Let me tell you how Camilla came to be my best friend. I used to hate her. Ma kept going on all the time about how her father is president of the bank and the richest man in town. "Why don't they invite you there to play?" she kept asking. She knew some of the others in our class had been invited. It made me so mad. I didn't care about not being invited. Anyway, I'm prettier than Camilla. Then last fall Camilla said, "Come to my house on Saturday." I said, "No, I don't want to." Ma was furious when I told her and *made* me go. It turned out I had a good time and now Camilla is my best friend. It was her idea to start a club. We named it The Ten Musketeers Club. We were very careful who we let in. Camilla asked Marjorie White first. I don't like Marjorie as much as Camilla does, but we needed a place for our secret meetings and Marjorie's house has a big cedar closet in the cellar that is perfect. It has a lock on the inside of the door, so once you are inside you can lock everyone else out. There is a fur in the closet. It has the animal's head still on it and the paws and the tail. The eyes look right at you and it has sharp teeth and a pointy black snout oh so *real*. Marjorie's Ma wears it around her neck.

*T*hree U.S. ships have been sunk by the Germans. Daddy said we will soon be at war. "This is the last straw," he said. Then he got into a fight with Ma, who said he was making mountains out of molehills and it will all blow over. "You call three ships molehills?" he said. Then he made Ma madder than ever by bringing up Elsie Janis. She is a star on Broadway in New York City and Daddy knows Ma thinks she is pretty. He started reciting this poem Elsie wrote:

> Where are you, God?
> I can't believe that you have seen
> The things that they have done,
> And yet upon this earth of Yours
> There still exists the Hun.

Oh Diary, if only you could have seen the effect this had on Ma. She got so mad she couldn't get any words out of her mouth. I thought she was going to choke. But instead she went out and slammed the door. Now they are not speaking or even looking at each other.

*M*a got a letter from Cousin Martha today. She gets lots of them and is always writing letters back. Boston is all Ma talks

8

about. She says "Why do you think I save slivers of soap and heat them up in a saucepan? Why do you think I scrimp and save? It is so we can get out of Evanston, get to Boston and start our new life." What will happen to my books and things if we move? What will happen to Puddin and Pie? What will happen to The Ten Musketeers Club? I wish Daddy and I could stay here and Ma would move to Boston. Tooka could go with her, I wouldn't mind. I mentioned this to Daddy but he kept shaking his head, so I have not mentioned it to Ma. It's true Ma melts soap slivers down and when the melted soap cools off she cuts soap cakes from it. I didn't know why she did that until now.

*T*here are elm trees all along Davis Street. There is one behind our house. Now that the snow is going away I can climb up onto the highest branch where no one can find me. It is the best place to be, believe me. Maybe Daddy is making a tree house for me. Maybe that is what the surprise is. Then I will be able to stay in my tree even when it rains. He is the only one who knows about my secret hiding place, except you, dear Diary. If it is a tree house I will move out of this house and live there. No one will know where I am except Daddy. I am so mad, mad, mad at everybody except him. Tooka makes me sick. I wish Daddy would change his mind about getting Ma and Tooka to go to Boston and leave him and me here. I keep praying to God but so far He has not done anything. What sort of trees are there in Boston? Skinny twiggy trees I bet, with branches that snap off if you hang on them and no leaves, only a few here and there.

*U*gly-wumps! That's what I call the Campbell Soup Kids. Camilla thinks they are cute. Whenever she sees them in a magazine she cuts them out to paste in her Diary. She calls her Diary her Memory Book. From now on that is what I shall call you. Mem for short. How do you like that? I like it very much so I hope you do too.

*T*oday Daddy gave me the surprise he has been working on. Oh Mem, do not be disappointed because it is not the tree house. It is something even *better*. It is a chest made of cherry wood. It has brass hinges that look like gold. The little key is gold too and it is hanging on a gold chain. I shall wear it around my neck and *never* take it off. Daddy made the chest especially for me to keep my treasures in. It is *perfect*. I have put it in my room at the foot of my bed. The first thing I will put in it is you, dear Memory Book. No one will ever find you. I love Daddy so much. He is the best Daddy in the world.

I have not yet told you about The Ten Musketeers Club's initiation ceremony. We all sat around in a circle. President Camilla Foldes gave me a pin and commanded me to hold it while she lit a match. Then she held the match under the pin. This was to sterilize it. The other members leaned forward to blow the match out. Then we passed the pin around the circle and pricked our arms one by one. Then we pressed our arms against the arms of the ones sitting on each side of us. So now and forever we are blood sisters. We call each other Retsis which, as you know, Dear Diary—I mean Mem—is sister backwards. Next we joined hands and made an oath to keep our club's secrets forever. Then Vice President Starr Wyman presented the secret code she had invented. This is it.

<u>The secret code of The Ten Musketeers Club</u>
<u>of Evanston, Illinois in the year of our Lord</u>
<u>Nineteen Hundred and Seventeen, and forever after</u>

To write A, use F	H, use M	O, use T	V, use A
B, use G	I, use N	P, use U	W, use B
C, use H	J, use O	Q, use V	X, use C
D, use I	K, use P	R, use W	Y, use D
E, use J	L, use Q	S, use X	Z, use E
F, use K	M, use R	T, use Y	
G, use L	N, use S	U, use Z	

The name of our club in code is YMJ YJS RZXPJYJJWX.

I saw part of a letter Ma was writing to Cousin Martha. I know it isn't honest to read other people's letters but it was on her desk. The letter said mean things about Daddy and how terrible it was to live in Evanston. Ma wrote that she had saved up enough money to travel to Boston and if Cousin Martha heard of nice rooms for rent to let her know. She was also considering moving to New York but Boston would be her first choice because she wanted Tooka and me to grow up to claim our rightful heritage. What does that mean? She asked Cousin Martha to let her know as soon as poss. her opinion on all this. New York is so fast-paced and Boston seems far more suitable. That is where the letter stopped. Ma had not finished it. Oh Mem, what can I do? I do not want to leave Evanston. I wanted to tear the letter up but didn't because then Ma would know I had read it and be furious.

*P*resident Wilson has asked Congress to declare war! He says the world must be made safe for democracy. Daddy said to Ma, "See? What did I tell you?" That started another fight. It was the worst ever ever. I climbed up into the elm tree, but I could still hear them. Tooka hid in the coat closet. When I saw Daddy run out of the house and get into his car, I climbed down and tried to catch him but he was running too fast. He did not see me or hear me.

A man came to our house. I didn't like him. Ma took him everywhere. He said, "I will take that and this." He pointed at different things. Ma kept saying, "How much?" She is selling our furniture and dishes. He wanted to buy the goblets with the family crest on them but Ma said, "Oh no! We will require them for our dinner parties in Boston." Tooka was crying and Puddin and Pie were barking. Ma told me to take them into the yard, but I refused to go. When the man saw the chest Daddy made for me he said, "Nice work, how much?" I threw myself on it and screamed. Tooka started screaming too. Ma got the man out of my room fast. They'll have to kill me if they want to take away my chest.

I am on the train. In the morning a big truck came to our house and took away most of the furniture. At 4 o'clock Ma called a Blue Cab and we went to the station. There was no time to say good-bye to Camilla or anyone else. Before we left Ma put their collars on Puddin and Pie and tied their leashes to the back fence.

She said the neighbors could have them. But the neighbors weren't home. Puddin and Pie kept barking and pulling at their leashes. They tried to follow us and were choking. It was cruel, Mem, but no one could prevent her. She was afraid Daddy might come back and stop us from going. Since we left, Tooka hasn't stopped crying. I feel hungry but when I tried to eat dinner I threw up.

We are in Boston in a house on Beacon Street. Cousin Martha found the rooms for us to rent. Everything is mixed up. Ma is worried about her hats, which got crushed in the suitcase. "Ruined, ruined," she keeps saying. She tries to fluff up the flower on her straw, but it is too squashed. Tooka will not stop crying. How will Daddy know where to find us? I want to die.

Why did we have to leave Evanston? Why? I didn't even get to finish 5th grade and will have to start it all over again in the fall. Tooka and I have to sleep in a bunk bed in one room. I have the top part of the bed and Tooka has the bottom. It is no fun sharing a room with her. Ma says we will get used to it in no time. She says soon we will be settled and that we should be thanking God we finally made it to Boston. I hate her.

I started to write to Camilla to explain why I left without saying goodbye to her and my other dear Sretsis. But there was too much explaining to do and I was so tired I could not do it. I ended by tearing up the letter. I sent her a postcard instead. It is a picture of Boston Common with the swan boat in the lake. I promised to write her a long letter very soon. I miss her so much. Also I miss Puddin and Pie.

O Memory Book—how to begin to tell you about these cousins of ours? I do not know how to begin. The day before we went to visit them Mamacita had a Marcel wave at the beauty parlor and Tooka and I went with her. She looked *gorgeous*. On the way home she bought us new dresses. We went to the house in Jamaica Plain for tea. The house is bigger than Camilla's! The butler let us in. His name is Ashton and he has been with Cousin Andrew's family forever and ever. The cousins were waiting for us in the drawing room. Cousin Martha was wearing a black dress. She is very quiet. Cousin Andrew is taller than Daddy and bald and he talks a lot. Their two children are Mary, who is fifteen, and Lucy Edwina, who is my age and quiet like Cousin Martha. There are four maids, maybe more, besides the butler. Cousin Martha sat in front of a table covered with a lace cloth and on it was a silver pot with a spirit lamp underneath to keep the water inside hot. The teapot and the sugar bowl and creamer were engraved with some writing that I could not make out. There was a silver toast rack on the tea table with buttered toast and next to it a crystal pot of dark honey. "It is from our own bees at Dover Farm," Cousin Martha said. The maids served Lucy Edwina and Mary and Tooka and me strawberry parfaits with whipped cream on top and little cakes. Each one was covered with pink or yellow sugar icing with silver beads dotted around. I had never seen anything like them. Some were round and some were square and some were shaped like stars. "What delicious petits fours," Ma said. I asked her later about petits fours so I would know how to spell it when I was telling you about them. They are French and everyone in Paris has petits fours instead of cookies. After a while Lucy Edwina and Mary invited me and Tooka to see the ballroom. I had never seen a ballroom before. It is *beautiful*. Everything is white. There are chandeliers and mirrors on the walls. "This is where I shall have my coming out party," Mary said. "So shall I," sniffed Lucy Edwina. "But mine will be first," Mary said, "because I am older." Then they took us upstairs to see their rooms. Lucy Edwina's has wallpaper with forget-me-nots and a blue rug. The bed is painted white and so are the shelves for her doll collection. Mary's room is pink. Her rug has pink flowers on it. She told me it was woven especially for her in Atlanta, Georgia. It has her name on it in one corner and the date. Mary P. Peters—1916. Each cousin has her own bathroom with a white basin and tub with "Hot" and "Cold" on the taps. There are white towels with initials. Lucy Edwina's initials are blue. Mary's initials are pink. They hang on pipes which are heated with steam so the towels are always warm. Mary said, "Mummy took the idea from the Ritz in Paris." Then we went into Cousin Andrew's room. Mary said, "Our Daddy was born right here in this room in 1872," and she patted the four-poster bed. We all stood around looking at it.

His room also has a desk piled so high with papers there is no room for anything else. On one wall there is nothing but shelves for books. I wish I had shelves like that and a room of my own. Cousin Andrew is a very important person and has a lot on his mind. On our way home Ma could not stop talking. "A fortune in antiques," she kept saying. "Every piece belongs in a museum." She told us the silver tea set was the trophy given to Cousin Andrew after he won a yachting race. And the cloth was Battenberg lace, the real thing. Many of the paintings on the walls were portraits of our ancestors. It was the most wonderful day. To think we are related to Cousin Martha and Andrew J. Peters! I never saw a house like the one they live in. It is so big and beautiful and quiet and they are all so happy. Do you think Lucy Edwina liked me?? I would like more than anything to be her friend.

*M*a goes on and on about Cousin Andrew. He was an important lawyer until he started representing Jamaica Plain in the State Legislature. Then he went to Congress in Washington, D.C. and after that President Wilson appointed him to the Treasury Department. Ma says the President doesn't make a move without him. Now he is thinking of running for Mayor of Boston. Someday he will be President!!! That is what Ma says. He belongs to all the clubs—the Tavern, the Tennis and Racquet, the Somerset, the Exchange, the Eastern Yacht Club and the New York Harvard Club (even though he lives in Boston). I mustn't forget the Country Club in Brookline. He belongs to that, too! Cousin Martha is going to take Ma to the D.A.R. so she can join the Boston chapter. Ma says we can hold our own anywhere because our lineage goes back before the Revolution. She also says, "Friendship is a garden and a garden has to be cultivated."

*D*addy has found us. He and Ma got into a fight right away. He said, "How dare you take Starr out of school!! How dare you!!" I never saw him so angry. Ma screamed back at him, "How *dare* you be so stupid and not see how much more important it is to be here in Boston close to my cousins. What could be more important than *that?* We're not muck, you know. There's blue blood running in our veins." Daddy kept saying, "Shut up, Hel, shut up." But she didn't. Now they don't speak to each other. I asked him about Puddin and Pie. He said, "I'm sorry, sweetheart, but I don't know." That's all he said. Oh, Mem, it is terrible.

*M*a told me and Tooka that we are to call her Mummy, not Ma from now on. That is what Lucy Edwina and Mary call their ma. "Too late for that, Helen," Daddy said, and they got into another fight.

*L*ucy Edwina asked me to come over to her house to play to-morrow. She goes to Miss Sheraton's School, where I will be going next fall. If I did not have to repeat 5th grade I would be in Lucy Edwina's class. O misery! Ma got us new dresses to wear to church with the cousins on Sunday. She says we are Episcopalians now and not Baptists anymore. "What does that mean?" I asked her. She said I'll see when we get there.

I met some of Lucy Edwina's friends. Did they like me, Mem? I don't know. I think Bettina Deans and Patsy Pierce did like me. I'm especially glad about Patsy because she lives near us—only a block away. None of the girls is as pretty as I am. Neither is Lucy Edwina. She introduced me as her cousin. Bridget, who is one of the maids, brought in a tray of cherry tarts. She called Lucy Edwina "Miss Lucy Edwina" and me "Miss Starr." Ma says that this is the correct way for servants to address the children of the family. From the moment Lucy Edwina was born she was "Miss Lucy Edwina" to all the maids and the butler too. Isn't that something, Mem? No one in Evanston ever did that, not even in Camilla's house.

I didn't like the new church much, Mem. I liked the church in Evanston better. Besides, Daddy did not go with us. He refused. Ma thought he would change his mind but he didn't. "Baptist I am and Baptist I will be," he said. Ma was mad but what could she do? The church is called St. Paul's Cathedral. It is very grand. There was a lot of kneeling and then standing but not much sitting. I was afraid I would stand when we were supposed to kneel but it turned out all right because I was next to Lucy Edwina and did whatever she did. We did some singing but not as much as in Evanston. Here the choir mostly sang and we listened. There were candles too and something that smelled like one of Ma's perfumes. Lucy Edwina said it was incense. The preacher is called the priest here. After, we went to the cousins' house for dinner. I wanted Daddy to be there but he didn't come, though a place had been set for him. No one said his name and before dessert Ashton took his plate and silverware away and even the chair. Then Mary moved her chair closer to Cousin Martha's. His place disappeared. When the Indian pudding came in for dessert I almost threw up but I didn't. I excused myself and went into the bathroom and locked the door. There was a big to-do over that but I'll tell you the rest tomorrow. All I want to do now is go to sleep.

Cousin Martha has been most generous, Ma says. She has arranged for Ashton's cousin Minna to come to cook for us and take care of things. Now Ma won't have to slave so. We all went to a parade today to see the soldiers who are going to France to fight in the war. Everybody was cheering. On the way I saw a yellow dress in Filene's window with a matching hat but Ma said it wouldn't suit me and it was too expensive anyway. She said our dear cousins have been more than generous helping us get settled. What did she mean? I asked her, but she wasn't listening. When I am grown up I will have a hundred closets full of beautiful clothes that suit me perfectly. Hats too. I was born into the world a Star Child, so why should I not have all the dresses I desire? When I am grown up everything is going to be the way I want it to be.

Guess what!? I am to have a tutor. Cousin Andrew is arranging it. This tutor will teach me what I missed by being taken out of John Dewey before the school year was over. Do you know what this means, Mem??? It means I will *not* have to go back and take 5th grade all over again from the beginning. When Miss Sheraton's starts in the fall I will be right there in 6th grade with Lucy Edwina and Patsy and Bettina. Tooka is not going to Miss Sheraton's. She is going to Miss Chatwick's. Ma says she will meet new friends there and we will have more friends that way than if we both go to the same school. Cousin Andrew is arranging it. He is also arranging to give me pocket money, same as Lucy Edwina. Twenty-five cents a week!!!

I am going to write a letter to Camilla. She didn't answer my postcard. Maybe she didn't get it. How does this sound?

Dear Camilla,

How are you? Did you get my postcard? I hope it did not go astray. I know I sent it to the right address. I am having a great time here in Boston. My Cousin Lucy Edwina is my best friend *here* but that doesn't mean I don't think of you every day and miss you. I miss all my dear Sretsis. Please tell me what is going on at the meetings of The Ten Musketeers Club. Are there any new members? My cousins live in a beautiful big house and they invite me over all the time to play. You would like them, I know. Can you come to Boston? I will introduce you to my cousins and we will all have fun together. Guess what? I am to be tutored so I will not have to repeat 5th grade next year. My cousin Andrew, who is a very important man here, is making the arrangements. That's all for now. I'd better go. Please write soon.

I miss you so much.

Love,

Starr

I wanted to ask Camilla about Puddin and Pie, but I started to cry thinking about them.

*T*oday I started with the tutor. Her name is Miss Merrick and I like her. I told her I *hate* arithmetic and do not understand it. She said, "Don't worry because you will catch up in no time."

*C*ousin Andrew is interested in my education. He thinks I have the potential to be intelligent. He took Tooka and me on an architectural tour. It was to Cambridge. On the way we drove past the biggest tent you ever saw. "Is there a circus?" I asked. He said, "No, the only circus in that tent is that fool Aimee Semple McPherson." He went on and on about how she preaches to thousands of people who are stupid enough to listen to her. "Look at that damn thing," he said as we passed the tent. He meant her car, Mem, which is called her Gospel Car. It had JESUS IS COMING SOON—GET READY written on it in big gold letters. "What does that mean," I asked. "Never mind, child," he said and told the chauffeur to step on the gas. I looked out the back window as we sped away and saw the other side of her car. It had gold letters on it too, which said WHERE WILL YOU SPEND ETERNITY? "Stop oogling," Cousin A. said and pulled my head down on his shoulder. Soon we were in Cambridge walking along Brattle Street. Cousin A. pointed things out to us. "Those are wineglass elms," he said. I told him we have elms in Evanston too, but I didn't tell him about my tree. Then he showed us Harvard Yard and we admired the buildings. Some young men were walking by and one of them waved at me. Cousin A. looked at his watch and said it was time to go home. Then Tooka starting whining for some candy, so he went into a store and bought peppermint sticks for all of us. "I hate peppermint," Tooka said, and threw hers in the bushes. After that Cousin A. said she should ride in front with the chauffeur on the way home. There was a window to roll up between us so Tooka could whine all she liked and we would not hear her. He asked, "Do you like sailing? Will you come sailing with me on my yacht?" I said, "Oh, I would love it." Of course he doesn't know I have never been sailing. What difference does that make? I know I will love it. Yes, I will.

Cousin A. encourages me to study hard with Miss Merrick. He wants me to be not only beautiful but a highly educated young lady and he is going to see to it that I am. We went on an historical tour today. Tooka didn't come because though she was old enough for the architectural tour, Cousin A. says she is too young for history. We went to Paul Revere's house and then on to the Old North Church and Bunker Hill.

My head is bursting with studying but Miss Merrick says I have done well and Cousin A. is proud of me. Today we went to get my uniforms for school. Oh, I am so *excited!*

Today was the first day at Miss Sheraton's! Lucy Edwina came
in the morning with the chauffeur to pick me up and we drove
there together. She is going to do that every morning and the
chauffeur will come for us in the afternoon. I'm still scared of
arithmetic but I will try hard. I must not fail Cousin A.

The teachers at Miss Sheraton's look sort of like Cousin Martha only not so quiet. They tell us to listen carefully and digest
what they are saying. Our English teacher is the nicest. I hate
hockey and cannot wait until we start swimming because I like to
swim. All the girls I met at Lucy Edwina's party are in my class
and we go around together and are on the Green Team in hockey.
I still like Lucy Edwina the best and hope she likes me as much as
I like her. It is hard to tell sometimes. My next favorite new best
friend is Patsy. She sits next to me in History class. Clementine
Rood is on my other side but doesn't talk to me much. Maybe she
doesn't like me. What do you think, Mem?

I wish Ma would stop telling me to show more gratitude to
Cousin M. and Cousin A. She says I am not smiley enough. She
says that I sulk. I don't know what she is talking about. I do my
best not to have bad thoughts about anything, even hockey. Only
you know how much I would like to step on the Blue Team's fat
faces when they run at me across the field. Did I tell you that
Cousin A. definitely decided to run for Mayor? The election is in
December. He is the candidate of the Good Government Association. He is running mostly against Mayor James Michael Curley,
whom everybody in school hates, including me. Mr. Curley is
Irish and Cousin A. says he is a crook.

Did I tell you that we have a sister school down the block that
is full of boys? Isn't that funny? It's called Lowell Academy.
Three boys from there came around today and serenaded Clementine. They hid in the bushes near where her chauffeur was waiting to pick her up and sang "Oh my darling, oh my darling
Clementine." She was mortified and ran back into the school.
Soon a big fuss was being made and out came Miss Sheraton and

some of the other teachers. "I am vexed, most vexed," Miss Shera-ton kept saying. "This will be reported immediately to Mr. Ice-wick." (He's the headmaster at Lowell.) But by that time the boys had run away.

*I*sn't this picture great, Mem? I found it in a newspaper and can't stop looking at it. Isn't Mata Hari the most beautiful thing you've ever seen? It says she was "the most fascinating, the most beauti-ful, the most astonishing and the most conscienceless woman spy ever." It also says she was "a talented dancer and a courtesan and a devastator of men's hearts and pockets." The French shot her be-cause she gave secrets to the Germans. I think it was hateful of them. When I grow up I want to be like Mata Hari. I especially want a dress like hers with jeweled things to hold up my bosoms. The newspaper said she wore a neat Amazonian suit specially made for the occasion of the shooting and a tricorn felt hat and a pair of new white gloves. What does Amazonian mean, Mem? Better look it up in the dictionary right now before I forget, so wait a minute. It means "characteristic of or like an Amazon; powerful and aggressive, warlike." Well, Mem, what do you think? And courtesan. I must look that up too, but I don't have time right now.

*M*a says the family hardly sees Cousin A., he is so busy getting votes. Everything Mr. Curley says about Cousin A. is mean and horrid. He said that Cousin A.'s head resembles a complete vac-uum and that Cousin A. is trying to fool people with a cloak of dignity and that he has purchasable camp followers. It is very bad, Mem.

*D*addy came home for Thanksgiving and it was wonderful. We went to the cousins' house in Jamaica Plain. There were new cousins there I hadn't met—Betsy Peters, Kate Phillips' little brother Adam, oh so many new cousins I can't remember them all. Everything was so beautiful. There was a horn of plenty in the center of the table made of silver with fruits and flowers spilling out down the table, and two silver birds with long tails standing among the fruits and flowers. There were raisins that were still on their branches, and nuts in silver holders like trumpet flowers. There were silver rosebuds to hold place cards with our names on them. I sat between Lucy Edwina and Kate. I think I forgot to tell you, Kate goes to Miss Sheraton's too. She is a year behind Lucy Edwina and me. I would have been in her class without Miss Merrick's tutoring. There was cider to drink and all the fires were lit. Cousin Andrew sat at one end of the table and Cousin Martha at the other. "You are next to me," Cousin A. said to Ma when we went into the dining room. She sat on his right and Cousin Elizabeth, Kate's Ma, was on his left. Daddy sat next to Cousin Martha. After dinner I was so stuffed I felt sick, but I wasn't. It was the best Thanksgiving I ever had.

*L*ast night Daddy came in late and he and Ma got into a fight. It was about Cousin A. I could hear them through the door. Daddy was saying that a dog looks up to you, a cat looks down on you, but a pig looks you in the eye, and that he had absolutely no intention of voting for Andrew Peters because *he* was a cat and he'd pick Curley any day even if he is a pig because at least a pig looks you in the eye. I didn't hear the rest because I put my pillow over my head. This morning Daddy left.

*T*oday I went with Clementine and Patsy to the Five and Ten. When we came out Clementine took a brooch in the shape of a rose out of her pocket. She had *stolen* it. Then Patsy took something out of her pocket and said, "Well, look at this, smarty pants!" She had stolen one too, only hers was in the shape of lily. They said stores charge too much for such cheap things. They looked at me—what had I taken? I had to admit I hadn't taken anything. At first I wished I had, but now I'm glad I didn't. What would have happened if we had been caught by Mayor Curley's police?!

*P*eters Elected! Peters Elected!" The newsboys are shouting it all over town!!! Oh Mem, I am so happy. Not that I ever doubted that Cousin A. would win. I can't wait to see him and hug him and tell him how much I love him. Soon, Mem, oh—I hope it will be *soon*. He got 37,924 votes and Mayor Curley only got

28,850 votes!!! The Boston *Herald* said, "It was a triumph for good government, as well as for the Good Government Association."

*L*ucy Edwina and I are the most important girls in school now that Cousin A. is mayor of Boston. We are treated according to our importance even though the teachers pretend nothing has changed. Do I imagine this, Mem? No, definitely not. Miss Shera-ton stopped me in the hall twice today just to smile and say what a beautiful day it was.

*C*ousin A. made time to take me and Tooka skating at the Boston Arena. Lucy Edwina couldn't come. She was Christmas shopping with Mary and Cousin Martha. We both got new ice skates and skated hand in hand while Cousin A. watched us. On the way home we walked down Huntington Avenue. Lots of people stopped him to say "Congratulations, Mr. Mayor." He introduced Tooka and me as his little cousins. He said, "I feel obliged to take them under my wing in their father's absence." What did he mean, Mem? When we got home I showed him the picture of Mata Hari. He said I would grow up to be far more beautiful than she was. I told him how much I liked her dress, and he said, "Holy Moses, would I like to see you in a costume like that— what a vision of loveliness that would be." He winked and patted my face. Oh I hope we will see him again soon. It is such fun to be with him without Prune Face around. That is what I call Cousin Martha because she looks like a prune, but *no one* is to know, Mem, except you. I asked him what a courtesan was. He pre-tended not to know what I was talking about. When he left I looked it up. Courtesan means "a prostitute or paramour esp. one associating with noblemen or men of wealth." Now I'll have to look up prostitute and paramour. Paramour must have something to do with *amour*—French for Love. Yes, definitely. Did I tell you I am studying French in school? It is one of my best subjects.

*L*ess than a week until Christmas! Minna was to have the after-noon off but couldn't leave because Ma came home late. She was out shopping for presents to give the cousins. She bought silver wrapping paper with glitter on it and tags to write each cousin's name. She got a handkerchief case for us to give Cousin Martha. It has a real lace border. Then she showed us two baskets filled with camellias, only the camellias are made of soap. These are for Mary and Lucy Edwina. She got chamois gloves lined in cashmere for Cousin Andrew. "They cost a pretty penny, but he deserves the best," she said. She put all the presents out on her bed and we stood around looking at them. "Nothing here to be ashamed of, eh, girls?" she kept saying. "No one can say your little Mamacita doesn't know how to do things right." We were so busy wrapping that she said jelly sandwiches would have to do for our supper. Minna had left. Ma said I could write on the little tags in red ink and attach them to the packages. "What should I say?" I asked her. "Write Merry Christmas to our dear Cousin Whichever from your devoted cousins. Then we will sign our names." I put Daddy's name under mine and tried to make it look like his writing. He'll be back in time for Christmas. Yes, definitely.

*G*uess what??? I am going to the cousins' tomorrow afternoon to spend Christmas Eve and I will stay the night and be there for all of Christmas Day!!! Tooka was invited but she has the sniffles so Ma said she has to stay home and anyway she and Ma will be going there Christmas Day so stop pestering. I am to sleep in the guest room next to Mary's room. Oh Mem, I can't wait!

*T*here is so much to tell you I don't know where to begin. Best start with the day before Christmas when I arrived at the house in Jamaica Plain. The door to the ballroom was closed and no one was allowed to go in. It was late afternoon. Snow was falling. We got into our nightgowns and had soft hot rolls with melted cheese and bacon for supper in the library in front of the fire. Not Cousin Andrew and Cousin Martha, silly. Just Lucy Edwina and me. After supper Cousin Martha came in with green and red petits fours on a plate to put by the fireplace for Santa. We had some too. I was so excited I was awake all night. In the morning our stockings were full of presents. The one I liked best was a marzipan mouse. Lucy Edwina got a shoe. My mouse was ever so much nicer. Later Cousin Martha started the music box on the landing and it played "Hark the Herald Angels Sing." That was the signal. Lucy Edwina and I ran down the stairs. The door to the ballroom was open. Oh, Mem, there were garlands of silver around the tree and silver balls shaped like apples and pears. There were little wax angels in glass bubbles reaching out their arms and smiling. And there were so many presents they were piled up one on top of the other all wrapped in gold paper or in red and green with fat bows. "This is yours," Cousin Andrew said, and handed me the biggest package of all, and guess what, Mem. It was the most beautiful coat you ever saw. It was made of brown squirrel. Yes, Mem, a fur coat!!!! But not only *that*—in another box there were earmuffs. I now have a fur coat and earmuffs like Lucy Edwina's, only mine are better. Later Ma and Tooka arrived to open their presents. They brought our presents for the cousins. Cousin A. put on his new gloves right away and pretended his hands were two ducks—quack quack quack. The ducks' beaks sniffed around my ears. They made me giggle. Everyone else did too. Ma said Daddy would arrive any minute but he never did. There were presents under the tree for him, which we took home. He can open them when he comes. I am getting sleepy now, Mem, so I'd better stop.

What a treat I'm going to have! Tomorrow I am to spend the whole day with Cousin A. and Lucy Edwina. He came by this morning to arrange it with Ma. He brought her another Christmas present. It is a bottle of French perfume with a golden crown on top. It is called Chypre. Hurry up, tomorrow tomorrow. I can't wait!!!

Mem, today was the most wonderful day of my life, even better than Christmas. I hardly know how to tell you. I guess I'll just start at the beginning. At first I was sad because when Cousin A. came to our house he said Lucy Edwina had caught Tooka's cold so she couldn't come. But Cousin A. said, "Never mind, she will come another time," and we went down the stairs and got into the car. I was wearing my squirrel coat. Cousin wouldn't tell where we were going, only that when we got there there would be a "presentation." I asked what that was and he said it would be a surprise. The car was cozy, with pillows and a rug. There was a picnic hamper and a suitcase too. We drove and drove. Cousin A. had a deck of cards and we played Snap. I won four times and he won three times. Then I got sleepy. Cousin A. asked if I would like a nap. He pulled down the curtains. I stretched out on the seat and put my head on his lap. He tucked the rug around me and patted my head. Soon I was asleep. Then the car stopped and Cousin A. said, "Here we are!" And there we were, in Providence, Rhode Island! He took my hand and said that what we were doing now was a big secret, like running away from the grown-ups. "You are a grown-up," I said. He laughed and said, "You're getting to be pretty grown-up too, so pretty pretty, my pretty little cousin." When we got out of the car we were in front of a hotel called the Narragansett Hotel. Oh, it is a magnificent place. I have never seen anything like it. There were two great marble staircases with a skylight in the ceiling and the *hugest* chandelier I have ever seen. It was like fairy land. In our rooms the carpets on the floor were like the decoration on the walls. In the bathroom, which was enormous, there were mosaic floors, like the Romans had, and the taps were gold. It was all wonderful! Cousin A. laid out the picnic from the hamper on the bed and then he spread his arms out and said, "Come, my angel, let's pretend we are sitting outdoors under a sweet magnolia tree with blue sky overhead and a babbling brook bibbling by—bibble, babble, bibble." This made me laugh. But he told me to hush, and then he said, "I trust you are not too hungry, because before we partake of this bounty we shall partake of—of—the presentation, so close your starry eyes now and count to ten." I counted fast as I could and when I opened my eyes the suitcase was open and inside there was the Mata Hari costume!!! Oh Mem, it was exactly like the picture. I took it and ran into the bathroom to put it on. When Cousin A. saw me he started clapping his hands. He said, "Oh you beauty you, beauty, what a beauty!" And he started singing, "Here we go loopy loo here we go loopy light." It made me so happy. I swayed to and fro as he held my hand. "Yes—dance, precious angel, dance loopy loo loopy light," he sang. I danced over the carpet and up on to a chair and onto the bed. The little sandwiches and other things on the bed danced too. I tried to pick up a cherry with my toes. Cousin A. laughed and got down on the floor and tried to put the cherry in his mouth. "Bow wow," he said, and I patted his head. We laughed and laughed and he said, "Dance some more." I twirled round and round until I got dizzy and fell. He picked me up. He was saying things like, "Starr baby, Starr beauty, my twinkling Starr." His voice was so very soft and gentle. I was still dizzy but soon I wasn't. I felt warm and snuggly. Then he kissed me on the mouth. His mouth was soft and it was so nice. I kept my eyes shut, because I knew that soon as I opened them he would stop. Then he kissed my neck and I opened my eyes and when I did he stopped. He patted my cheek and we ate lunch. I was so hungry I finished all the sandwiches and everything else. He said, "We're having fun, aren't we?" "The best fun I've ever had," I told him. He asked if I wanted to play games with him again sometime. Oh yes yes yes yes yes. He said that someday maybe I'll be a ballerina, because I'm so graceful and such a good dancer. He put the empty dishes back into the hamper while I went into the bathroom and changed into my dress. He put the Mata Hari costume into the suitcase and said he'd take care of it until next time. Then we went down the great marble staircase and drove away. On the way back he said to tell everybody we had been to the Boston Children's Museum and after that to the Parker House Hotel for lunch before the symphony. Then he gave me the program to show Ma. He said I should promise, cross my heart hope to die, never to tell anyone ever as long as I lived where we had really been. He said secrets are magic and if they are told something evil happens, and besides, if I told I'd never be friends with him, or go on adventures with him ever again. When I got back Ma asked, Did you have a good time? and I told her Yes, but that's all, because my lips are sealed. But if I didn't have you to tell about it, Mem, I would surely burst. And telling you doesn't count, does it? It would only be telling if someone found you and read this, but no one can, because no one but me has the key to Daddy's chest and that's on the chain around my neck safe and sound.

1918

Well, Mem, the new year has started with dancing feet. Lucy Edwina and I and all our friends are to join Miss Bonnie Mae Murphy's dancing class. It is to be held once a week in the ballroom at Jamaica Plain. There will be boys in the class, too. They are all in the sixth grade at Lowell. I have a new blue velvet dress to wear and white stockings and black patent leather shoes. The dress has a lace collar. I asked Ma whether I would have to wear the same dress each time. She said, "Whatever has to be done will be done." I guess that means I will have more than the blue to wear. Lucy Edwina has four party dresses. The first class is day after tomorrow. I can't wait. Got to run now. Bye.

Mem, don't say I have been faithless to you just because you haven't heard from me in a while. Truth to tell I have been too too busy. There is hardly time to *think!* Please forgive me, dear Mem. You will, won't you, *please?* There have been three dancing classes now. Miss Bonnie Mae has a long cane and she taps it on the floor in time to the music while we dance. Mr. Juro plays the grand piano. There are not enough boys to go around so the girls take turns dancing with each other. I dance mostly with Clementine because we are the same height. The boys are all shorter than I am. I can never think of anything to say to them. They don't talk much either. Miss Bonnie Mae says we are going to have such fun. So far it has only been tap tap tap and don't slouch. So far the best part is dressing up before dancing class begins. Ma got me another dress. A pink taffeta with rosebuds around the collar. It is beautiful. Sometimes Cousin A. pops in while we are dancing. So does Cousin M. Only they do not pop in at the same time. It is either one or the other.

Saturday, January 26

Dear Mem,

Today is my birthday. I am 12 years old and I have decided I am going to write you a letter on every birthday forever and ever until I die. I am going to live to be 100 so you will have 90 birthday letters to remember me by. I wish Daddy were here, but he's not. He didn't forget, though. He never would, would he, Mem? But to tell you the truth, I was afraid he *had* until yesterday, when the package arrived. On the brown paper it said "TO BE OPENED JANUARY 26." Inside was *The Secret Garden* by Frances Hodgson Burnett. I love the cover of the book. It is a drawing of a girl with long wavy yellow hair. She is wearing a red coat over her white dress. Her stockings are white too and she has black boots that go up to her ankles. Oh, and she has a little red cap on her head. She is holding a key and leaning forward to unlock a door in a wall hidden with ivy. Daddy wrote inside the book "Happy Birthday—may my darling little girl find her secret garden. With all love from her Daddy." I cannot wait to read this book. If only I were grown up so Ma wouldn't treat me like a baby. Then I would be able to make Ma and Daddy be sweet to each other and Daddy would be here all the time. Cousin Andrew is busy these days, but he says we will go on another trip soon. Soon soon, it must be soon, sooner than soon, for I yearn to wear my Mata Hari costume again!! Cousin A. kept saying he had something special for me for my birthday. I kept trying to guess, but I didn't even come close. Well—are you ready? It's a gramophone!! And records! All my favorite songs. Ma said I drove her bananas today playing "K-K-K-Katie—Beautiful Katie—You're the only g-g-g-girl that I adore," but I told her it was my birthday and I should be allowed to do anything I liked.

Bye, Mem, for now. Happy Birthday to you too. I love you.

Starr

P.S. Did I tell you I made the swim team? I am the only one from the 6th grade who did.

I've finished reading *The Secret Garden*. Oh I love it, I love it. It is about a girl who is orphan. Everyone says she is the most disagreeable-looking child. After her parents die she is sent to live with her Uncle at Misselwaite Manor in Yorkshire, England.

There is this boy who lives at the Manor too. He's also an orphan or a part orphan. Anyway, his ma is dead. His name is Colin and he is pale and sickly. It is too long for me to go into right now, but Mary discovers a door in an ivy-covered brick wall and then she finds the key that's in the drawing I told you about on the cover and lo and behold it fits and when she opens the door she discovers the garden. It is choked with weeds but Mary makes it come to life by caring for it. Now, listen to this. At the beginning of Chapter 27, it says, "To let a sad thought or a bad one get into your mind is as dangerous as letting a scarlet fever germ get into your body." Then later it says, "Whatsoever things are honest, just, pure, lovely and of good report—think on these things." Oh I do, I do, and I will, I will. After the garden blooms Mary and Colin do too and look how happy it makes them in the end. I just know our Peters cousins never have a sad or bad thought. They are like Mary and Colin in the garden.

*C*ousin A. took me to the Hotel Toulaine today for tea and Boston cream pie. He came and got me at school. Usually only the car comes for Lucy Edwina and me but today she wasn't in school because of the sniffles. She gets sniffles a lot. So no cream pie for Miss Lucy Edwina. Cousin A. had something really serious he wanted to talk to me about. After the inauguration next week he will be very busy and he is concerned that boys will soon be paying more attention to me than they should and that it might turn my head. I told him I have no interest in silly billy boys. He gave me a pat on my hand and said to always use my head and be the intelligent little girl I should be. Well, I'm not so little and he sounded like Ma does sometimes. So I pulled my hand away. He tried to take it back but I told him to leave me alone. He wanted me to have more cake but I said no. I was angry and told him he was the one who was silly billy. The waiter came to ask Mr. Mayor if everything was all right. I said, "No, it isn't all right." "What would you like, Miss?" the waiter asked me. Cousin A. said to bring the check. He kept trying to be friends all the way home, but I will never make up with him. I mean it, Mem.

*D*addy came in the door while we were having supper. I was so happy to see him. Ma said, "Well, Frank, at least you have the decency to show up in time for Andrew's Inauguration." "What makes you think I have?" Daddy said. He was angry and they got into a fight. Oh how I wish they would stop stop stop.

$\mathcal{M}$on., Feb. 4, 1918—Inauguration Day!! Because of this most Special Day I didn't have to go to school. Instead we all went to the City Hall Reception with the cousins. When I say we I mean Ma, Tooka and me. Daddy did not go. He was leaving town any- way in the afternoon and said he was too busy and had too much to do before he left. Ma didn't say anything when he said this so they didn't get into another fight. Ma was busy fussing about what we were going to wear and how we would look. We had to look our best so Cousin A. would be proud of us. We sat with the cousins during the ceremony at City Hall. There were also three newly elected members of the City Council, but none was so handsome as Cousin A. Just think, Mem—my cousin is the Mayor of Boston!!! Now that he is so famous I hope he won't forget about me. Tell me please, I beg you, tell me that he won't, because if he does I will die and then I will never see him again. Oh dear, I'm not making sense, am I? I guess I'm too *exhausted* by all the festivities, as Ma says. I love you, Mem. Good-night now.

$\mathcal{V}$alentine's Day is next Thursday and everybody at school is talking about who she will send valentines to. No one signs a name to a valentine so we can send dozens to all the boys and they will never know who they are from. Bettina is sending a valentine to only one boy. She made me swear cross my heart and hope to die that I wouldn't tell who it is if she told me. And I have kept true to my vow and told no one. No one except you, Mem. You don't count. I don't mean you don't count, because you do count more than anyone, but if anybody can keep a secret, you can. Any- way, she is sending it to Charles Thornton Gilbert. "Who is he?" I asked her. "You don't know him," she said in an uppity way. "He's a boy I met in New Orleans. He's handsome and tall and he's moving to Boston any day now." Then she told me he is her one and only. Do you think that is true, Mem? I am sending more than one valentine, that's for sure. The first and most important one will be to Daddy. He is at the top of my list and I am going to draw a picture of him and me together holding a heart between us and on the heart I will write "I love you." He will guess right away who the valentine is from but I don't care. I want him to know how much I love him. The only thing is, I do not know where he is right now so I have no address to mail it to. I will also send cards to all the boys in dancing class and to my boy cousins. Why not? Cousin A. will receive one too. I will send it to him at the Mayor's office!!! I will make a very special valentine for him with my own special message on it.

*I*t was getting late, so I made Cousin A.'s and Daddy's valentines at the same time. I got the biggest envelopes I could find and then I put two pieces of red paper together and cut out a heart shape to fit into them. For Cousin A.'s I pasted silver stars all around the edge of the heart to make a border and give him a hint and in the middle I wrote

XYFWW QTAJX FSIWJB

I put it in the envelope and addressed it to Mayor Andrew J. Peters. Do you think he will like it? He will never ever be able to guess what the message says. Only you and I know that. When I started decorating Daddy's it turned out like the one I made for Cousin A. instead of the way I'd planned. I started to write I love you, Daddy, but it ended up I miss you, Daddy, please come home. On the envelope, I wrote Mr. Frank Wyman. I left a space under his name for the address when I know where to send it.

*A*ll the girls in my class are jealous, I can tell, because I got the most valentines. I have them tied together with a satin ribbon and will keep them in Daddy's chest. I take them out every night before going to sleep and look them over. Who are they from? Some I can guess—others not. Some are from the girls in class. We sent valentines to each other even though everyone agreed not to. Bettina got almost as many as I did but *I* think she sent most of them to herself. My favorite has the stump of a tree on it with a heart perched on top of the stump and the message "As long as the vine grows round the stump—you'll be my darling sugar lump." Who do you suppose sent that?? There was none from Daddy. I would know even if he didn't sign it because it would have a postmark from far away. But maybe he did send one and sent it to someone living in Boston asking him to mail it to me from here—you know, to keep me guessing. Could it be Daddy who sent the one about the stump and the sugar lump? Or is that one from Cousin A.? What do *you* think? Maybe the one Daddy sent got lost in the mail.

*G*uess what?? Cousin A. got my valentine and he loves it! He took me for tea at the Hotel Toulaine again and that's when he told me. He didn't say anything about not being able to read it. Then after a while he asked me to make up a "sweet secret name" for him, something mysterious and difficult so others couldn't understand it. His eyes were twinkling so of course I knew what he was up to. It was a game to make me explain the valentine. I said I couldn't think of anything so quickly, but when we were back in the car, just as we got home, I pretended to have the most amazing brilliant idea and as soon as we got in the door I pushed him down in the big armchair and told him, "My sweet secret name for you shall henceforth be—Fou." "Fou?" he said. "What is Fou?" To my surprise Fou did not please him. So I told him that Fou was his initials AJP in the sworn secret code of The Ten Musketeers Club of Evanston, Illinois, of which Starr Wyman is Vice President. I told him that no one in the entire universe knows this code except the members of the club because I invented it. Then I got a piece of paper and wrote it all down. I thought this would make him happy, because of course he had won the game. Instead he got more upset than ever and said I was making a fool of him because a Fou is a fool. I truly hadn't thought of that. I said I was sorry and gave him a kiss. "Call me Fou or whatever you like, you little minx," he said and soon he was laughing. "Fou Fou—Fou—Fou—yes Fou Fou—Fou Fou—why not?"

I keep Daddy's Valentine on top of the pile in my chest so it will be easy to get at when I see him. I'm glad it's there. Better to give it to him personally and be sure it doesn't get lost in the mail. He will be here soon, definitely. That is one thing we can count on. He goes away—he comes back. Pretend we're on a seesaw, Mem, and when it goes up Daddy goes away and when it comes down he's back. What would happen if he fell off the seesaw? We'd fall off too, to be where he is.

Today I went to the farm in Dover to the cousins' Easter party. While the grown-ups played croquet or sat on wicker chairs under the sycamores having tea, the rest of us ran around looking for colored eggs. Whoever found the most was to get a prize. I was near the house searching in a patch of crocuses when Cousin A. came out the door and saw my basket almost empty. "Come, come, we can't have our Starr of Stars with an empty basket," he said and winked. Then he nodded toward the kitchen garden. "That's where the chicks go to lay their eggs." I ran over and sure enough, hidden among some hedges there were enough surprises to fill my basket. None of the others had followed me, so I got them all and I won the prize. It is a white rabbit made of velvet with cornflower eyes. It is beautiful. But now I think the rabbit should not belong to me. I didn't win it fairly. What should I do, Mem?

I told Ma how I won the rabbit. She said, "Why child, don't be silly, it only shows how highly dear Cousin Andrew thinks of you to favor you in this way. You should be grateful instead of mooning around with a long face." I do not know what to think. I feel awful.

I hate the rabbit. It is not really soft and it smells like garlic. I told Ma this and she sniffed around but could not smell it. She told me I was a bad girl to make up stories about the lovely lovely rabbit. But I am not making up stories. I smelled it in my dreams last night and the garlic smell is under my fingernails. All day long I kept picking at my nails to get it out. Ma was at me every minute to stop, stop it. "Stop it, Starr, stop it! What's gotten into you?" I kept trying to explain about the garlic but she wouldn't listen.

Today I put the rabbit in a paper bag and left it on Patsy's doorstep. Then I rang her doorbell and ran across the street and hid behind a tree. I waited there until I saw the butler open the door. At first he didn't notice the bag but then he did and took it inside.

*I*t was so balmy today that during history class Randy opened the windows. (Did I tell you we call Miss Randolph Randy? Not to her face, of course.) The sun shone in and the flowering trees outside smelled so sweet. I couldn't concentrate on what Randy was telling us. Instead my thoughts drifted out the window, and Randy tapped on the blackboard and said, "Our Starr's dreaming again—pay attention *please*"—and then I sat up straight and tried to do better while she talked on about the Ottoman Empire, which was founded by a Turkoman nomad named Osman the First. It was the last successor to the Byzantines and chose to fight on the side of the Hun. See? I *can* retain information if I put my mind to it. I must remember to tell Cousin A. about the Turkoman nomad. He often asks me about my studies. He says everything we do should be educational.

I've got to tell you what happened today with Cousin A. When I got out of school he was waiting for me. Lucy Edwina and Elaine Newbold have started taking piano lessons at Elaine's house and they were going there together in her car. So no Lucy Edwina. It was just Cousin A. and me. "We're going for a little drive," he said when I got into the car. "A little drive to see the spring posies." The chauffeur was a new one named Morris. As we set off Cousin A. pulled down the shades at the windows. How can we see the spring posies? I asked him. I started putting the shades up so we could, but he tapped my hand. "Tut tut, little one, the spring posies are going to posy nosy up right here with us in the car so pull the shades back down and close your starry eyes." I did as he told me and he said, "Open your palm." Then he put something cool and smooth into my hand and asked me to guess what it was. "It's something to smell," he said. "Perfume?" I asked. "No, no—not perfume." "Cod liver oil?" I said this even though I knew it would not be that. He laughed. "Adorable child," he said. "Guess again." But I couldn't wait and opened my eyes. It was a little green bottle. Cousin A. told me to open it. He said what was inside was much nicer than perfume. I was to take deep breaths and I'd see what he meant. So I opened it and smelled it and, oh Mem, it made me feel creamy dreamy, as if I were floating away on a cloud. I floated and floated oh so far away. Then he told me to count the buttons on the front of his trousers and after that I could unbutton them and I did. There was this little pink thing in a nest of hair and he said to pretend it was a baby ear of corn and we were going to play a game called "make the corn grow." All I had to do was pat it and pinch it but not too hard and the little ear of corn would grow. This sounded silly to me, like a baby game, but he said to try it and see what would happen. So I did and it did start to grow! The more I patted it the bigger it got. It got hard too, like a real ear of corn. Cousin A. said what a clever girl I was and he took off my shoes and stockings and rubbed between my toes and up along my legs under my skirt. His fingers tickled what he called my beaver. I was still floating and floating. He said from now on we would have our very own secret club much more important than any other, in Evanston or anywhere else. He said other things, too, which I forget except for the part about how important it was not to tell anyone our secrets and did I understand how important this was? Then the car stopped and the ride was over. He took my hand and we went into the house. I was still feeling floaty, but not so much. He opened the front door with the key and took me up to my room. Ma and Tooka were out and Minna was in the kitchen making dinner. He got me settled on Tooka's part of the bed because I was still too floaty to climb the ladder to mine. Then he tiptoed away.

*A*ll day today I kept thinking about the fun Cousin A. and I had in the car yesterday. I wonder when I will see him again. I mean just us. Of course, I will see him in church tomorrow. The little green bottle doesn't look like a perfume bottle because the top screws on and it doesn't have any decoration on it. It is only a plain green bottle. But oh, Mem, inside there is creamy dreamy. It is far better than any perfume Ma has from Paris. I wonder what it is. Did Cousin A. invent it? He is so clever and important, I bet he did.

*G*uess what? My bosoms have started to grow. I wonder what Cousin A. will say. I cannot wait for him to see how I will look in the Mata Hari costume now that they have. They have, haven't they? I'm not just imagining it, am I? No, definitely not!!! The mirror does not lie! Help me to think of a way of getting him to ask me to dance for him again.

*E*veryone is talking about what she is going to do this summer when school closes—all will be going away except Lucy Edwina and me. Cousin A. is so busy with his mayoral duties that the cousins have decided to be at the farm in Dover instead of Vinal-haven Island. Cousin A. will be in Boston during the week and drive to Dover on weekends. Tooka and I are invited to spend the summer at the farm too, but Ma says we must not wear out our welcome and she will only allow me to go on weekends. I am to drive up with Cousin A. on Fridays and back to Boston with him on Sundays. Tooka is to go to Camp Wigawam in Maine where she will learn to do lots of things. Cousin A. says during the week we will have many opportunities for cultural pursuits. What does he mean by that, Mem?

*L*ucky me! Cousin A. popped into the ballroom today to watch us dance. He only stayed a minute but when I saw him leaving I excused myself and said I had to go to the bathroom. I didn't really have to but who could guess that so I went upstairs to Lucy Edwina's bathroom and ran the water and when I came out Cousin A. was sitting on Lucy Edwina's bed. "How lovely to see my Starr," he said. "How I'd love to see my twinkling Starr danc-ing!" You just did, I told him. "Clever child." He winked. "But I didn't mean in the manner of these ballroom formalities, I meant in the manner of a certain private performance where Mata Hari danced. Come, come, angel." He held out his arms and I went and sat on his lap and gave him a kiss. I asked him when it would be. When when when? "Soon soon soon," he said. "On Friday next." Then we heard footsteps on the stairs and he bounced me off his knee and hurried out. I went after him but he was nowhere in sight. Instead Prune Face was there. She asked me why I wasn't downstairs dancing with the others. I told her I had to use the bathroom. "Oh," she said. "Well, hurry on back, they're all wait-ing for you." I went down the stairs but they hadn't been waiting for me at all. They were twirling around and around and Miss Bonnie Mae was tippy tapping as she always does. I can't wait until Friday. But how are we to go all the way to Providence after school and get back in time for supper?

*F*riday at last, and Cousin A. kept his promise as he always does. At first I was afraid he hadn't because the car and chauffeur were not there as they usually are. But when I saw him, I knew it would be all right. And it was! First he had a surprise for me. He had driven *himself* in a Model T car! He said the car was to be our own gypsy caravan because from now on, more often than not we would be going places without a chauffeur to drive us. "We'll be gypsies like the rest in their Lizzies tooting around town, all alike, all alike." He leaned over and gave me a smacking kiss on my ear. I yelled ouch but he just laughed some more and mumbled on about happy days ahead. Then he pumped at the pedals and turned the wheel and off we went. And you'll *never* guess where! Not to Providence but to Chinatown!! One of Cousin A.'s friends has a room at the corner of Tyler and Beach. When we got there Cousin A. let me in and lit a lamp standing by the door. He said he'd be right back soon as he parked Lizzie. The room was in a cellar. It was a big room with no windows and no furniture except for a long sofa with lots of pillows and next to that a table on which there was a gramophone and a pile of records and another lamp. It was spooky and I was getting scared until Cousin A. came back. "Isn't this razzamatoo?" he said, lighting the lamp on the table. I said I liked the Narragansett Hotel better, but he paid no attention. "What have we here?" he said, opening the door of a closet. You guessed right, Mem. It was the Mata Hari costume. He wound up the gramophone and put on a record. "That's Hawaiian hula music," he said as the music started. "Like it?" Oh Mem, did I! "Don't look," I said, and went into the bathroom to change into Mata Hari. I'd brought cotton along to stuff inside the brassiere part under my bosoms because I didn't think they were big enough yet to fill it up and I was right. But with the cotton they looked plumper. The music was making me sway this way and that as I went back into the other room, and he beckoned me to come closer, but I didn't because I didn't want him to notice the cotton. "Aren't you pleased?" he asked, making a frowning face. So I danced a bit closer, and blew him a kiss and twirled away again. He blew me a kiss back and started swaying his hips too. It was funny to see. I got the giggles and was so giggly I had to stop my dancing. "Don't be a silly girl," he said. "You were dancing superbly and most interesting from a cultural point of view for it was more like dancers I've seen in Constantinople than in Hawaii—and now you ruin the whole effect with girlish giggles." "Have you really been to Constantinople?" I asked him and told him about how we have been studying the Ottoman Empire in history and about the Turkoman nomad. "What an excellent student you are," he said. "But hush, hush for the moment. You're spoiling the mood, and we must not let this mood slip through our fingers, for it too is part of the cultural picture." He was looking down at the corn between his legs, which had turned back into a baby ear. He was peevish, so I went over and sat on his lap. "Don't be an old grumpy-wump," I said. "But why did we have to come here? Why didn't we go to the Narragansett?" He was annoyed and said now that he was Mayor of Boston he just couldn't pop off to Providence every other minute and what's more it was a much longer drive from Boston to Providence than from Beacon Street to Tyler and Beach so we'd be able to see each other more often. Wouldn't I like that? I said I would, but I still liked the Narragansett better and what about his friend? Wouldn't he be coming back soon? "What friend?" he said. Then he remembered. "Oh ho yes yes—the friend, yes, a close dear friend—Who knows, who knows when he will return? But I do know it's getting very late and I have to get you back home—what will dear Helen say if we're not back soon?" It all sounded a muddle to me, but I was ready to go anyway. The cotton was slipping and I was afraid he would notice. Then he said that next time he would bring the little green bottle. Would I like that? Oh, would I!! I clapped my hands and twirled around and around and the cotton slipped out! I swooped it up and hid it behind my back. Did he notice? Well, maybe, but if he did he pretended not to. So maybe I did fool him after all.

I've been so busy busy studying for exams I've hardly had a moment to talk to you. You do understand, don't you? But now they're over and I got an A in English and an A in French—all the better to please Cousin *A*. Also a B+ in History. And, dear friend, I save the best for last. Even though it is only a B−, it is in Arithmetic! Hope you are proud of me.

$\mathcal{M}$y first weekend at Dover Farm is over and oh Mem, you'll never guess what! There when I arrived was a horse to be my very own! She's black with a white star on her forehead almost like the one I made the secret wish for when I blew out the candles on my eleventh birthday! I say almost, because then I wished for a white horse with a black star, but how could Cousin A. have guessed it right unless you told him, Mem, ha ha, for no one knew but you. Anyway black with a white star is far better and now I am learning to ride and Cousin A. is teaching me. We have named the horse Star and I am the luckiest girl in the world. I kept wishing I could stay at the farm all the time and not have to go back to Boston on Sunday with Cousin A., but then that turned out to be the best part. I mean when we were driving back this afternoon. He asked me if I was a happy girl. Oh yes yes. I hugged him and told him he made wishes come true. "Well, well," he said, "happy girls can never be too happy for me, so put your head in my lap and let's see if we can make a wish come true right now." So I did and he said, "Close your starry eyes," and I did. "Don't move—good girl—now—make a wish but don't tell me what it is because if you do it won't come true." I squeezed my eyes tight as tight could be and wished hard as I could and right away my wish came true. There was creamy dreamy under my nose. I kept my eyes shut and didn't say a word. I could feel Cousin's hand touching me here and there. It felt so good I couldn't stop myself from wiggling even though he told me to stay still. Then all of a sudden the car stopped and he was pushing me up. "Sit up, sit up," he said. "Here we are, here we are." When Morris opened the door I tried to get up but my head kept falling back on the seat. "Miss Starr's been napping," Cousin A. told Morris. "Upsie time, upsie time." But I couldn't move. Finally Cousin A. said not to disturb me and Morris picked me up and carried me into the house. "Hasn't had her nap out," Cousin A. said to Ma. "It's such a long drive." Ma invited him to stay for supper but he didn't. Now I am sleepy again, but I wanted to tell you about all this before going to bed. Goodnight, Mem.

. . .

A very terrible thing has happened in Russia, Mem. The Bolsheviks executed Czar Nicholas II and all his family. Just like Louis XVI and Marie Antoinette but they shot them instead of using a guillotine. Ma said I mustn't look at the newspaper photographs but I'd seen them already. I tried to find out more about it from Cousin A., but all he said was "Politics—politics—don't bother your starry little head about politics." Ma's worried about the tiaras and other jewels. "What is to become of them?" she asked. "That's the least of the worries," Cousin A. said.

*Y*ou ask me what I do during the week between Monday and Friday when I am here in Boston. It's a good question, because I really don't do much of anything but lie around on my bed and read or look out the window. I do see Cousin A. sometimes to go on walks, which he calls constitutionals. Yesterday we passed by a house that had petunias in window boxes. Cousin A. loves flowers. On the way home he bought me a basket of daisies. I put them on my window sill. I like yellow daisies better than white ones—don't you? The ones Cousin A. gave me were yellow. I used to like the white ones better than the yellow, but lately I've changed my mind. I do that a lot. One minute I think one thing and the next minute the opposite.

*T*his weekend I learned to post. Cousin A. says at this rate I'll be Lucy Edwina's equal by the end of the summer. Cousin A.'s daisies on the window sill were fine when we left. When I got back from the farm they were gone.

*E*ven though the heat is killing, as Ma says, and even tho' I didn't want to go, Cousin A. insisted and so yesterday we went to China Heaven. What a surprise! Fou does think up the most wonderful things to surprise me with. There were hundreds of balloons, blue, red, yellow, pink, and every color you could imagine, and they were moving around, floating on the ceiling and everywhere, because he'd put in two electric fans to make a breeze. I ran around trying to catch them and he ran after me laughing and

calling out, Follow me, follow me, and I did and ran after him
into the bathroom. There were more balloons there and he kept
reaching up to catch them. Then he turned on the taps of the tub
and started testing the water and dabbing his fingers on my face,
tickling. "How's that? Too cold?" No, I like it, I like it. "Well,
jump in, then," he told me. "With my clothes on?" I asked.
"What an idea, child," he said, laughing. "No, no, undress, undress, let me assist you." He undressed me slowly and gently, so it
was nice. When I was little Ma used to pull my things off in such
a rush. What about the plug? I asked him. "Forget about plugs,"
he said. "Just get in the tub and let the water splishy splash splish
over you. It will refresh you. You'll see." Then he took his hands
and whooshed it over me. Oh it was cold, and I squealed. "Too
cold, eh?" He took his tie pin and poked it at one of the balloons
and it popped. He kept laughing and saying pippity pop and telling me to sit down and he would make the water a little bit
warmer. He fiddled with the taps and told me to tell him when it
was coming down pippity pop, not too cold, not too hot, not too
strong, not too weak. Now. It's pippity pop right now, I said.
"Lie back then so the stream of water runs over you," he said.
"Let pippity pop find the little piece of candy." I didn't see any
candy but he said it was hidden between my legs waiting there to
be discovered. "I'll show you," he said, and he took his hand and
rubbed gently inside my beaver. Then he put his hand to my
mouth. "Taste that," he said. I touched my tongue to the tip of
his finger, but all it tasted like was water. "Of course, of course—
how stupid of me, how could you taste the candy with water running over it? We'll have to wait until later when I'll dry you off,
after our tub—you'll be able to taste it then." Will I be able to
take it out and eat it? I asked him. He thought that was v. funny.
"No no," he said, and popped two more balloons. "This little
piece of candy is extra special and stays inside there all the time
just getting sweeter and sweeter. It never comes out." After that
he started touching my feet and between my toes. It felt so good,
with the water softly coming down between my legs. Then all at
once I wiggled a certain way and the water found the sweet little
candy. I knew right away because all at once I was floating. It was
like creamy dreamy. Then he told me to lie back and rest for a
while. He took a package out of his pocket and said I could un-
wrap it. It had pale green paper around it with golden scrolls and
inside was a cake of soap that curved to fit my palm. It smelled *so*

good, and he told me it was Jasmine. Then he put the plug down so the tub would fill up and while it was filling he took off all his clothes! There he was naked in front of me. I had never seen him like that before. He was much fatter than he is in his clothes and his tummy hung down a little over his corn with the curly hair around it and something else hanging down like a pouch that I hadn't seen before. I couldn't stop staring while he climbed into the tub. "Between my legs there's a little fishy, see if you can catch it," he said. I said I thought it was corn. He laughed. "That was a different game," he said. "Now we're playing catch the fishy." He took the soap and we rubbed our hands over it so we could make ourselves soapy together and I kept putting my hand under the water trying to catch the fishy. But it was so small I couldn't catch it and not only that, he kept rolling over every time I almost got hold of it. He has the *biggest* bottom, Mem. I gave it a smack. "You devil," he said and laughed and I did too. I kept reaching around under it and all at once the little fishy got bigger and bigger and I grabbed it. He was very jolly and huffed and puffed and then all of a sudden the fish got teeny again and he gave a big sigh and said it was time for a nap on the sofa. But even with the fans it was so hot we couldn't sleep. Instead we went to the Hotel Toulaine for lemonade and cake. Then we went home. Don't laugh about what I'm telling you. It is *true*, every word, and I have a balloon to prove it. As we were leaving Fou said to take as many as I liked but I only took one. It's white and it's tied right now to the back of my chair.

This weekend I galloped on Star for the first time. Cousin A. said my seat was excellent. Later he and Lucy Edwina and I rode over to the Phillips farm to visit Kate and Adam. Did I tell you that the Dover Farm was in Cousin Martha's family? She inherited it and Cousin John Phillips inherited another farm close by. Cousin John is Kate's daddy. And Adam's. It is complicated keeping the cousins and the houses straight. There are so many.

Something terrible happened today, Mem. This morning when I got up I found blood on my nightgown. I was too scared to tell Ma, but I had to so I did. I closed my eyes first. It was the only way I could tell her. She said, "My my, it was bound to happen sooner or later. It is called The Curse." She told me to buck up as it will stop in a week or so but I will be getting it every month for the rest of my life!!! It is called that because it is a woman's Curse to bear. I asked, What about boys? "Don't be stupid," she said. "They get off easy. Their only Curse is having to shave every day." I begged her to swear to keep my Curse a secret from Daddy. If he hears what's happened to me I will kill myself. He must never ever know. No one must ever know, but Daddy more than anyone. "Don't be absurd," Ma said. "Silly child." I kept begging her to listen, but she wouldn't. Then she said now that I've gotten The Curse, I can get a baby. I didn't understand but she wouldn't explain. Who can I ask, Mem? I wonder if Lucy Edwina has it. I can't ask her in case she doesn't. Besides, how can I go to the farm this weekend? How can I be with Cousin Andrew if I'm bleeding? I asked Ma but she said, "Nonsense, child. Of course you will go. I will tell Cousin Martha you are indisposed. She will know what to do." But what about Cousin A.? I asked. "What about him?" she said. Oh, Mem, I would die if he knew. What if he has creamy dreamy for me in the car? I will have to lie to him and pretend I don't want it and then maybe he will get angry and think I don't like creamy dreamy when I like it more than anything. Ma gave me 8 cotton napkins and showed me how to pin them on inside my drawers. When they get too bloody I am to soak them in cold water to get the blood out. After that I am to scrub them clean. She says it will be easier if I quickly wash one as soon as I take it off. Eight will be plenty and she will not have to get me extras. Ugh!!! She says from now on I must count the days, 28 until it comes again. In 28 days school will be starting. What happens if it comes when I am at school and there is blood on my jumper when I get up? What will I do? What would you do, Mem? Die. That is what we will both do. Ma told me to stop giving her a headache with my stupid questions. I looked up indisposed in the dictionary and it said, "Unwell, disinclined."

*W*ell, the weekend is over and I am home safe. It turned out Cousin Martha did know what to do and she had explained to Lucy Edwina that I was indisposed so we would have a quiet weekend with no swimming or riding. We found a tent in the attic and pitched it on the lawn and pretended we were camping out. Cook made us a picnic lunch. After that we played Parcheesi. Of course what worried me most was the drive up and then the drive back. I didn't want Cousin A. to put his hand down there and feel the napkin. Everything turned out all right, though. Cousin A. just told me to stretch out on the back seat while he settled down on the jump seat in front of me. "I don't mind riding backwards this once," he said. "You make yourself cozy." And then he told me stories. The best of all was about Mata Hari, and guess what, Mem! He *knew* her. "It was in Paris, my first trip there," he said. "One of our stops on the Grand Tour. My dear mother was a close friend of a Russian lady who had a beautiful house with a winter garden." What's that? I wanted to know. "A greenhouse, child," he said. "But this greenhouse had been transformed into a Hindu Temple with thousands of mirrors twinkling in the lamplight, and the most delicious scents wafting around. There was twinkling from the jewels in the tiaras of Russian Princesses too and from the decorations worn by the Grand Dukes, not to mention my dear mother, whose paroor of diamonds and rubies outshone them all." I'm sorry, Mem, but I didn't want to interrupt him to ask about paroor and afterwards I couldn't find it in my dictionary. I'll try to remember to ask him next time. Anyway, it turns out that Mata Hari was trained to serve Siva from childhood—that's S-I-V-A, Mem, and he is a Hindu God. Her dance was a tribute to him. As she danced, the veils drifted from her body oh so gently like clouds caught by a whisper of love. Those were his exact words, Mem, and oh it was thrilling to hear them, for it was as if *I* were Mata Hari. And then all the veils drifted off, and when they did—there she was, *naked*. But if she was naked, what about her costume? I asked him. "Pay attention, child," he said. "Education is what is retained, otherwise a story is just a string of words. You must listen more closely. I said veils—meaning that on this occasion her costume was only veils, many veils, and not your costume." He became stern all of a sudden—"Besides, this performance was to educate us about Siva and so on, otherwise I would not be telling you about it." And it *was* educational, Mem. Ma is calling me so I have to go. Bye.

$\mathcal{T}$his is the last weekend I'll be going to the farm at Dover. Oh, it doesn't mean we'll never be going there again, it means this summer is over and I do not want it to be. If I could have my wish this summer would go on forever and ever with a weekend always ahead to look forward to. I will miss Star so much and the ride back to Boston on Sundays. I don't have to tell you why, eh Mem? The only good thing about it being over is that maybe Daddy will come back. Do you think so, Mem? Do you think that this Sunday when I get back from the farm Daddy will be waiting for me? So even if the summer is over it won't matter a bit, because that is what I wish for most of all—my Daddy to come home.

*I*t's Sunday night and I'm back home, but Daddy is not. I got all my valentines out of his chest and spread them out around me on the floor. They made a big circle with me in the middle. The one I made for Daddy I took out of the circle and tore up. What's the use of waiting anymore? It was a dumb valentine anyway.

*T*he summer is really over. Tooka got back from Camp Wigawam this afternoon. She has a suntan. Well, so do I, only mine is prettier. It is, isn't it? I know you agree with me as you always do. I wish we didn't have to share a room.

*T*oday was the first day in 7th grade. School seems different from last year. What I mean is everyone looks the same except *me* and that is why it is different. Do you suppose I look the same to everyone else but they feel different?

*T*his morning we were informed by Miss Sheraton that each student is to let Miss Umgar know those certain days during the month when she is "indisposed" so she can be excused from gym until it's over. So now it's out! All the teachers will know when I have The Curse and that means others in our class have it too. I don't think Lucy Edwina does, though. Wouldn't she have told me about it? But then I didn't tell her about it, did I? I only told you, Mem. The 28 days are up tomorrow. Ma told me to wear a napkin to bed tonight just in case and I am to wear one to school tomorrow, too. She says sometimes it isn't 28 days exactly. Sometimes it is less or more. O misery.

. . .

*T*oday at lunchtime we were talking about babies and where they come from. Lucy Edwina says a stork brings the baby to you, but only if you are married. If you are not you can't get one. Patsy says they come out of your behind like #2 but Clementine says that is ridiculous—they pop up out of your belly button. Of course I know babies and The Curse go together but I was afraid to say anything until Bettina did. It turns out that she got it this summer, too, and so did Patsy! Now that I know some of my friends have it, it doesn't seem so bad. And guess what? We are going to call it Aunt Margaret. Nice idea, eh, Mem? I wish I could say I thought of it, but it was Patsy's idea. We won't tell our Mamacitas. Nobody will know who this Aunt Margaret is except us. That way we can bring her into the conversation no matter where or with whom and no one will know what we're really talking about—ha ha. Nothing on the napkin I wore today. I hope it comes tomorrow. I want it to be over with.

*O*h Mem, I have something dreadful to report to you. Miss Sheraton called us together this afternoon to tell us that the Influenza, which has killed thousands and thousands of people all over the world, has come to Boston. She says it will be in all the newspapers tomorrow. She was informed in advance by Mayor Peters, who was the first to know what is in store. Afterwards we went on with our class, but we were too scared to learn anything.

*T*oday the newspapers told about the epidemic. Prepare yourself, Mem, for I am about to tell you word for word what Dr. Blue says in the Boston *Herald*. "The disease is characterized by sudden onset. People are stricken on the streets, while at work in factories, shipyards, offices or elsewhere. First there is a chill, then fever with temperature 101 to 103 degrees, headache, backache, reddening and running of the eyes, pains and aches all over the body and general prostration. Persons who are so attacked should go to their homes at once, get into bed without delay and immediately call a Doctor." It sounds even worse than I thought. Dr. Blue says you must be careful to avoid complications like bronchial pneumonia, which may have fatal termination. That means Death. I am so frightened. Ma cut instructions out of the paper and has tacked them to the door of the icebox in the kitchen.

HOW TO AVOID THE DISEASE

Spray nose and throat daily with di-chloramine.
Get plenty of rest in bed.
Keep windows wide open.
Eat meals regularly and do not curtail on quantity.
Beware of persons shaking their handkerchiefs.
Don't use common towels, cups or other articles
which come in contact with the face.

Ma says that we must not worry about anything as our cousin Mayor Peters has taken charge and so everything will be all right.

Cousin Kate Phillips and Cousin Elizabeth died today. Ma said Cousin Elizabeth was dining with friends yesterday evening and went home feeling fine and this morning woke up dead. I mean she was dead in her sleep. It is so terrible, Mem, because it is The End. Even though Kate was in the grade below me and I didn't know her very well, knowing that I'll never see her again walking on this earth is a very terrible thing to know. I cannot put this thought out of my mind. Ma said Cousin Kate and Cousin Elizabeth went to Heaven, which is where we will all go if we do what God tells us in the Bible and are always good. I'm scared I won't go there because even if I'm good, how can I be good *always*? Please God, don't let me die until much later. It has got to be later, much much later, because I have plans and things I want to do in the world even tho' I don't yet know what they are and it's going to take years and years to get them all done. Ma keeps talking about what happens "after life." There are only two possibilities—Heaven or Hell. Listen, Mem, I would only tell this to you. I've decided I do not want there to be any "after life." I may be so bad I'll end up in Hell.

Miss Sheraton has closed the school and we are to go to the farm in Dover where we will be safe. Ma and Tooka are coming, too. We should have gone before, she says, but we had to "carry on" because Cousin A. is mayor. Now that school has closed we can go but it is too late for Cousin Kate and Cousin Elizabeth. I am so worried about Daddy. And Cousin A., who must stay behind in Boston.

*G*uess what, Mem! A postcard came from Daddy! He's in Mexico! Morris brought the mail out here to us from Boston. And my Daddy is not only all right—he is rich!! He's discovered a silver mine in a place called Guanajuato and asks how I would like to be decked out in silver bracelets with rings on my fingers and bells on my toes. I'd like that fine. Tooka got a postcard too, but she won't let me see it. There is no address to write back to. He didn't say when he was coming home either, but better not because of the Influenza. Do you suppose he's heard about it in Mexico? Ma said she doesn't believe for one minute that he is in Mexico or that he is rich. Now I'm sorry I tore up the valentine I made for him. I must be less hasty in future.

*A*t last it is over. We came back to Boston yesterday. Ma took down HOW TO AVOID THE DISEASE. We went to church today and everyone was thanking God. I thanked Him too but I am still scared. If no one knows how the epidemic started, how can we know it won't come back?

*S*tarted school. It was so quiet going back. Almost everyone was wearing black armbands. Besides Kate, two other girls and one of the teachers died. But nobody in my class died and my teachers all escaped too. We will have to work very hard to catch up, Miss Sheraton says. Randy had the disease but recovered. Bettina's little brother died. Patsy told me Billy Evans from dancing class died, too. He used to step on my toes a lot. Miss Bonnie Mae was very ill and has gone to a sanitarium in New York State for a rest cure. We won't have dancing class again until next year.

*N*ov. 11. The war is over!!! It ended on three elevens. The last shot was fired at the 11th hour of the 11th day of the 11th month of the year. What can it mean? It must mean something v. important.

*M*y bosoms ache and one is growing faster than the other. I have to check on it every night. I looked up brassiere in the dictionary. It is an archaic French word for a soutien-gorge, which means a support that enhances the throat. Also called a cacheseins, which means breast-concealer. That is what it says. Sometimes I wish Elsie Dinsmore were around so I could talk to her about God. Ha ha. No, Mem, I mean it. She sure seems to know all about Him and always gets an answer from Him, which is more than I can say about you, Mem. But maybe I just have to keep trying, so here goes again. God, please please make my Ma let me wear a brassiere. She told me again that I am too young to be concerning myself with such things, but if I have got The Curse, why can't I wear a brassiere? Why did I have to get Ma for a mother? Why isn't Frances Hodgson Burnett my mother? I wonder where she lives? If I knew I would certainly go and visit her. Right now. She would listen to me and we would have tea and creamy dreamy together. Don't laugh, for I am certain that anyone as intelligent as Mrs. Burnett knows about creamy dreamy. We would never have disagreements about anything. Isn't that a marvelous word? Yes, I love it. Dis-a-gree-ments.

*W*e went to the Cousins again for Thanksgiving. Prune Face hardly spoke to me. I asked Ma what she was angry at me for. She said that grown-ups have moods too and to stop imagining things. She's always telling me that I am imagining things.

*D*addy came home today! Oh Mem, I *knew* he would. He says there is a revolution in Mexico and so his silver mine is closed down for a while. He brought us jewelry made from his own silver. For me a bracelet with turquoises around it, for Tooka a butterfly pin with turquoises dotted here and there.

*M*a called the presents Daddy brought us tourist junk. She said he'd probably picked them up in some cheap shop. I was so mad I hit her. She slapped me back hard and Daddy went for her but then instead he ran out the door. Oh God. What is going to happen?

*T*oday everything is as if Daddy never came home, except that I have my silver bracelet so I know he did.

*F*rom now on when I'm writing I'm going to refer to Cousin A. as AJP. I like the look of the three initials together, don't you? But when oh when Mem will we ever be alone together again? I would do anything in the world to make it be *Right now.*

I know it's *hopeless* but I can't stop wishing and praying oh so hard that Daddy will come back for Christmas. Even when I try not to think of him I always am.

*C*hristmas arrived but Daddy didn't. Ma kept at me to look cheery—"What *is* the matter with you?" One of the presents AJP gave me was a velvet scarf. "The color of your peachy skin," he said when I opened the package. He placed it around my neck right away and everyone admired it. Later he took me aside and whispered that there were other uses for a scarf than draping it around pretty necks. What? What? I asked him, but everyone was gathered around the tree opening presents and Prune Face and Ma were close by. "This isn't the time and place—later, later," he kept hissing. It was disgusting. I hate him and I hate the scarf even more. It is so pale, too pale, and he is much too pale too, and anyway the color certainly looks nothing like my skin, no, not in the right way or any way. I held it up to my face in front of the mirror as soon as we got back home.

*M*em, I should have told you last night soon as it happened but I was too excited and besides you were already put away. But guess what! Mamacita *finally* got her Favorita a brassiere! It was lying on my bed under my nightgown. So I *discovered* it, which is *better* than a Christmas present. It is cotton and very plain, but I don't care, it is still a brassiere and I plan to wear it every day!!

I feel better now about AJP and the scarf. Maybe he isn't so disgusting after all. I started missing him again as the days went by after Christmas so I let him fetch me today in dear old Lizzie and even wore the scarf. When we got to China Heaven—Oh it was *beautiful!* There were no balloons but he had put branches of holly all around and hanging on the branches were trinkets and sugar canes. It was Christmas all over again, only better. He was so happy, clapping his hands and bustling around turning the heaters on and putting water in a pot to boil. Then he fussed with a tray and cups and took out the chocolatiest cake you ever saw. Sit sit, my angel, he kept saying, so I sat and we had tea and cake and I had two pieces. He took another piece too and stretched out on the sofa and put a pillow on the floor beside him and I sat on it and took the scarf from around my neck and together we patted it down his body. "What have we here?" he said, patting his pocket, and out came the little green bottle. "Ho ho—a most interesting combination with velvety-welvet." And in a moment, there was creamy dreamy, and he was taking my hand and touching it to his trousers, where a molehill was rising up like one on Prune Face's croquet lawn. I patted it to please him and the more I did the more it kept rising. After a while though, all I wanted to do was float, and I took my hand away. "No no no," he said. He kept pulling my hand back onto the molehill but I kept pulling it away. "Oh, all right, all right," and he took some cotton out of his pocket and sprinkled it with creamy dreamy and put it right down on my nose and started undressing me. But did he have a surprise, for I was wearing my new brassiere. "Holy Pete—what's this?" He was running his hand over it and pulling a strap off my shoulder. "How did this come about?" he asked, and he gave the material over my bosom a tweak. Ouch, I said, sitting up. "Ouch or not," he said, "this isn't soft enough for my starry one. This is coarse cotton, not worthy of a starry one. I shall get a satin one—satin to cherish your satiny skin. Then he threw my cotton brassiere behind the sofa as if it were an old rag and took took the velvety welvet and started touching it between my legs with one hand while wafting creamy dreamy back and forth under my nose with the other. I closed my eyes and felt the velvety welvet oh so soft and furry as he drew it oh so gently up and down, back and forth between my legs. I was floating floating, but then the mole escaped and started demanding attention, so I pitty patted it, but too fiercely I guess, because he pulled away quite startled. He looked so funny I had to laugh and he did, too. "No harm done, no harm done," he said. Then I got dressed, all but the scarf, which he wanted to keep. I said no because it was a present, but he said he'd get me another to give me when he gave me the satin brassiere. How am I going to keep Ma from noticing the scarf is gone? How will I keep her from seeing the satin brassiere and asking how I got it? "Never mind, never mind," he kept saying. And he was right. She never noticed the scarf was missing. I guess I'll worry about the satin brassiere when the time comes. Scarfs and satin brassieres and creamy dreamy are still floating around in my head. I hope I haven't left anything out—don't think I have. Night, Mem.

*I*t's the last day of 1918. The year 1918 will never come again. This day will never come again. It's Tuesday. Tuesday December 31, 1918 will never come again. It will never be this year or this day on this earth again. Kate Phillips will never run on the lawn under the sycamore trees of Dover Farm again. Kate Phillips will never walk along the halls of Miss Sheraton's again. She will never walk through a door anywhere on earth again. I will never see Kate Phillips again.

1919

*D*addy came back on New Year's Day. I still can't believe it, but the door opened and there he was! At first Tooka didn't recognize him because he has a beard, but even though I was amazed I knew it was Daddy right away. He looks like Abraham Lincoln.

*D*ancing class has begun again, finally, and guess what! Do you remember that boy named Charles Thornton Gilbert Bettina sent the Valentine to last year? He has just moved to Boston *and* is attending Lowell *and* has joined the dancing class! Now all the girls, not only Bettina, have a crush on him. He likes me best, though. I can tell. I call him Bonnie Prince Charlie—not to his face, of course, silly, but when we're all talking about him. His family has a plantation near New Orleans called Aurora. Don't you love that name? I just love it and the way he talks. He likes to read too, so we have something to talk about when we dance. Not like the other boys, so clumsy and stupid. Besides, Mem, he is tall, taller than I, and he has one green eye and one blue! What do you think of that?

*M*a kept nagging Daddy about his beard, so he left. Maybe he'll come back tomorrow. Maybe he went out for a short walk. He told me he would be back soon. Yes, he did.

*A*JP took me to the matinee at the Symphony for a special "birthday treat" even though it isn't my birthday yet and even though he knows the Symphony isn't exactly what I'd call a "treat." Lucy Edwina was supposed to go, but she was "indisposed." Yes, Mem, Aunt Margaret has arrived at last. So Fou and I went without her. After, we had tea at the Vendome. They have the best profiteroles. Cousin advises me that I must tell him everything and have no secrets from him. So during tea I told him all about Charles Thornton Gilbert and his one blue and one green eye and what an interesting person he is. "What is it exactly that's so interesting about him except for his eyes?" he said. Oh, he's not like the other boys, he likes to read so we have things to talk about. "Things? What things?" Fou was anxious to know. Things in books like Elsie Dinsmore about Elsie and sin. Charlie teased me and said, "Sin? What is that? Never heard of it in New Orleans"—only when he said sin it sounded like "see-un" and I giggled, but Charlie didn't mind. He says no one from the South can pronounce sin without having it come out "see-un"—who knows why? Fou didn't think it was funny and kept tapping his fingers on the table, which he does sometimes. It helps him concentrate when he's thinking deep thoughts. Then he said it was time to go even though I hadn't finished my profiteroles.

Guess what? Lucy Edwina says that Fou knows all about The Curse. Oh, he hasn't *told* her he knows, but her Mummy tells him everything so he must know. And he must know I have it. He must've known all along. Well, at least now that I know he knows I won't have to worry so much. No, I won't have to worry about it at all. What a relief. One less worry to worry me. But I worry anyway. It's confusing, it really is.

Sunday, January 26, 1919

Dear Mem,

I don't ever want to talk to anyone except you. Nobody understands me except you. Nobody likes me except you. AJP doesn't count. I wish I could live alone. The only time I am happy is when I am home by myself reading. That's better than anything. One thing I am going to promise you, Mem—I *will* stop biting my fingernails. *Definitely.* I know I can do this because I did it once before. Before the garlicky rabbit, remember? I swear I will do this, swear that from this day, my 13th birthday, in the year of our

Lord one thousand, nine hundred and nineteen, I will stop biting my nails.

Daddy promises every time he goes away that he will be back soon. I do *not* believe him anymore. I will never believe him again.

This isn't much of a birthday letter, so I'm going to stop now before I make you even sadder than I already have.

Anyway, you know I love you. And I know you love me.

OOO and XXXXX

Starr

P.S. One nice thing to report: I'm becoming an excellent swimmer, the best on the junior team, although most of the others are in eighth or ninth grade. Patsy made the team this year as an alternate. I like to hold my breath and dive far under, pretending I'm a mermaid and that the feet of the other swimmers splashing above me are other mermaids moving around so fast I can't make out who they are or which is which. No one knows I do this except you.

*P*atsy discovered the most fascinating book in her parents' library. (They have a real library, a room with books all around, on every wall.) The book is called *Myths and Enchantment Tales,* and in it are pictures of the Greek gods and heroes. One in particular more than enchants me. His name is Adonis and he is a very handsome young man who was slain by a wild boar but permitted by Zeus to pass four months every year in the lower world with Persephone, four with Aphrodite, the goddess of love and beauty, and four wherever he chose. (That's what the book says, anyway.) None of the boys at Lowell looks anything like Adonis except maybe Charles Thornton Gilbert, a little.

*T*here was a sketch in the newspaper today of Abraham Lincoln because it is his birthday. Well, he may have been our sixteenth President, but he sure does look like my Daddy. I cut the sketch out of the paper and shall frame it and hang it on the wall beside my bed. There isn't too much room, but room enough for Daddy Lincoln. I am not telling anyone about this except you.

.   .   .

*V*alentine's Day and guess what?? I got not one but two Valentines signed Adonis. I know one of them is from Patsy. (I wonder if she knows that the one she received signed Adonis is from me?) But who is the other one from? Clementine, I bet. I got more Valentines this year than last. I didn't send one to Fou this year. I'm mad at him. I don't know why. I don't really like profiteroles anyway. Maybe it's his bald head. Yes, definitely. Compare it with Adonis Charles Thornton Gilbert's yellow hair. Much nicer to pitty pat than AJP's bald pate. Still, now that I think of it, Fou's is like a drum to drum-de-dum and have some fun. Better stop now. I'm getting silly. But seriously, who do you think the other Adonis valentine is from? Could it possibly be Charles? O bliss!!

I touch myself and slowly run my finger inside the creases. When I take my finger out there's something white and creamy. What is it? It looks like cream but different. I tasted it and it was salty but not really. Some days it is not there, but when it's not I can touch myself and make it come. I wish I could tell someone about it but who?

*C*ousin A. told Ma he is most pleased about my interest in classical music (?!). He got tickets for the Matinee at the Symphony again but this time when he came to fetch me he kept looking at his watch and saying we'd better hurry otherwise we'd be late. He kept humming a few bars of something classical as he took my hand and off we went, but instead of Morris, the Lizzie was waiting for us so I knew we weren't going to the Symphony after all. On the seat beside his satchel there was a speckled gold box with gold ribbon around it, and inside "a special something for just the two of us, my Starry one." He said this as we bounced along and I was excited, for I was sure he meant the satin brassiere he promised me last time. But when we got to CH and I tore off the ribbon and lifted the lid, there was no satin brassiere inside. Instead, there was row on row of chocolates. I cried I was so disappointed, and I threw the box on the floor. You *promised* me a satin brassiere, I said, and ran to the door. I was going to leave—leave *him*— even though I would have been stuck in Chinatown with no way to get home. He came after me saying how sorry he was and "next

time, next time," but I kept saying, forget about next time—
there's not going to *be* a next time. That's when he started fumbling around with the satchel where he keeps the green bottle,
trying to open it, but it was stuck. "What's going on with this
damn thing?" he said. Locked, maybe? I said. I had decided to
stay. "Yes, yes, clever girl, of course," and he took his key ring out
of his pocket and opened up the satchel and soon creamy dreamy
cotton was wafting around close to my face and I started feeling
floaty, so I didn't mind much when he started going on about
how it had come to his attention that I was occupying myself with
myths and enchantment tales. As you know, Mem, I hadn't mentioned that book to him or said anything about Adonis. He must
have heard about it from Lucy Edwina. He said he would be responsible for my education in these matters, and I should rely on
him. He sounded just like Randy, but since there was creamy
dreamy right away, no teasing as there sometimes is, I didn't
mind. After he had undressed me, I settled down beside him on
the sofa and he put his arm around me and said he had a story to
tell me, "Yes, yes, an enchantment tale about a maiden and a
horse—yes, a handsome stallion named Sultan. How do you like
that for a name, my Starr?" Sounded fine to me and anyway by
then I was quite floaty so I hope I've got the rest of it right, Mem.
I think I do, most of it. He went on about how the maiden was in
that particular time, in that particular country—yes, yes, there
she was, bathing in a pool among water lilies, when who should
come by but Sultan. He came over to the pool and kept looking
at her with eyes like a person's eyes instead of an animal's. She
kept looking at him, too, and noticed that his dingle was dangling. Why not dingle-dangle it? she thought, and she put her feet
on the edge of the pool just the way your feet are now on the arm
of this comfy chair and she took his dingle-dangle between her
toes and rubbed it gently. Sultan was most pleased and pleasured
and the more pleasured he was the more it encouraged her to rub-
a-dub. Sultan was encouraged too to put his head down and snuz-
zle her bosoms while her lovely bottom swished around making
even the water lilies tremble with excitement. The maiden became
all creamy inside and kept moving her feet faster and faster up
and down, up and down his dingle-dangle." By now, Fou was
huffing and puffing, "Do that, keep doing that" and "Yes, yes,
that's what the maiden was doing." Then he gave a loud groan
and a fountain spurted up all over my legs and down onto my

feet. That's all I remember of the story, Mem. Guess I drifted off. When I woke up he touched my feet and told me it was time to do as the maiden did and wash them in the pool. What pool? I said. "The tub, the tub. Have you no imagination, child? The tub in the bathroom is a pool." So I went in and stuck my sticky feet under the running water in the pool. It was dark by the time we drove home and I sat with the gold box of chocolates open in my lap. Each one was filled with a sweet-tasting syrup. By the time we got home there were none left.

I woke up mad this morning because I realized he had made me forget all about the satin brassiere. Ma asked me why I looked so angry and said to stop it because I have nothing to be mad about and if I continue it will make furrows in my brow which will imprint themselves permanently and then how will I feel? It made me even madder, her saying this, even though it is true that I am mad. I am mad about a lot of things. I'll make you a list if you like. I'll make you a list even if you don't like—so here goes.

(1) I am mad at Ma for telling me I have nothing to be mad about.
(2) I am mad at myself because when I look in the mirror I know it is true.
(3) I am mad at Daddy because he is away and we do not know where he is or when he will come back.
(4) I am mad at Tooka for messing around with my things.
(5) I am mad at Fou because he broke his promise to me about the brassiere.

There, that is 5 reasons I am mad. Does that satisfy you, Mem, or do I need to list more? Easy for me to do if you ask. Just speak up.

*T*oday he really did take me to the Matinee at the Symphony. Lucy Edwina couldn't come because she and Elaine are practicing day and night. They are to play a duet in the Easter recital. I didn't want to go but Ma said I had to. My mind kept jumping to other things and without knowing it I started biting my nails. They started bleeding. I could taste the wet on my fingers in the dark. When we came out, Fou said, "Why do you look mad? What are you mad at? Didn't you like the music?" It was maddening music, I told him, so why shouldn't I look mad? Ha ha. As we were getting into the car, he saw my nails. "What's this, what's this? What have you been doing to yourself?" Shut up, I told him. He wrapped his handkerchief around my hand and tried to soothe me. I thought for sure he was leading up to creamy dreamy, so I put my head in his lap. "That's better, that's better," he said and kept soothing my brow with his hand. I felt harmonious for a while after that, until all of a sudden he pulled out his watch. "Oh my, oh my, I'm late, very late," he said. So there would be no creamy dreamy after all. Fou Fou White Rabbit, I shouted at him—late late for a very important date. "Ho ho," he said. "So my little girl has been reading *Alice's Adventures in Wonderland.*" He made a droopy face and wiggled his ears. "Cheer up, babykins—dwell on what we have to look forward to next time." I didn't think this was funny one bit and stuck my tongue out at him and moved as far as I could over on the seat so as not to be sitting close to him. He tried kissing me but I pushed him away. Then the car stopped and Morris was opening the door and I jumped out without saying good-bye. He kept calling after me but didn't get out of the car, and I pretended not to hear. When I got into the house I went straight to the mirror. I didn't look mad at all and kept smiling into the mirror for ages until Ma called me to come for supper. When I sat down at table she saw my fingers and had a fit. She said she was going to get to the bottom of it no matter what and after she put iodine on the raw places she called a doctor named Snodgrass who came right over. He said I'd have to stop hurting myself by biting my nails and gave Ma ointment to put on my fingers. "You're much too pretty to keep on biting your pretty nails, little lady." He went on and on like that. I hate him. By the way, as you have probably guessed, when I bit my nails I only did it on the left hand. I didn't touch my right because he was holding it. That's the reason I can write this. I couldn't if it was like the left is right now. It's bandaged up. Night, Mem.

I've decided to hang a curtain up around my part of the bed. It will be almost like having a room of my own. I'll do it tomorrow. It will be marvie-dar. (That's a word Patsy invented.) Just took a look in my mirror to check freckles—still there. I pray every moment that I'm not doomed to have them for life. So far none of my prayers get even a peep out of God.

Well, Mem, I take it back about God. It was Friday and Fou was in the car when it came for me after school. At first I didn't want to go with him, but Morris was holding the door open, so I had to get in. When I did I saw at once that there was a package on the seat. "For my Precious Angel," he said and gave it to me. Oh Mem, inside was the most beautiful silk underwear. Two brassieres with chemises to match and panties with tea roses sewn about here and there. "For your little garden," he said. "Beauties who go to Paris don't wear cottony wottony underwear, no sirree!" I couldn't believe it, Mem. He is going to take us to Europe this summer. "How would that suit you?" he asked. I couldn't open my mouth I was so excited. We are to sail on the *Aquitania*. What about the others? I asked him. "What others?" he said. Oh you know—Ma and Cousin Martha and Lucy Edwina. He put his finger over my mouth and said, "Only you and I, sweetkins." Then he gave me a big hug. I still can't believe it, Mem. Everything is more than marvie-dar and I am the happiest girl in the world!

I've just come back from the Parade to welcome home the Yankee Division soldiers—Oh how to describe it to you, for my heart's bursting out of me and my fingers are still stiff from the cold so it's hard to hold the pen. My voice is hoarse from cheering for hours along with the multitudes. The sound of it still rings in my ears. There were flags everywhere and bells ringing and horns blasting and thousands of soldiers oh so proud and brave marching. Ma was crying and so was I. It was so—so—thrilling, Mem, so unlike anything that had ever happened, and not only to *be* there, but to be one of the girls chosen by the Mayor's Entertainment Committee to toss chocolate bars, oranges, and cigarettes to the soldiers as they passed! We were on the great stands at Tremont Street with our dear Cousin A. and other dignitaries. I will never forget this day, Mem, and don't feel left out please, for if I was there, you were there too. Always remember that.

$\mathcal{T}$he suspense is over. All arrangements for the summer have been made. Instead of going to Vinalhaven Island or Dover Farm for the summer, Prune Face, Lucy Edwina and Mary are going to San Francisco to visit some Phillips cousins. Ma and Tooka have been invited to go too, so it works out perfectly because AJP can't go to San Francisco. His brother, who is a diplomat in Paris, has to see him on urgent business. And I am to go with him to keep him company and at the same time further my education, improve my French accent and so on. I'm jumping out of my skin. Tomorrow I'm to have a photograph taken for my passport.

$\mathcal{H}$e has sent me a Vuitton Innovation trunk! It's as big as a house! Well, almost. When it's closed and standing on the floor you'd never guess that when it's open there are four drawers on one side and on the other a rod with hangers so it's a closet. Oh, it's marvie, Mem, and I've new clothes and traveling things to put in it. Are you wondering where I am going to put you so Fou won't know you're along with us? Have no fear. You'll be cozy under the flannel cover of my hot water bottle. You fit perfectly and he won't guess a thing.

$\mathcal{Y}$ou ask me how I will feel about leaving my Mamacita and Tookacita behind. Well, truth to tell, your Favorita won't miss them one bit. Why should she? No Mamacita and her "do this, do that." No Tookacita and her "give me this, give me that." It will be a relief, I can tell you. Of course, I'll be glad to know they are in the world *somewhere*. I wouldn't want them to drop off the face of the earth. But I'll feel so much more grown-up without them around, don't you agree? What I don't feel so happy about is Daddy. What if he comes home? How will he know how to find me? Help me, Mem, to find a solution to this problem, should it arise. At first I was sorry that Lucy Edwina wasn't coming. I could tell she was disappointed to be going only to San Francisco. Then I was sort of glad she wasn't coming because we aren't such good friends as we were last summer. Patsy and I go together more and Lucy Edwina goes with Elaine because of their piano lessons. But anyway, at the last minute everything turned out perfectly because Prune Face let Lucy Edwina accept an invitation from Elaine and her parents to go with them on their yacht to the Galapagos Islands. Cousin A. and I are to leave day after tomorrow. I can't wait.

I'm taking my Daddy Lincoln picture out of its frame to carry with me between your pages, Mem. That way he will be safe and close to me.

*O*h—the *Aquitania* is even more more more *more* than I could have imagined!! So big, so *gigantic*—How can it float all the way across the ocean? As we went up the gangplank I had to bend over backwards to see the top of the huge smokestacks and even then I couldn't because I got dizzy and had to hold on to Cousin A. The corridors are everywhere so clean and bright and smell of metal polish and rubber. We have two staterooms with a connecting door and the furniture is like furniture in a house with everything oh so luxurious. There were flowers and baskets of fruit on the tables, champagne too, and my Innovation trunk and Cousin A.'s. The rest of our luggage is down in the hold of the ship. Before sailing everyone was bustling around happy and weepy saying goodbye goodbye and soon men in mess jackets (that's what AJP says the jackets are called) were running around with chimes playing a little tune and calling out "All Ashore Who's Going Ashore." So now here we are at last, Mem, you and I sprawling on a deck chair two days at sea. So far it's been chilly, so I have my hot water bottle with me—and you, Mem—besides being covered by three lap robes. Fou is off attending to something he has in store for tonight. What can it be? Can it have anything to do with the color green? He hasn't given me any creamy dreamy since we left Boston, which seems ages ago even tho' it's only been three days! All the way down on the train he kept talking about how *urgent* it was to get to the deck steward soon as poss. once on board, to make certain he would "navigate" our deck chairs properly. He's so fussy—everything has to be done the way he wants it. I have to stop now. I see him coming.

*T*here are more Adonises on the ship than I can count. You can't help but notice. Fou's in a constant flibberty flub about it.

There is one in particular, named Roland Roberts. He is a member of the MCC Cricket Team who's been visiting an aunt in Milwaukee and is now on his way to meet his fiancée in Paris. (Roland Roberts is a most euphonious name, don't you think so, Mem?) Every time Fou sees Roland and me talking together he gets suspicious and I have to listen to the lecture about "fooling around in dark corners with fellows." I assure him I'm not fooling around. Mr. Adonis Cricket and I have philosophical conversations, I tell him. "What manner of philosophical conversations?" He's determined to find out. Educational philosophical conversations regarding cricket and—Alfred Lord Tennyson—he's very taken with Alfred Lord Tennyson as I am myself (even tho' I may not have mentioned this to you before, Mem). And anyway, I keep telling Fou, he's engaged to be married to Miss Amanda Rhys-Loftus from Cornwall, so what's all the flibberty flubberty about?

I spend as much time as I can swimming in the pool, but it's hardly worth it as I have to listen to Fou's tirades afterwards about "strangers" ogling me not to mention how smelly the pool is with disinfectants and how noisy with sounds made by other swimmers laughing and enjoying themselves. Well, it is noisy with the laughter and splashing around echoing off the walls, but—why not come in? Join the fun. He pretends not to hear. He won't swim because he can keep a better eye on me from the sidelines. If he was in the pool I might slip away from him—yes, slip away, mermaid that I am, and never see him again—slip away through a tunnel in the bottom of the pool, on down until I get out into the ocean where I'll be safe. No such luck, tho'. There's no tunnel in the *Aquitania* pool (believe me, I've made a thorough search).

*M*eal times are almost the best times, Mem, for we are sitting at the Captain's table and everyone thinks I am much older than thirteen. You, Mem, may be wondering how I know this. Well, smarty, I know it because everybody talks to me in a much more grown-up way than people do back home. I'm dying to find out how old they think I am. Sixteen maybe? Seventeen? Older?? O bliss! Anyway, only important people sit at the Captain's table

THE MEMORY BOOK OF STARR FAITHFULL

and of all of them, dear Cousin A. is most important of all because he is the Mayor of Boston. I sit next to Adonis Cricket. Fou sits near the Captain quite far from me. The two ladies sitting beside Fou do keep him busy, but not busy enough for me. He's constantly looking down the long table in my direction. At dinner last night I got fed up and kept waving at him. He didn't wave back. I guess he was embarrassed, but it served him right. He's at me constantly. If it's not about Mr. Adonis Cricket it's about Officer Hallibut. It so happens that Mr. Hallibut is an erudite conversationalist—even more so than Adonis Cricket. But every time Fou sees him coming in my direction he gets in a huff and a puff and makes up some excuse to hurry me away. Mr. Hallibut loves to dance and so do I, as you well know. And thanks to Miss Bonnie Mae I know all the steps. There's dancing every night, but Fou is the dreariest one on the floor. He holds me far away and never looks at me. He says he is "practicing proper behavior," but he turns me into a stuffed doll. So last night I left Fou at our table twirling his thumbs while I twirled about the dance floor with Mr. Hallibut. Finally I had pity on the silly thing, and when the music stopped I went to the table and sat beside him. He insisted we go back to our staterooms, where he went on and on about his "duty" to protect me from strangers, especially junior officers like Hallibut. He called him "Fishy Fish" and it put me in a fury because it was so unfair—there is nothing even remotely Fishy about Officer Hallibut even though his name may bring fish to mind. I told him there was only one person a bit Fishy on this ship and his name was Fishy Fou and he was the one who was spoiling the trip. Then I ran out of the room and he came running after me. I could have escaped, but his face was so red from running down corridors and up steps that I had pity on him again and let him catch up to me, yes, he was breathing hard and I got scared and I took his hand and led him back to his stateroom. He had to move slowly and hold onto the rail as we went down the stairs. When we got there he collapsed onto his bed. I knelt beside him and held his hand and tried to remember the words of "Roses of Picardy"—you know how he loves that song, but even the tune had gone from my head so I couldn't sing it, only hum, and what came out was the sound of an insect buzzing around. He was startled at the sound, so at least it brought his mind back for a second. I told him I was trying to sing "Roses of Picardy,"

64

and at that he began singing a few snatches of the song himself
and then it all came back to me and we were singing together,
nowhere near the exact words, but he closed his eyes and squeezed
my hand and that was good enough for me. "Don't stop," he said.
So I kept on singing, and after a while he fell asleep. I lay down
beside him on the bed and soon I was asleep too. When I woke
up he was in the bathroom and when he came out nothing was
said about what had happened. Tonight I'll say I had too much
sun when Fishy Fish asks me to dance with him.

Well, Mignonette, here we are in France. (Hope you don't
mind, now that we're here, if I call you that sometimes?) We arrived in Marseilles on the train this morning. A grey and black
Duesenberg car was waiting, along with Claude, who's going to be
our driver during the trip. He knows every twist of the hazardous
corniche so we shan't miss a thing. Right now I'm in my bathroom in our suite at the Hôtel de Paris in Monte Carlo. Fou
hasn't given me a minute to myself and I've locked myself in here
to talk with you a little. The last two days on the ship were *awful.*
You see, it got rough, Mem. The sea, I mean, and I was sick as a
dog and Fou was even sicker and we missed the fancy-dress ball. I
wanted to go as Delilah (she's my new favorite) and I thought he
could go as Samson. But that idea made him peevish. He said it
would be inappropriate for the Mayor of Boston to appear as
Samson, and as for his little cousin, when it came to costumes she
should be dwelling on Bo Peeps instead of Delilahs. I'm not little,
I screamed at him, but anyway the wind started to blow and we
never did decide on our costumes, and the ball was cancelled anyway. I have to stop now, though. He's knocking on the door fran-
tic that something's happened to me in here—ha ha.

I spotted a daisy ring in Cartier near the hotel and AJP bought it
for me. I love it. I'm wearing it now and intend to leave it on even
when I wash my hands. The soap can't harm it because it's real
gold and the center of the daisy has real little diamonds twinkling.
At dinner in the dining room of the hotel everyone was dressed in
splendid clothes and jewels. I wore my blue with the flounces and
my daisy ring of course. For dessert he ordered meringues and

vanilla ice cream with raspberry sauce for us both. Then the waiter brought more champagne. "No more for Mademoiselle," Fou said, but too late, for my glass was already filled.

*T*oday we went to the Oceanographical Museum and Aquarium at Monaco. I leaned over a tank of tortoises who were having naps but now and then opened their eyes to look at me. After, we came back and had tea on the terrace of the Hôtel de Paris. We had violet sandwiches! Picture it, Mem—sandwiches made of violets. Oh, if only you could taste them. All through tea he kept talking about what we had seen at the Aquarium, especially the turtles. He said he had "secret information pertaining to sweet little turtles," but then he refused to tell me what it is. He can be so infuriating. "Soon, soon" was all he'd say.

*H*urry, hurry, hurry," Fou said when we woke up this morning. "We mustn't miss a moment of this glorious day." He was still in his dressing gown calling to me from the balcony and I could tell he had something special in mind. I was ready before he was but soon we were speeding along in the Duesenberg with Claude. Suddenly I heard a band in the distance and Fou's eyes were twinkling and he said, "All for you, Mademoiselle Etoile—to welcome you to Menton!" For that's where we were going, and soon there we were in the jardins publiques, oh so gay with the band playing and people walking among the beds of white pansies, or were they nasturtiums? Anyway, Fou was holding my hand and we were happy. He let me ride on a white donkey led by a woman in a black pleated dress and a black hat like a pancake, and he took a picture of me with his Phanex flash camera (the latest thing). Oh, if only you had been with me, Mem, for words can hardly describe how it was. I had never felt so clean and bright.

*L*ast night *finally* he told me the secret of the turtle, and you're going to faint because the secret is that *I* have a little turtle between the two parts of my beaver!!! And that's not all the secret—there's another part, which is that every girl's turtle is different. Some are plump and smooth and placed high on the pubis, while others are placed low. This knowledge of the placement of the turtle is from the Taoist culture, which instructs that the high ones are best but most Chinese females are "low-cut ones." Fou made me write all this down, otherwise, he said, I'd forget and he wouldn't want me to do that. He was right, too, because there's so much to think about my head is aching and I never could have remembered it all to repeat it to you now if I hadn't. (Written it down.) The Hindus call low-cut ones lotus girls because their vulva is no bigger than a lotus bud. Then there is the "shell girl," whose vulva is as large as a sea shell, and the "elephant girl," whose vulva is as big as a baby elephant's, and that girl would definitely be one of the high-cut ones. Naturally I asked which one I was, but he wouldn't tell me. By this time my head was spinning around with turtles and shells and what not, so I was glad when he said I could stop writing and we'd go on to the "practicum." I was sure he meant creamy dreamy and I was all for that, since I hadn't had any since we arrived in Monte Carlo. But I pretended I didn't care one way or the other because I knew if he thought I wanted some too much he might decide to tease me and who knows when he would relent, although he always does eventually. Well, he said, show me where your little turtle is and we'll see what we can do. No, I said, I'll never be able to find it until I have some creamy dreamy "practicum," for isn't that what that means? He laughed and called me a naughty girl and pulled me onto his lap. "It's only naughty girls who can't find their turtles so now I'll have to find it for you," he said. Oh no you don't, I said. I jumped up and ran to the door, but he caught me before I could get out. He held on to my hand and led me over to the bed. Look under the bed, he said, and when I did there was the satchel where he keeps the green bottle. Open it up, he said, and while I did he took off his trousers. I stretched out on the bed and pulled up my skirt. Now, now, he said—you try to discover where your little green turtle is hiding while I try to discover if there is anything in this little green bottle. He took the stopper off and sniffed inside. We're in luck, he said, turning the bottle upside down and shaking it over the cotton. Hurry up, I said, and he came over and lay down beside me on the bed and brushed the cotton over my face oh so gentle, so soft, so loving. Yes, Mem, AJP loves me I know. He makes me so happy.

*Y*esterday we drove to Grasse to a place where perfume is made and AJP bought me samples in aluminum flagons. As I smelled each one, colors came to mind—white for Gardenia; lavender for Mignonette (that's you, Mem); yellow for Tuberose; pink for Jasmine; peach for Patchouli; and for Violets—Violets might be grey but I'm not sure. Oh—and Musk, I mustn't forget Musk; Musk was green, definitely. Of all the scents, Fou went Fou over the Musk, especially a blend called Rose-Musk. He kept rambling on about the sweetest flower wild nature yields, which is a fresh-blown musk-rose. Yes, Mem, that's what he was going on about, and it was throwing its sweets upon the summer, which comes from a sonnet by Keats. When we got back to the hotel he spent the whole evening patting my beaver with Rose-Musk and reciting poetry while I had creamy dreamy.

Listen, I have so much to tell you. Starting out on the drive to Paris Claude drove us along the coastal routes so we wouldn't miss a thing. He kept pointing out this and that while lamenting that it wasn't spring, for had it been he would have taken us by the road through the Cévennes. "Ah, Mademoiselle Etoile," he said—Etoile means Star in French, as if you didn't know—"high in the mountains in the spring you would observe great sheets of white and think they were patches of snow that had not yet melted, but closer, ah yes Mademoiselle Etoile—closer you would see they were fields of narcissi—sooo beautiful—quelle tristesse that you will miss this sight, but perhaps another year you and monsieur will come in springtime and—" "Ça suffit, Claude," Fou said. He never encourages conversation between Claude and Mademoiselle Etoile. "Enfin—" Claude said, shrugging his shoulders, and that was the end of snow and narcissi. But not the end of jasmine and roses blooming around us or my feeling so grown up, so mademoiselle, so—so enfin. I had dabbed on a bit of Rose-Musk at my earlobes before we'd left the hotel and to complete the effect I'd put more than a tat on a little ball of cotton tucked inside my brassiere. I read about doing this in a magazine on the ship. Romantic, n'est-ce pas, Mignonette? It was going to be a long drive and who knew what might happen? Nothing much did until after lunch. Our picnic hamper was with Claude on the front seat and as we passed a piney glade he suggested we stop there. Then he spread a cloth out over the pine needles beneath the trees and opened up the hamper. I was so hungry I ate most of the pâté, not much left for anyone else. Anyone else meaning Fou, for once the hamper was opened he had told Claude to go into the next hamlet and lunch there—no hurry—come back in two hours. In the hamper there was a glass-covered dish with Petit Suisse and thick cream in a stoppered jug to pour over it and brown sugar, lots of brown sugar, to put on top. Oh, it was sweet and good. After, I stretched out and closed my eyes. It was quiet and hot, and the scent of cork and of the greeny pine needles warm beneath me and the scent between my bosoms made me hazy and heady, but then I knew it wasn't that—it was creamy dreamy and Fou was beside me oh so close and I knew nothing could harm me. I knew he'd take care of me always and that he wouldn't go away. You'll never go away, will you? I whispered to him, but he didn't hear me because he'd pulled up my skirt and his mouth was kissing me through the silk of my chemise. After, when I came back into myself I was sad, I don't know why because he was there, asleep beside me with his arm over me. So why did I cry? Why did I slip out from under his arm and walk out of the glade and onto the highway not knowing which way I was going? I kept seeing Fou asleep under the trees, how he'd look when he woke to find me gone. Yes, gone and never coming back. But then suddenly I heard a shout behind me and it was his voice calling. He was running towards me and in front of me a car was rushing towards me. Between Fou and Claude there was no escape, Mem. So here I am with you at the Ritz Hotel in Paris in rooms overlooking the garden. Oh, it's v. grand, I can tell you, and I like it. But tell me, what do you make of it all?

*H*e says he's let me distract him with too many frivolous demands—running in and out of shops trying on dresses and hats and the like. Then there's Marcel's, where I went to have my hair rinsed with henna. It was his idea first and he was the one who took me there. His idea too that I have a manicure and pedicure. My first, Mem! He told them no lacquer on my fingernails but they could be buffed and for my toes he selected a lacquer called Sea Shell. It is so pale it's hard to see, but it has a pearly shine. So he has a nerve complaining! Since then, of course, it's true I've been back constantly, but he complains that it takes time away from him and from now on a new schedule is to be set up so our studies will no longer be as sorely neglected as they have been of late. Such things as henna hair-dos, pearly toes, and Paris dresses are charming but not important in the grand scheme of things. What *is* the grand scheme of things? Well, your future, Starr— that's the grand scheme of things. My Starr must be guided so she finds her place in the firmament. This sounded like it had a hidden meaning—but what? What, Mem? Sometimes he makes no sense and when I ask him to explain he tells me I am too young to understand but someday he'll explain, when I'm ready. It's *infuriating*.

*H*e made a discovery on the Left Bank yesterday, in a bookstore to be exact. He said it was v. educational and we'd need lots of time to study both the pictures and the text because one cannot be studied without the other. I asked what he meant by that but all he'd say was later—later. Hold your horses, Starr. I thought I was in for a long tease but later came sooner than expected. Instead of going out for dinner or anything else we had dinner in our suite, and as soon as the table was removed Fou put the sign on the door so the maids wouldn't be interrupting our studies by coming in to turn down the beds as they usually do. Come, he said, and we sat down on the divan holding the book between us. It turned out to be a book about Chinese and Japanese art and it was v. heavy. Open to the first page, he said. There was a drawing of a room and in the room a man lying down on a couch like the one we were sitting on and on the floor beside the man, sitting on cushions, was a girl playing the flute. What's her name? Fou asked. "Lady of the Vase," I read. She was wearing red trousers so transparent you could see everything underneath—her body I mean. The man's name was Hsi-men, but Fou said to pronounce it "she-men," and to go on to the next page. There we saw Hsi-men and the same lady. Fou explained that the lady was going to play the flute for Hsi-men, though in the picture she had put her flute down and was holding Hsi-men's corn in her hand. "Treasure is what this particular lady calls *that*," Fou informed me, and he went on reading from the book, where it said the Lady would like to suck the treasure all night long. Would you like to do that? Fou said. I didn't know what to say. What was I supposed to do? I pointed out that the lady had put her flute down. "Precious Angel," he said. "Turn the page." There they were again, Hsi-men and the Lady. See? Fou said. This time she was holding the treasure in her mouth and Hsi-men was smiling. Fou leaned over the book and read some more, about letting the essence flow and how she sucked it into her mouth, but couldn't drink it fast enough. Next Hsi-men was telling the Lady to put his Limpo back in her mouth and suck it while he drank some wine. He said that if she played the flute well he would give her a silk robe. Yes, yes, the Lady said, and she took his Limpo in her mouth and played the flute till dawn. It was *fascinating*, Mem, and I couldn't wait to go on to the next picture, but Fou excused himself and went into the bathroom and took the book with him. He stayed in that bathroom forever it seemed, which made me mad. Finally I just went to bed and when he came out I pretended to be asleep. He turned the lights off and got into the bed next to mine. Did I tell you that my bedroom has two beds that are pushed together so they look like one? Anyway, he fell asleep right away and now I'm in the bathroom with you telling you the events of the day. I didn't want to risk turning on the light and waking him up. I'm getting sleepy now. Goodnight, Mem.

We're sailing from Le Havre in two weeks and guess what! We are to take the Duesenberg back to America with us! Today I saw an aeroplane fly *under* the Arc de Triomphe!! There were huge crowds, but AJP had sent Claude on ahead hours before to get the best spot for us to see it. When we arrived AJP held my hand and pushed his way through. People who had been waiting for hours made angry noises and kept glaring at us but AJP paid no attention. So there we were in the best place near the Arc. After that it was back to the Ritz for a nap. Tonight we're going to the Folies Bergère and after that to a cabaret in Montmartre. Tomorrow Claude leaves for Le Havre with most of the trunks and the Duesenberg. We have four more days in Paris.

I wanted to spend these last days shopping, not to mention having my hair and nails done, but Fou was intent on cramming culture and education into me. He took a sudden notion into his head that time had gone by quicker than even he could have anticipated and that I must be fully informed and equipped to relate in detail all that I had seen in Paris. "Yes, knowledge is all. Culture is all," he keeps saying. He says it so often that I want to scream.

He's dragged me back to the Louvre *twice*, and for the hundredth time I've showed him my Travelog scrapbook with the postcards on each page, proving how studious I am. Anyway, I guess he's convinced because in a few minutes I'm dashing off to Marcel's, and after he's meeting me at Madame Lucille's. I've been asking and asking him to buy me one of her robes de style and he's been adamant against it. He says a robe de style is much too grown-up for me. But at last he's given in. Oh he is a dear sweet Fou, isn't he, Mem? Tomorrow we leave for Le Havre.

We're on the train, Mem. Can you hear the sound the wheels make? For a while I thought we wouldn't make it. AJP was so upset I was afraid he would have to go into the hospital. The Duesenberg was being hoisted up onto the ship by a pulley and the pulley broke and the car fell into the sea! Fou really loved that car. He walked around in a daze muttering, "Now all the happy memories are down there along with the fishes swimming in and out of the windows—that is if they're open." "Oh, the windows wouldn't have been open while they were hoisting it up onto the steamer," the shipping official, Mr. Moulin, told him, but all AJP did was wring his hands. For the longest time, he just sat staring out the window into the garden. I'd never seen him so not himself and I began to get really worried about him. Then I thought of the book of Chinese Art and asked him where he'd packed it. At first he didn't seem to know what I was talking about but then he said, Yes, yes, and soon we were lying together on his bed looking at the pictures and he gave me some creamy dreamy and had a few whiffs himself. I said, would you like it if I played the flute for you? Oh, you remember, he said. Now he was smiling, so I took his Treasure in my hand and pretended it was a flute and he liked that a lot. Soon he seemed better, and I kept playing the flute and all at once milk was spurting into my mouth, only it tasted *terrible*. Swallow, swallow, he kept saying, but I was gagging and ran into the bathroom, spitting it out into my hands. He ran in after me and gave me Floris Rose Water but I was so scared I swallowed it. Then I kept rinsing my mouth out but nothing I did could get the taste of the fishy sticky milk away and my face got red and swollen and all I did was cry. I couldn't stop and he was running into the bathroom all worry worry and putting a hot towel over my face and begging me to be all right. He rocked me in his arms and

I breathed deep into the towel and the steam brought me back to myself and when I looked up he was himself again too and I told him I was fine—everything was fine. Of course it is, he said, fine, everything's fine—keep smiling, keep smiling keep smiling.

W e're sailing on a French ship this time, called *La Lorraine*. No news about the Duesenberg and AJP said he never wanted to hear the word Duesenberg ever again. He looked so sad, but there was a band playing as we boarded and it put him in a better mood. Once we got out to sea he was even better. I've tried to be good, Mem, not teasing him or anything. I haven't so much as looked at an Adonis—altho' there is one—well, never mind. I stay by his side day and night and he gets pitty pats and sweet kisses every few minutes. I'd be happy going back and forth on this ship forever.

H ere we are, Mem, back home and listening to Ma raving about the San Francisco cousins and the fine time they had while I'm raving about Paris and Monte Carlo, so everybody's raving at the same time. Divine, divine, Mamacita keeps saying, but oh how I wish I were in divine Paris or on a divine steamer going there. I hate being in Boston, hate Tooka, hate Ma. Daddy wasn't here when we got back and there was no message from him. There is one good thing. Everyone says I look more grown-up. That's more than fine by me. I can't wait to grow up—then everything is going to be different, we know that, don't we?

S omething wonderful has happened and something dreadful, both at the same time. The wonderful something is that Daddy came back. When he walked in Ma took one look at his beard, grown oh so long, and made a lunge to pull it off as if it were a fake. But then instead she turned her arm around and hit the top of her head three times, like a woodpecker peck peck pecking away at a tree, and Daddy started laughing at her. Then he asked, did she have any idea what a pretty pass her dear Cousin Andrew had brought the city to? He meant the something dreadful, Mem, which is that the policemen in Boston have gone on strike and since last night there have been mobs rampaging in the streets.

"Of course we know about it, you fool," Ma shouted. "We haven't been out of the house all day and Minna couldn't come, but what do you mean by saying *Andrew* brought us to this pretty pass?" Daddy said he'd seen James Michael Curley speaking to the crowds from the running board of his car outside of City Hall, and that he (Curley) had hit the nail on the head about how Cousin A. was spending all this time gallivanting around Europe instead of running the city and now he's not lifting a finger to settle the strike. Daddy said the policemen are only striking because their pay has not gone up since the war, though prices have gone up very much and Cousin A. must think they can live on air, that is if he thinks at all, and Ma was screaming at the same time that what the police were doing was illegal, so why blame Cousin A., and after all everyone must tighten his belt. Oh, it was a fierce battle, Mem, and I kept trying to understand. It was very bad. I hate Curley. After his speech he got in his car and had the chauffeur drive the wrong way down Washington Street. I asked Daddy why he did that and he said, "To thumb his nose at your cousin the mayor." Yes, Mem, those are his exact words. He said a few other exact words, too—about how if Cousin A. was what reform meant he preferred good old-fashioned corruption. How *could* Daddy say things like that about Cousin A.? Ma kept screaming "Shut up, shut up! Lies—lies—it's all lies—you're jealous—that's what *you* are, Frank Wyman, eaten up with jealousy because our Cousin Andrew J. Peters will be a hero after he settles the hash of those damn strikers, and then, Mr. Nobody, what will you have to say for yourself?" Daddy didn't say anything after that, not to Ma. He told me he was going out to see what was what and he would be back. I was scared something would happen and he wouldn't come back even though he'd promised, but he did, in time to say goodnight to me. Tooka was already asleep. He and Ma are in the kitchen but everything is quiet. I can't even hear whispering.

I kept waking up in the night oh so restless and *sick* hearing over and over again the things Daddy said about Cousin A. Why can't they love each other, since I love them both so much? Of course I love Daddy most, more than anyone, even you, Mem—yes, it's true. Don't be angry, I beg you, try to be fair. After all, he came first. I'm not making sense, I know, but I kept waking up and hearing Daddy's terrible words against Cousin A. and made up my mind to talk to him in the morning and confirm what I am sure is so—that Daddy only said those things because Ma had driven him beyond endurance—yes, that's definitely it. Definitely. After a while I fell asleep, but when I woke and went to find him there was no one there. He was gone. "Gone, Gone," Ma kept saying, "gone and *not* coming back." I don't believe it—that he's not coming back. What does *she* know?

*L*ater. Morris came to bring some things we needed, since Minna still couldn't get here. He said AJP has ordered the militia to be called in. Gov. Coolidge is to come this afternoon, but by that time Cousin A. will have settled the strike and everything will be fine again.

*M*inna finally reached us today, as Ma puts it. She (Minna) says there are soldiers everywhere, so we must not go out yet. Being cooped up here with Ma and Tooka is making me crazy. Not knowing where Daddy is makes me more crazy.

*C*ousin A. came by today full of news about how what the mob needed was a firm hand and how tomorrow he would be oh so busy hiring new policemen because the old ones had been fired. "Can't tarry long," he kept saying, "but you know how important my little cousins are to me and I couldn't rest until I saw firsthand that there had been no damage done down this way." He has everything under control now, there is nothing more to fear.

*T*his just came.

> Precious Girls,
>   Writing in haste, great haste as hastening to catch the 9:06 to Memphis. Got out of Boston all right, so don't worry. Will be in touch again soon. Have business in Memphis. You are my little angels. Never forget that and how much your Daddy loves you.

It was addressed to me and Tooka on stationery from the Pickwick Arms Hotel on West 38th St. in New York City. But what help is that? He's already left for Memphis so it's no use writing back.

Sunday. Oh how inspiring to sit near Cousin A. in our family pew. I couldn't keep my mind on anything but the back of his handsome Fou head in front of me. If only I could have leaned over and given it a pitty pat. My, wouldn't he have been surprised, not to mention Prune Face and the others, for the church was full, everyone so grateful that order has been restored. Then I got another crazy notion, to lean over and not just give the back of Fou's head a pitty pat but draw a face on the shiny smooth pate of it, a smiling Campbell's Soup kid face for all the congregation sitting in back of him to see. Of course I restrained myself, but I got such giggles I had to pretend it was a coughing fit and Ma kept shushing me and whispering to stop drawing attention to myself. Finally even Fou looked around at me, frowning severely and shaking his head for silence. Anyway, it turned out all right because after church we had dinner at Jamaica Plain and no mention was made of the occurrence. Tomorrow we can start school. Morris will be by as usual. It makes me so proud that such a great man is my cousin. Ma says we need more leaders like him in the world. Before he left he gave me a kiss and whispered, "Soon, Precious Angel," in my ear. My heart is bursting.

Oh Mem, I could die. I was dancing with Charlie Gilbert at the first dancing class since school started and Miss Bonnie Mae said, "Too close—too close—six inches apart, have you forgotten everything over the summer holidays? Tut tut" and she tapped her cane on our toes. Charlie pulled back and twirled me away, yes away, six inches apart like all the others dancing around. But then he twirled me right on out into the hall so fast we slipped and fell against each other and then he kissed me—and right then there he was—Fou—behind us. He was outraged—angry as could be. I was commanded to go straight to Lucy Edwina's room and soon the chauffeur would be in attendance to take me home— "and as for you, young man, I shall deal with you anon." Oh God, Mem—what does that "anon" mean? No one else saw anything—at least I don't think they did. Only Fou. That makes it less terrible, doesn't it? Or maybe *more* terrible—can't decide. Oh, Mem, what's going to happen?

I'm frozen with fear. There's been no mention of it. Everyone in dancing class that day thinks I was excused because I had a sudden indisposition. No one knows anything.

*T*his letter came. Oh Mem, listen—

My dear Starr,

It distresses me to be forced to take pen in hand and write to you in this manner over your display of vulgarity with the Gilbert lad, which occurred recently outside the ballroom during your dancing class at Jamaica Plain. Luckily I was the only unfortunate witness. I must say that this episode more than puzzles me. I have not been able to find any explanation for your behavior, and, as it is difficult, nay almost impossible, to forgive that which we cannot understand, it has taken me some time to gather my thoughts to write you this letter. Surely you are aware of the fact that your mother, dear Helen, is not only a cousin of Martha's but also a close friend. We have taken you and Tooka not only into our lives but more importantly into our hearts ever since you came to Boston. Your behavior reflects badly not only on you but on our family and indeed on all members of the Peters and Phillips families, of whose position and heritage you are well aware. As to the Gilbert lad, I have made my sentiments clear. You will find him a perfect gentleman when your paths cross again.

I need say no more, except that I am content that there will be no further exhibitions from Starr Wyman save of the decorum appropriate to a cousin of mine. Take heed, my dear, and let this unfortunate incident not be mentioned again.

Your concerned but always loving
Cousin Andrew

Oh God, Mem. Doesn't he just *know* I'll never ever do such a thing again? Should I write back telling him I vow not to or should I do as he says and not mention it? If only I could explain to him how it all happened so fast—and I still don't really understand why what happened was so bad. O Mem, I miss him something awful.

I keep trying to figure things out, but it's no use. I even went back to *Pilgrim's Progress*—do you remember it, Mem? I thought maybe if I could *see* those places Christian has to go through before he gets to the good places like the Delectable Mountains and the Celestial City it would help. So I drew this map. It's not exactly like the book because I added some things of my own, but I don't think Christian will mind. Anyway, Mem, here it is. Do you think if I show it to him he will see into my true heart and understand my true intent and forgive me and love me again?

*T*hought I'd die walking into the next dancing class, but nothing happened. No one knows anything. Charlie just laughed and whispered, "Mr. Peters sure gave me a talking to, but he calmed down when I told him we skidded together because the floor was so slippery." Cousin A. wasn't there. I keep praying for everything to be all right again with AJP, but it isn't. Now Thanksgiving is coming and we are invited as usual and I don't know what to do. I want so much to see him again—I do love him, Mem, and he loves me, I know. He's the only one who truly cares about what happens to me even if he hasn't gotten in touch with me since his letter. Yes—he's done everything in the world for me, hasn't he, and if only I could see him I'd be able to show him how much I love him—oh yes, Mem—if I could see him only for a second everything would be all right.

*S*till no word. If I'd heard from him I could go on Thanksgiving, but as I haven't—no, I'm not going. Clearly his opinion of me hasn't changed since The Letter, even tho' it did end "your always loving Cousin Andrew." Ma thinks we are all going as usual, but she is wrong. This will be one Thanksgiving I will *not* attend. I'll stuff cotton up my nose and speak in a whisper as if my throat were sore. Yes, haven't you noticed, Mem, that I'm definitely losing my voice? Soon I shan't be able to speak, but only shake my head from side to side or nod it up and down, up and down. No, side to side is best, side to side means *no*.

*H*e came *today*, and acted as if nothing had happened, very jolly. Ho ho ho. Not angry, no, not at all. I could have jumped right through the ceiling I was so relieved. All he said was, "Heard about your sniffles and brought a present for my sweet cousin." It was the *Just So Stories* and I couldn't wait to get my hands on it but Tooka was lurking around and Mamacita was in and out, in and out with cookies and fidgety fuss so we didn't have a minute to ourselves. After he left I locked myself in the bathroom to read. *Quelle* disappointment. It's a book for *children*. The best thing in it is Fou's inscription, which says "For Starr—Just so you'll keep busy until you are well enough to resume our studies. Your friend and cousin, Andrew." I guess I'll go to Thanksgiving after all.

.   .   .

*A*ll is well now, Mem, as you'll be happy to hear. When he picked me up in Lizzie I knew we were going to China Heaven. At first I was a bit worried, because we rattled along without talking. Thoughts bounced around in my head this way and that, rattling me more than Lizzie was, for I wanted so much to please him but couldn't get a sense of the mood he was in or what was ahead. As it turned out I shouldn't have worried, because when we got to CH it was clear that my education was to continue as we settled ourselves side by side on the sofa with a new book called *Studies in the Psychology of Sex*, Volume I, between us. This book is by Professor Havelock Ellis and it is *most* educational—is v. thick and with lots of v. small type. He opened to a page with a poem in French and said in a kindly manner, "Lis, s'il te plaît." Here it is, Mem. It's word for word because after I read it he said I must write it down to memorize.

> J'ai calculé mon age,
> J'ai quatorze à quinze ans.
> Ne suis-je pas dans l'age
> D'y avoir un amant?

After I read it he asked me if I knew what it meant and of course I did. "Translate it for me," he said.

> I've calculated my age,
> I'm 14 going on 15 years old.
> Am I not of an age
> To have a lover?

"Excellent, Starr, parfait!" he said. "Do you realize that in less than two months you will be fourteen years old?" Of course I do, Mem, and at first I couldn't see what this was all this about, but then I did. It was about the Gilbert lad—that's what it was leading up to. Of course he didn't bring up the Gilbert lad by name—what he brought up was *modesty*, in "The Evolution of Modesty," which is the title of the first chapter of Professor Ellis's book. At first I thought he was going to read the whole chapter to me, but after a few pages, about Casanova, and about this Madame Celine Renooz wavering between the laws of Nature and social conventions and scarcely knowing if nakedness should or should not affright her, he turned to page 82 and told me to read aloud the following, which I also had to copy down, for I must memorize it later.

In the art of love, however, it is more than a grace; it must always be fundamental. Modesty is not indeed the last word of love, but it is the necessary foundation for all love's most exquisite audacities, the foundation which alone gives worth and sweetness to what Sénancour calls its "delicious impudence." Without modesty we could not have, nor rightly value at its true worth, that bold and pure candor which is at once the final revelation of love and the seal of its sincerity.

He made me read it aloud three times and after that he sat there as I copied it down. "Good girl," he said. "Now—a reward—yes, yes, a change of scene," and he bounced over to the cupboard and waved his hands around like a magician hocus-pocus-crocus-wocus and then opened it wide. Out fell clouds of white gauze, oh so floaty, so soft and drifty. "It's called chiffon," he said, "c-h-i-f-f-o-n," and he scooped it all up in his arms and held it out to me. I ran to him and it was so appealing, Mem, so inviting, so feathery, so soft, like clouds or the wool of the lambs at Dover Farm. I took it in my arms and closed my eyes and melted into it. "Not so fast, impulsive child." He sounded stern and I opened my eyes and pulled back. "Remember, we are here today primarily for studies and perhaps you have forgotten the subject at hand is modesty—so disrobe, please. It's time for the practicum to begin." I turned my back and let my dress and everything slip down onto the floor and stood there without moving waiting to see what was going to happen next. He came up behind me and turned me gently around, and as he did he started draping me in the heavenly folds. "Ah yes," he kept muttering—"yes, yes, modesty in the art of love is more than a grace"—and he put a fold around my head like a turban and draped it to cover my face, yes my entire face except for my eyes, which were left uncovered. The chiffon was so drifty I could easily breathe through it. Then he kissed me through the layer that covered my lips and murmured, "Yes, it is fundamental, not the last word of love but necessary for the foundation, necessary for all love's most exquisite audacities." As he said this I could feel the chiffon being wrapped down over my breasts, on down between my legs, then drawn up into a snug bond around my bottom and tied around my waist, and finally left free to float on down again, around my feet. "Precisely," he said. "What a pretty package." And he stood back to admire the effect. He seemed quite taken with his handiwork and led me tenderly to the chair, the big comfy one, and bid me recline just so, for he had a pleasure in store. I lay back and closed my eyes, pushing lightly and down against the soft fold of chiffon that he had so cleverly positioned between my legs, and then, oh so heavenly, the creamy dreamy wafted across my face. Oh Mem, I'll never be able to describe it to you as it really was. On the way home he commended me again and I can honestly say that he loves me as much if not more than he ever did before the Gilbert lad fiasco. You too, Mem. Good night.

*I*t is not true that all is well. I do not think that Daddy will be home for Christmas. But I don't care. Not at all. I'm going to run away—on a train or a bus—run away from everybody except you. Of course I'll take you with me. We'll never leave each other, will we. What would I do without you? There's no answer to that. Soon it'll be 1920! Oh, Mem, will I ever see Daddy again? I can't write any more.

1920

I didn't run away, I'm still here, though more serious than ever about disappearing somewhere. I just can't make up my mind how to go about it. Positively, that is. Where is Sister Aimee, do you suppose? But let's not be hasty. Now that it's 1920 maybe everything is going to be different, everything is changed as of right this minute, isn't that true, Mem, because it's time to say Happy New Year.

January 26, 1920 — Monday

Dearest, dearest Mem,

I am 14 years old today and I woke up different! — Yes, I definitely woke up feeling different, and yes, I am! More than anything I aim to think for myself and there is so much to think about my head is bursting. I have to run around to clear it, to let one thought come in at a time. I just know this is how Joan of Arc felt with the voices swirling around in her head — but how to ·know which voice to listen to or which is the right one?

I can report to you on this birthday morn that I have *permanently* stopped biting my fingernails. I have also permanently stopped feeling sorry for myself. This proves I can be firm of character, and firm in my resolve once I decide to pledge myself to whatever it is I'm pledging myself to.

My biggest worry is that I don't make the kind of impression on people that I'd like to make. The problem is that I'm not really sure what that impression *is* — and if I don't know what it is, how can I make it? See, Mem? Ma calls me her Starr Baby in front of

THE MEMORY BOOK OF STARR FAITHFULL

people and I hate it. Sometimes, if Tooka's not around, she tells
them that I'm Mamacita's Favorita. *That's* not the impression I
want to make. No, not at all. First, even if I am the Favorita—
I'm *not* a baby. I am a firm-of-resolve 14-year-old person. The future is ahead of me, and I can be anything I want, even tho' I don't
know yet exactly what it is. Sometimes I wish I were Catholic so I
could become a nun of the Dominican order. They wear white
habits all the time, not only the day of their marriage to Christ
when they take the vows of poverty, chastity and obedience.
There's a poem I'm particularly in love with—"The Eve of St.
Agnes," by John Keats. The nun is dressed "in raiment white and
clean," so she must be of the Dominican order, don't you think? I
feel best when I'm wearing white, muslin especially. Nuns also get
to live in convent gardens where white lilies grow and doves fly
around. This must be a fact because there is a painting by Charles
Allster Collins called *Convent Thoughts.* I saw it in a book in Patsy's
house. A nun is standing in a garden by a pool holding a flower in
her right hand and an open book in the other. She's gazing into
the flower, and oh how I'd like to be she, so serene there in that
setting. I may not have mentioned it at the time, so many other
things were going on, but when Fou and I visited Notre Dame de
Paris—well, I felt very much at home inside even tho' it was so
huge, vast and the light so dim—I felt très spirituelle lighting the
candle, yes, infinitely definitely I did. I can't understand why I
didn't go into it with you at the time, but maybe I did and have
forgotten—anyway, now you know. I must also tell you that
there are other times when I am determined not to retire from the
world, but to do the exact opposite—get out into it. But before I
can do that I will have to know what the true way is, because I
fervently desire to be out there leading others along it. The true
way is what I'm trying to find. Does this sound silly, Mem? If
only you could talk you'd tell me.

Happy Birthday
Starr

I didn't do very well last term—you know why, Mem—and
wanted to make it up this spring, but it seems the more I try to
study the more my mind drifts off to who knows where. Now I
have failed two math tests in a row, and there are to be no more

84

visits to China Heaven until the end of the school year. Cousin A. is displeased with my failures and this is what he has decreed.

*O*h Mem, I can't find words not a one to tell you how I feel. I try to study but he is all I think of and whenever something else comes into my head I can only hold on to it for an instant because there he is, back again, his initials going round and round in my head AJP/PJA/JAP/APJ—well, you get the idea.

I flunked my mid-term in math, and did badly in every other subject except Eng. Lit. Even French. Ma is beside herself because Cousin Andrew and dear Martha are more upset than ever. It's because they take it personally, Ma says, especially Cousin Martha, when she's treated me like a daughter and—and it's doubly hard to understand my failure when I'd showed such promise. I don't understand it myself. My head's all jumbly.

I thought things couldn't be worse, but they are. AJP is taking Prune Face, Lucy Edwina, and Mary to Europe this summer—but not me. After they return they will go to Vinalhaven until the end of August. I am to go back to Miss Merrick. I hate them all and HIM especially. Not a word from him—not one word. How can he do this to me? If he cared for me at all he never could. How can he leave me alone in stuffy old Beantown while he goes to Europe with Prune Face and the rest?

*T*he final blow. *Tooka* is to go with them. They are to sail on the *Aquitania.* How could he—*our* ship. Oh Mem—oh Mem—he'll be sorry, I swear it.

*G*uess what! *They* have gone but my Daddy's back!! And not only back but here for good! And he's rich!! He arrived all spruced up with sporty new suits and a Tiffany gold watch. And he was driving a Packard!!! "A lucky streak," he said. I am so happy I'm not along on that dumb trip. Think of it—Daddy would have come home and I wouldn't even have known it. This makes up for *everything*.

Started with Miss Merrick on Monday. I'd forgotten how much I like her. Once I'm there we settle in and the hours fly. She's sure I'll do well and be top of my class next term. Yes, she believes in me the way you do. Daddy believes in me, too. I know he does. It's just that he finds it hard to put it into words in the clear way Miss Merrick does. He's rented a boat for the whole summer and we're going sailing tomorrow. Just we two. It's hot here, but not too hot for Ma to pick fights with Daddy. She's at him all the time about letting her take charge of his money. He has no intention of letting her take charge of anything.

Miss Merrick and I have started reading the Boston philosophers, and I am *immersing* myself in them. While we were boating on Saturday I told Daddy something Emerson said and asked him what he thought of it: "A nobler want of man is served by nature, namely, the love of Beauty." Fine words, fine words, he said, and it turned out that he knows all about Emerson. Oh, I am happy. Now we have so much to talk about, like something else from Emerson: "The eye is the best of artists." I think I understand what he meant by that, for a highly evolved sense of beauty is one of the attributes I most aspire to. Yes, I aspire to beauty, not only within (I insist on that first) but without. And I don't mean simply Paris frocks. I mean beauty of face and body, which I may already be well on the way to having, considering the effect I have on those around me. I can tell by the way they look at me that they think I'm not so bad looking. Daddy says I look like his Ma, who was a famous belle. She died the year I was born, but he has a picture of her, so I know it's true.

Stopped by the library on the way home and got into conversation with a boy named Clark Amis, who has a job there for the summer. He loves poetry as much as I do—especially Keats. He can recite all of Book I of *Endymion.* Imagine! And he's already memorized half of Book II. He has a beautiful voice and he's handsome, too.

I never give a thought to what the cousins and Tooka are doing or where they are or what I'm missing. I'm missing nothing because Daddy's here. I asked him if he liked Keats. He said, "Sure thing," the way he does, so I brought along my copy of his poems when we went sailing today. We were drifting along and he started reading out loud where the book fell open.

> I had a dove and the sweet dove died;
> And I have thought it died of grieving:
> O, what could it grieve for? Its feet were tied,
> With a silken thread of my own hand's weaving;
> Sweet little red feet! why should you die—
> Why should you leave me, sweet bird! why?
> You liv'd alone in the forest-tree,
> Why, pretty thing! would you not live with me?
> I kiss'd you oft and gave you white peas;
> Why not live sweetly, as in the green trees?

Oh, it was beautiful, Mem—the most perfect moment I've ever had. It reminded me of something long ago, something I couldn't remember. Why are you crying, Angel? Daddy said. Then he asked me if I'd ever tasted white peas. I said no, but I had lived in green trees, ha ha, and he knew I was thinking about the elm in our backyard in Evanston.

*T*old Ma about Clark and she made a trip to the library to get a look at him. When she got back she pointed out to me how short he is and what a low forehead he has, which proves he's not intelligent enough to memorize anything, much less Book I of *Endymion*. I don't care what she says, I like him. He asked me to go for a walk on Sunday. I said I was going sailing with Daddy but why not come along with us? He said he couldn't do that. He's shy, I guess.

*T*oday stopped by the library with the express purpose of seeing Clark and insisting he change his mind and go with us on Sunday.

Daddy had said he sounded like a nice fellow and to bring him along. But when I got there Clark was nowhere in sight, so instead of seeing him I just fooled around and got the notion to look up the Dominicans in an encyclopedia of religions. While doing so I came across this. It's from something called the Dhammapada—

> He who wishes to put on the yellow dress without having cleansed himself from sin, who disregards also temperance and truth, is unworthy of the yellow dress. But he who has cleansed himself from sin, is well grounded in all virtues, and regards also temperance and truth, he is indeed worthy of the yellow dress.

Am I worthy of the yellow dress? I think not. You are, of course.

*T*hey're back—each and every one of my dear loving cousins and of course Tooka. Oh yes, they had such a good time they stayed away longer than planned, so no time for Vinalhaven Island before school starts. Tooka especially had a great time, not to mention AJP and Lucy Edwina. They had a great time, and you'll be happy to hear that Prune Face did, too. They all had great times. But what care I how great these times were—we had a better time here and I can't wait for school to start. We'll show 'em, won't we, Mem.

*A*merican women have got the vote! Isn't that great—the right to vote. I'll be first in line when I'm 21. Maybe AJP will be running for President. Wouldn't it be something if my first vote were for him even tho' he'll never know it because I hate him so much and intend never to see him again.

*S*hould I try at the library to get Clark's address in Ithaca? Or I could write to him at Cornell. Yes, *much* better—less embarrassing than inquiring in person at the library. They'd think I'm running after him.

Dear Clark,
How are you? I guess you had to leave in a hurry. I know just how you feel because I feel that way myself most of the time, only I

don't know where to hurry to. Maybe you could help me. Not that I want to bother you. Quite the contrary. I would just like to talk to you and be your friend even tho' I'm a girl. Maybe we could write to each other and get to know each other that way. I find it much easier to write than talk about how I feel. Do you agree? Somehow face to face with someone I turn into a different person and do not remember who I am. It's the same when I look in a mirror—the reflection I get back isn't the one I expect. It is the face of a stranger and then I become a stranger, too. Please don't think me foolish. Please answer this letter. Even if you do not, I want you to know it was nice meeting you. I hope you have a great time at Cornell. I can tell you are a very studious person. So am I.

Bye for now,
Starr

Of course I won't mail this. I have my pride.

I have no interest in hearing from my dear cousins any details of their trip and even walk out of the room whenever Tooka starts going on about it. I have also refused to see AJP ever again. Absolutely. But I told you that already, didn't I? The first day back at Miss Sheraton's I felt funny but now I don't. I'm way ahead of everyone in my studies and intend this to continue. Even in Latin. (I hope.)

*T*ooka and I spent this weekend at Dover Farm. AJP was in Washington, D.C., which is the only reason I would set foot there. Nothing has changed at the farm, but—and I'll only admit this to you—it was funny without *him* around. All during the weekend Prune Face was in a good mood and kept on about what a "charming young lady" Tooka is growing into and how much they all enjoyed having her on the trip. They went everywhere! To Grasse? I asked. "No, not Grasse, we didn't have time to go there." Daddy and Ma came to Sunday dinner and Daddy and I went riding. He kept calling out to Star, "Heigh-ho-giddy-yap" in a most merry way, as if to a rocking horse, but I didn't mind. It made me happy to hear him calling my name.

. . .

*L*ast night Daddy told Ma that we should have our own Thanksgiving at our own home as other families do, instead of going to Jamaica Plain. Ma said, that's what you think, Frank. Oh, it was the bitterest fight ever. Ma was saying things like, right back where we started, you fool, like the night you—and Daddy was cutting her off with, you and your damn bigoudies—None of it made sense, and then Ma started hitting him and he hit her back and I ran between them and they collapsed into chairs and started to cry. Oh Mem, it was v. terrible. Then they stopped crying and we all sat for a long time saying nothing until I said, What are bigoudies? and Ma said they were chamois rolls she used to twist strands of her hair around to sleep with overnight so her hair would be curled by morning. She kept twisting her hair around her finger as she spoke while Daddy sat slumped in his chair looking at her.

*W*ell, on Thanksgiving Day Ma and Tooka went to Jamaica Plain and Daddy and I stayed home and dined on tinned meat and Campbell's Soup. Daddy read aloud from Keats's "Lines Written in the Highlands After a Visit to Burns Country." I asked him to take me there someday and fill my arms with heather the way Heathcliff did to Cathy in *Wuthering Heights* and he said he would. Later I showed him the picture I'd framed of Lincoln—didn't he think it looked like him? "Well—I'll be darned," he said. It was the best Thanksgiving I ever had, but oh, Mem, I just know he will be leaving again soon. When Ma and Tooka got back he turned quiet, the way he used to be before. Before what, you ask? Oh God—I don't know. I have no answers to Befores or Afters—only questions that no one ever answers.

I was right. I hugged and hugged him but he went anyway. I'm coming back soon, sweetheart, he kept saying, soon as I can. How soon is that? How soon? He couldn't say exactly because it depended on things. What things, Daddy? He told me he couldn't go into it now and to take care of Tooka.

*M*a's tight-lipped at me for being so upset about Daddy leaving. What did you expect? she says over and over. What I expected was that he'd never ever leave again after the heavenly summer we had together. Oh I don't understand anything. Talk to your Cousin Andrew about it, is all I keep getting from Ma. Meanwhile, I am to spruce up and prepare myself to go to the cousins' for Christmas and that means you Missy, she says. But I am not going. I have vowed never to set eyes on his fat bald Fou head again and those piggy eyes—I mean cat's eyes—well, I don't have to, do I? Ma can't drag me there.

*A*t the last minute I changed my mind about Xmas Day and went with Ma and Tooka to Dover Farm, where the cousins had the tree this year instead of Jamaica Plain. Altho' I went I was absolutely *determined* to pay no attention to him or acknowledge his presence in any way, but I couldn't help but notice him out of the corner of my eye and he looked so sad and thin that I got scared and then without knowing why or how I found myself going for a walk with him alone in the snow. We walked side by side without speaking or looking at each other. But when we got out past the barn he put his arms around me and words tumbled out so fast I couldn't make sense of what he was saying. "Martha's doing—Europe—Tooka—leaving you behind . . . not my fault, I beg beg—not my fault—can't bear that we don't see each other as we used to—" He said he hadn't thought of anything during the trip except me and since he's been back, busy as he's been, he thinks only of me. I got scared and patted his ears the way he likes but that only got him more upset. "Don't you miss it? Don't you? Don't you?" he kept saying. Miss what—what? I hadn't a thought as to what he meant—all I wanted to do was soothe him and make him all right again. Please, please, I begged him, I love you, I love you, and I put my arms around him and kept kissing him and crying too. After a while he took his handkerchief out of his pocket and dabbed my cheeks and blew his nose. What a honk, I said, and we both started laughing even tho' we were still crying. There there now, he said, and he took my hand and we went back into the house. Guests were arriving for the tree and to have some of Cousin Martha's famous mulled cider, and pretty soon he was himself again and gave me a glass of cider and after that another. I was so exhausted I almost fell asleep during dinner and did in the car on the way home. When we walked in our house I was still so sleepy I forgot Daddy had left and called out to him. What's gotten into you? Ma said. She was v. put out with me. Can't write more, Mem, too tired.

*H*e came by this evening with some mango tea to go with the rosemary honey from Dover Farm that Ma likes to use instead of sugar. And for me an egg made of polished brass. It has what seems to be a ball inside. There is no way to open the egg to find out for sure, but you can feel the weight of it. The egg fits in my hand so smooth and *right*, as if it were meant to be there. It made me feel harmonious to hold it and after a while the brass got warm from my hand. He didn't stay very long, not long enough even for tea, but he said he'd like to take me on an outing on New Year's Day, could I be ready at 3 o'clock? Oh yes, yes, yes. I took his hand and spread out three of his fingers and gave each one a kiss. What an enchantment you are, Starr, he said.

*E*very minute seems a year since our parting and I count the days until he comes. How could I have gone almost a whole year without seeing him? From now on I want to be the most important thing to him in all the whole wide world. That is my New Year's Resolution.

1921

New Year's Day

*H*e arrived on the dot—even inside the center of the dot—of three. I was ready and waiting, having taken extra special time and care with my appearance. He approved, I could tell, and kept saying, What a way to start the new year—an outing with my own Precious Angel! I gave him a kiss and as soon as we got in the car I said, Look—and held out my hand. I had brought the brass egg, and did he smile! "You like that, do you?" Oh, yes, Cousin Andrew, I like it a lot. "I'm glad you brought it," he said. "We'll play a game with it later." I spent the rest of the drive trying to imagine what that later meant, but when we entered China Heaven all thoughts of eggs were thrown from my mind by the vision before me, for China Heaven was—well, *transformed*, Mem. "Not too much pêche, is there, sweetheart?" He seemed suddenly unsure of himself, and it was true there *was* a lot of pêche. Everywhere you looked it was pêche on pêche. But I kept exclaiming and running around touching all the pêche things trying to show him how pleased I was. I half expected even the books to be bound in pêche but Fou had drawn the line there, for they were just the same as they had been when I saw them last—the special dictionary and the book of Chinese art and dear Professor Ellis, all our familiar old friends in their worn morocco covers. Do you remember this? he said, taking down Vol. 1 of Professor Ellis. Oh do I! I answered in my most enthusiastic yet studious manner. And he took the book and turned to page 82, just as he had last year, and there was the paragraph about modesty you already know, dear Mem. He asked me to read it aloud, and I did. "Alors," he said, "alors, alors—" and he went over to the cupboard and there was the chiffon, and, as he had before, he scooped it up in his arms and held it out to me. Remember this? he said

93

again, and I turned my back to him and let my dress slip down onto the floor and stood there without moving as he came up behind me. You are so lovely, he said. So lovely. And I could see what he meant, for I watched in the mirror as he started draping my body in the heavenly folds. I could hardly believe what I saw, Mem, because it wasn't just a girl, it was a beautiful grown-up girl, grown-up as a Paris model. I couldn't take my eyes off her as he swathed her in chiffon and he had to pull me away from the mirror to lead me to the chair, where I lay back and closed my eyes. "Now," he said, "now for the game," and he sat down on the floor beside me. "Let's see what's inside the pretty package," he said, and he untied the bow he had made at my waist. It was nice having it released, for it was a bit tight. Then I felt something smooth being rolled around under the folds of chiffon between my legs and I didn't have to see it to know it was the brass egg with the ball inside oh so heavy and sweet, as sweet as the creamy dreamy, Mem, for he had inserted it in the place where the candy is, yes yes yes, and he was saying, "Now I'll tell you about this egg, which is described by Professor Ellis in his book. It's called Little Man, and the better acquainted with him you become and the more you pleasure yourself with him the more pleased you will be and the more pleased you are, the more pleased I will be. Are you pleased, Precious Angel?" Oh, I was, Mem, I was *fainting* from the bliss of it. He smiled and congratulated me on the delicious impudence of my modesty, but then, suddenly, he took Little Man away and it rolled over on the carpet and disappeared under the sofa, and he started fumbling with the veils, but so quickly they got tangled up and fell around him on the floor, covering his corn, which was demanding attention. To tell you the truth, Mem, he looked quite funny there on the floor with the chiffon draped over his corn, but I didn't dare laugh. Then all at once the chiffon was wet, and he flung it off and flung himself onto the sofa with a huff and fell sound asleep. I went to the mirror and got quite caught up practicing modesty with the veils, draping them this way and that (not the wet ones, silly) until he woke up with a snort and I couldn't stop laughing. You sound like two elephants, I told him. "Elephants, elephants," he said sleepily, "ah yes, elephants have corn to ho-ho and they grow it by entwining their (I think he said pro-bo-si-deeze) and the corn grows bigger and bigger and then one elephant opens its mouth and lets the other tickle the roof of it." Then he sat up suddenly and grabbed my hand and put my finger in his mouth, saying "Tickle, tickle, tickle," and I tickle tickled as he kept waving his arm around as if it were an elephant's trunk. He made me laugh so hard I got a stitch in my side.

Wednesday, January 26, 1921

Dear Mem,

It's early in the morning and I am 15 years old. I'm writing to you before I have to get up and go to school. Tookacita's still asleep under me and snoring away. Actually, it's not real snoring, it's a sort of snoozing sound, lovable in its way. Anyway, I'm doing my best to organize myself starting today, but how can I, when everything's so wrong. Is this a mood that may pass like my other little moods, which Mamacita keeps complaining about? "Temperamental," she calls me. *Me*, temperamental? Don't make me laugh, Mem, this is serious. Listen. If only I could get away from here I'd be happy, because I'd have the opportunity to meet people I could communicate with, which is what I ardently desire. There's no one around here of that description, that's for sure. Actually, the more I think about it the more I believe I don't belong anywhere except with AJP, and even though there are times when I hate him, the times I love him count most, and at least I've got *that*, because he loves me I know. But what help is that to me in the times when I long to go far away from *everyone*, yes even him? (What is he anyway but an old Fou)? Or—maybe what I really want is to go far away *with* him, on his yacht maybe. I can't decide. Maybe the two of us could sail off together like the Owl and the Pussycat and never come back. Would that be fun? Or not? Better still, Mem, you and I could sail off *alone* in the pea green boat with a pot of honey and plenty of money. Yes, honey and money. That's what I'd *really* like, and never ever have to hear noisy noise or see any of them, even the Fou, ever again. Especially the Fou, if you really want to know. You and I know a noisy noise annoys a noisy oyster and Fou Fou's the biggest oyster of them all. Tooka's stirring now so I've got to stop and get ready for school. I don't like to end on this gloomy note on our birthday, but if I can't be honest with you I can't be honest with anyone. And now that I'm speaking my mind, I'd like to say I do wish you could speak yours—Daddy his. But where is he? It's my birthday and he's who knows where. If only you and

Daddy (when he is here) would open your mouths and Ma shut hers things would be a lot different around here.

So long for now.

Your loving sister
Starr

*M*iss Dailey wrote these words of Saint Peter's on the blackboard and asked us to copy them.

If you will stand fast as you ought and grow in grace, esteem yourself as an exile and a stranger upon earth.

Then she assigned us to compose an essay on Self-Respect, for that is the message behind those words. It is difficult for me to do this, Mem, because I don't know exactly what it means. People tell me I'm pretty but I don't believe them. I never think when I look in the mirror that the girl I see has anything to do with me. So how can self come into it? Patsy says Self-Respect means feeling good about yourself. Well, I feel good about myself when I win a race but—well, I have to admit that what really makes me feel good about *everything* is Fou holding me close and giving me creamy dreamy. Does this have anything to do with what Saint Peter is talking about? I don't think it does, but if creamy dreamy makes me feel so good, how can it be bad? Who says it is bad anyway? Fou doesn't, so why should I? But if it's good why is it such a big secret? Why doesn't Fou tell everybody about it? Anyway, it's no use going on about this because none of it can be in my essay. Must get down to work and think up what to write. Do you think Miss Dailey will flunk me if I bring underwear into my essay? I used to think it didn't matter if my underwear had a rip or needed a wash if it was covered up by a clean dress and no one could see it. But I've changed my mind. It does matter, because even tho' no one can see it I know it's there. Well, got to stop procrastinating, as Ma would say, and get to work on my essay. I guess I'll leave out the underwear.

I have a v. important question to ask you. It's been on my mind for a while but I haven't had the courage to talk to you about it because it might make you think less of me. I have to admit I sometimes tell you things in a way that will make you think I'm a better person than I am. You have thought that, haven't you, altho' I hope not, because I don't ever want to deceive you because you're not only my best friend, you are my *real* sister. It's only when I want to impress you that things come out differently (maybe) from how they really are. So I hope you'll forgive me. I'm going on and on like this, using it as an excuse to put off the moment of truth. I'll tarry no longer—here goes. It has to do with Aunt Margaret's visit, which, as you know, is scheduled for tomorrow. When she is about I want more than anything to have AJP touch my beaver instead of doing it myself. Oh, it's bliss just thinking of creamy dreamy and his finger touching me. Dare I ever speak of this to him? Would he still love me if I did? Do *you* still love me? It is a fierce dilemma, as you can see. Do you see? I pray you do. Don't stop loving me.

Who do you think I'll marry? I'd like to be married right now and not have to wait any longer. If I were married it would mean I was definitely, absolutely, positively grown-up. I would wake up every morning and the first thing popping into my mind would be—no school today. I do look older than my age. And isn't it true, Mem, that I could so easily be a little "wifey" to AJP? You can't deny I know how to please him, to make him love me oh so much, better than anyone else. It makes me laugh sometimes when I see Prune Face fussing around her "dear Andrew," doing every little thing to please him in every little way. Sometimes I'd like to tell her who and what really pleases him. Other times I feel sorry for her.

Why is it that when I'm with him I love him and when I'm not I hate him—yes, more and more. Why isn't Daddy here?

The Cousins took Ma, Tooka, Lucy Edwina, and me to see Douglas Fairbanks in *The Mark of Zorro*. I tried saying I was sick so I wouldn't have to go but Ma started having one of her spells and I gave in. She was nice as Boston cream pie as soon as we got there and kept simpering to Prune Face about what a treat it was to be on an outing with the family. It wasn't often dear Cousin Andrew had time, being the busy important Mayor that he is. This isn't *my* family, I said. Daddy's not here. Nobody said anything to that. When we got into the theatre AJP maneuvered it so I was next to him, but Prune Face put herself on my other side and I kept leaning toward her during the movie to get as far away as I could from Fou, who was pressing toward me. I put my knees tight together and bent my head down and put my arms over my head pretending I was an ostrich. Sit up, Starr, Ma kept whispering to me. People around us started telling her to shhh. After, on the way out of the theatre, I told them I'd vomit right there on the street unless I went home immediately, for I had no intention of being forced to be in their company a moment longer. "The poor child," Prune Face kept saying, while people were looking at us as they walked by. "Starr-baby," Ma said, "what's gotten into you? You don't look sick to me." I feel it coming on, I said. They couldn't risk that and hustled me into the car and told Morris to get me home fast as he could. When we got there he wanted to help me upstairs but I told him to go away, go away, go away and leave me alone. There was no one in the house and I ran upstairs and made it to the bathroom basin in time. Then I climbed up to my bed and lay there waiting for Ma and Tooka to get back. It was a long wait, but finally I heard them coming in the door, babbling about lovely tea at the Vendome blah blah blah. Then Ma went into the bathroom—Disgusting! Disgusting! Oh, the shock of it. I'd put the plug down in the basin when I'd vomited and left it there. I'd like to wear a mask like Zorro and be a man.

No word from him since the Zorro movie. Ma said I acted in a very babyish way that day and any other 15-year-old would be ashamed of herself. Well, I don't care—I'm ashamed of her and the way she treats Daddy and the way she carries on about a new house we may move to. It's in Hampton, about 20 minutes away from Boston. She talks about this all the time, but hasn't made up her mind yet—there are "all aspects to consider." If she does decide we're to move, Cousin Andrew will "arrange it." Ma has only to say the word and off we'll go. What has Daddy to say about this? Does he know about it? If only I knew where he was so I could write to him. But there is nothing I can do except wait until he gets back.

I do miss him. AJP (as if you didn't know). Guess he really must be mad at me. Maybe I'll never see him again. Just us two, I mean. No wonder, after my unpardonably babyish behavior at the Cinema. What could have gotten into me?? Ma's right about it, but what can I do now? Nothing. Nothing. It's hopeless. Why did I think I hated him?

*N*o word from him today. Will he ever ever speak to me again—Oh God—

*W*ent to the annual Easter Party at Dover Farm. I was scared to death dreading what was in store when I came face to face with him but the killing moment came—and there he was loopy looing up the hill to greet us. Yes, there he was loopy loo, there he was loopy light, just as though nothing had happened. He winked and said, "If spring is here, can summer be far behind?" That means Vinalhaven, Mem! That means everything is all right.

*D*etermined to get highest grades in exams. *Determined.* How pleased Cousin A. will be. How worthy I shall be. Not only prettiest in—dare I say—the entire school but brightest too. Ah yes, to be beautiful and best will please him most of all.

*C*ame in 7th. Pray Cousin won't be too disappointed in me. 7 is a lucky number after all. School's almost over. I went to St. Paul's and sat for ages thinking of Daddy, trying to pray. Turns out I was only there four minutes. I looked at my watch when I came out.

*D*on't know where to begin, my mind's in such a tizzy what with the scent of pines around me as I sit here under trees that reach so far above me I can hardly see their tippy tops, much less the sky. Oh, 'tis wondrous, Mem, at Vinalhaven Island. It would be hard to imagine a more perfect place. A little village, you might say, only that isn't really what it's like since even tho' there are cottages and cabins dotted around here and there, no one is crowded, for each has space around it and in the space are trees and rocks and blueberry shrubs. And even tho' many people are here, Cousin Martha plans things so well that everyone always seems to be doing exactly what he wants to be doing. We are forever off on hikes and fishing expeditions with guides to supervise. Mary and Adele are in Pokaku Cottage (each cottage has a name), which is next to Kacudo Cottage, which Lucy Edwina and I have to ourselves. Every day is busy, even a painting class Cousin M. has organized outdoors in front of the Big House, where Cousin M. and Cousin A. reside, and there are sailing races too, so there's never a moment of what shall we do now? The days are warm but the nights are cold, lovely and cold, so fires are lit and we sleep with more blankets. In the morning there are buckwheat cakes and hot maple syrup with as many pats of butter as you want. At night there's dancing to the gramophone with Cousin Martha and Ma chaperoning everything. Yes, Ma and Tooka are here too and loving it. AJP hasn't been around much but he does have a summer office here with a secretary, Mr. Parke, who doesn't seem to have a lot to do and keeps to himself, as if he's got a lot on his mind. He's interesting. But the one who's really interesting is this Harvard boy named Pete Haddon who came to visit Mary. Last night I danced with him twice and then Prune Face cut in and suggested it was his turn to dance with Adele. It made me so mad. He kept looking over at me with a soulful look all the time he was dancing round and round with her.

Dreamed that Pete Haddon and I were dancing in the white ballroom at Jamaica Plain. Couldn't tell where the music was coming from because the room had no ceiling and snow was falling around us through the crystal chandeliers as he held me close. Alone we were, and I love you, I love you, he kept whispering.

Everywhere I go on the island I keep looking around for Pete Haddon, all day I kept doing this, but he's nowhere in sight. Later found out he went at the crack of dawn on a camping trip to one of the nearby lakes. Not expected back for days. Miss him, yes I do, even tho' he is Mary's beau.

*W*hy can't Fou go on a camping trip at the crack of dawn and leave me alone? Instead he pesters me, trying to get me off somewhere. Finally succeeded long enough to give me an apple, instructing me it's to be peeled tonight and put under my arm to sleep with it there until morning. He said when I wake it will be saturated with my sweet sweat. He's going to do the same thing with another apple and tomorrow we'll exchange apples to inhale. "Love apples"—that's what they were called in the Elizabethan age. Weird, eh Mem?

*T*he half-eaten apple was soggy when I woke up, but I was going to take pity on him and try to sneak it to him sometime during the day anyway. It started falling apart, tho', so I threw it into the bay instead. His fell apart too before he could get it to me. He was disappointed, but said we'll try it again later. Even tho' it's cold here at night he thinks we'll have better luck when the winter weather comes to Boston. Uggy wuggy, eh Mem? But I do like to please him.

*C*ousin A. has done the most wonderful thing. He telephoned from his office up here and directed that the time of registration for voters for the state primary be extended two days. It was to have closed at 10 o'clock last night but now it will continue to 10 o'clock tomorrow night. He did it because few women had registered so far—they didn't really begin to come in until this week. He has asked our Boston women to lead and urges them to show the way in exercising their newly conferred power. Even tho' according to the law he can't run for mayor again, he's taken charge of *everything* about the election. He'll see to it that "women will have their day." Isn't it thrilling, Mem! I just wish they could vote for him—It's not fair.

*I*t's in the newspapers—31,809 women registered to vote in Boston! The booths were so crowded right up until midnight with women lining up to get on the voting list that extra police and clerks had to be called in. Oh Mem, if only I could vote. Until then I keep telling myself I'm part of history being here with our cousin Mayor Andrew J. Peters at his summer office on Vinal-haven Island. I get to hear news of what's happening before any-one else does. He is the most wonderful man in the world.

*T*he summer's gone so quickly, Mem. I hope you aren't angry with me because I may have neglected you and not written in you as much as you would have liked. (I haven't even had time to read.) There's something going on every single minute—you know it's true, Mem, so no need for apologies, is there? Day after tomorrow we leave this heavenly island—to get ready for school. Oh how I hate to go. Wonder if I'll ever see Pete Haddon again???

*D*addy *was* home when we got back, but it's been *awful.* I haven't had the heart to talk to you since school started. Not awful that Daddy's home but awful with Ma's mean looks and— oh God—Daddy is so unhappy. He doesn't say anything about what he did this summer except that he's "working on a project that can't be discussed until everything is finalized." "Finalized like your silver mine, eh Frank?" Ma laughs as though he's told a big joke. Yes, it's awful around here. But God, I don't want him to go away again. Even though it's awful it's much more awful when he's gone.

*M*a announced to Daddy she'd come to a decision and that we were moving to Hampton into a big house. "Over my dead body," he said—quiet and looking her straight in the eye. It was a thrilling moment, Mem!!

*A*re we moving or not? Today's been the worst. Ma told us to get ready, for Cousin A. was coming by to pick us up and take us to see the house we are moving to in Hampton. Daddy refused to go and I did too. Ma knew we were determined, so she and Tooka drove off without us. Daddy kept shaking his head "no no no no no no." Minna was away and I made us some hot cocoa. He definitely doesn't want us to move, and I only want to if he comes with us. He left after we drank the cocoa, saying he had to get away for a while and think things over. I begged him not to go but he did. When they got back from Hampton there was no one here but me. Ma acted as if she didn't even know he was gone and she and Tooka kept on raving about the Hampton house. I couldn't stand their hateful faces so I shut myself in my room. AJP had come in with them and tried talking to me through the door but I refused to come out. I can't stop crying.

When I got back from school today Daddy's things were gone. The space in the closet where he hung his things is empty and the hangers are hanging there empty. Ma said, Isn't that nice, now we can spread out more. I keep looking around for a letter, under tables and things, thinking he might have propped one up somewhere and it fell off behind a chair. Ma says she hasn't a clue where he's gone and doesn't want to talk about it. He came in while we were at school, packed his things and left without a word. That's all she'll tell us. This is the first time he has taken all his things. I never really believed this would happen even though I was afraid all the time that it would—afraid the seesaw would go down and never come up again. Tooka whimpers around making Ma jumpy and crazy. "Stop it, stop stop stop," she shakes Tooka till her teeth rattle. "I'll be a nervous wreck if you children don't stop it."

Mem, I'm going to write this letter to my father. Please let me know what you think of it before I send it—not that I can send it, because who knows where he is? If Ma does she's not telling us, but I don't think she's lying when she says she doesn't know where he is or where he's gone—so writing to him will be like dropping a piece of paper into a well, but anyway that's what I'm doing.

Dear Daddy,
Is it true you are never coming back? Ma's lying, I'm sure, so it's not really true. You are just on one of your trips and will be back soon. If only you had told me you were leaving, everything would be different. I love you. Daddy, please come back. Come back and tell me what I can do so you'll never go away again.
Your loving daughter,
Starr
P.S. I have no address to send this to, but I'm going to put your

name on the envelope, stamp it, and put it in the chute at the P.O. It will shoot the chute. Do you remember the day you took Tooka and me to the Carnival and we went down the shoot-the-chute in a yellow boat? It was before we moved from Evanston. Ma wasn't with us and we had such fun. It was a good idea then, so why not now, eh? Why not come back from wherever you are and take us away. Tooka has been crying so much Ma sent her to stay with Cousin Martha at Jamaica Plain, so I am alone here with her. I hate her and everybody else. It's her fault you left us. I'll do anything to get you back—only tell me what it is. I know your way is the right way, if only you will tell me what it is.

I look around the walls and up at the ceiling knowing Daddy looked at the same walls and ceiling that my eyes rest on. The nails on the walls are dotted around with no pictures hanging, only shadows outlining the places where they used to be. His Harvard crew photographs and pictures of his family, the ones in Natchez Ma never speaks to—all gone. Maybe Daddy didn't take them with him. Has Ma hidden them? Thrown them out?

*N*o one in my class at Miss Sheraton's has had a Divorce. This is what Ma says will happen because Daddy's abandoned us. I asked her if Prune Face and the other cousins know about it. "Of course they do, and are outraged," Ma says. But they shouldn't feel pity for her, she says. She's glad he's gone. Tooka and I were witness to the living hell it was around here having to put up with him and anyway the cousins had known for a long time that she and Daddy would Divorce when things got better. What does she mean by that? Better than what?

I know Daddy left a letter for us and Ma's burnt it or torn it up and thrown it away. Oh Mem, would she do that? I wish you'd give me some opinion. Not that I'm complaining. Just to have you to talk to means all the world to me.

*T*ooka came back home, but she looks different even though she's only been away for a little while. She's almost the age now

that I was when we left Evanston and moved to Boston. Is that
how I looked then? Hope not ha ha. Guess I sound mean. I can
tell Mrs. Prune Face likes her a lot better than me even tho' I'm
prettier. Anyway, my little sister's home after having had a marvie
time at Jamaica Plain and all she wants to do is go back there
again soon as poss. She had a room and bathroom to herself. She
doesn't miss Daddy anymore.

*F*orget the things I said about Tooka. She cries at night and
wants to sleep with me in my bed. Ma won't allow it and says
we're acting like babies. Why did he leave like that? It's still so
hard to believe that he's gone for good. I don't believe it. I'm sure
I'll be hearing from him soon. Any day now a letter will come
explaining everything, and saying when he's coming back. He'll be
back for Thanksgiving. Yes, *definitely.*

*W*ell, there's no mistaking it now, we are moving to Hampton.
Cousin Martha's already gotten us into the Country Club and we
are to have our own car and chauffeur driving us to school each
day. What about Daddy? I wanted to know. "What about him?"
Ma said. How will he know where we are? When I said that, she
got mad and told me to get him out of my head and stop worrying about things, because even tho' she'd scrimped and saved to
get us out of Evanston it was due to the kindness of her Cousin
Martha that we'd gotten even a toehold in Boston when we first
arrived—yes, yes, Cousin Martha's sense of family had helped us
out in the beginning and now it was Cousin Andrew's generosity
that had made everything possible. "Look around you, Missy,"
she kept at me—"everything we have—yes, yes—" I'm in a
rage, oh God, Mem, a rage. I can't stop crying even tho' I never
cry in front of anyone. No, I can't stop. Tooka can't either. I
thought I was going to die—die—die, yes. Ma slapped me hard
and told me I'd better shape up and be extra nice to the cousins
now that I know what's what and how good they are to us and
what a mess we'd be in if they weren't. "What's got into you,
Missy?"—she kept raising her voice—"You ought to be on your
knees thanking Andrew"—on and on she went until I couldn't
stand it another minute and almost told her about the little green
bottle, and *everything* else, but instead I slapped her back. Well, she

can't *make* me get on my knees or see AJP or do anything else if I don't want to. I'll shut myself in my room and starve myself to death. I vow to, Mem. Yes, by Christmas I'll be dead and then where will you be? Come up with an answer to that if you can.

Christmas is over and I'm not dead so you're alive too, Mem. Not only alive but so busy helping to pack and running around because by New Year's Day we'll be out of these rented rooms on Beacon Street and moved into the house in Hampton. I've finally seen it. AJP drove me there the day after Xmas. I had refused, absolutely refused, to go up till then, but I must admit it's not bad. In fact it's quite good—a house with a garden and trees outside and more than enough rooms inside—a huge house in fact. No more bunk beds—it's bedrooms and bathrooms for each of us and many more to spare, and fireplaces everywhere. I'm only telling *you* this. As for Ma and everyone else, they think I don't want to move. He can't fathom why I'm so sulky about it and says "Ho ho ho" more than I care to hear and is extra jolly. The old Fou—silly old Fou. I'm not going to give in and shall sulk or do anything else I choose from now on. That is my New Year's resolution. Daddy will be back soon anyway. He'll understand and make everything all right.

My name is Starr Wyman. But who am I really? Speak up, please. Do I really exist? I do not want to live in Hampton. I want to live on a farm somewhere. With Daddy. It will be far away from Boston. We will have animals and grow vegetables. I will cook and when it rains we will take turns reading out loud to each other. It's the last day of 1921.

1922

We've moved to Hampton, and there's so much space I feel the way I used to visiting at Jamaica Plain or Dover Farm, only now I'm not a visitor—the house I walk into is mine—yours too, Mem. And oh! it's grand, to look up at the canopy of Tiffany glass floating over our front door. There's a new Packard too and a chauffeur named Herbert and a staff of servants to do our bidding. I must admit we like it, don't we, Mem, very much indeed. My room has a bed with a canopy—not glass, silly, dotted swiss—and I have my own vanity table, kidney shaped with dotted swiss skirt and ruffles. Over it there's a Venetian glass mirror with rosettes you could pick off and eat like sugar candy. Our staircase curves beguilingly and the halls are so wide there's room for tables—"consoles," Ma calls them—against the walls and mirrors with paintings over them. In my room are two large bookcases, so big my books only half fill them, and I've wallpaper—ribbon bows and flowers—prettier even than Lucy Edwina's in her room at Jamaica Plain. Tooka's room is pretty too, so she's not jealous of mine. Cousin A. took us into each and every room the day we moved here. I gave him a big hug before he left.

Don't you thrill to the mention of a Chinese Robe?—Who but our dear Fou is there to mention this to? Who but he to give us this mention for our birthday—magenta satin it must be with friendly dragons and lotus blossoms embroidered in golden threads. We shall accept nothing less, and with it a sash (satin, wide) fringed with tassels to wrap ourselves around and around, and a fan would not be amiss—a fan of perfumed silk to open and release the scent of rose-musk. Yes, we're quite carried away by these thoughts, aren't we, Mem, and he shall receive more than a little hint as to what we'd like for this birthday.

*W*ent to China Heaven today and there it was spread out on the sofa—a magenta satin robe with a smiling golden dragon friendly as could be and peonies and yellow butterflies on long flowing sleeves and beside it the sash with silken tassels just as we wished.

*H*e took me to his office at City Hall. That secretary of his was sitting behind her desk buffing her nails. Nothing much was going on even tho' he's moving out of his office any day now and the hated Curley is moving in. He told her he wasn't to be disturbed on any account and on we went into his private office. He locked the door and suggested I take all my clothes off—interested to see what kind of dance I could improvise on his desk. The desk isn't that big, but I jumped up on it and swayed around and did my best while he hummed some dim-dumb song that I couldn't get the beat of, even tho' he was waving his hands around in time to it. Nervous I was with Miss Biffer Buffing sitting right outside the door. I'm tired, I told him, and got off the desk and put my clothes back on. When we went out there she was—Miss Buffer still buffing her nails. She didn't look up or say anything. Maybe she'd been looking through the keyhole and was too embarrassed. "Any calls?" he asked. "Mrs. Peters called and asks that you call her soon as you receive the message." "Of course, of course," he said, "immediately, immediately." He took me to the door and gave me a wink. It's the left eye. He never winks with the other one. I wanted to poke both of them out.

I intend *never* to see him again. That's my new New Year's resolution for 1922.

I have been informed that Prune Face is to give Lucy Edwina and me a Sweet Sixteen party on Valentine's Day. Not *me*, I told Ma. From now on I am going to have definite say in what goes on around here. Especially when it pertains to me. That's fair, isn't it? Ma thinks I'm moody because Aunt Margaret came to visit but it's not so. She'll see. Aunt Margaret may come and go but I shall remain forever firm in my resolve. I shall have nothing to do with Prune Face and her party plans because it will mean having to see *him* and I have sworn never to see him again. "What about Lucy Edwina—she is your best friend, what will she think?" Ma goes on and on about that. *No*, she's *not* my best friend. I have no best friend but you, Mem. And anyway I don't care what Lucy Edwina thinks. Or any of them. All I care about is what *I* think.

January 26, 1922 — Thursday

Dear Mem,

I intend from now on to be in charge of what happens to me. To further this resolve I'm making a study of how to make myself ugly, so he'll leave me alone. He thinks he can tell us to do anything he wants and me in particular. Well, if he thinks that, he's got another think coming to him. We may be living in this grand house in Hampton with dozens of rooms—but so what? I'd rather be with Daddy in a tree house in Evanston any day. I'm sick of listening to Ma going on about what a darling Martha is, what a fine man Andrew is for seeing to everything, on and on till I could die. Ma's on the verge of a nervous breakdown because I told her I never want to see him again and this time I mean it. She says if these indulgent sulks of mine continue there's no telling what will happen. If they only knew how I hate them all—everyone except Daddy, even though he's left me here alone with Tooka who constantly draws attention to herself with mewing sounds so soft no one can make out what she's saying. I know Daddy will be back to take me with him and the sooner the better. Tooka can go with us. That's the only fair thing because she's his daughter too, even though she mews and I can't stand her. I can't understand why a letter hasn't come from him—not a word since the day he left. Perhaps it was sent to the old address and wasn't forwarded. That must be it. Ma keeps threatening to take away my gramophone because of my moodiness, for it is my surly attitude that is keeping dear Andrew away. Even though I have intense hatred for my cousin the former Mr. Mayor of Boston, I have to admit I miss you know what. Ah yes, Mem, as the days and nights go by I miss it more and more. If you'd like to know what I'd really like for my birthday—it's that little green bottle. Instead I'm keeping to my room reading. I'm not in school today because I've decided I have a slight cold and Ma agrees it mustn't develop into a definite one because if it does I might miss Prune Face's big party. Actually, I've got an idea about that party. You'll hear about it later, if I pull it off. Happy Sweet Sixteen, Mem.

Starr

A package arrived from Daddy—*A Garden of English Verse.* Inside the book he wrote, "Happy Birthday to Starr—the fairest flower in my garden. I love you, baby, Daddy." Oh, Mem, he hadn't forgotten (tho' it arrived late). There was no return address but the postmark is Mexico City! No package for Tooka. Perhaps it got lost in the mail?

*W*ell, Mem—it was a *great* party. Bettina came by our house in the morning with Ma thinking she was going to drive over to town with us—so when she arrived with a suitcase Ma thought nothing of it, just that she'd brought her party dress to change into. And indeed she had except that there were other things in the suitcase too. Later, when the knock came on my door and Ma's sweet voice called out—"Time to go, are you ready, girls?" Come in, come in, I said, very sweet, too. Well—when she saw me! Bettina had brought her brother's suit and cap. They fit me well (considering) and I'd pushed my hair under the cap so I really did look like a boy. Mamacita kept sputtering that it was not a costume party, it was my sweet sixteen that dear Martha was going to all this trouble to celebrate and how could I be so rude, perverse and ungrateful. But it was too late to do anything—she knew nothing could make me take off that suit or the cap and Herbert had been waiting and waiting to drive us there and we were v. late already, yes, she knew I was *determined.* I wish I had a photograph of everyone's faces when we walked in. Ma tried to be jokey about it but Bettina and I stayed arm in arm and kept flirting with each other. I pretended Bettina was Charlie Gilbert even tho' she's shorter than I am and he's so tall and it drove Ma just crazy! Everyone tried not to notice but they did! AJP wasn't too crazy about it either, but it's hard to tell sometimes what he's thinking. Prune Face rose above it, as if nothing was amiss. But no one was fooled. I felt swell in the suit and cap and will definitely dress like this from now on. So Mem, it was as happy a Sweet Sixteen as it could be. I love you.

I vow I'm never going to swim again. Never never never. Everyone stares at me when I'm wearing a bathing suit and it's like knives going through me. I *hate* my body, and in a bathing suit attention is brought to what's underneath—nakedness, and it's *mine.* If I make myself ugly, AJP will stop wanting to look at me.

*T*o think I once dreamed of cabarets and pleated frocks from Paris. Such things now make my insides churn. I must confess these vain pursuits possessed me, but now they are in the past where they belong, in the Vanity Fair I had to pass through before suspecting my true destiny, which is to be a Joan of Arc or something similar. It's clear to me now that revealing my body in a bathing suit hinders what I hope to achieve, for it draws attention away from the spiritual. It is also clear that I must find a way to ease the suffering of others, for it is the only way I shall ease my own. I need time to think this out more, because it's not clear to me yet who these others are who suffer as I do. Perhaps they are also star-children, marked as I from birth. Do I make any sense to you, Mem? Of course I do because you understand everything, but would you please help *me* to understand what I'm trying to get at? Why do I feel guilty all the time and, as Saint Peter said, "an exile and a stranger upon earth"?—Of course Saint Peter was saying that each one of us in the world is unique and that's why we should respect ourselves, but I can't seem to get it into my head because of this dread I feel, dread that something terrible is going to happen, that is if it hasn't happened already.

*M*iss Umgar refused to accept that I am quitting the team. She said I'm the best swimmer Miss Sheraton's ever had and I owe it to myself and the team not to quit. I don't give a damn about the team or myself, I told her. What's more, I'm not only quitting the team, I'm going to quit school. I mean it.

. . .

*H*ow he used to love kissing my feet, in between my toes, playing games—"This little piglet went to market"—well, he's the piglet who will never ever see my feet ever again, much less touch a toe, nor will anyone else. When I sit I pull my skirt down over my feet so no one can stare at them. Ma laughs— "Starr-baby, don't cover those lovely legs—why do you do that?—only draws attention to yourself in a bizarre way, and makes people wonder about you." Well—let them wonder—I don't care.

I wish I could believe in God, but I'd be lying if I said I did. I'm still trying to figure it out, but I can't fit what I see going on in church with what I see going on when we get back home. Why does God let people treat each other as they do—killing each other with harsh words and meanness? If there really was a God he'd help people to get along and be good to one another. Isn't it a lie for me to keep on going to church and pretending I believe in God when I don't know what I believe? In the library I found another book about Buddha and it describes the Golden Flower as a symbol of the Self, whose body resembles the roots of a lotus and the flower is the spirit. The roots remain in the mire, yet the flower unfolds toward the sky. I wish I had someone to talk to about this. Buddha, I mean. Not Buddha himself, silly, but someone to talk to *about* him. It's hard to figure out by myself but I'm determined.

*N*ow that I've quit the team, at least I don't have to make a spectacle of myself in a bathing suit. I do miss swimming, oh how I miss it, but no one will ever know except you how the missing gets me down. At least I have more time to be in my room. I'm safe here and can read, play the gramophone and make my plans. Oh yes, plans are shaping up more and more as each day passes. I haven't told anyone yet, but I'm not going back to Miss Sheraton's next year—and I refuse definitely, positively ever to set foot at those dances Prune Face keeps talking about. Even if I have to run away. Yes, Mem—running away's on my mind again, but to where? Well—I'm not without resources—even if I can't grasp exactly what Buddha is trying to tell me—surely the Dominicans would not deny me? No, they'd not turn me away. I'd be safe there in my white habit among the doves and the lilies. Don't laugh, Mem.

*M*a told Tooka and me that she and Daddy are officially DI-VORCED and that we are to stop speaking his name in her presence. If we do there's no telling what will happen because she's a very sensitive person and her nerves won't be able to stand it. She's told us this before but we haven't listened, so now that the divorce is final Daddy is out of our lives and she'll not only have nervous breakdowns if his name is mentioned but something much worse because she's been having fainting spells lately and that's a warning—a warning—a warning of *heart attack.* On and on she went—this was the Snodgrass's diagnosis of her condition, and we must pay heed if we have any feeling for her at all. We must do everything possible to keep her calm and the way to do this is to forget Daddy ever existed. He's *dead* as far as she's concerned. Tooka and I must make every effort to be good girls and obey because her only hope now is to make a happy new life for us here in Hampton. "Especially you, Starr-baby, who have been behaving so irresponsibly lately, wearing strange clothes that hide your beauty, making yourself look ridiculous, being rude and ungrateful to those who really care for you and have your best interests at heart—it's so unlike my baby." All right, all right— oh God, make her stop.

*H*elp me, please. What shall I do? The cousins have invited Tooka and me to go on a vacation with them on their yacht. I have positively refused to go, but if I don't I'm "a wicked ungrateful girl after all the lovely things Martha and Andrew have done for us and are doing every day of our lives." Ma's at me more than ever to show cheerfulness and gratitude in my attitude. (Sorry, Mem, but that's what she says, word for word.) If I don't stop behaving as I am right now I'm going to ruin our chances for happiness not only now but in the future—blah blah blah on and on. Of course I know there's more than one reason why she wants us to go. It's so she'll have more time to see this new man she's met—Mr. Faithfull. I'm fed up with the whole rigmarole and anyway I do agree with her about the way I look in the knickers and other getups I've devised to hide my body. I hate them, but I'll die before I admit it. As an alternative I'm looking around for a man's suit, a suit and a cap to hang in my closet where I can see them. Even when I can't see them at least I'll know they're there if needed. Also, I resolve to go on a diet of green grass soup which was the staple of the starving Russian peasants before the Revolution, if it was good enough for them it's good enough for me. But on second thought maybe 'tis not, on second thought why subsist on greeny grass soup when I can have greeny creamy dreamy instead? Maybe we should forget about the suit and cap, eh Mem? Maybe yachting's not such a bad idea after all.

When I informed Ma of my change of mind about cousins and yachting, you'd have thought she'd won the Irish Sweepstakes—"Thank heaven you're your own sweet Starr-baby again—you'll be pleasant from now on, won't you?—pleasant to everyone—won't you, darling girl?" Oh yes, you stupid fool, I know how to be pleasant. I'm more than tempted to tell her the real reason why I'll give in to seeing him, but only you and I can know that, right, Mem? She's sweet as pie to me, scared I'll be packing wooly underwear or other dreary getups to take on the trip. Little does she know I have other things in mind and intend to look pretty as a pearl, so she's wasting her time being sweet as pie to me.

School's over. Thank God. Made valiant efforts and passed exams if only just.

Ma won't leave me alone, suggesting ways to be extra nice. You need never fear, dearest Mamacita, I'll be particularly nice to dear Andrewcito, I'll give him the time of his life, the sky's the limit, anything to reacquaint myself with the little green bottle. I do miss it—no doubt about it—and I have to admit it does make me feel like a queen to be so desired, even if I have to put up with his face slobbery with wanting when I tease and pretend not to know what he's after. He knows I'll never let him do the things he does to me without a whiff or two of creamy dreamy, but what do I care? It's all a game, isn't it?

*T*ooka was mewing most of the night. I thought a cat had gotten into the house. Cat or not, Tooka's unable to go on our little trip with the cousins and Ma's taken her to Boston to see the Snodgrass to find out what this night spell is all about. Yes, hurried away with her at the crack of dawn so they wouldn't be around when the cousins arrived.

*T*he yacht's called the *Lady Godiva* and we're on our way who knows where without another cousin in sight. No Prune Face, no Lucy Edwina, no et cetera. They've all vanished to Vinalhaven Island instead. So it's AJP and me alone (except for the crew), comfy as can be. We each have our own cabin and mine has white linen curtains printed with cherries in a row and there's a bedspread to match. The armchair has the same cherries on it with the colors in reverse, cherries white on red. Very chic—cozy too and ooh-la-la—does he have his eye on this chair. I'm sitting on it now as I talk to you. You know how he loves to do things with me sitting in chairs and I can tell he can't wait to get me down here in my cabin sitting with him on the cherries doing God knows what. It'll be a tight squeeze and one I've been able to avoid so far. Right now he's up on deck talking with the captain, rigged out in captain's clothes himself, taking charge, as it were, and making himself absolutely ridiculous. Well, he's not going to take charge of me. This time I'm the one in charge.

*L*ater same day: One thing he did that's really nice. When I went back to my cabin after a look around on deck there on my pillow was an envelope and inside this note:

Sweet Starr,

> My child—Star—you gaze at the stars,
> and I wish I were the firmament
> that I might watch you with many eyes.

The Greek philosopher Plato wrote this. I wish the words were mine and feel they are, for they echo my sentiments most truly,

Your devoted cousin
Andrew

Despite Plato and the poem, which I have to admit pleased me, I haven't made any effort to please him as I used to. Most of my time is spent reading. Reading what? you ask. *Salomé* by Oscar Wilde. I really like the Beardsley drawings. But the best part is what Fou does when he sees me reading it. When I first unpacked it I waved it back and forth under his nose so he couldn't help but notice. He had a fit, Mem, absolute apoplexy! "How the hell did you get ahold of that? Who gave it to you?" He's crazy to find out. How I got it is my little secret, I told him. Actually—*he* gave it to me. Well, not gave it—I, well—borrowed it. Check your library, Fou, you might be missing something from your "special" shelf. He kept trying to grab it out of my hands until I got really mad. Any book I'm reading is sacred to me and I don't want his dirty paws on it. It's private, mine, and belongs to *me*. For him to touch it would spoil it for me. And even though this *Salomé* belongs to him—for the time I have it, it is mine, isn't it? Yes, I'd say so. Definitely. You'd say so too, wouldn't you, Mem? My reading it without him really gets to him, I can tell. He does everything to distract me, everything that is but shake creamy dreamy in my direction. It would be quite heaven here on this boat if 'twere you, Mem, and me, along with Oscar, Eugene (*Anna Christie*'s with us too) and creamy dreamy—let's not forget that. But, alas, Fou just keeps fou-ing around trying to interrupt my concentration. There's not even a hint in the offing of creamy dreamy. Oh, if only he'd leave me alone. Jump off the boat. Stand on his head. Peel a banana. Choke on it.

We're drifting lazily along. The three in the crew are silent and discreet as the three monkeys—"Hear no evil, speak no evil, see no evil." Yesterday when we moored in a bay with not a soul in sight, I took pity on him and decided it was time for a swim, so I went to my cabin and donned a terry robe (it's got hearts on it) and went back up on deck. He didn't know I was naked underneath.

Well, not naked, but almost. I'd gotten this daring new bathing suit—just in case—in case of what? you may ask. You know I'm always dead honest with you, so you'll believe me when I tell you I really don't know what made me get it. I'd thrown all my bathing stuff away since I quit the swimming team and my ugly body had been the last thing on my mind for ages, except to conceal it as best I could with knickers and so on. Anyway, before I left, I'd found myself in Filene's trying on different bathing suits and my body didn't look so bad after all. "Ah, I see you're wearing the robe I gave you," he said, pleased as punch when he saw me. He'd given me this terry robe the day we set sail, but I hadn't worn it until now. Every word out of his mouth annoys me and I could have punched his fat face, but I paid no attention and went over to the railing and climbed up and sat there for a while with my back to him looking out over the sea. But then it got so hot I let the robe slip over my shoulders onto the deck. He bounded over, but I pushed him away and jumped into the water. As I did the top of my bathing suit slipped down and the hot sun burned my nipples before the cold salt water struck my skin. It was dark, oh so cold and dark, there under the sea, with the breath I'd taken gone. There was nothing but the cold dark, heavy upon me. There was only water to breathe—another breath, maybe two or three, and I'd be dead. Dead and out of it all, and they'd be sorry. Sorry and sad, wondering the why of it and never understanding how sick I am of this lie, how sick I am of myself. Then the cruel weight of water forced my eyes open and there was a monster mauling my bosom, my hips, and I fought to push it away, but it was fierce and strong, pulling me up, up and out onto the deck, and I knew then who it was, who my savior was, bringing me back into hell. I was choking but he was pushing his hands up and down on my back and soon he turned me over and breathed into my mouth. Then he held me close and carried me down into the cabin where we lay together, his breath smelling of the sweet Champagne we'd had at lunch, close so close, he rocked me while he pressed the cotton against my face, telling me sweet things and humming that song he sometimes hums, barrel organ music from far away, heard through an open window on a hot summer afternoon.

I'm restless and it makes me spend my time dreaming up ways to torment him, instead of reading and improving myself. Oh so restless, guilty too, guilty about everything, everything that is except Prune Face. Whole days go by and I never think about her at all. So why bring her up now? It's all a game, isn't it, and if no one's the wiser—who cares? Yes—who cares? Who cares? Who does care? And why haven't I heard from Daddy? Oh, not on this boat—I don't expect to hear from him *here*—but before, before we got on the damn boat. Why, Mem, has there been no word? For sweet God's sake, *speak*. If ever it was time to end your silence it is now—Do you hear me? Sorry, friend, but I get so mad at you sometimes.

When are we going back? When? When? I ask him. "Back where?" he says. What a dumbo. Back to Boston, stupid. "Aren't you having a good time, Starr-baby?" Sure, but I've things to do at home. "What things? What things?" He went on and on about that. Friends, I told him, and I'm expecting a letter—yes, yes, a letter, but forget about the letter—it's my friends I miss. What friends? Who are these friends and from whom are you expecting a letter? He even brought up Charlie Gilbert again and his blue eye and green eye. "Is *he* the one who gave you *Salomé*?" He got all dizzery about it and wouldn't stop, but no matter how much he went on I wouldn't elaborate. Let him think whatever he wants.

What a "lucky girl," Ma said when I got home—"no need to ask if you had a good time—radiant and healthy you look—your old self again!" I lie abed, under my canopy, sick to death of the games we were playing on the yacht, sick to death of how I made myself sulky as poss. (which you know I'm pretty good at if I put my mind to) to torment him. I knew he was punishing me because of *Salomé* and would deny me more creamy dreamy until I told him how I got a copy of it. I was determined not to give in and finally he knew it and gave the order to sail back—I hate him.

Tooka's her old self again. No more night mewings, only day mewings. "Overtired" was the Snodgrass's opinion and that it was best she didn't go on the yacht, as it would have "overstimulated" her. She doesn't see it that way and is mad at *me* instead of Ma for making her miss it. I've been trying to get her to tell me what's been going on while I was away, but she's cranky all the time.

*T*ooka finally told me that Mr. Faithfull's been around more frequently since I've been away. And? And? What else? Well nothing else, except Ma wants Tooka and me to go to Vinalhaven Island for the rest of the summer and not come back until school starts. I *refuse* to go—let Tooka go. I don't care what she does. I don't care what anyone does. I'm tired all the time and have headaches. I want to be by myself and read. That's all I ask.

*N*ot a word from AJP. Ma's still trying to get me to go to Vinalhaven. No! No! No!

*F*inally Ma sent Tooka off without me. I'm blissfully alone, blissfully happy. I don't mind that my friends are away in their summer places. Ma and I get along better when Tooka's away. I like this Mr. Faithfull. He takes her dancing and they laugh together. I can hear them sometimes.

*M*r. Faithfull strung a hammock between the oak trees on our lawn especially for me. He was worried about how I stay inside, not wanting to do anything but lie abed and read, so now I settle into the hammock with tons of pillows and read outdoors to my heart's content with a pitcher of lemonade on the grass beside me. I'm happy when alone—no one around to change me into someone else. Mr. Faithfull said to "please call me Stanley." Ma likes him, I can tell, and he is nice, I guess. But he's too short. I've definitely decided that. He is too short. Don't you agree, Mem? Stanley Faithfull is *too* short.

I went with Ma and Stanley to Pleasure Bay Beach to swim. Ma took along a parasol to protect her from the sun but Stanley seized it and started pirouetting around with it, pretending he was an acrobat on the high wire, making a complete fool of himself for all to see. But was Ma embarrassed? Not one bit. She applauded, egging him on. So did the crowd gathering around. I ran away, far away along the beach and into the sea, far out I swam, so far that the only thing I could see were little dots on the sand. I couldn't tell which dot was Ma, which Stanley, but I didn't care and kept swimming out farther away from them, until my arms and legs got heavy, then I turned over and floated looking up at the sky. But the sun was too bright so I turned over and floated with my face looking down into the dark sea. I heard voices calling my name from far away and when I looked up the little dots were lined up along the edge of the sea waving to me. So I swam towards them and someone was swimming towards me. It was the lifeguard and he made me lie afloat so he could escort me back onto the beach. All the little dots made a fuss about what I'd done, swimming out so far from shore. Ma kept it up on the way home, but I fell asleep and put an end to it.

$\mathcal{M}$y new name for Stanley is The Faithfull One.

$\mathcal{T}$ooka's back. Everyone is back and school's started—it's so noisy and I don't like anyone, especially at home. I don't like anyone at school either. If only I could be alone again, left alone to read and be myself. Ma's threatening to take the hammock down. She says "summer's over and besides it only encourages you to lollygag." She's mean and horrid, don't you agree?

$\mathcal{M}$y dear Cousin Andrew hasn't called or anything. Why, Mem, do you bring his name up? Why, Mem, do you give him a thought? I certainly haven't.

$\mathcal{C}$ame across a book in the library about the ancient Egyptians. It was their belief that they possessed an immortal soul called ba, and that it's represented by a bird or—a star! Yes, Mem, I was riveted—a Star! Could this be what the fortune teller had in mind when she told Ma I would be born into the world a Star-child? This would mean that I too have an immortal soul and therefore a Self—because how could you have an immortal soul without a Self to begin with? Wouldn't that follow, Mem? And what's exciting to me is that I seem to grasp this ba-star idea better than anything else so far (Buddha, for example). Then there is the ka, the shadow double, which fascinates me for it unites with the ba to become One. I am making every effort to absorb all this and keep referring to my heart map. It makes it clear to me that I must not linger another second in the Land of Ignorance. I must make a giant leap over onto the Isle of Man, get my bearings there—never again find myself in places that deter me from my mission. And what *is* my mission? Good question. I keep floundering around trying to find out. Help me, Mem.

Listen to this—got hold of a letter from F. Scott Fitzgerald to his sister Annabel (from a magazine). It's a godsend, Mem. He advises Annabel to brush her eyebrows or wet them and train them every morning and night and says he advised her to do this long ago but she didn't listen. Well, I'm listening and starting to do it right now. He tells her that "they oughtn't to have a hair out of place" because boys notice everything about a girl subconsciously, even eyebrows. But now—the best part—he gives her a list of leading questions to use while dancing. I'm writing them down to memorize.

Leading Questions to Use While Dancing

(a) "You dance so much better than you did last year."
(b) "How about giving me that sporty necktie when you're thru with it?"
(c) "You've got the longest eyelashes!" (This will embarrass him, but he likes it.)
(d) "I hear you've got a 'line'!"
(e) "Well who's your latest crush?"

AVOID

(a) "When do you go back to school?"
(b) "How long have you been home?"
(c) "It's warm" or "The orchestra's good" or "The floor's good."

What a windfall, eh, Mem? I'm going to pass it on to the others. Isn't that sweet of me?

. . .

*M*a and Prune Face endlessly back and forth about the Junior League and the Vincent Club, sooo easy for Mrs. Andrew J. Peters to arrange memberships for her lovely little cousin Starr—sooo, soon, yours truly will be meeting "Ten Thousand Men of Harvard" (as it says in the song), going to football games, dances and having more fun than a barrel of monkeys. Everyone is ever so grateful for Scott's letter to Annabel. Elaine said it's a good idea to be peppy to all the boys, even the pills, because that's the way to get popular and have a rush. I can hardly keep up with homework. So excited I can't concentrate. What's uppermost on my mind is what to do to make myself appear older and more grown-up. I'm training my brows into butterfly eyebrows and use Ashes of Roses powder on my face (the latest thing), but does it help? Pinching my lips helps some, but not enough to suit me.

*H*alf of our class from Miss Sheraton's was at Lucy Edwina's house in her room talking about boys, boys, boys, and the dances. On and on it went—will there be boys we know from Miss Bonnie Mae's or boys we don't know? Who? Who? Who? Elaine had put "April Showers" on the gramophone—it's her favorite song even though it's December. She calls it her Xmas Carol and wants none other. She and Patsy were fox-trotting around when who pops his head in the door but AJP! It was the first time I'd seen him since the *Lady Godiva* and I hadn't given him a thought. He was full of ho ho ho's and I smiled a lot. He twirled around a bit with Lucy Edwina and ho ho hoed some more to everybody—then out the door he went. I didn't want to but I followed him out into the hall and he took my hand and down the stairs we went into the library. The grown-ups were in the ballroom decorating the tree so we were alone. He said he'd missed me so and had I missed him even a little? More than a little, I told him, and I guess it was true. "Well, well," he said, "the missing days are over and we're going to celebrate that right now this minute," and he handed me a package to open quickly, right away. It was wrapped in Christmas paper and around it a gold ribbon with a silver star tied into the bow. His own handiwork, he told me. It was a shame to take off the paper and bows they were so pretty. But he kept saying "Hurry, hurry" and looking towards the ballroom. Inside the package were orchid silk teddies with lace and an orchid silk brassiere to match, but then—guess what?!! Tucked in one of the brassiere cups was a velvet box from Shreve, Crump & Lowe and inside two star pins made of blue enamel with a diamond in the center of each one. Oh so dainty and pretty, I said. Thank you thank you, Cousin Andrew. "No daintier or prettier than you and much less than you deserve," he said, so happy. Then I told him I'd use them to pin my brassiere straps to the teddies to keep them in place when I wiggle around. He loved this practical aspect and insisted I put the teddies on then and there to show him exactly where the pins would go. Not now, I kept saying. We were alone in the library and he seemed to have forgotten that Prune Face and others were nearby fussing with the tree and that the door was open. "It'll be all right if you hurry up—hurry up—" he said and shut the door and turned the key in the lock. But as he did that we heard voices coming closer so he turned the key back around again and the door flew open and who sailed in but Mamacita and Prune Face. "Oh, there you are," Prune Face said—"time for tea." "There they are," Ma said. "Here we are," Fou said, clapping his hands, and they all tripped on into the living room where the tea table was ready. I went back upstairs to Lucy Edwina's room, where the girls were still fox-trotting away. I'd pushed the teddies and everything else under the library sofa when we'd heard the voices, but retrieved them later with none the wiser. He'll have some other trinkets to present to me around the tree on Christmas morning "so the others won't get suspicious but"—he winked—"but we know what the real presents are." He'd made me swear when I opened the package to say I'd bought the teddies myself if anyone asked—his name mustn't come into it. Silly old Two Fous—he didn't have to tell *me* that. Of course I haven't and wouldn't breathe a mot to a single soul except you. I was really happy to see him again and to know he's not angry with me, because I guess I wasn't v. nice to him on the yacht, to say the least. I've missed him even more than you know. I have really. It's not only the creamy dreamy.

Wish you could see my little Mamacita running around blah blahing to her friends about her "sub-debutanta Favorita"— that's me, in case you didn't know! She took me in to Boston, shopping for dresses for the parties I'll be attending and also bought me a bottle of Chanel Number Five. The first party is the Friday Evening dance at the Somerset and Prune Face is having a dinner at Jamaica Plain before. Herbert will be driving me, not that I need him or anyone else to get me there—I'm so excited I could fly. When we got home after shopping I tried everything on with Ma and Tooka standing around to admire. Fou keeps calling and asking me to tea. Ma doesn't seem to mind that I'm too busy and keep putting him off. I'm so busy and excited I haven't thought of creamy dreamy until right now.

*E*veryone keeps telling me how beautiful I am, but I never believe it unless I can get to a mirror and see for myself. I do look all right, don't I? I mean I'm not deformed or anything. I'm not a dwarf either because I'm 5 ft. 7½ and I can't be too fat because I weigh 125 lbs. It's when the mirror's not around that I get panicky and feel I don't exist even tho' I can look down at my bosom, see my arms with the hands attached and a torso merging on down into legs and feet, but what help is that without a face? That only exists when I'm looking in a mirror. Everyone would think I was crazy if I told them this but I know you understand. Luckily I have a little compact to carry with me in my pocket or handbag. It's with me day and night, readily at hand to pop open and it never fails me. Once I can look in that little round mirror I know that I do have a face, for there it is, inside the lid looking back at me. But without that to look into I lose faith. I'm also fast losing faith as Friday evening looms closer. I could of course not go to this dance at the Somerset. The more I think about this possibility the better I feel. It's nice to feel you have a choice about things, isn't it? I'm only happy when I'm talking to you, Mem, so why don't we spend that Friday evening together going over this and that. Then I wouldn't have to worry about mirrors or anything else.

I'm in my room resting before the party, that is I'm trying to but my mind is elsewhere and everywhere, whirling around so I'm talking to you in hopes that it will calm me down. My crêpe de Chine underwear's out on the chair beside the bed and my dress is hanging on the chandelier. It's twinkly and silvery with a frill of white feathers at the knee—soon I'll take a gardenia-perfumed bath and after my limbs shall be dusted with powder. Oh Mem, I'm all aquiver.

Oh Mem—Powerful—Triumphant—Victorious! But these are weak words to accurately describe how your friend feels since last night. Listen to me, Mem—since last night your friend knows the secret of keeping people under control. What a simpleton—how unaware until now. I'm referring to myself as "your friend" because before I arrived at the party I couldn't connect the girl in the mirror with the girl we know as Starr Wyman. Who was this girl in the silvery dress floating down stairs, in silver slippers dancing over a rainbow as stars fell around her? Sounds like twiddle twaddle to you, doesn't it—well—twaddle twiddle it is not!—for 'tis true, 'tis true, every word of it. It was none other than Starr Wyman they turned to as she floated through the portals of the white ballroom. Yes, girls in flowery dresses of many hues and young men in starched white shirts and dinner coats— all turning to gaze in wonder. And there was Prune Face coming forward with some old, bald fatso beside her . . . AJP? But Prune Face also different, changed. For it wasn't a Prune Face but a pigeon on mincing feet in dove grey shoes with arms stretched out to welcome, wearing not black, but grey chiffon, oh so soft and pretty. "You look charming, dear," she said. "Starr looks charming, doesn't she, Andrew?" But though my beauty dazzled others, the fatso Andrew was not amongst them. No, dear fatso Andrew turned away and started a conversation with his Lucy-Boo, who was standing around unpeppy as could be, ill at ease in a lace dress. The flowers at the hem brought attention to her legs, which are not her best feature. She does have nice hair though—too bad she'd plastered it down with so much brilliantine. Oh, forget I said that—it's mean of me to say unkind things about Lucy-Boo. I've never felt I belonged in that white ballroom at Jamaica Plain or anywhere else for that matter but last night I *more* than belonged. Henceforth I *must*—no I *will*—perceive myself differently—respect myself and know at last what the word means. Henceforth I will belong in ballrooms, white or otherwise, no matter where they may be. Who needs a mirror when I know now that every eye is a mirror?

· · ·

*T*alk about a rush!!! It's tea-dancing with Denny Holbert at Shepard's Colonial and football games at Cambridge with Sam Filley and Billy Robbins. They wear coonskin coats and take sips out of silver hip-flasks and tell me I'm "smooth." Yes, everywhere I go, there's not a boy who doesn't reiterate it until I'm quite deaf from hearing it. I wear nail lacquer (pink), lip salve (orange) and you'd think they'd clash but no—it's dashing, it's fascinating— it's smooth. My shoes have 3-inch heels and did I tell you green is my new best color ever since I found those green shoes at Hovey's with a felt cloche hat that exactly matches. I'm mad about green (as if you didn't know already, ha ha)—everything's going to be green from now on. Yes, from now on, everything green, I'll wear nothing but green and write in green ink. Don't you *love* that idea? Then there's Freddy Norman and Tom Curtis, Petey Dearborn, Jake de Forest and Willy Johnson and dozens more begging to take me out. Jake's maddeningly persistent but he is divine and the other girls are pea-green—Lucy Edwina especially. She tries to hide it by saying she's mad about Benny Wilburn and he's mad about her but we know better don't we, Mem, for Jake's after me day and night. Yes, boys buzz around me like busy bees, but do I show favoritism? Not I! Treat all busy bumbling bees equally is my motto, for I refuse, absolutely refuse at the end of an evening to sit in a car in some out-of-the-way place for cuddles and coos. You'd think they'd drop me, wouldn't you, for girls who do, but the more I say no the more they chase after me, for Starr is in control. This is not only for today, nor is it one of those New Year's resolutions usually forgotten by Valentine's Day—it is a Forever and Ever resolution which came to be after that fatal Friday evening. Starr Wyman is in control, but not only since that evening of earth-shaking revelation—Starr will be in control Forever and Ever—but I went into that already, didn't I—so won't bore you going over it again, now that it's settled for good and all. I only keep bringing it up so you'll know how firm I am in my resolve. Yes, truly and definitely. Everything is going to be great from now on. Happy Happy New Year, Mem!

1923

New Year's Eve. The Faithfull One took Ma, me and Tooka to the Copley Plaza. We had lobster thermidor and "ginger ale" with swizzle sticks made of wood to swizzle around in it to get some of the bubbles out. Tooka fell asleep at the table. "Let her be," Ma said. No one at the other tables seemed to notice. It was pretty noisy. Just before midnight everyone put on paper crowns and necklaces of paper flowers and tooted horns at each other. There were also whirligigs to spin around and add to the noise. The Faithfull One has been around more and more. When everybody was wishing everyone else Happy New Year he raised his glass and said, "Not only happy in the New Year but always if I have a say in it." Ma giggled and gave him a big kiss. I took my swizzle stick home as a souvenir. It wasn't stealing because the waiter said they were "compliments of the Copley."

I was on my way out tea dancing with Jake de Forest when The Faithfull One showed up with licorice cats from Louis Sherry in a lavender tin box with painted violets on it. I had on my pleated silk with the fringe and by chance a lavender posy in my hair— same color as the Sherry box. We smiled about that, and The Faithfull One said my "countenance resembled a gentle, fragile doe" (he does have a courtly way about him) and would I be averse if he started the New Year by calling me Bambi from now on? Indeed, I would not be averse! On the contrary—I like it! I like it! Jake likes it! I more than like it, I love it!! Everyone shall call me Bambi not only in 1923 but forever and ever. You too Mem, so don't forget. We shall inform everyone.

· · ·

*T*he holiday parties are over and things are pretty ho-hum. The bumbling bees are back in school, yes gone away, and I do miss the attention. Can't get my mind on school work. Although I'm deluged with letters from boys it's not the same as gallivanting with them here, there and everywhere. Tons of letters pile up especially from Jake de Forest (don't you love that name, Mem?), but I take my time answering. The other boys I take pity on with an occasional postcard (scenes of Boston in spring to cheer these wintry days). Postcards are divine but there's hardly room on one for even a sentence since I've developed my new scrawly handwriting. Yes, the green ink inspired me to write much larger and in stretched out curlicues. How do you like it, Mem? Hope it's not too hard to decipher? Oh well—so arresting, why fret? What fun to keep busy bees guessing, trying to read my handwriting and falling for me more than they already have. Speaking of falling— what about my falling out with AJP?—he must be pretty loony having gone so long without the pleasure of my company. Wonder if he knows everyone calls me Bambi? Wonder if Lucy Edwina's told him about Jake de Forest and how hard he's fallen for me? And what about the others? All starry-eyed about Starr. He must have heard about them too? Something, anyway.

*H*e certainly has dropped off the face of the earth. Well, we do remember, don't we, that he paid no attention to me, no not even a glance, after my thrilling entrance into the white ballroom. Who cares! Who cares about old fuddy-duddy one or two Fous. Not I—no, certainly not. I have more important things to think about—school work, par example. I'm behind in History but can't think of anything except boys and clothes and—wonder if I'll hear from the dear cousin on my birthday?

January 26, 1923—Friday

Dearest Mem,

Seventeen today! Sweetie-pie Faithfull gave Bambi a bunny jacket and a snappy little hat to go with it. I'm crazy about both and insist on wearing them (the hat too) even when I'm inside the house. I go to a mirror every chance I get and when not in front of one I'm looking at everyone around me to see the effect I'm making. Thank heavens there's always my trusty compact to turn to in a crisis, which happens more than I care to think of because I forget what I look like. Then Emily Post's *Etiquette* came with a card—"Happy Birthday with Love from your cousins Martha and Andrew" (her handwriting). What do you think of that? But guess what else! Stanley gave Ma a Beckwith piano right out of the Sears Roebuck catalog—yes, it arrived today, on my birthday—a present for being the "Ma of two great girls." He's so generous, Mem. Ma used to play piano as a child and "once you know how, it's something you never forget"—and sure enough "Roamin' in the Gloamin' " is tinkling through the house and is she happy, oh yes—I can tell. Think of it—today we're 17 whole years old!! Well—you, Mem, are only 6 years old (so why are you so smart?) because I only started knowing you when I was eleven and started this diary. Little did I know then we were to become best friends—yes, so close that it's fair to say you're 17 too. Congratulations! I love you so much, Mem.

Happy Birthday,
Starr

*G*uess what? *He* called on Wednesday—Valentine's Day! He asked Ma if he could take me out on Sunday. Maybe drive to Concord, visit Orchard House, Louisa May Alcott's family home. I'd like that, wouldn't I? Ma's delighted. More than delighted. She'd been hinting around (more than once) that it was odd we hadn't seen dear Cousin Andrew since the holidays. "Have you been rude to him, Starr? Think back—carefully. Have you?" I kept turning away, not deigning to answer. Don't you think it significant that he called on that particular day? I certainly do.

*O*h, Mem, dearest, dear Mem, how can I ever tell you why I haven't been talking to you until now . . . the whole world's caved in. I'm broken, crushed, shattered, no longer the confident Triumphant chattering away to you about bumbling bees, coonskin coats, Jakes and Billies and—Oh God—what'll I do? Help me, help, help. If only there were some way of dying without actually doing so. There's no room for the pain and I'm praying that it bursts inside me, now, right away, so I'll be blown away and taken out of misery. Listen . . . listen and don't blame me, please. I have to tell someone or I won't be able to take another breath, which is what I ardently desire anyway, so what the hell am I saying? I'm going to try to make one last stupendous, gigantic effort—so here goes and for God's sake *listen* to me, don't interrupt, hear me out. First, I have not seen or heard from him since it happened. What? you ask. What is the it that could have happened that is so terrible? Well—shut up, I'm trying to tell you. Don't judge before you hear me out, I beg you—*Please*. Sunday—that Sunday we were to see each other after my not having seen him for so long. He was mad at me, I knew. Well, he was to pick me up, take me for a drive. After Orchard House he'll take you to a nice place for tea, Ma said. Yes, it was to be a drive in dear old Lizzie, a simple sightseeing drive to Concord to see Orchard House. Ma'd been apprehensive all day about my attitude, which was cool, to say the least. Although I was dying to see him I didn't want him to know and wasn't going to let him think I'd forgotten his ignoring me the night of my triumph. That night of nights he'd barely glanced at me in my white-and-silver and it made me so upset and still does, every time I think of it, and I wasn't about to let him forget *that*. He was going to have to be more than awfully nice to me for me to forget it even for a minute. So when he arrived—ten minutes early—I barely said hello—let *him* see how it felt to have *me* be cold, ignoring him as he ignored me at dinner before the Somerset. So there was Ma as usual hovering around, clucking over me when he arrived, but he was eager to take off, and once we did, I have to admit it was like old times as they say, ha ha, with Ma waving—"drive carefully—have a good time"—and the usual twiddle-twaddle. It had started snowing and as we drove along he said the roads were getting icy so instead why not go to Jamaica Plain and make a cozy fire? Yes, I said, but won't the others be there too? But when we got there they weren't—there wasn't a soul in the house—it was real spooky seeing it so. In my head it was still filled with people as it had been that Friday night of the dinner before the dance. Now it was empty—Prune Face and all of them had gone to Dover Farm and it being Sunday the servants were off, no one there except him and me. I'd never been alone with him in that house before. It was as if we'd run away—escaped in the nick of time and were safe at last. He was in a scurry to get me up to his bedroom—"hurry, dear one," he kept whispering as I followed him up the stairs—but when we got there and he'd lit the fire he quieted down. He didn't even bother to draw the curtains. The snow was swirling against the panes of glass and I went to the window and looked out into the street. It was empty and I knew soon I'd feel even more quiet and safe than I already did since he'd started in the car giving me whiffs from the little green bottle—and soon there'd be more. He came up behind me and put his arms around me and we stood looking out at the snow. I wanted to stay there—that way—forever. He took my finger and put it in his mouth—then held it to the window pane and drew his initials on the glass and around his initials he drew a star. Then he turned me around and led me to the bed. By then my teddies were off and I was creamy dreamy as he put his hands around my waist—he knows I like it when his hands circle my waist just right—his hands warm against my flesh and I feel thin, so thin as he holds me firmly and I straddle his knees, facing him just right for him to take my rosebuds in his mouth, one after the other, and he makes them pointy and pretty and oh Mem—it feels so good. Yes, there he was doing that and bouncing me slowly up and down and starting to sing—Ride a cock horse to Banbury Cross . . . Oh God—how can I say it other than saying it—the door opened and there she was—Prune Face, back earlier than expected. It was the most terrible terrible thing that's ever happened to me. He let me fall to the floor and got himself dressed like the house was on fire while she gasped and choked, pointing at me, pointing—"Get this Bambi creature out of here." Over and over again she kept saying it. He hustled me out like I was a sack of hot potatoes. He was dazed on the drive back—not a word was said. I was left at my door heavy with wooziness—he didn't even help me up the steps into the house. The maids were off and Ma and Tooka were out but I got upstairs all right. I lay in the tub and ran the water—hot, hottest— and slid my head under to hide and not breathe. My hair floated up over my head, falling, falling, sinking down, falling, falling into the watery sleep, but I didn't drown. I never thought that I'd have to be writing to you like this, ever. Oh, God help me is all I can say. I'll never get Prune Face out of my head ever again, the pointing arrow of her finger is burnt into me for as long as I live. Pray with me please to be struck dead for only then will none of it matter. At least Lucy Edwina and Mary weren't with her—that's something, isn't it?

I haven't been in school all week. How can I look at Lucy Edwina—how can I look at anyone? Who knows and who doesn't know? Oh God, it's killing me. I'm feverish, craving sleep, to be out of pain—out of pain and never to wake. Ma wants me to see a doctor, it doesn't have to be Snodgrass, but to hell with any doctor I don't care who it is. I'll kill Ma, I'll die if she brings any of them anywhere near me. Leave me alone, I'm all right. But she won't listen. Poor Stanley's hovering around all the time but too scared to venture into my room. Sometimes he opens my door a crack and peeks in—"What's wrong, Bambi, what's wrong?" Wrong, wrong, what do you mean—Wrong—everything's Right Right Right, yes Right in the night but get out of sight, I can't see the light.

*M*a keeps calling dear Martha but can't reach her. Prune Face is mum to Mum. (Forgive these puns but they help me think.) We'll never see AJP or any of them again, that's for sure.

*S*hould I write to him to apologize? Is that what I should do? Is it a good idea? Maybe not. What could I say? And no matter what I said what good would it do? It wouldn't change what happened. I'm so alone. You tell me that's not true because I've got you, but I still feel it.

*W*hat's been going on in that bedroom in Jamaica Plain since it happened? Has the fire been lit since? Forget about the bedroom—what's happening in the rest of that house? Does Lucy Edwina know and Mary? If they know, surely Charlie Gilbert and the whole school does. Oh God.

*D*oes he miss me? Or am I out of his mind as tho' I never existed?

I went back to school. They were glad to see me. Lucy Edwina especially said she'd missed me. Bettina too—yes, the whole class. Perhaps none of it happened. Maybe it *was* all in my head. The teachers say I'll make up the time I missed "quick as a wink." Wink—why did they say that?

I am more of a fool than I thought if I keep trying to pretend it was only in my head—it *did* happen. What about writing to him at his office and telling him how sorry I am and that I know it was my fault? I'm sure of that now because if it wasn't I wouldn't feel so bad. It's killing me. Yes, that's what I must do, write to him now this minute before I lose my nerve. I must beg forgiveness. But then what about Prune Face? What about her? What can I do? Ever. When it comes to that I can't come up with anything. I'm speechless—yes, when it comes to what to say to her—speechless is the very word—no breath left to breathe in or breathe out. Maybe Fou can explain it to her. No, I'm the fou for trying to believe that—even for a second. Oh God, if I do have the nerve to write to him, it would be better not to go into details, sound casual—"rise above it," as they say around here. Dear Cousin Andrew, I'll write—It's been dreadfully long. I'm lonely and bored. I need to see you. And then I'll sign it—simply—your Cousin Starr. Even if he hates me and never wants to see me again a brief note such as this won't make him hate me more than he already does, will it, Mem?

I hated him when he made me wait for it, teased too long, but in the end he always did open the little green bottle, soak the cotton, and soon I'd be safe and warm, loving and loved. Safe and free. Is that what ecstasy is? But whatever it is, it was always over too soon and now I'm longing and missing, oh yes—wanting. I'll die if I never see him again.

I wrote the letter. Better, Mem, I feel better.

. . .

I went to the post office and mailed the letter myself. Nothing in it about how sorry I am or asking for forgiveness. I couldn't bear risking the answer—also who knows who'd open the letter before he even saw it? Of course I wrote Private on the envelope but what good is that with that Miss Biffy Buffer sitting around with nothing better to do than read his mail. I'd forgotten about her until now. She probably was looking through the keyhole that day in his office. Yes—I'd put that out of my mind too, but when I mailed the letter it thudded back in along with other things forgotten—things like "Get this Bambi creature out of here"—and now I'm back in that room again only he's left me and I'm alone and it's dark and I can't breathe.

*O*n the way to the library I found myself instead on Boylston Street in the Parisian Hairdressing Parlor requesting that my hair be bobbed. Snip snip went the scissors. I closed my eyes as it fell around me to the floor, free, gentle as rain. Yes, I felt light and free—like someone else—but who? Someone happy—that's who. I had a manicure too and when I got out onto the street, walking along in the sun, men flirted with me. I forgot about everything for a while. Does my new bob make me appear older? Now I wish I hadn't mailed the letter.

*W*hy did I mail it? I haven't heard from him. It's been over a week now. How will I live if I never hear? How will I live if I do?

*I*f I ever do see him again what will he think of my new bob?— have a fit probably. How he enjoyed twirling my long curls around the corn to make it grow—leave it to him though to dream up something new. How about dangling earrings to swing around as I toss my head to show off my new bob? See the pretty lady, I'll tease him. He loves it when I pretend to be grown-up with sophisticated ways. My little Mamacita's so funny—while she's thrilled at my success with those boys who give me such a rush, at the same time she's relentlessly warning her Favorita against them. I'm sick of it—anyway, those busy boy bees do nothing but bore me. AJP's not a boy—he's a man like my father, only he used to care about me and Daddy doesn't. No, I never hear from Daddy Lincoln. Tooka and I don't even talk about him anymore, but who cares.

When I got home from school today Ma said she'd "heard from our dear Cousin Andrew and she had a lovely surprise for me." He said he "hadn't been attentive lately—so busy!" That's what Ma said he said. But the surprise is that he's taking me on a trip this summer. It's to be a motor trip. I'm stunned, Mem. You know I'd lost all hope. But what about Prune Face? I'm totally mystified. Does she know about it? This trip I mean. "Stop asking foolish questions, child," Ma keeps telling me. Not hard to do, when you're so scared about what the answers might be.

Ma should have warned me but she didn't, she didn't, and if it hadn't been for you, Mem, I would have kept running and never come back. Yes, Prune Face came to our house without Ma letting me know she was coming to her Saturday bridge party. I just *happened* to go down the stairs when they were there in the living room and I overheard them talking—something about Fatty Arbuckle and a girl at a party at the St. Francis Hotel in San Francisco. Something about a Champagne bottle—and then a voice saying—"Well, what can you expect from those Hollywood people"—and it was Prune Face—no mistaking it. Laughter after that and I ran down past the living room door, on out into the driveway. To run and run and never go back, that's what I intended, but I thought about you, Mem, left alone there in Daddy's chest, and I ran, back into the house, and up the stairs. Ma waved and called out to come and say hello to everyone, but I pretended not to hear. How could I—how could I go in there and come face to face with *her*? How can I ever ever be in the same room with Prune Face again? Now I'm in my room holding you close, oh so close, holding fast to you instead of running.

Oh God, now I have been in the same room with her and I didn't die, because here I am telling you. Right after the bridge party, after they'd all left, Ma said we were going to Dover Farm the next day for lunch. Stanley too. I said no no no, I couldn't, but Ma was adamant, adamant. I must pull myself together and Go. "Cousin Martha is expecting you." And what about Cousin Andrew—? "What about him?" Ma said—besides he's away, busy busy on business somewhere or other. At least that was something. Anyway, Mem, I went. Soon as we got there Lucy Edwina said, "Come on, let's go riding," and there was Star waiting for me as if nothing had happened, and off we went galloping around in the meadows while Prune Face and Ma stayed inside. There were sandwiches to take with us which we had for lunch sitting by the pond. I only saw Prune Face to say "Hello" to when we arrived and "Goodbye" to when we left. Still it was *awful* having to be in her presence even for a second and I could not bring myself to look at her.

$\mathcal{M}$a and Prune Face are seeing more of each other than ever. I'm certain Ma knows nothing about "this Bambi creature." But—? I can't understand or figure any of it out. I worry myself sick.

I'm doing so badly in school I have to be tutored again by Miss Merrick during Easter vacation. It's *imperative*, Ma says, otherwise I won't be able to go on the trip this summer with Cousin A. I haven't seen him or heard from him directly but he's informed Ma that it's to be "a motoring trip, motoring around to educational places in our own U.S.A."

$\mathcal{T}$omorrow is Easter. I've been with Miss Merrick every day. She says I'm making progress. Will *he* be at Dover Farm for the Easter party tomorrow?

$\mathcal{H}$e *was* there, but stayed with the other grown-ups sitting around as they always do on the lawn under the sycamores having tea. Lucy Edwina and I went riding again. I hardly saw him. No one said anything about summer.

I'm back in school. I think I'll at least pass exams. Oh God, Mem, what'll we do—what's going to happen?

*M*a took me shopping for summer dresses—also a muslin nightgown with eyelet lace around a sweetheart neckline and around the puffed sleeves. "It will be cool even on the hottest nights," said the girl at Filene's.

*M*em, we are en route as they say, but this is the first moment I've been able to get you out of the flannel hot water bottle cover. He's been hovering over me every minute since we left. Oh—I wish you could have seen his face as he walked in when he came to pick me up—jolly as could be as if nothing had ever happened—mumbling on about how busy he'd been and how glad he was to see us again, ho! ho! ho! handing out presents—for Ma Chypre perfume (she's got a big collection by now)—for Tooka a big box of candy—for me a "Grandmother Shawl" from Paris—where he'd just been—yes, yes, purest silk, the latest fashion there. Tooka grabbed it from Ma, who had taken it from me and was pirouetting around—"what a lucky girl—what lucky girls we all are." Then she waved "goodbye, goodbye, goodbye—have a good time, be a good girl"—and off we went in Lizzie, just the two of us. Got to stop now, Mem—I hear him.

*S*till not one word about any of it. Not a word about Prune Face. No, not one word about anything. But a great deal to say about my new bob—can't get over the fact that we could easily register at the hotel as a Mr. and Mrs.

*W*e're at the Lafayette Hotel in Portland registered as A. J. Peters, Boston, and S. Wyman, Boston. We're in rooms 304 and 306, adjoining. So far no mention of creamy dreamy.

. . .

*S*pent an hour caught up in a Ping-Pong game with him on the porch. "What a charming daughter you have," a couple from Cleveland said. He reached over and patted my cheek with the paddle. I aimed mine and whacked him one with the Ping-Pong ball—bull's-eye right on his bald fou-fou dome.

*H*e has one heavy suitcase he hasn't opened yet. Bricks? I asked him. "Witty creature!" he laughed—"No, no—books, but— we'll get to our studies later."

*T*he desserts here are really good. Last night there was Apple Pandowdy but I shook my head no thank you to annoy him. He knows how I love sweets. I just sat there watching him eating his. He's the slowest eater I've ever encountered and I'm the fastest. Anyway, I know he eats slowly simply to infuriate me. We never finish a meal at the same time. I have to sit there with my empty plate while the old bull chews away on his cud. Finally the ordeal was over and we went upstairs to our rooms where he ran water for my bath and watched me undress. The tub's huge and sits on claw and ball feet. He'd filled it too full and water splishy splashed out onto the floor while I lolled back and he put sweet-scented foamy stuff over my body, cooing a to-de-do lullaby, swishing the water around to get it just right . . . Then he turned me over and whooshed the bubbles around some more, touching me. It was warm but not too hot, nice. He was holding his hands under me, rocking me oh so gently to and fro and putting his finger up the back of my sit-upon, no fear the cradle would fall, ha ha. It was so pleasurable I had about fallen asleep when he lifted me up out of the tub, wrapped me in a towel and carried me to the bed. Now I said—You haven't given me any and I want it now, but he said no, it was too soon—maybe in a few days. Why a few days? I got real mad and finally he gave me some to calm me down, but not nearly enough, only a whiff to settle me. He didn't touch me anymore and it took me a long time to fall asleep.

I really like this hotel. The veranda wraps around with lots of cushioned wicker chairs to sit in and tables to put things on, lemonade and cookies. Everybody's friendly but we keep to ourselves. He told me not to talk to people unless it was absolutely called for—if someone says "Good morning" I'm to say "Good morning" back, but that's all. Today an old lady tried to be friendly and I smiled politely. "Good morning." What would she say if she knew what I was really thinking, which was that tonight I may go very mad and dance naked on his chest.

*T*onight for sure. He's easy to bamboozle if I put my mind to it. After the fireworks, after the party—I have my ways of making him give me enough.

*J*ust now he came in without knocking and said we weren't going to the party. He almost caught me writing in you, but I hid you quickly under the quilt as I heard the door opening. "What's my Starr-baby doing?" Resting, I told him, resting up for the fireworks tonight. "Who needs that?" he said. "We'll make our own fireworks." About time. He looked at me and closed the door.

*W*e had dinner on trays in the room. It was hot, really hot, the windows all open, not a breeze. He'd pulled the shades down. We could hear the people on the lawn where the fireworks were to be, laughter and music—a carousel, but coming from across the lake. The potato salad got hot and runny. It's gooey, I told him. "Well, you have to eat something," he said, "can't let that sweetie tum-tum stay empty." Clap clappity clap, I quacked at him and went into the bathroom and locked the door. I pulled up the shade and leaned out the window. I could see shadowy figures on the lawn, tall boys and the girls in their summer dresses, and I tried climbing out on the roof but it was too steep so I came back. He kept tapping on the door, but I wasn't going to come out even if I had to stay there all night listening to his needling and wheedling, begging me. There was no place to sit except on the toilet seat and finally it got so hot and boring I yelled at him to stop stop stop, to stop and I'd unlock the door. When I came out he had it ready for me—no games or anything this time.

· · ·

*H*e's been much more amenable since last night. He even gave me some more this afternoon at nap time. I feel so languid and so creamy dreamy it's an effort to write, but I like to keep you up to date, Mem. Now if only he'd go away, just disappear so it'd be only you and me and my white muslin nightgown. I have it on right now. The lace isn't scratchy at all.

*L*ast night we had Champagne from his "private stock." He put his finger up in me and it felt nice, yes, oh so pleasurable. No, you're not ready yet, he whispered. Ready for what? Couldn't hear him at first—didn't care, all I cared about was turning loose. His voice—some insect, most annoying, buzz buzzing in my ear, interfering, making me aware of him, intruding, when what I wanted was to be left alone, to breathe deeply in and out, to get as much as I could from the cotton he was teasing back and forth under my nose. I kept turning my head into the pillow so the buzzing would stop, but his voice kept after me, buzz buzz buzz, pulling me out of where I was, back into the room, kept at me until it wasn't a buzz buzz buzz anymore but the sound of the sea when you hold a seashell close to your ear and a wave of salt sea, hot from sun, pushes up inside you.

*L*eft suddenly for Camden. Stayed there two weeks and four days. Started for Canada. Stayed at an inn somewhere around the borderline of Maine. Got to the Château Fontenac, Quebec, at about six next day. Stayed there two nights. Started for White Mountains and stayed at the Newport House in Vermont overnight. Reached Breton Woods in the White Mountains next day. Stayed there about three days. I hate him.

*S*tarted for New York. Stayed at the Mohican Hotel, New London, overnight. Got to New York next evening at about six. Stayed at the Plaza Hotel. Left in about five days for Springfield. Saw Smith College in Northampton. Drove and drove. Next night, stayed at the Bancroft in Worcester, Mass. Motored to Marblehead the next morning. At least think we did. Sorry this is such a travelog, Mem. He's at me day and night. I can't get a minute to myself to talk to you. I hate him.

*S*tayed Sunday night at the Narragansett Hotel in Providence. He kept bringing up the happy times we'd had right here in the same hotel we were in now and how about a little dance? No no no—all I want to do is sleep. He pesters, asking why I'm so tired all the time.

*H*e bought a pillow for me to use in the car—"for your tuffet to sit on while we're driving." I'm not Miss Muffet, I screamed at him, and threw it out the window.

*W*ent to Barnstable. After two days motored back to Portland, Maine, and here we are again at the Lafayette. He wants to stay for another week.

*W*e stayed two days. Oh God, this moving around, back and forth, back and forth gets me dizzy, but at least I know whenever we get to wherever we're going, even if I don't have time to talk to you, there'll be creamy dreamy if I play my cards right. So it doesn't really matter where we go, or what we do, I'm always thinking up new ways to get him to give me as much of it as I want, yes—must have.

*F*inally—home. Ma unpacked for me. Where's your pretty nightgown? she wanted to know. Didn't answer. (Left it at the Lafayette, but why tell her?) Ma eager to hear about the swell times—"Tell me about New York, New York—what did you do in New York? Well, Ma, we did this and that, Ma, saw a revue, *Runnin' Wild*, that's just moved from Harlem to Broadway, oh yes—saw the sights. "What fun, baby," but she wasn't listening—she was so excited about the lisle stockings he'd bought me in New York with clocks running up the back seam. I told her, Take them, for I've no interest—when I put them on they slither

up my legs like a snake. "What a peculiar thing to say, Starr—
how can you part with them—are you sure, baby?" Yes, yes, Ma,
sure—*take* them—

I'm trying to rest up getting ready for school to start. Everyone
from Miss Sheraton's is still away for the summer. Tooka's on
Vinalhaven Island and Ma says I am to go there too, for the rest
of the summer, but I *will not*. I will stay here in Hampton and get
thin—thin enough to fade away—rise up into the sky and evaporate. The only thing that soothes is listening to my gramophone.
I play it all day and all night too—so low no one else can hear.

*T*ooka's back, everyone's back getting ready for school. She has
a crush on one of the guides at Vinalhaven. His name is Clark,
but she doesn't know his last name. Could it be Amis? Oh what
the hell, let her have him or anyone else she gets a crush on. I hate
them all.

*M*a is over-excited about my Debut party, which is to be with
Lucy Edwina's. "What an honor," everyone says—"those dear
Peters cousins treating you as their own daughter, and why—
why so moody when you're the luckiest girl in the world?"
"Sulky," they call me. I am to wear white. A white tulle dress,
white feathers in my hair in that white white Ballroom—

*S*chool started. I hate it. I hate everybody except you, Mem. I
never want to see him again.

I miss him. He makes me laugh.

I'm not doing well at Miss Sheraton's. How could I when no
one likes me anymore? Lucy Edwina looks at me in a peculiar
way. Has she finally found out about "this Bambi creature"?
Could one of the servants have still been in the house that Sunday
at Jamaica Plain, not taken the day off like the others? Why

hadn't I thought of that before? The maids' rooms are in another part of the house, such a solidly built house, built long before 1872—that's the year he was born—yes, not only born in that house but in the very bedroom we were in so happy, singing away—Ride a cock horse to Banbury Cross—when in she came—the Prune Face—to spoil it all—the more I go over it, the more I realize it was *her* fault. Weren't we happy until she opened that door—and—well, you know the rest, I don't need to go into it again, but I will if you want me to. If only we had been in another room and not the room he was born in—it would have come out differently.

*M*iss Merrick is tutoring me again in math on weekends. She must think all I'm interested in is the math my scale adds up to because I'm forever asking her if she thinks I've gained too much weight. "What does the scale tell you?" She smiles. Nothing. I laugh. "You're a thin lovely young lady—so stop worrying about that and put your energies to the task at hand—I expect you to graduate in the spring with honors."

*H*e's traveling again—Paris. But why is he there without me? Ma got a postcard of cancan girls romping at the Moulin Rouge—"Dear Helen, busy as can be but know my dear ones keep the home fires burning until I return. Love to all, Andrew." What do you make of that Mem?

I work day and night over math. It churns around in my brain but I can't grasp it. Everything's upside down when I look at it on paper—the equations, I mean. Miss Mooney (Moo Moo), my teacher, looks at me and says—Starr, you just don't get it, do you. It's not a question, it's a statement—and truer words were never said—everything I learn from Miss Merrick's tutoring flies out of my head. Let me explain the concept, Moo Moo keeps saying, but when she does, the dread returns and I feel—no, *know*—there is something terribly wrong with me. He'll hear of it soon, you can be sure—that is if he hasn't already. They're in constant communication, Moo Moo with AJP and the lot of them, and don't think I'm not aware of it—even if they're positive I'm not. My poor little Mamacita's worried about me, I can tell. She doesn't want me to "lose my looks—that's the important thing." I haven't any looks to lose, I hollered at her. "Now now, Favorita—now now—" and she brought me a little glass of The Faithfull One's bathtub gin to soothe me. She had some too.

*H*e's back from Paris. I know because he brought Lucy Edwina a silk scarf from Hermès. He hasn't called.

*D*amn it, Mem—I'm being forced to pretend I'm excited about the dances coming up—not to mention the debut I am to make with Lucy Edwina. "Like sisters they are," Ma tells everybody. I'm sick of hearing it. No one understands my serious character or that my deepest wish is to shun any participation in such frivolous pursuits. No, I shall not attend the dances.

I've come to the conclusion that it is *imperative* I go along with the rest of them—Lucy Edwina and the others—yes, I shall attend the holiday dances. Why the sudden change? you ask. Simply that I've decided I'm not fat after all—too thin perhaps? When fleeting doubts cross my mind, I run to the nearest mirror. Is that really *moi*? Yes, definitely, and it confirms my decision to press on. Press on to wondering what I'll wear and what about hair. Is mine fluffy enough? Too fluffy perhaps? Fluffy enough or not, I am determined once more to be the most rushed sub-deb at the dances. And won't we love it, Mem. There we'll be far far above him—old Fou down far below, part of the crowd of Jakes and Billys, Phillips and Dennys, dozens reaching up, jumping around, calling—"twinkle twinkle little star, how I wonder what you are, up above the world so high, like a diamond in the sky—" twinkle twaddle isn't it, but who cares? I'm so preoccupied with these plans I hardly think about creamy dreamy.

*D*id you think I dropped into a well—or was simply faithless beyond forgiveness? Oh me, Mem, I have no excuse for not keeping you posted regarding my activities of late but I've been too busy having fun fun fun, and when you are having it—there's no time for anything else. You will understand as you always do and will forgive this lapse in confidences. Anyway I must tell you before further ado that I am the belle of the ball, although Lucy Edwina does look prettier than last year. Alas, however, this has gone to her head and she is under the impression that Jake de Forest has a pash for her. Little does she know how he pesters me even tho' I've no interest anymore in him, beyond flirting. There is no doubt about it, I am the most sought after beauty in Boston. If only Daddy Lincoln were here to see my success he'd be impressed and love me more than he already does. AJP doesn't approve and has ignored me during these holidays—well, practically. What an old Fuddy-Fou he does look when he gets in these moods. But what care I? Let him stew while I twist him around my pinky toe any way I choose. But right now I'm much too busy choosing among Peter, Charles, Jake, Phillip, Randall, and David—oh, it goes on and on, but you get the gist of it. Oh I'm in such a whirl—can't think, but having fun is much more fun than thinking. Why not have fun and think at the same time? Don't ask me serious questions for I'm in no mood. My mood is frolicsome, impetuous, and anything else you can come up with at the moment. Seriously, Mem—I'd better get to sleep. 'Tis almost dawn and Phillip's picking me up for something or other at noon. Night, Belle of the Ball.

$\mathcal{G}$ot into a fight with Phillip on the way to the matinee. Can't remember what it was about but made him take me back home. Called Denny and left word I could see him tonight after all. He's been after me but I've been putting him off. He called back and wanted to take me dancing but I told him I was all dated up until school starts. "Why did you call and get my hopes up?" he asked and hung up. Who cares?

$\mathcal{T}$omorrow is New Year's Day—1924. Why am I blue? All I do is lie on my bed thinking. What about? I know not. Things drift in and out of my mind, but I can't hold on to a one. It's only when I get up and look in the mirror that I feel real, and when I'm talking to you of course. I could be a hundred places tonight but the only place I want to be is with you.

1924

*I*t's back to Miss Sheraton's and all my efforts are put into trying to concentrate. It's true what Miss Merrick says. I *must* graduate with honors so AJP will be proud of me. Daddy Lincoln will surely hear of it too one way or another—don't you think? I must keep that in mind. I told you, didn't I, that no one in our class except Patsy is going to college. All everyone else talks about is summer after graduation—and plans for the coming-out parties in the fall. It's to be nothing but fun so why do I feel guilty and peculiar about it? Speak up, Mem. Yes, everyone's looking forward except me. There must be something really wrong with me. Maybe what's wrong is that I should be doing what Patsy is doing and going to college. But Ma's never taken it even as a consideration. Oh why am I blue one day and the next day everything's rosy again? It's either up or down. I can't make up my mind about anything. I must stop brooding and get to work. But I wish I had some idea what you thought of all this. Maybe if I work harder I *could* go to college. Is it too late? Patsy's family applied to Radcliffe ages ago. Who am I, Mem? I feel like a nobody who wants to be somebody—but exactly who I don't know.

January 26, 1924—Saturday

Dear Mem,

Eighteen today and taking time off to write my usual Birthday letter to you, my dearest darling friend. First I must report that math still stumbles along, but when I passed Miss Sheraton in the hall yesterday she said, "Good girl, Starr," which must mean she has heard of my sincere efforts concerning the hated subject. So that counts for something, doesn't it? Now I must tell you about my birthday present to myself. It's bookplates I found in the stationery store. *Ex Libris* at the top, space below to write my name and between an engraving of ancient volumes, a candle and a skull. This morning I started pasting one in each book and it makes me feel that I now have a real library—something solid to rely on. All around me are my old friends going back to *The Secret Garden, Pilgrim's Progress,* and *Elsie Dinsmore* and so on. Soon I'll need more shelves. AJP doesn't know it, but I still have his copy of *Salomé* (no bookplate in that!). It's sandwiched on my shelf between *Elsie* and *Pilgrim's Progress.* It's in good company, n'est-ce pas? But now comes the moment of truth, for I have something to reveal to you, something I'm deeply serious about, something I haven't told you about before because I've been waiting for the right moment, but that could go on forever (the waiting), so here goes—the moment's arrived. I don't think about college anymore because I am deeply serious about becoming an actress. Yes, a deeply serious very famous movie star. Let me tell you how I came to this momentous decision. If I become an actress I might—no, *will*—find myself in whatever role I'm playing. Because if you're a nobody the only way to be anybody is to be somebody else. I hate to have to say this but I haven't been able to really absorb, much less hold on to the ba-star theory that gripped me so that day in the Boston Public Library. In fact it slipped away from me almost immediately. Altho' I did try, Mem. Honestly. So doesn't what I'm saying to you now make sense? More than ancient Egyptians and even the Dominican nuns I felt so drawn to. From what people say I certainly have the looks to be a movie star and wasn't I more than convincing in my first role as Mata Hari—ha ha. Yes, that's what I intend to do and it's a relief to tell you about this definite decision I've come to. I'll start by getting a part in a play—something Shakespearean—Hero in *Much Ado About Nothing* perhaps. Why not! Think about it please and let me know what conclusion you come to as soon as poss. I want your support and value your opinion, as you well know. You're probably puzzling (you who know me so well) about why my future plans keep changing, one day's it's one thing, another day another. Oh Mem, perhaps even now you are questioning the soundness of my character, since I always seem unable to come to any definite decisions. I can tell you're losing patience with my going on like this when we both know that what I really do want (forget about nuns and movie stars), what I really want is some of that little green bottle. No, not some of it—a lot of it—*all* of it, in fact, and I'm furious because I have to depend on AJP to get it. So far, I haven't been able to get around that little problem, though I'm clever when I put my mind to it—maybe I haven't been thinking too clearly lately, what with our graduation day ahead and one thing and another, and even tho' I try to erase it forever from my brain it grinds itself deeper into it—and altho' it happened a year ago it's as if it's *about* to happen—a terrible event foreseen, as a fortune teller predicts when she places the Tarot cards on the table in front of the doomed one. Don't laugh at me, Mem, don't tell me to stop being dramatic for I go over it again and again—that terrible Sunday at Jamaica Plain, and the slap stings and hurts and I can't swallow and want to die. I didn't want to frighten you but last week two nights in a row I had dreams about Prune Face, and her finger pointing at me was a poisoned arrow which found its mark in my skull. I've been trying to pull it out ever since, but parts of it are stuck in my brain, which has knitted over the tip of it—the arrow, I mean, and there's a kind of glue in there that cements it in, so that now it's actually part of my head. If you have any thoughts on this, Mem, let me know, I beg you. But don't worry, please, and don't tell anyone about the other plan I've revealed to you. No one but you would take it seriously. And don't worry, I intend to have a happy birthday—just wanted to keep you posted—none of this is important except to you and me. Hugs and kisses,

Starr

I keep puzzling over President Wilson, who died in his sleep. He told a friend a few days before he died that he felt like a broken piece of machinery and when the machinery is broken . . . What was he dreaming about before he died? Have you any ideas on this, Mem?

*M*y little Mamacita's being jazzed around more and more these days by The Faithfull One, and when she's not doing that, she's playing mah-jongg with her friends. They wear Chinese robes (none magenta, or gorgeous as mine) and burn incense and carry on like fiends in an opium den with ciggies, dry martinis and gin fizzes made with The Faithfull One's bathtub gin. "Ain't we got fun," they say to each other, joking around. But then Ma gets serious and calls Mr. Faithfull her "intended," and her friends nod—"so amusing, so quaint." She's real proud of his having been born in England and being descended from one of the three oldest families there (one of his ancestors is Oliver Cromwell). Do you think they really will get married? I know Ma likes him. They never fight. But does she love him?

*V*alentine's Day. It's going to happen. Mamacita became officially engaged to Stanley Faithfull today! And when they marry I am to be rechristened. I am no longer to be Starr Wyman. I shall be Starr Faithfull. Pretty swell name for an actress! I'm sure Daddy Lincoln will understand when he knows how serious I am about my career. The wedding is to take place during Easter vacation at Dover Farm. They really are happy—Ma and The Faithfull One. And he doesn't shut us out of things and he takes us places and oh yes, those licorice cats keep coming. Tooka's crazy about him and I like him too, but I refuse to call him Daddy even though Ma says I must. Let Tooka call him Daddy if she likes, but that's no concern of mine. Tooka insists she be called Tucker from now on. Soon she'll be Tucker Faithfull. Pretty swell too, eh?

*I*t was a sunny sunny day—Mamacita wore a pearly beigey dress and floated over the lawn to where Stanley was waiting under the sycamore tree. AJP gave the bride away and Prune Face didn't wear black. Her dress was dove grey but not the same dress she wore the night of the Somerset dance. Tooka and I were bridesmaids in lilac dresses and tulle hats with lilacs on the brim. Ma carried a bouquet of white lilacs. Afterwards there was dancing and lots of "ginger ale." Guess who caught the bride's bouquet? Miss Starr Faithfull! I could go on and on about it but why bother when you can read all about it on the society page of the *Herald*. Ma's bought up every copy in town.

*T*wo days married and they've suddenly decided to go to Niagara Falls on a spur-of-the-moment honeymoon. Ma's enchantée and it's all working out perfectly, because while they're away AJP's taking me to New York. He has to go there on business and I can go along to "meet some lovely young people who are friends of a lovely niece of a friend who lives there." Tooka's to visit at Dover Farm. It happened so suddenly I'm in a whirl.

$\mathcal{D}$o we want to go on this trip? No, we don't. Then we do. Creamy dreamy no?—creamy dreamy yes? stay? go?—go or stay—yes or no—which will it be?

$\mathcal{O}$h Mem, I'm still in a state. In a little while he will arrive to pick me up to take me to New York. We're to go there by train and stay for five days. Will it be too short? Too long? Don't ask me. I never know in advance. When I think of what will probably take place I shudder. And yet, I long for that little green bottle, or rather for what is in it, for what it does, where it takes me. Even now, after all the times I've spent with him, I can't be sure of what will happen. Often it is something new. What would people say if I told them about that little green bottle and what it does to me and what it makes me do? And Daddy? Oh God—what would he say if he knew about it? I don't care—that's what he'd say.

$\mathcal{A}$ll the way down in the train he kept questioning me about those Harvard boys I saw so much of during the holidays. Jake de Forest especially. Now you know I didn't encourage Jake, but, well, he is so handsome and not only handsome but extremely intelligent. I went on and on about that particular aspect of Jake's character—it helped pass the time, but poor Fou Fou went crazy. What's so extremely intelligent about him? he kept wanting to know. Well, he's even more well-read than I am and sure to graduate magna cum laude. He could do and be anything in the world he put his mind to. Fou pounced—"And it's *you*, cutie-pie, that this magna cum laude is putting his mind to." Don't act like a crazy cat, I told him—I'm not your mouse or anyone else's for that matter, so leave me alone. He was getting on my nerves. But he wouldn't calm down, he kept wanting to know what "this de Forest" and I had talked about and where we'd gone and what we did—"What? What? What?" Of course I had no intention of telling him—not that there was anything to tell.

*P*laza Hotel: Our rooms are next to each other—we're registered this time as A. J. Peters, Boston, and S. Wyman, Boston.

*B*illy Lossez's band is playing at the hotel and he took me downstairs for tea-dancing. "Bet your magna cum laude wouldn't take you places like this," he said. Why do you say that? I said. The Copley Plaza's just as nice and Jake took me there twice. As the music played Fou sang in my ear . . . *Come to me, my melancholy baby . . . Cuddle up and don't be blue . . .* Oh, stop! I said, pushing him away. I'm not blue and anyway, they're looking at us. And they were, not only the couples dancing near us but also the people sitting at tables. He didn't stop tho'—except to lower his voice and lean closer.

*W*ent to Tiffany's and tried on bracelets and things. While I looked around I could see him out of the corner of my eye whispering to the sales clerk and knew he was up to something. He couldn't wait to get me back to the hotel for a game of Hide and Seek. I finally "found" the box hidden in his coat pocket, where it had been all along, as I well knew. In it were earrings, emerald-bead tassels like the ones I'd been hinting about. I jiggled around, turning my head this way and that—see the pretty lady, mincing the way grown-ups do when they show off. I knew he'd like that but after a while it wasn't fun anymore, no fun at all because he'd hidden the little green bottle too, and I couldn't find it. He was being mean and teasing, as he so often does.

*H*e took me to a play. I wore the earrings and some new crêpe de Chine underwear he bought me from B. Altman's. There was a new dress too with a swag at the hips. He'd been promising we'd have supper at the Marguery after the theatre—Chicken à la King, spun sugar and pistachio ice cream, but at the theatre during the intermission he started going on about Jake de Forest again. I screamed at him that I was sick of hearing about Jake, but

he told me to lower my voice and pay particular attention, because he had very serious things to tell me regarding Jake de Forest, so serious that they couldn't wait another sec. and we had to
go back to the hotel right then and there. What about the 2nd
Act? To hell with the 2nd Act, and he rushed me into a taxi. Hush
now—hush—no talk now in front of the driver, he whispered.
He scurried me fast through the lobby of the hotel up to his
room. Once there he let out a flood of angry words—oh Mem,
there was no calming him. On and on he went about Jake being a
"bad influence—yes, a bad bad influence" and he hadn't been the
Mayor of Boston for nothing and had his ways of finding out
things. What things? He was taking deep breaths now and trying
to be reasonable. "After all, I am responsible for your education
and these young Harvard fellows have newfangled ideas about
things, things you must be sheltered from—this Jake fellow especially, despite his extreme intelligence, has a bad reputation, a very
bad reputation." Don't be ridiculous, I told him—you just don't
want me to have any fun. "Fun!" he shouted. "You call that fun,
being pawed over by every Tom, Dick and Harry!" Who said I
was? I shouted back. "Listen to me, young lady—actions speak
louder than words"—he was getting really crazy—"and *your* actions speak volumes—yes, you're a walking encyclopedia to me,
Miss Starr—you don't fool me for a minute." Jake Jake Jake.
Shut up about Jake—what about the Chicken à la King you
promised me? "Chicken, chicken," he said. "You've already had
enough chicky chicken from your Jakes and Charlies," and he
started shaking me, getting all purple, and then I got scared and
told him I wanted to go home. "You are home," he shouted, and
threw me on the bed. I was scared he was going to kill me—I'd
never seen him like this before—as if he didn't know who he was
or who I was or where we were or what was happening. I tried to
get away, out the door, but he caught my leg and I fell to the floor.
We'll see about your Jakes, and he ripped off my dress and threw
me onto the bed and pushed his tongue into my mouth, but I
shoved him away and he got madder and rammed his finger way
up inside me hard, pinning me down and telling me to stop
screaming—stop it stop it, and he put cotton over my face—
then instead of his finger ramming up inside of me it was the
white corn pushed up hard so hard it cracked me open and—Oh,
Horror, Horror, Horror!!! I was crying and begging him to stop,
but he wouldn't—it went on killing me and I died but then later

I woke up in the dark and I wasn't dead because I was hurting so and everything under me was wet and I put my hands between my legs to stop it from pouring out of me—the blood, because I knew that's what it was even though it was dark and I couldn't see it. My hands didn't stop it and the blood kept coming, the pain getting worse. He was far away from me on the other side of the bed, like a dead body only he was snoring, and I knew if the blood didn't stop soon it would reach him and drown us both. I called out to him for help and put my hand out to wake him but pulled it back before I touched him because it was so wet with the blood. I was afraid to have him see the sheets and have him know that it was my fault they were so bloody but I couldn't do anything because it kept on pouring out of me, but then he turned over in his sleep and threw his arm across my chest. It was like a tree had fallen over me and I was too scared to move. Then the pain got less and so did the flowing between my legs. I lay there hardly able to breathe until light came through the windows and he woke up. Oh, it was very terrible, Mem, seeing in the daylight all that blood on the sheet. My, my, what happened—what's all this? he said. He sounded surprised—very surprised—seeing the mess. I'm sorry, I'm sorry, I kept saying. Maybe Aunt Margaret decided to pay a little unexpected visit, he said—yes, that must be it. No, no, I told him, she came ten days ago. Well, well, he said, let's sit you up in this nice chair and order some breakfast—then a nice hot bath and you'll be fit as a fiddle in no time. He lifted me off the bed and carried me into the bathroom. Better tidy up first, he said, and while you're doing that I'll call down for those nice waffles you're so partial to. He started running the water in the tub, testing the temperature to get it just right. Don't want my Starry-eyes in hot water, he said, winking. When the tub was half full he turned the tap off and draped a bath towel over the toilet seat. There now, he said, you'll soon be right as rain. He went out and shut the door. After a while I got in the tub and sat there without moving except to keep rubbing soap on the wash rag, squeezing the water into it and letting it trickle over me. A long time went by and then there was a knock on the bathroom door and he was calling me to hurry on out or my lovely waffles would get cold. I let the water run down the drain. It left a pink shadow on the white tub. My robe was hanging on the back of the door and I put it on and went back into the room. The spread had been put over the bed and it looked as if the maid had come in and done the room only I knew it was he who had covered the bloody sheets. He fidgeted around putting too much butter on my waffles, too much syrup, but it didn't matter because I couldn't eat anyway. He suggested we spend the day at the Botanical Gardens, but that meant walking around which I could hardly do because I could barely stand up. I told him I didn't feel like walking around much and after I said that he couldn't do enough to please me and suggested a Hansom cab ride around Central Park instead. It was awful. The jigging of the carriage made me hurt more. And then suddenly my head split open and my brains spilled out down over my face and into his lap. He kept saying, What's gotten into you, Starr-baby (he didn't understand what had gotten out of me — the brains, I mean) and the driver kept turning around and looking at us while he clicked at the horse to go faster and Cousin kept me alive with soothing words that made no sense. How could they with my brains scrambling out of my head? Some were left, of course, but not enough so a sentence might be formed into an idea. Home, he called out — home — hurry. Oh yes — home. He's downstairs in the lobby taking care of the hotel bill right now as I write this, sitting on the bed in our hotel room. I'm waiting for him to come and get me. A bellboy will be here soon to take the luggage down — I think that's what he said, Mem. I'm taking these moments to tell you — don't worry about me. My brains are back inside my head — at least I think they are — some of them. In place, let's say. Yes, let's. But dammit, the tip of that arrow is in the part of them that's still there.

All the way back to Boston on the train he kept mumbling on about the noise I'd made in the hotel last night, yelling so he was sure the hotel detectives would be up knocking on our door to see what was going on. What with the yelling and screaming and making so much trouble there was no other way to quiet you. It's *you* who were yelling and screaming at me, I told him. Quiet — honey, be quiet, he said — I don't mean to upset you. *Upset* me — ? Then he made me swear and repeat after him that I'd never mention to anyone about yelling and screaming or anything else — especially about the chloroform. What do you mean? I asked him. Never you mind, never you mind, I only gave you that to calm you when you got so upset — so — so out of hand — we had a nice time, didn't we? Didn't we? You're feeling your own pretty sweet starry self again, aren't you? Aren't you, baby? And he hugged me, but I pushed him away. He lapsed into a daze and closed his eyes and started twiddling his thumbs. Stop that, stop that, and I hit the thumbs with my fist. Then I went into the cabinet where the toilet was and stayed there until the train stopped in Boston. He got me home in a big hurry and just left me at the door, didn't look at me or say goodbye. He was not himself. He was some terrible stranger I'd never seen before, but then of course how could I have seen him before if he was a stranger? I was too scared and hurting too much to figure it out. The hurting between my legs had kept getting worse all the way to Boston. When I saw Ma she thought it funny that he hadn't come in to say hello and I told her I had to go to bed because I was so tired. "You do look a bit peaked dear—ah yes, but as they say in that lovely poem—something about, Bliss was it in that dawn to be alive, but to be young was very Heaven! but what your Mamacita says is get a good night sleep and you'll be your twinkly self again." Oh God, Mem, what's happened?

I keep crying, Mem, and I can't stop. Ma says I'm doing it on purpose to draw attention to myself and throw a wet blanket over her newfound happiness—and that I'm never satisfied, never happy, always discontented. Why, any other girl would be thanking her lucky stars for her new Daddy. I haven't a new Daddy, I yelled at her, but she only went on—not to mention the opportunities you have—trips to New York, lovely young people to meet—tell me about them. Tell us, what lovely things did you do? Where did you go? Who did you see? Tell me, Starr—tell me, dear, and for God's sake chin up, get out of bed, stop your snivelling, it'll ruin your looks. What *is* the matter with you? Buck up, missy—graduation's ahead, and summer and your debut with Lucy Edwina. How can you behave so—how how—you'll ruin *everything.*

I haven't been able to go back to Miss Sheraton's because I can't stop crying. Ma tried to force me—what will people say?—but . . . Oh Mem—

· · ·

*S*tanley got real worried about me and made Ma take me to the Snodgrass to find out why I can't stop crying. I told the doc I don't stop because I can't stop. We'll see, we'll see, young lady— we'll see about that. He made me undress and get up on a table and spread my legs out in some stirrups. I screamed but he didn't stop and two nurses came in to hold me down while he poked around inside me. After the examination we went back to where Ma and Stanley were waiting. I was fighting to breathe, fighting not to tell them about what happened. But they were determined to know. Snodgrass kept after me, insisting. I screamed "Melancholy Baby Melancholy Baby," but they didn't understand because I was choking and my nose started bleeding. Blood was pouring out of me. Snodgrass yelled at the nurse to get ice and I lay on the floor and they tried to stop the bleeding, but it wouldn't stop. Then it did, because it was flowing backwards into me, going up through me and then down again and coming out between my legs. I heard a voice telling them what had happened at the Plaza Hotel in New York even tho' I was firm in my resolve not to, a voice telling them about the hard cornstick that was pushed up inside me, splitting me open and killing me, telling them that I'd died but hadn't gone to heaven, because before I could get there he'd taken the cornstick out, and made me swear never to tell anyone what he'd done and that if I didn't obey I'd be a bad girl and something terrible would happen. A voice was mumbling about chloroform and how he'd given me that instead of the little green bottle it went over my face otherwise the hole inside me wouldn't start filling up, and if it didn't fill up, I wouldn't be safe even tho' he was holding me, and even tho' I was bad and it was my fault, I wasn't afraid anymore once the cotton was over my face because it was dark and I stopped breathing. I have a hole inside, you see, that only he knows how to fill, no one else on earth or in heaven knows how to do this except him. I'd sworn never to tell anyone about the little green bottle, and now that I have God will punish me. Chloroform. Yes—it was my voice saying that, too, telling what I'd sworn never to tell. Oh God—strike me dead.

I don't know what day it is or how much time has passed but I want to get this down before something else happens to make me forget what's already happened. So please listen to me—don't interrupt until I finish—wait a minute—I've lost my train of thought—I can't seem to remember how they got me into the bed because my legs couldn't move, my feet couldn't either, both were tingling so that I couldn't tell which was which. There was a nurse in the room—Angel by name—but I didn't believe her or any of them. The room was dark with the shade down. Where was Stanley? There was seaweed on the walls but they certainly weren't going to hear about that from me. It was sticking to the walls with more on the side where my bed is. The bed was pushed up against the wall as you well know, and to avoid the seaweed I had to lie on the edge of the mattress as far away from the wall as possible, which is why I fell on the floor and why Angel had to get Stanley to help her get me back up into the bed because I was heavy as lead and couldn't do it myself. I still won't be able to until my legs and feet are home again and God knows when that'll be. I was scared to death He would show up, but they told me if I obeyed the Snodgrass he wouldn't. They kept telling me this but I didn't believe it—and still don't. Angel says it was the seaweed that was making my room the mess it was and still is, I may add. What a fool. Does she think I needed her to tell me that? The seaweed has spread onto the floor too, but I've kept quiet about it. I want to be in a clean room, is that too much to ask for? I demand to be in a white room, snow on snow, falling on snow, with me in it, sun on crystal. It is goodness that will make the evil slime go away. Ma cries and cries and Stanley sits there white, as if lightning had struck him.

I'm making every effort to study the map I made—my heart map inspired by *Pilgrim's Progress*—and the more I study it the more it speaks to me. Look up, not down—that is what it tells me. You hear that, don't you, Mem? It's very important. But I need you to keep reminding me so I won't forget. You will do that for me, won't you? I know I can count on you. It'll be different this time I know. Why do I know this? I'll tell you about that later. Right now all I care about is that I'll never have to see Him again no matter where we are. I know these things because I keep studying the map and I know I am now located in the House of the Interpreter, and what I interpret is this: New York is the Celestial City and once there I will find Faith, Virtue and Enchanted

Ground. No longer will I have to fight against drowning in the Sea of Hate and Malice or battle in the Grove of Furies—but all this depends on whether I can really trust them. After all, Angel lied to me about the seaweed. It's still here, only I don't let on for fear we won't move and I'll have to stay on in Hampton, which I now know for a fact to be the City of Destruction. And tho I've gotten somewhat used to it I refuse to accept this, I'm determined to get myself to New York one way or another even if they're lying when they tell me we are moving there and will never have to go near Boston again. Now that my legs and feet are home again I have some say in the matter, surely—haven't I? When I look in the mirror I'm there too. I know now that I won't have to go back to Sheraton's, back to its Love of Gossip (that's on the map too). And they tell me my room in New York can be painted any color I choose. White, for Virtue, of course. I'll settle for nothing less. I haven't told them that the seaweed's still here on the floor and have no intention of doing so, because in the Celestial City it'll be different. They say we'll leave as soon as I'm more on my feet. I never see Lucy Edwina or anyone from school. I wonder if they know I'm sick. I wonder what they all think? What terrible gossip they've heard. Is that why they haven't come to see me? I can't think anymore. I must get well so we can get out of here. I don't even care about leaving my bed with the dotted Swiss canopy, all I care about is you, Mem, and Daddy's chest where I keep you. I am in constant fear something will happen to you—a fire, or worse . . . ? If you were to burn, Mem—I would cease to exist. My books are important too—they must come with us wherever we go—but it is you, Mem, I worry about most. If I lost you or if something happened to you—I would cease to exist. I know I'm repeating myself but I want you to know how serious it would be if I lost you—I would cease to exist—do you understand? Yes, we are moving to Greenwich Village—which may prove to be the Village of Morality—we are to live there in a house on Grove Street and I am to have my own room exactly the way I choose—but I told you that already, didn't I? Don't forget all the things I am telling you. Especially about taking care of yourself. They are not just idle words when I say if it were not for you I should not exist.

We're in New York—I know that but how long has it been since I talked to you? The last thing I remember is getting you quick as I could into Daddy's chest. It's hard to write because Angel's around all the time and so are Ma and Stanley. The Snodgrass was in and out too much too much, but that was before we left I think. I do remember locking you safely in but after that it's been figgy-foggy until now. I have been able to get *some* information from Stanley. Christmas is over. Or is it? That means Thanksgiving is, too. See how smart I am, Mem? Have to stop. I'll tell you about Green Witch—I mean Greenwich—later— have to stop now—someone's coming.

Tonight's New Year's Eve. Well, I'll be around for that. Ma and Stanley are staying home to be with me and we are to have cake with white icing and candied cherries for dessert. It's so quiet around here and I suddenly noticed—where's the Beckwith? I asked Ma. The one Stanley gave you on my birthday. Never mind about pianos, dear, she said. Well, I do mind, I told her. Look around you, baby. Where would we have put it? She's right. There's no room for a piano. I wish they'd stop tippy toeing around and whispering. I feel better. I must put Boston behind me, Ma says, because I'm going to love it here and we'll all be happy again, and aren't we already? I don't know what she's talking about. How can I put Boston behind me, in front of me, or on the side of me, because I don't remember anything about Boston or Miss Sheraton's, but then maybe I didn't graduate, maybe the math finally did me in. Ma says, "It doesn't make any difference. Your health now is the only important thing so you'll get your looks back." She keeps saying that as tho I haven't heard it the first time, the second time or the hundredth time. I'm sick of it. Oh Mem . . .

1925

I'm coming from one country, crossing the boundary into another territory, but I don't remember much about the place I'm leaving—I've been on a train, a slow, slow train, a train going in and out of tunnels—and I've been groping in the air for the light switch. But now I'm over the border, crossed over into a place which I'm told is New York. And it *is,* I keep telling myself. We're out—away from Boston. That is a v. great and big accomplishment. I thought no matter what they said that they were lying to me about coming here, but it wasn't a lie. It was true all along and here we are, Mem, in a room in a house on Grove St. in Greenwich Village, New York City. The room is painted white, as I requested, and the bed I sit up in as I write is clean and white with a painted headboard—white too, and on the table next to me is the frame with the drawing of Daddy Lincoln and no one says take it away. There are no paintings on the wall because bookshelves take up the space, tho my books haven't arrived from Hampton. Soon, Angel says. She and Stanley say they'll help me unpack but I don't want anyone to touch them except me. We drove down from Boston in a hired limousine. Angel and you (in Daddy's chest) and I. Ma and Stanley went ahead by train. Angel's going to stay with me for a while. I dread the day she'll leave. I trust her even though I know Snodgrass put her here. I don't think she likes him either but as he's the Doc and she's the nurse she can't show it. Yes, I like her v. much. She's not too tall, she's not too short, she's just right. Nothing about her irritates or annoys me. I wish it were Ma who was going to leave instead of Angel. How could we arrange that? Maybe you could do something, Mem. Think on it. I'm tired now—

Did I tell you that Tooka's been sent to boarding school? Seaton's Academy near Brewster in New York State. She'll get to ride there. She cried and didn't want to go even when they kept telling her it would be as much fun as Camp Wigawam and that she'd be allowed to come home weekends. (Well, some, anyway.) I cry too, every time I remember that I didn't graduate with the rest of my class at Miss Sheraton's. I keep picturing them—the graduating class—dancing around the maypole the way they do on that last day before the ceremony—yes, around and around, I see it clearly even tho it's past—Elaine, Patsy, Bettina, Lucy Edwina and Camilla and the rest of them—in my head dancing around that maypole, but I'm not in the picture. Why the hell is Camilla there? She's not a Boston girl, she's in Evanston, but I definitely see her there with the others going around and around. Tooka got thin before she left for Seaton's. I'm thinner too. At least I think I am. It's hard to remember what thinness I was (exactly) before we came to New York.

I worry about the girls in school, go over and over it again, trying to remember what happened. I think it was that I got sick and couldn't go back to school after the spring vacation. Then I got really sick and couldn't go back at all. (So it was not due to failing math.) That's how and why I didn't graduate with the others. That's why I don't remember much about the summer—don't recall much of anything until we got here. I could check back with you, Mem, to find out, but I'm too scared. Best leave well enough alone for a while anyway. Perhaps the whole school and the teachers came to see me when I was sick but if they did I can't remember. What I do know is that I haven't heard from a single one since we moved to New York.

I'm up and around more every day. Angel took me for a stroll even though it was cold out. She's leaving tomorrow. We looked in the shop windows. I saw a hat that reminded me of something but can't remember what. Everything looks different—even Angel. I don't like her. No, definitely not. Her face is squiggly and there is something about her fingernails I don't approve of. Her wrists are thick and she wears shoes as thick as her ankles—

odious. She'd look nice in that hat tho'. Do you agree? Maybe I do like her.

I pretended to be asleep when Angel left so I didn't have to say goodbye.

My beloveds (books) arrived at long last. They're in boxes still, but I'm going to spend the day unpacking and putting them in place. My gramophone and records are here too. I feel better. Yes, much. But I miss Angel.

Ma goes out early every morning to be the first one at the shops when they open. There's money to burn, money to burn, chirps my little Mamacita. Stanley tries to calm her down—please, Helen, please, you're spending money like it's going out of style, please, Helen, don't let it burn a hole in your pocket. Then he sits down with a sigh and says, What'll we do now? Ma pays no attention to him, none at all. Yes, I have my own room, as promised, and it's painted white, everything's white and my books are around me (not painted white, silly). We're in an old brownstone on Grove Street in Greenwich Village in New York City and it's 1925—no, they didn't lie to me, everything's come true, exactly as they said it would.

Angel left without a word—but I told you about that already—didn't I?

Shaky—snaky—whenever I try to get up—shaky. Whenever I'm not putting my books in place on the shelves what I like best to do and do best therefore is lie abed and do rien—rien at all. But while I'm doing rien my little brain isn't a zero, it's working, busy every minute making my plans, so that's doing something, isn't it? Though what these plans are is hard to say right now. I'll delve into it deeper later.

*N*o one around here minds if I turn the gramophone up loud. Sweet Stanley got me a new record and it's on and loud, loud as it can go—*Rhapsody in Blue.* Oh, my tiny heart soars up into the blue of rhapsody—soars up, up into the rhapsody of blue. Like a bluebird, did you say?—why not!—up, up and away—soaring—and disappearing through the clouds. You think 'tis twaddle I twiddle—oh hell.

*M*a's busy with shopping and getting the place fixed up and Stanley's busy mixing "things" and I'm busy being left to myself, which is fine by me. I've all the time in the world to read, but now that I do all I do is rien, rien, rien. Ma has no time to pick at me the way she used to in the old days. We're in new days now. I can do whatever I wish. That's a new one, eh?—no homework to worry about—no first thought waking, school today and the looming math—all I have to do, I'm told, is "get your looks back." What I wish right now is that Stanley would stop going on about Ma's pocket and the burning money. I'd like to put tape over his mouth but never would as he's so sweet to me—his manner, I mean. I still don't look at calendars or read the newspapers. What month or day it is I know not and care less.

*W*e don't know a soul in town, but how could we when we keep so much to ourselves? Maybe in a few days, weeks, months, years—I'll feel like going out and meeting people, people I can talk to. There must be hundreds in New York waiting to meet me. I went out yesterday for about an hour, but I can't go into that now as I haven't formed any opinion of what I saw because I can't remember but that's between us. I trust only you.

I slept better last night and woke to hear a bird singing in the tree outside my window. I made my body into a sieve (I have that facility, you know) and let the sweetness of the sound flow through me. Or tried to, because this time something kept clogging the sieve (icicles?) and the sweetness clogged up. Still, I kept trying . . . There's a bird outside my window singing as I wake . . . and no matter what the day brings little difference can it make

. . . for somewhere, someplace a bird is singing . . . with it love and beauty bringing—oh what mishmash. I got so mad at myself I shut the window and the damn thing flew away.

I was lying abed per usual, exhausted if you must know from forcing you know who out of my head. There are times he pushes himself into my mind—little things, memories let's call them, for want of a better word—ah, yes, as a dark shadow he comes towards me, but when the shadow gets closer, it's not dark—it's Fou's smiling face lit up, glowing so merrily I can't restrain myself from smiling back and reaching out to him—but then he disappears. You know, I still have that pearl bead from the Mata Hari dress, the one that fell off that day in the Narragansett Hotel—remember?—when I was in the bathroom getting ready to leave and he was fussing around packing up the picnic. Yes, it fell—tiiiiiiing! tiiiiiiing!—onto the mosaic floor and rolled under the tub, but as you know, I retrieved it, and right now as I'm talking to you it's in my mouth, sliding over my tongue, smooth pearly ball that it is. There's something pleasurable—the gentle bite over the bead, before I roll it back under my tongue, pleasurable yes, not to mention the thrilling danger inherent in this activity—a few seconds ago I almost swallowed it and if I had would have choked—perhaps to death, and if so, wouldn't be here now telling you about it. But that's obvious, isn't it? Anyway, as I said, there I was abed rolling the pearl bead around in my mouth when what should save me but a tap tap on the door. Who could it be? Come in, come in, I took the bead out of my mouth and called Enter! Lo and behold, it was sweet Stanley with a puppy in his arms. Hope you like your new friend, Bambi, his name's Congo, but rename him anything you want. Congo—Congo—no, I like it! Congo! Why not! Not only like it, I love it. Love it. Why change something that's perfection? Congo's good enough for me. Oh he's adorable. Congo I mean, but Stanley too. What will Ma say? Oh she knows about it, he told me. We don't want you to feel lonely. While you're getting well again and until you meet new friends let Congo be your first in New York.

*M*a and Stanley are getting acquainted with the speakeasies around town. Not that she and Stanley have to go out, because nothing can top the stuff he makes in our bathtub, but they like to dress up, mingle, make new friends. Their speakie admission cards are stuck around the mirror over the mantel in our living room—any time we want we can get into the Mona Lisa at 36 West 56 St. or the New Ball and Chain at 56 East 52. But the one for me is the Son of the Sheik at 77 Washington Street. I've walked past it on my outings with Congo and have become obsessed with discovering what goes on there. I'm flirting with the idea of going one night. Dare me and I'll do it.

Went!!—Felt funny going unescorted but I was at my best I must say and the owner must have liked the looks of me because I had no trouble getting in. Of course it was the admission card I'd borrowed from the mirror over our mantel that probably did the trick so I'm not fooling myself thinking it was simply my fatal beauty. Inside it was so gay, people laughing and talking and in no time at all I was one of the party. Out of the blue this prune-faced woman started picking on a girl who was wearing silk stockings, lecturing her that a British medical journal has warned not to wear them in cold weather because they puff and chafe the skin, causing a dangerous illness never reported until they came into fashion and anyone wearing silk stockings with short dresses will be in trouble if she doesn't mend her ways. I got so mad. Listen, Prune Face, I said—we all know about Vanity Fair so if you don't like it here, why not leave, stop spoiling the fun—and anyway, it's none of your beeswax. Everybody applauded but that didn't stop her from pointing at the stockings—"Hus-seeeee—hus-seeee." Finally the girl told her to "stop kissing parrots." (Never heard that in Boston, eh, Mem?) Anyway, the poor old thing left. I had such a good time sitting there, talking and laughing—yes, like a normal person laughing and talking—as tho' nothing had happened—I mean Snodgrass and—well . . . The silk stocking girl and her friends walked me home, waving goodbye as they left me at my door—calling out "See you soon—see you soon." The girl's name is May Lark Loomis.

A couple of days had gone by and I'd lost hope of ever hearing from my new friends again, when who showed up at our door but May Lark herself. We spent the whole afternoon talking. She's

only been in New York a few months—came here from the
Ozarks against family wishes determined to be in the theatre—
but she sure knows this town inside out even tho' she hasn't got a
job yet. She supports herself with odd jobs here and there—ran
an elevator at Altman's, sold notions at the five and ten—doesn't
stay long in any one place—"I spent my childhood in the wildwood," she says. She has dozens of beaux from Princeton and
knows everyone around town and is going to teach me the Too-
dle and the Turkey Trot, new dances that are all the rage. Also
how to make the most of myself, what shade of powder to use
and how to shape my lips beestung—things that are most important, things I'd lost track of since the Snodgrass got hold of me.
Wear green, she advised, bring out your hazel eyes. Oh yes, May
Lark really knows how to make the best of herself and will help
me do the same. She showed me how to roll my stockings, and
rouge my knees in just the right spot. And get a Boyishform
bra—they're the best—the one you're wearing is too pointy,
much too pointy. Tell me more, I kept begging her. I never get
enough of these girly preoccupations, they sure do take my mind
off things. Oh yes, my mind is off things. I'm ready to go—no,
not bananas, but itching—itching to have F-U-N—that's what.
I've been too serious all along, that's always been my problem.
Oh, Mem, if only I could find words to describe May Lark, with
her blackberry hair and cream-colored face and eyes like blue
crystal marbles floating around in milky white. Sounds discon-
certing, but take it from me, it's most beguiling. She is my new
best friend.

*Mickey—pretty Mickey . . . With your hair of raven hue . . . With your
smiling so beguiling . . . There's a bit of the Blarney, bit of Killarney, too! . . .
Childhood in the wildwood . . . Like a mountain flower you grew! . . . Pretty
Mickey, pretty Mickey, can you blame anyone for falling in love with you . . .
Boom, boom!* Oh, stop it, Mickey May, stop it, I beg her—she's
restless as can be, singing that song every time I see her, and now I
can't get it out of my head either. She's taken me under her wing
in a big way and we've been jazzing around together all over town.
Not with each other, silly—there are more beaus around us than
there are stars in heaven. She told me she has dozens crazy about
her but she only likes to do it with Hughie and Rex. I couldn't
understand why because they aren't very good dancers. She

thought I was pulling her leg. Not dancing, she said—*you* know
... IT. What is IT? I asked her. IT, she told me, is having a man
put his ding-dong inside your biscuit box and having more fun
than a barrel of monkeys. Biscuit box? "Call it what you like,"
May Lark said, "but without it there'd be no making whoopee,
making love, or fooling around. Oh, Starr, what desert island have
you been on?" Well, I wasn't on a desert island that night at the
Plaza, but I didn't go into that. That wasn't making love, it was
Horror, Horror, Horror!!! May Lark gave me a hug and said, "I'm
older than you are, little lamb, and I know you already have a
good Mamacita but you need a real tough one for this city and I
volunteer. You're much too pretty to be floating around town
without knowing what's what. And while we're on the subject,
first rule is no M.M.'s—that's married men, if you haven't
guessed, and it's strictly hands off." Then she told me that the
M.M.'s will be after me anyway, along with all the other fellows,
not to mention certain girls. What do you mean? I asked her.
"Well, honey, be prepared because there'll be lots of girls after
you too." Girls after me? "Absolutely," she said, "because some
girls like to do IT with each other." How is that possible? I asked
her. "Well, first you have to want to do IT with a girl—have the
urge, so to speak, and then—well, you do whatever you feel like
doing. I only did it once," she said—"just for the hell of it.
Someone was crazy about me but then she went and spoiled it all
by pretending a cucumber was her ding-dong." What's a ding-
dong? I asked her. "Oh, that's my name for what a man does IT
with. Still," she laughed, "you never know—I might change my
mind, but I don't think I'm a lesbian by nature." A lesbian?
"That's what they're called—girls who like to do IT with each
other. Live and let live, I say, but you take it easy, Starr, because
the woods are full of mysteries." So you see, Mem, I've got a lot
to mull over. May Lark sure is full of fun and doesn't get serious
about things the way I do. I must try to be more like her, do the
things she does and learn how to have fun and laughs. "Yes, have
as much fun as a barrel of monkeys, but you've got to be careful,"
and she told me a surefire way to avoid getting preg. because
doing IT is how it can happen—having a baby I mean. Well—
listen to this. After you do IT you take a bottle of Coca-Cola and
shake it, get it fizzy-wizzy, then squat down over the bottle and
put it inside you, then the fizzy-wizzy shoots up into you. But you
have to do it right away, soon as poss. after you've done IT, other-

wise it won't work. May swears by it and so far it's never failed her, "so kiddo, better make sure there's a Coke nearby when Vesuvius erupts."

Oh, I do like May Lark, Mem, and admire her get-up-and-go. She likes me, too, only she can't fathom why I haven't done IT with anyone yet. Why not do it with Hughie Prentice? she says. She thinks he's cute and wouldn't mind as it's only whoopee between them, not love. I'm scared—but??? The way she talks makes IT sound like fun. What do you think?

Well, I did IT. I wore my soft dull-rose frock and the getting-dressed-up part before was fun, but then once out on the town we ended up at Maxie's Speakie with lots of bouillon. May Lark was with her new fella Sammy and when she saw how Hughie Prentice was going after me she leaned over and told me to have fun, but don't forget the Coke, and remember *everything* so I could tell her about it the next day. The trouble is I can't remember much because by the time Hughie got me to his place I was feeling no pain, as May Lark would say, and as far as I can remember we did IT on the sofa, or was it the floor? I do remember my frock was still on as he humped away on top of me, urging me to "let 'er rip," and after that he went into the kitchen and came back with a glass tube that had a rubber ball at one end. It looked like the thing Minna used to use to pull up the juices from the pan she roasted the turkey in. That tube was mean-looking in Hampton and it was mean-looking last night. It was filled with something (?) and he told me be quick, put it in and squirt. What do you think I am—a turkey? I screamed. "Hurry up, hurry up—you might be getting preg. right now," he said. I begged him for some Coca-Cola, but he said he didn't have any and hurry up, hurry up or it'd be too late. I got panicky and put it up in me fast and squeezed. Ugh! It stung. What is it? What is it? I kept asking him. Vinegar—only vinegar, but the white kind so I shouldn't worry. Why does the color make any difference? He told me to stop asking dumb questions and then suddenly he fell over and went to sleep. It happened so fast I thought he was dead. But he was breathing and I left him there and walked home with the vinegar stinging and dribbling down my legs. There was no one on the streets. Oh God, if only I had some creamy dreamy right now. And my new dull-rose frock—I'll never be able to wear it again. And Hughie—I can't get his smile out of my head—his lips are full and fleshy and when he smiles they have no place to go and they fold themselves up onto his face, leaving spaces above and below his gums, and as this happens, his teeth loom out, presenting a row of elfin tombstones.

I'm still burning inside from the vinegar. How was IT? May Lark was dying to know? Great! Simply Great! Yes, I know now what you're talking about—Hughie Prentice sure knows how to do IT. Why do I lie? Well, why not? How can I even begin to explain things that I don't understand myself. What does "let 'er rip" mean? I asked her. Oh, you know, she said, it's just a way of encouraging someone to let go. Let go of what? I asked. Oh Starr, she giggled—use your imagination.

*M*ay Lark's landed a part in *The Garrick Gaieties*—music by Richard Rodgers, lyrics by Lorenz Hart. The director's Philip Ives, and he says she has beautiful legs and she will be in the chorus at $35 a week. There's a song in the show, "Manhattan"— *We'll have Manhattan, the Bronx and Staten Island, too—it's lovely going through the Zoo*—yes, the zoo's lovely, but right now it's the movies I'm going to. Back later.

*O*h God, something quite wonderful has happened!!! I have the biggest crush on someone I haven't met but soon will, I know. I must calm myself, but this passionate intensity I feel cannot, simply cannot, go unrequited. And altho' he is not in New York, he will be drawn to me across oceans and clouds and whatever else separates us. His name, Sweet Mem, is Clive Brook, British naturally and oh so elegant. He's in the movie *When Love Grows Cold* and you, cautious friend, might call it only a crush, but it's far more than a crush, oh so *much* more. Yes, it is—love at first sight—he's in the fiber of my being, heart and soul constantly day and night, night and day. This is serious, so listen and heed. Rollo Fairbanks took me to *The Green Hat* last night and even the play, fascinating as it was, could not tear me away from Clive. I couldn't keep my mind on a thing happening on the stage, not even the divine Katharine Cornell in her green hat kept my attention for more than a second. Later we went on to a bottle club called—what? I don't remember—but it was fun, even though, caught up with dreams of Clive, I fell down the long flight of stairs going into the place, yes fell and almost broke a leg. What a disaster that would've been since I've become such a cutup on the dance floor. Heads turned when I entered in my emerald pleated chiffon—if only Clive could have seen me. Rollo had a bottle with him and they set us up with bouillon cups. It was difficult to keep up with the crowd we were with—in from Chicago and out for jolly-wollys with countless cups of bouillon. Oh and guess what? Legs Diamond was there with his moll of the moment but I missed seeing them because I was beside myself with ecstasy, having spotted Clive sitting a few tables away—but then he stood up and my heart fell into a pit because he didn't look anything like Clive. Quite the contrary—bald and pudgy. How could I have been so misled, even in the dim light? It was a heady coincidence, though, because I'd been seeing Clive all during the day, here and there, on the street—yes, there he'd be—getting in a taxi and so on, but on second look that too kept turning into a cruel joke, for it wasn't Clive or even anyone like him. (Sigh, sigh.) Who knows what hour it was when I got home and who cared? I knew I wouldn't be able to sleep. Anyway, what diff. does it make whether I'm home or anywhere else? I get no sleep, preoccupied as I am with Clive. At least I was left to toss alone on my bed, alone to go over my fevered plans concerning our future together. Rollo'd had so much bouillon he wasn't interested in me or anything else and the taxi driver had to carry him into the cab to get him home. What a break, none of the usual hustle-tussle.

Oh God, oh God—my feelings for Clive reach fever pitch. I become breathless, trembling, inarticulate, weak in the knees (fill in anything else you can think of along these lines), but even then you wouldn't come even close to my passionate longings. Oh, if only I could articulate them. Dare I try? Surely these feelings swirling around in my brain tell me something. Tell me I need, must find—must have the love of a man who is fine and true, and now that I've seen Clive Brook it becomes clear to me that HE is the one. Now a meeting between us must take place for he will

fall in love with me and when this happens I'll be cleansed, transformed, no longer sinful. But let's not delve too much into that.
It'll pour water on the flames of Hope and Happiness, for even
now Hope purifies me (a bit) so picture how it will be when he
loves me. I'll be reborn, yes, that day will be my true baptism—
not that flimflam I had to go through in Evanston with the river
swirling around and those fools on the shore not even having the
wit to sing "Amazing Grace" (my favorite hymn). And to think,
Mem, it was May Lark who had to *drag* me to the cinema to see
Him. To think I'd hardly listened to her ravings about the handsome, distinguished Clive Brook playing at the Roxy in *When Love
Grows Cold*—oh Mem, what a perfect gentlemen he is, what culture, what sex appeal. I could kick myself for days lost—life
lost—before I went with her to see the movie, which she'd been
to twice, and to think I only finally went to shut her up. Worse
still—I might never have gone and so missed the most important
event of my life. You always sensed, even though you never told
me, that if I followed my instincts they'd lead me to a man who
has the traits of character I most admire. And so they have, but
why did I have to find him in a stuffy old movie theatre, an image
on a screen, so near and yet so far. But patience, child, patience—
discipline and hard work will make you not only a person but *the*
person worthy of meeting him. And once you have, redemption
will come . . . *Patience* is to be the watchword henceforth.

*I*f I think about him day and night, and I do, I do—it will draw
him closer to me. I must dwell on nothing else. Last night—
rough—constant dreaming—on a cruel sea—yes, Mem, tossed
about like a salad, well at least it was salty enough ha ha so I
didn't have to add that to the dressing as up and down I went
with that damn Hughie and his leering "let 'er rip."

*M*en find me pretty, yes definitely a beauty—so why shouldn't
Clive? I'm certainly well-read, more so I bet than those flibber-
tigibbet actresses he has to associate with most of the time, even if
they happen to be beauties too. He's highly evolved and intelligent I can tell, strong and stalwart, a man who will take care of
me, a man I will be able to depend on. Oh, give me courage, God,
and the stamina of my watchword, my motto PATIENCE—the

patience to wait until I am worthy to meet him, but once I have—*cleverness* is what I'll need then, yes, I must be clever to not mess it up as I have everything else.

I've booked passage for England. Not another moment is to be wasted. I found out that his real name is Clifford Brook. Well, that's not bad either. Still, Clive suits him better, don't you think? I can't wait to find out if he has sandy hair. It must be, I'm sure. But it's hard to tell just from seeing him on the movie screen. Soon—soon, Mem, I'll know for certain, for I'll be oh so close to him and—oh darling Mem, I faint and cannot go on.

*B*etter dreams the last few nights. Clive and I in various settings. No intrusion of others (you know who I mean).

*H*ad to cancel my passage—his new movie, *Enticement*, is opening the day I was to sail. I'll be first in line when it opens and go again the next day, ditto the following one and so on unless I change my mind and am on my way to England. The *Franconia*'s sailing in a couple of weeks—I could be on that.

I sat in the first row, but had to move back to the fourth as sitting so close to the screen gave me a headache not to mention a dreadful stiff neck. Oh, He was . . . he was . . . no words can convey how . . . he was . . . how he is. I am more in love than ever. We shall meet soon or I shall die.

*D*espite this raging impatience, I've decided the wisest plan is to wait here in New York. The reasoning behind this is twofold: (1) I need to work on self-improvement and (2) Picture me arriving in London not knowing where he was or where to find him— calling film studios and being treated like any other smitten fan. Or worse still, wandering the streets knocking on the doors of strangers in Chester Square and other likely squares where he might live. The upsetting part of this decision, however, is my inability to control the restless fever that possesses me. Nothing distracts me. What am I doing here in New York? Only marking time—nothing's moving—only my boiling brain, making one plan and replacing it with another. If you think of something every single waking and sleeping moment, you can make it happen. I can't tell you how I know this, but I do.

I'm solitary by nature, so what pushes me to do things I don't really want to do? Every time I go against my nature it leads to gossip, yes, there's awful gossip circulating about me right this minute, which I keep putting off telling you because I'm so upset, Mem. Well, here goes—my so-called intimates (except for May Lark) have nicknamed me the Flame Girl. Can you believe it!! Apparently to them I'm just a jazz-baby firecracker like the rest of them, frolicking around drawing attention to myself to amuse all and sundry. Little are they aware that I *am* a Flame Girl but not in the way they mean. I am a Flame Girl because a flame burns— yes, a flame burns inside me, a purifying flame purifying me so that I will be worthy to be loved, to be loved by Clive, for if he loves me I will be *somebody*—my real self will emerge. I never want to see any of them again.

*G*uess what! May Lark has a new boyfriend—Arnie Rothstein. Yes—even though he's a gangster and one of the M.M.'s we vowed to stay away from—May's nuts about him.

*J*ust read *The Great Gatsby* and it's not that I'm untrue to Clive, but oh I must confess I'm wrapped in a web of longing. If only it wasn't too late—if only I could meet him. Scott, I mean. But— oh God, it's always the *buts* that tell the truth of the matter. He's married. The *Gatsby* dedication says

Once again
to
Zelda

I sigh at the words, for had he met me first—if it weren't too late—'twould be my name upon that page . . .

.   .   .

I'll never stop praying that I'll meet someone fine and true. I'll never give up. I'll go on hoping forever even though I'm reeling as a result of recent developments. Yes, you might as well know now—there's no point in putting off the horrendous moment. Clive Brook too is one of the M.M.'s—a fact I discovered in the cruelest way when I picked up an old magazine in the beauty parlor. They have stacks of *Tatlers* lying around mixed up among our American magazines and oh Mem, it was more than a shock—it was a blow—and he's not only an M.M., there's a daughter, Faith (very forward in the background, ha ha). At least with May Lark's Arnie the wife is pretty much out of the picture. Not so in Clive's case. Well, I'm no home wrecker, as you well know. It's been a battle, taking all my strength of character to relinquish my claims, but I know now—to think I would ever have to write these fatal words!—the union of Clive and Starr is not to be.

*O*h—the tempestuous mood I am in . . . pressing on despite sleepless nights and restless days, with Clive still invading my dreams. There is no surcease. If only I were stronger of character and had more control over my feelings, but they overwhelm me and I can't help but think there's something terribly wrong with me, something even more terrible than the hole that won't fill up. It must be true because whenever my tempestuous mood swings away it is replaced by a dark cloud which hangs over me, if you'll forgive the use of such a cliché. But there's no other way to describe it—and I know if I wait longer to express how I feel, I'll get so scared I'll end by telling you about some silliness that has nothing to do with my true self. Even now I feel myself sidetracking as my mind starts to wander to what happened yesterday when May Lark and I went to a party on a battleship moored off Pier 16—we took bathing suits and there was oodles of champagne and oodles of giggles and oodles of diving off into the water. My bathing suit nearly came off and Boo Pickins (I think that was his name), this amusing officer, handed me a safety pin to keep it up. There were lots of laughs and the two of us—Boo and I—ended up in someone's cabin. He locked the door and tried to push me against the wall. Take it easy—slow, I kept telling him—slow, but he wanted no part of slow—so what the hell, I let him do it fast—not that I had much say in the matter. People kept trying to get into the cabin while it was going on, making a big racket outside. It distracted me somewhat from the fatness of him lunging at me, making me ugly, ramming me against the wall until my bones cracked. Yes, they did. Even though I hate him and hope I never see him again, I'm going to keep the safety pin he gave me when my bathing suit almost fell apart. Maybe I'll figure out a way to pin it to my skin so my body won't fall apart (ha ha). No matter. It'll be another souvenir of sorts to keep company with the pearl bead from the Mata Hari dress. Besides, it might come in handy again some day. Well, it was fun until he got me to go down to the cabin with him. Yes, up until then it had been fun, but he went and spoiled it all. Oh what the hell— at least he had sandy hair.

*I*t's back again—the seaweed—even on my face when I look into the mirror—not only my mirror here at home, but any mirror—including the cracked one I carry with me in my purse at all times. I can't remember how the crack got there, but it *is there* and I mustn't put off getting it fixed one second more. It's supposed to mean seven years of bad luck.

*W*hen I saw Rollo last night he said I'd better rest up a bit—get rid of those circles under my eyes and what's got into me—why aren't I so peppy lately? Well, of course it's the blow of finding out that C.B. is an M.M. It'll take me time to recover, that is if I ever do. And then there are those other things I'm trying to tell you about. There are men, Mem, not only the ones you know about, but others whose names I can't recall at the moment, but definitely in the picture at one time or another. Please don't think I've been deceitful or kept them from you on purpose—they blurred one into another the way the days and nights sometimes do and none of it seemed important enough to mention at the time and even if I had there were no details to speak of that I could remember—so what was there to say about any of it? Of course now that the seaweed's back they float up out of it—some face up, others face down—and when not doing that, they are bobbing around—here and there I catch an eye or a bit of a nose.

· · ·

*I*t's gotten into my nose and mouth, the seaweed's choking me so I can't breathe. It started exactly three days ago when I first looked out and saw AJP standing across the street looking up at my window. There is a girl with him. He stands there hour after hour in an unfamiliar coat (where's the black vicuna he was so partial to?) waiting for me to make a move. But what's the girl wearing? I can't make it out. Sometimes he has his arm around her and her head is resting on his shoulder—other times he's just standing there with her standing beside him.

I've stopped going to the window for fear he'll catch my eye— instead I've devised an important system which I must patent before it's stolen by some outlaw like Boo Pickins (he's the type to do this). I creep on the floor up to the sill and peek out. This way he can't see me, no not possibly, but it helps to know he hasn't gone away even when I'm not looking at him. Does that make sense? What I mean is—remember those debates we got so heated up about at Miss Sheraton's—if a tree falls in the forest and no one hears it fall, has it really happened? (that kind of thing)—anyway, he's still there—I'm not imagining it. Yes, he's still there. The girl too. I'll never set foot out of this house again, even my room. I mean it.

*T*his morning he was gone. Ma and Stanley thought I was stay- ing in my room because Aunt Margaret was in here with me. I let them think that. Anyway, he's gone. The girl too. I'd like to get on a bus—any old bus that's leaving for who knows where—get on and close my eyes—end up somewhere—somewhere peace- ful where no one knows me, or my name, or anything about me—then I'd be free.

*M*y mother and Stanley are up to something. They whisper and stop talking when I come into the room. Does it have any- thing to do with AJP? She's been to Boston twice this week.

*M*y head hurts and also my shoulder. I've been struggling to pin my Ma down to tell her about a preserved fragment of Damascius I read about which may have bearing on my predicament. Damascius believed the soul possesses a certain shining (*augoeides*—I copied it down from the book in the library) vehicle (*ochema*) which is also called Star-like (*asteroides*). Significant, eh Mem? It is eternal, and it's situated in the body, either in the head or in the right shoulder. I'm going into all this now because of my hurting head and the pain *is* in my right shoulder. And of course "star-like" has a direct meaning for me, doesn't it? A message, definitely. That's what I want to ask Ma about, but when I try to talk to her I can't get much out of her. Nothing, in fact. How could I when she hardly listens except to say sure, honey, sure, that must be why I call you my star-baby.

*T*he choking got worse and I couldn't breathe, otherwise I wouldn't have let them hustle me up there. It was hustle rustle hustle to get to the Snodgrass in Boston. If only I could get him out of my hair everything would be o.k. When we did get there he kept us waiting due to a commotion going on in his private office. Strange sounds and God knows what else emanating from there. Nobody in the waiting room dared look at each other. They kept on sitting, looking down into their magazines. Finally, the moaning stopped and our turn came up to go in. At first I thought he didn't remember me but then he got down to brass tacks about a place called Channing in nearby Wellesley where I can go to rest a bit if I want to. Everyone's friendly there, Snodgrass said, and it's clean. That means they won't let AJP in, doesn't it, Mem? Then I heard a loud, uncouth voice, someone begging to get sent there as soon as possible before the seaweed pulls her into the sand and she disappears as if she never existed. On the train on the way up to Boston I looked in the mirror and there was no one there—no reflection—nothing. Yes—nothing but the in and out of shallow breaths coming from somewhere. That's what makes me suspect the disappearing's already happened, but nobody's discovered it yet. Or they have and aren't telling me. But if I'm absent from myself, who's that begging in the loud uncouth voice to go back to New York and why do they keep on talking to me as if I'm still here? Then Ma and Stanley took Snodgrass aside and they told evil secrets to each other about me. They thought I couldn't hear what they said, but I did, every word, which I'll tell you about later. Then I was told Doc. says it's back to New York—I could calm down, rest there, maybe if I was a good girl I wouldn't have to go to Channing.

I'm supposed to rest but how can I when my heart swoops around like a roller coaster until the switch goes off and I start choking—can't get enough air—can't breathe.

*C*an't put off telling you any longer. I still can't find my face in the mirror—no reflection of my face, no nothing, whatever time of day I test it. How can I rest with that going on? It's up and down day and night looking in all the mirrors we have around the house—even in the kitchen I looked in the bottom of Ma's best frying pan, the one she keeps so shiny. I keep praying one of them might work but there's nothing wrong with the mirrors—all the rest of me reflects in a recognizable way. It's *me* that there's something wrong with, and I'm telling you this quickly before they take me away to the Sanitarium. It's finally come to that, and they won't let me take Congo with me. I'll have to leave you, too, Mem, for a while, have to hide you in our other secret place behind my volumes of Tennyson in the bookcase. Even though I can lock Daddy's chest, Tooka, who's back for Xmas vacation, has her little ways and I'm afraid she might pick the lock, yes pick the lock—her fingers are nimble enough to do it. No, Mem, I don't trust anyone but you. I'm putting you in the chest now and then the chain with your key—taking it off from around my neck and putting it between the pages of *The Secret Garden* Daddy Lincoln gave me. It's the only place I can think of—I'll have to keep trust no one will find it—they'll take it away from me at Channing—there's no alternative—they're coming—keep breathing in and out even tho' it's dark in there and no air gets in. In and out, keep breathing, and you'll be all right. I promise.

1926

Dear Mem—It's such a relief to be back holding you close. I was in a sweat every moment I was at Channing afraid that some-one would get hold of the key to Daddy Lincoln's chest, the key I hid in *The Secret Garden* seconds before they came to take me away. But no one did and I did remember where I'd hidden it even if there were times when I got crazed trying to recall where. Where? Where had I hidden the key? I kept imagining Mrs. Burnett sit-ting there in her garden (the secret one) and that if she knew where I was she'd come for me and be my real mother and we would enter the garden together. Oh Mem, it was bitter not knowing where to find Mrs. Burnett, bitter to have the key hidden between the pages of her book but not know where to find her— but then, the minute I walked in the door of my bedroom at Grove St. I *knew*, I remembered, knew I'd soon be opening Daddy Lincoln's chest and that you and I would be reunited and to hell with Mrs. Burnett. I knew too that Congo wouldn't go away. He wouldn't fail me. I knew that you and he would never lose hope that I would return no matter how long it took. I knew I could count on you no matter what—and the what that I had to con-tend with at Channing was fierce. Everyone there really was crazy and I knew the minute I was carried in that I didn't belong there. I belonged with you—but no one listened. No one let me alone for a minute, and now that I'm back with you—the *theys* here don't let me alone for a minute either except when I'm asleep which isn't often. There's so much to tell you that the thought of it exhausts me and I'd better take a rest now. Let's get together later—for tea maybe?

. . .

You'll be glad to know that Channing discharged me as a "non-mental" case, listing me instead as a simple case of "extreme nervousness." I still feel pretty "nervous" but thank God I'm out of there even tho being back isn't like being home (except for you) but I'll have to explain about that later. I'll be able to do that when they stop walking around pretending to be normal. They don't know that I'm on to them. I know they're really turkeys tippy-toeing, bobbing around in a decorated room that is really a backyard. Too bad they have names—Ma Turkey, Tooka Turkey, and Stanley Turkey—otherwise I'd eat them right away without waiting for Thanksgiving—yes, gobble them up with or without the cranberry. But I can't do this because you can't eat something once you've looked it in the eye—no, once you've done that you're connected and you can't kill what you're connected to. At least I can't. The only one around here who treats me like a human person is Congo, but that's because he's really a person and not a dog. No one knows about this except him, me and you. I knew it the minute Stanley brought him in that day and his eyes met mine. Did I tell you he has turquoise eyes? Exceptional. I mean Congo, not Stanley. Stanley's exceptional too in his way, but his eyes aren't turquoise—makes all the difference, believe me.

Angel—I mean Nurse Fisher—brought me back to New York on the train. She was the best of the bunch at Channing, not like the other apes parading around in their white. When we got to Grove Street Stanley opened the front door—Welcome home, Bambi—right on time for Tucker's birthday. I could have hit him, but now I hate myself because he was just trying to make everything sound normal and that made him nervous, so he left me out when I should have been included, because Tooka and I have birthdays so near each other. Anyway, what diff. did it make as it was already past both our birthdays, but Ma and Stanley were celebrating anyway and welcoming me home with presents—an old-fashioned nosegay of white tea roses with a lace paper hankie around it and starting in April a membership in this new Book-of-the-Month Club. Every month I'll be receiving a new book beginning with *Lolly Willows* by Sylvia Townsend. Stanley had put my membership certificate in a box with a lavender ribbon around it and in the bow was a gold mesh bag of Louis Sherry licorice cats (for old times' sake). Sweet of him. There was a yellow cake and champagne. Nurse Fisher had a glass too, saying she was "off duty" now that I was safely home, and Congo had two pieces of the cake. So Happy Birthday, Mem, better late than never, eh? Nurse Fisher slipped me a "goodbye present, honey, for being such a goody girl," a wee stash of Allonal.

*A*ll my books were waiting for me with not a one out of place. No strange hands have prodded the pages while I was away. I can tell. How? you may ask. Well, don't. If you don't understand I'll never be able to explain it to you because I don't understand myself, but I know as I take one down from the shelf—it's still mine. How reassuring to read over again pages of *Pilgrim's Progress,* especially the part when Christian gets to the City of Destruction and falls into the putrid bog filled with scum and human sinfulness. This bog is called the Slough of Despond. Hits the nail on the head, doesn't it. I love when I get to the part where Christian meets up with a person called Help—Help pulls him out and explains to Christian how men fall into the Slough of Despond when they accept how sinful they are. Oh yes . . . how well we understand about that. I read this part over and over again and each time I am stronger and more certain that Help will show up soon. Help is on his way hurrying towards us right this minute —yes, we're going to be rescued soon so hold on, hold on— Coraggio.

I've got to get Ma sitting still for a minute so I can tell her what I've got to tell her. Mainly that even though I did beg to go to Channing it was a mistake—I knew that once I was there—I knew that even though I'm different I wasn't different in the way that the others were. I knew I didn't belong with that crowd, no not at all, because all I really needed was rest, the kind of rest you get in a hotel with the Do Not Disturb sign on the door so you can sleep—sleep sleep—sleep, that's all I wanted—to sleep and never wake up, or if I did—wake up as someone else who'd never met AJP, someone who didn't have this hole inside, so deep it can't be filled. No matter how much breath is drawn in, it has to go out, and when it's drawn back in again, there's never enough to fill the hole and so I'm left gasping for more, which explains why I can't breathe right, and maybe never will until I die, and even then who knows? And even if they did know, no one will ever understand how large this hole is or how empty, except sometimes it fills up a little, but only for a moment and never ever enough, no never ever never enough. Do you grasp the significance of what I'm saying? Even if my mother did listen I probably shouldn't tell her—it might make her love me even more than she does now. Yes, definitely do not tell her.

I did tell her—couldn't help myself. This happened yesterday. I screamed—Listen, Ma—and kept on at her—Listen—and finally she did—that is if listening is shaking me and shouting back—Turn the page, honey, turn the page—that's what we have to do in this life—turn the page. Stanley couldn't take it and scooted into the bathroom. He means well, but he always has things on his mind, something about a rumpus that happened way back before he met my mother. He was president of Lactics then, and everything was going fine until he got indicted for using the mails to defraud (I think), and even though the jury acquitted him and it's way in the past, he broods over it, I can tell. I know, because I feel close to him though he doesn't know it. I tried to make those crazies at Channing understand but how could they, they had their own fish to fry. I kept dreaming about Daddy Lincoln all the time, wondering what he was doing right that minute and where he was. Have you heard anything about him or where he might be? I'd like to write him another letter. If he'd known about Channing he'd have come and taken me out even if they'd told him what I'd done. What have I done, Mem? I can't seem to remember. But how was Daddy to know where I was or what was going on? Maybe he's dead and I'm not being told. Once on the stairs at Fenway Court I ran after him—I'm sure it was him—the way he hunches over when he's in a rush going somewhere. Of course he could have spotted me and that's why he was hurrying. Anyway, who cares? It was long ago.

*M*a's still after me to call Stanley "Dad"—how can you not when he's so good to us and so loving to my little girl, my perfect Starr-baby? If not "Dad" how about "Pops"—"Pops" would be perfect. Well, not perfect enough for me even tho' I do love him and it's true he's kind and good to us. Yes—we're all back together again in New York City, aren't we? We live on Grove Street in Greenwich Village. It's spacious and Tooka has a room of her own when she's not at Seaton's and I have my own room, it's painted white, the color of my choice, but I went into that before. Didn't I?

I got in touch with May Lark to tell her I was back. I made her promise not to tell anyone else as I need more time to breathe in and out, but she keeps after me, says all the fellows drive her bananas asking after me—Rollo Fairbanks and Jay Sparks, Hughie Prentice, and Rex Toler, and the others—"Where's Twinkle Starr and when'll we see her?" Lots of new fellows in town too, panting to meet me. Well, they'll just have to wait till I'm good and ready. I'm not setting foot out my door until I can look myself in the eye and know who I'm talking to. I'm jittery, but I can't tell even you how scared I am—

*F*or two days now when I look in the mirror there's been no one there, so how can I put my lipstick on or anything else for that matter? The only time I'm at peace is when I lie down and put Congo on my chest and whisper secrets to him. Together we breathe in and out—it puts him to sleep, and soon I'm asleep too, up and down, in and out. Easy does it—not scared then—happy—I forget, but then remember—jump up—go to the mirror—there it is—same as before, only it's not there because nothing's there. If only I could sleep—wake up in a place where there are no mirrors. I dare tell no one of this, for they will send me back to Channing.

*I*t's all right. I slept for 12 hours—woke up—ran to the mirror—I was there. That means you're here, too, Mem.

*S*omething fishy's been going on for days. Yes, something fishy's going on and whatever it is *smells* fishy too not only in the rooms of this house, but in the walls. Perch? Sardines? No—

like—oh don't pin me down, I don't know, but fish—definitely some kind of fish. No matter where I go the smell follows, down the stairs, and even out into the street—that's the lengths it goes to. (Went out today for the first time since I got back.) Yes, it's in the walls and under carpets—even between the pages of you, Mem, it's seeping in here too and trying to come between us (at least the garlic never went *that* far). Congo knows about this better than anyone, but he can't speak up or tell me what it is or do anything about it any more than I can. Ma's got a lot on her mind and is going to Boston tomorrow to "attend to things." Stanley insists on going with her but she tells him to shut up—he'll only "cloud the issue." What is this issue? To hell with clouds. Fishy issue is what it is.

*M*a got back from Boston flip-flapping around like a fish in a hot skillet—so excited and talking so fast we couldn't make head or tail of the fishies babbling out of her mouth. Calm yourself, Helen, calm yourself, Stanley kept saying. She flung herself down on the sofa and took a big swallow of the drink he handed her. Then she took another and said—gather round, gather round—*you*—she pointed to Stanley, *you* sit here beside me, and Starr and Tooka—sit down—doesn't matter where, just sit down and listen to what I have to tell you. Stanley poured her more drink and she sipped that one slowly, looking at each of us in turn (Tooka and me, not Stanley, who was staring at his feet). Well—she said, I have news, great and wonderful news—news that must never leave this room or be heard by ears other than ours. Do you hear me? She took another gulp from her drink and looked at Tooka and me. My trip to Boston has been fruitful beyond my wildest hopes—not that I ever doubted our Cousin Andrew's continued generosity or that he'd do more than the right thing, fine man that he is—but still one never knows until the i's are dotted, the t's crossed and the bottom line bottomed—what with Cousin Martha and so on—well, she's never been a bother so no need to go into any of that—yes, our cousin, out of the kindness of his heart, our dear Andrew who as we know was more than eager to pay for Starr's rest cure and make up to our family for that which destiny has put us through—yes, la forza del destino—or the hand you are dealt—call it what you will—I always say, it's how you react to the hand that is dealt that determines character, and in this case everyone has behaved nobly—more than nobly. She looked up in the air for another word—Superbly! Yes, that's it exactly—behaved superbly, for the right thing has been done to one and all *by* one and all—especially Mr. Rowley, that nice lawyer of Cousin Andrew's, who made the meeting in his office so pleasant. So pleasant, Mem, that not only have my doctors' bills and rest cures been taken care of, but there is to be something else—a present, a lovely present to make up for any and all little misunderstandings of the past. Horror, Horror, Horror!!! Is that what it was—a little misunderstanding? Now it all fits into place—the move from Boston to New York—this house on Grove Street, the new clothes and money to burn, more than enough. More than we'd ever had before and now there is to be more more more. I've been a *fool* not to have understood—Now, now, baby, she said, don't try to reach Andrew to thank him— you never have to think of doing that—he's not here anyway and he wasn't in the office when I went to Peabody, Brown, Rowley & Story—those nice lawyers who have taken care of family matters before even dear Andrew was born—most trustworthy, I assure you—No, it was only that nice Mr. Rowley I saw, Andrew had sailed for Europe—aboard the *Leviathan*—only the day before. It's money, Ma, isn't it, Ma? Isn't it—say it—it's money money MONEY. Starr, don't be crass, she said as Tooka clapped her hands and crowed "Oh goody—is it a lot?" Yes, Ma said—a lot, and she stood up from the sofa proudly. A very great deal of money—we'll never have to worry about money or anything else ever again, and she smiled at me—you're an heiress now, so why the long face?—cheer up, my little goose who laid the golden egg—yes, cheer up—it's time to celebrate. I wish I were dead.

I'm sinking, choking, not enough air—oh God, if I can get Congo, hold on to him, breathe in and out, slowly in and out, I'll be all right, but Stanley's taken him out for a walk and God knows when they'll be back. I feel so strange . . . feeling as tho' I've committed a murder while asleep, but no one could understand that, could they? Not even you. Even if you did, how would I know? You can't tell me. I keep trying to remember the details of this murder. Not only why I committed it, but who exactly it was (that I murdered, I mean). Not only that—how and where this murder took place. If you know please tell me, and quickly, I beg of you. Maybe I'll have a drink. Often, when I do, a door opens and what it was clicks into place (the murder, I mean) and then the flat grey stone lifts off my head, but just as it does, the door closes again before I can remember, and it's back again, the stone crushing me.

Stanley knocked on my door a minute ago and trotted in with one of his silver cocktail shakers of martinis. Specialité de la maison, he said, trying to be gay. I'd already taken an Allonal but I took the glass he handed me and drank it down. He'd had some of it too, because he'd come out of the torpor he'd descended into when Ma first told us the news. Come on, join the party, Bambi, he said, your Ma's invited some friends over to celebrate. No thanks—send my regrets. Ah, come on, Beauty Bambi, he coaxed—won't be a party without you. Tooka stuck her head in the door and called out—Stanley's rightee-oh, Starr—what will the party be without the goose that laid the golden egg? I'll leave the shaker here by your bed, honey lamb, Stanley said. Hope you change your mind—don't forget we love you. He shut the door and now I'm pouring myself another drink. I can hear people arriving. Soon I'll be asleep.

Winds are sweeping mountains of snow against the window and we can hardly see out into the street. It's the worst snowstorm New York City's had in years—12 dead already. As the hours pass and the snow descends, I tempt myself to go out and pit my strength against the elements. I would feel strong, unbowed by nature and therefore able to contend with man—contend with little Mamacita. I can't stand being around her and here we are, Mem, snowbound—cooped up together—thank God you and I have each other.

Couldn't stand it another minute and went out. The street was empty—snow piled up over abandoned cars. Sun, but the wind piercing and my face froze, my lips couldn't move. The snow beaded my eyelashes—I could barely see and I lay down, sinking into a drift, far down out of sight into a white grave. I wanted to stay there—quiet, white, still—in that strange world. Maybe that's what it will be like to die. White all around with crystals and the sun dazzling the prisms with light, making me warm with happiness. But instead it got colder, oh so cold, and I finally made myself get up as otherwise I would have frozen where I lay, frozen there, unable to move. When I got back Ma said I was crazy to have gone out like that. She helped me take my frozen clothes off and made me sit by the fire in her Jaeger robe drinking hot milk with the gin that Stanley brought me. My skin was stinging from the cold and Stanley had to hold the glass so I could sip from it as my hands had curled up into little balls and it was ages before I could move my fingers or uncurl them and get them moving again. Ma kept rubbing my feet—What made you do a stupid thing like that, Starr? they kept saying—you might have caught your death! Tooka sulked in a corner and didn't say anything until suddenly she spoke up—I want to go out too, *right now*, and no one can stop me. Of course, Ma was having none of her guff and locked her in the bathroom until she came to her senses. The hot milk made me sleepy. Oh, it was nice, Mem.

The weather changed and so have I—my spirits aloft as I go every chance I get to Whoopee Cruise Bon Voyage parties. Not that I'm sailing (alas) or even know friends who are, but it's easy to pretend once I dress up and sally down to the pier, easy to invite myself on board, mingle with the merrymakers—oh yes my tiny heart does thrill to the brass band, the bustle of porters bearing baskets of fruit and flowers, the balloons and gay streamers. I wander from one cabin to another through confetti showering around me, the colors of happiness. What matter that I'm an imposter? No one suspects, for one or another is drawn to me as I join the party and altho' I bring my own flask there's always champagne and I'm more than welcome. I'm so happy to be there that it's even worth the sinking feeling when I hear the "All Ashore Who's Going Ashore"—and I know the moment's come when I have to say goodbye—altho' I don't say it of course, just slip away. Do they miss me after the ship's at sea? Does some fellow ask later, "What happened to that girl?" and realize she's not on board? Was it the brass band and merriment of Bon Voyage playing tricks, and the girl he thought he'd seen really some unknown girl he'd passed on a street long ago, one who'd caught his eye (the way it happens sometimes) and had come back into his mind much later for no reason and not someone real who'd been on the ship at all?

*M*et a most—oh so tall, dark and handsome perfect person— a person I could easily have a pash for. His name is Francis Peabody Hamlin and he's Cruise Director of the Cunard Line and when I told my little Mamacita about him she oohed and aahed because he's the grandson of Francis Peabody, a Mass. millionaire lawyer. I knew she and Stanley would be impressed—Stanley especially worries about some of the people I keep company with. I suspect he thinks I like to cat around even tho' he'd never put it that way. It's not true, is it? It's that I sometimes find myself in— oh well, let's not go into that now. Let's go into my telling you more about Francis. May Lark says it's better to keep "friends" separate from "lovers"—makes everything less "complicated." So—is he to be one of my pashes or simply friend? Only time will tell.

*S*obbing dream again. Again I can't remember—a blood blister on my lip (upper) when I looked in the mirror this morning. No, Mem, it's not a love bite. Must have bitten my lip while asleep.

I've come to a decision. The right one, I'm sure you will agree. Francis Peabody Hamlin is to be not pash, but friend. And a good one. There are times when I'm going out—who knows where—that I tell Ma and Stanley I've a date with him. They don't worry about me then—know I won't get into trouble.

*I*nvitations, I have more invitations and more and more—than I can say yes to—weekend invitations to go to the beach, to the green of Woodstock or Connecticut. But more often than not I say no thank you, I'm busy. Yes, busy, busy with guess who? Myself. For on hot weekends, when the fools leave the city, I make a date with myself to do as I please. I take my books and a sandwich to the park, to hidden places where no one can find me. No one.

Except Congo's with me of course. He nestles down beside me and oh what bliss.

*M*et a painter in Woodstock named Rufus Steinberg and he couldn't stop staring at me—says I have the face of the Botticelli Venus and that I could easily have a career as a model. It's not the first time I've been told this—illustrators and photographers I've met at parties often mention it and the more I hear it the more it appeals to me. Yes, enormously. How could I cease to exist with my image in magazines framed and hung on walls in rooms of strange houses I myself need never enter? *I* would exist. *I* would be there. I wouldn't have to do a thing.

*T*hink about it constantly—to be a model inspiring artists to do their best work—masterpieces. Yes, only masterpieces. I shall settle for nothing less.

*M*a won a ton of money at the races and came home chirping so I took the opportunity to tell her about my plan, but it plunged her into a fury. "Model," she shrieked—*"prostitute* is more like it—no daughter of mine is going to be paid to display her body for strangers to ogle. Think of your heritage, Starr—we are Daughters of the American Revolution—let *that* sink in before you permit yourself to sink down into the mire." There was no stopping her, no way to explain it wasn't like that. Now we'll have to think of another way of getting around this, for I am determined to be a model and the sooner the better. People will look up to me, want to emulate me. I am pretty, aren't I? Ma herself has said, "Your face is your future."

*C*onfided in May Lark and she told me about the Art Workers Club for Women. If I join I can become a professional model and my, that would certainly be no problem, as I am a beauty and what's more, May Lark knows Mrs. Janine, the woman who runs it, and will put in a word for me.

· · ·

*M*et Mrs. Janine and as of today I am a member of the Art Workers Club for Women and a professional model. Actually, Luna Moon is a member. Theatrical name, isn't it? But why not. Have to camouflage so Ma won't get wind of my capers, for if she did she'd surely put a stop to my career. Mrs. Janine is a cutie pie, with hair piled up on top of her head like a nest of spun sugar. She keeps her pencil stuck there like a hat pin, taking it out to scribble bookings on the chart in front of her on the desk and smiles and smiles. My first one is tomorrow. Luna Moon is to model a Madame Recamier costume at Lincoln Arcade near Columbus Circle. Yes—we're on our way.

*C*hanged my mind about Luna Moon—settled on Mary Browne. Wisely, don't you think? Less theatrical. Less chance of drawing attention to myself and having Ma ferret me out. I put the e at the end of Browne—oh, I don't know why—just did.

*M*ary Browne stood around in various poses pretending to be Madame Recamier and dreaming about—oh, something or other—forget exactly what. The only blight was worry that some friend of Ma's or Stanley's might be spooking around and recognize me—report me to Ma. Mary Browne must get over such thoughts if she is to pursue her career with confidence. No one knows who Mary Browne really is except May Lark of course and Rufus Steinberg—had to tell him as it was his idea—can trust him (I think).

*M*rs. Janine smiles and smiles—would I be interested in posing for the Review of Models? What's that? It's a meeting held once a week for aspiring professional illustrators—like a life class in art school—a different model poses each time—nude—would I? Of course. I am now a professional person and must take what comes accordingly. Still—?

*I*t was today, and once disrobed and standing on the platform in front of the twelve aspiring professionals I realized how foolish my maiden fears had been. To them I am just an anatomy and even had I attempted to be provocative nothing could have dissuaded them from their task (I admit I did try just for fun to take their concentration away from charcoal and paper). They let me look at the results after class was over. Scratchy versions scratched in charcoal on paper, supposedly of me, but not one of these likenesses pleased me. These drawings have no resemblance to me, do they, Mem? Henceforth I shall pose only for acclaimed professionals. Neysa McMein's after me for one of her *Saturday Evening Post* covers, not to mention James Montgomery Flagg.

*T*oday it was for dear Rufus. He's doing the illustrations for a Sears Roebuck catalog and the dress I wore cost $5.50. He went on and on about me—"sweet as a cupcake" and so on—and when it was over he said he'd call me soon to set up another appointment for me to pose in nightgowns which haven't arrived yet. "Best model I've ever worked with." That's what he said. Wish I could tell Ma and Stanley *and* about the money I'm earning. Rufus tells me my body's as impressive as my face. My feet also much admired. My second toe is slightly longer than the others, which denotes sensitivity—so willy-nilly now we know why I'm the way I am. I guess I do have pretty feet, but looking at my toes, having been told this, I see them from a new point of view, especially that one next to the big one. My hands aren't bad either, much larger than you'd expect—after all, my other features are delicate, fragile, but my hands have an unexpected strength. The right hand slightly larger than the left as I put my palms together (which I did a minute ago), but I'd better stop before my head's turned.

*H*e was in the street today—yes, I'm certain of it—following me—I was on my way home from Rufus's studio when I saw him—started running and soon as I got home I told Ma and Stanley—they said it was impossible and to stop imagining things. *Why* is it imposs.? Because, Ma said, it just is.

*O*h God, I thought she was going to kill me. She found out about Mary Browne. I thought she was going to kill me. I ran out of the house but she came after me—her words following me as I spun around the corner. I put my hands over my ears but I could still hear her. I was crying as I ran away but then I turned back and ran towards her instead, ran past her, back into the house, up the stairs to my room. Soon I could hear her through the locked door, no—she wouldn't stop so I opened it. Ma—*stop*, I told her. Told her I'd done nothing wrong. Told her I'd never go back to Mrs. Janine's. Told her all I wanted was for her to stop. Told her all I wanted was to be quiet. Told her to stop about Boston and what the cousins would think if they knew I was a prostitute. Told her I *wasn't* a prostitute. *Model—Model*—That's what I am. Went into my room and locked the door.

I've stayed in my room for two days—has it been that? Not sure. Slept most of the time. Haven't eaten and feel dizzy. Where's Congo? Everything is quiet quiet, quiet all around. The street outside too. No one seems to be in the park either. Is it a weekend—everyone gone to the country?

*T*his note was pushed under my door.

> Starr, baby,
> Please come out. We don't want you to get sick again. Let bygones be bygones. I'm making a nice dinner, sweet potatoes with marshmallows on top even though it's so hot outside.
>
> Ma

*C*ongo was lying outside my door waiting for me when I came out. I feel kind of dizzy so I've gone back to bed and lie here doing nothing. Reading makes my eyes blink.

*W*ent out today. I saw him again in the street following me. I'm certain of it now. So scared I told Ma. She wasn't mad this time. Tried to reason with me. I sat listening, saying nothing. So did Stanley. Then she raised her voice and called me an ungrateful girl to keep telling lies. But it is *not* a lie. I did see him. I make every effort to try to get her to understand, explain how it was, but my mind jumps back to—the street—Bank Street it was—and I see myself as though from a distance, slipping in and out of doorways running faster as he followed me, running—trying to lose him. But to no avail. No one listens. I should be doing everything I can to concentrate on the Queen of Rumania. Why think of *him* when I have *her*? She's arriving today on the *Leviathan*. He was on that ship going to Europe. The ship may be landing right now, the royal foot high-stepping down the gangplank as the brass band strikes up to welcome him, I mean her. Yes, definitely. I should be there and even more definitely the Congo should be there not to mention the Mamacita and the Stanley, they should be there too, yes, even the lowly Tookacita, but they will not be there. I forbid it. The Congo and I alone will greet the Royalness, yes alone together, but in tandem of course. We are to be the only members of the Royal Welcoming Committee. We Royals joining the other Royals, staying as long as we wish, never coming back, never having to see any of them again.

Queen Marie had already left by the time I got there. The crowds dispersed. Why couldn't she have waited for me? A man with a beard tried to get fresh but I was able to hasten into a taxi before he actually was and when I got home Ma said she was sorry she'd gotten angry when I'd told her about him following me. She was trying to keep calm and reason with me—he has his own life and family, dear, so much on his mind, he'd hardly have time to come down from Boston to wander around the streets of New York looking for you, such an odd idea, dear, no matter how you look at it. Shut up, I told her, stop talking to me as if I were an idiot. I made it all up anyway.

Weeks pass and as I lie abed things come to me—water running over pebbles in sunlight, sunlight shining into caves of crystal stalactites and stalagmites. I the center. Yes, water running over me—warm and soothing. It's gotten cold out. I feel so cold and nothing helps—even if my body gets warm my hands never are, they're always cold. Cold, that is, except when I fill the basin with hot water and stick them in—let them rest there for a while. I'm going to go and do that now.

· · ·

*P*atati-patata, my little Mamacita croons at me, her voice so sweet. She's worried—worried I might have to spend the holidays at Channing. They'd have to kill me first but I can't tell her that.

I'm feeling much better and full of plans, determined on self-improvement. What's Clive and the dear Mrs. Brook doing this Christmas, I wonder. And Faith. What will the dutiful daughter be asking Santa for? Whatever it is, she'll have faith enough to get it. And what you may ask is Starr asking Santa for? Oh not the moon—no, what she asks Santa for is simple. To walk tall and straight so she'll make something of her life. She never gets the faith to believe she can.

*G*ot myself together and went to a New Year's Eve party at Rufus's studio. Took one look in the door and left. Came back home and sat in a hot bath with a towel over my face. I'd soaped and soaped it first. My body too. Now I'm clean, so clean, in a dreamy dream talking to you on this New Year's Eve. There's a big racket outside in the streets so it must be midnight. Maybe I'll get dressed up again and go back to the party.

1927

January 26, 1927—Wednesday

Dearest Mem,

Today is my 21st and according to the world I'm of age. Grown-up at last, and knowing lots more than I did yesterday. But the truth of the matter is I keep thinking everything should be different but feeling it's not. How to explain it. The only thing I think and feel at the same time is that I want to improve myself and do better from now on. Yes, I must try harder. I must no longer be Starr the indecisive, Starr procrastinating as she so often does. It's this being unable to make a decision that holds Starr back. Let us linger now on thoughts of those who are *not* indecisive. Elsie Eaves, for example—the 1st woman elected to the Am. Society of Civil Engineers—and by her side include the woman who broke all male tradition by taking a seat on the Stock Exchange (can't think of her name right now). Surely they were *never* indecisive. Then there was Elsie Janis Ma admired so. These Elsies should inspire me to have high hopes for myself and they do. I meditate further, on another Elsie in my life, the most important of all—the Dinsmore girl. She, and this new Elsie Eaves, make me most ashamed and dismayed that I have nothing more of momentous achievement to report to you on this day of my 21st other than that I am 21. At least I can say that for myself. But Mem, heed, please—from now on indecisiveness is to be in the past. You have my firm resolve this moment, this very day, that from now on things are going to change. Oh God—the men I've slept with. So many, I've lost count, and the names forgotten (surely those don't count, do they?). But from now on, with my newfound awareness, everything will be different, so why bring them up anyway? From now on I'll be sane and worthy of being loved, I shall be able to listen to music with a quiet heart. I shall be able to go to bed with someone without having to anesthetize myself with Allonal or drink in order to let them come close to me—I hardly remember about it the next day (sometimes not at all), and because I don't, it means nothing to me. I want to be with a man and be with him as I am when I'm alone writing to you—my true self, not the girl who takes Allonal and drinks too much and goes crazy when she hears music, amenable to any suggestion, doing anything that comes into her head (or somebody else's). You know how it upsets me to be called the Flame Girl, but why shouldn't I be so named even tho' it be by fools who don't understand the true flame that consumes me? In fairness I must admit that it may be somewhat my own doing that people think I belong to Vanity Fair. Fools. Fools. But I the biggest one of all, giving credibility to the likes of them for I know that what they say about me is far from the truth and I am not of their kind. The truth is that I struggle to get out of the Iron Cage, knowing I'm there because I've sinned beyond all hope of forgiveness. Yes, I live in despair, shut up in this Iron Cage of my own making. I'm trapped and will never get out unless I can trust myself to be myself. Only then can I hope to get even a toehold in the House of the Virgins, catch even a glimpse of the Delectable Mountains. But if I could, oh Mem, then the hole I have inside me would be filled, wouldn't it? Then I'd stop thinking about AJP, his desire for me and how important it made me feel, yes powerful. He did love me. Didn't he? And in the beginning it was a game, wasn't it, and because it felt so good—how could something that felt so good be bad? Oh, even tho' I don't tell you—I still can't stop thinking about him—he's in my head like glue. These sound like excuses, I know, but between one game and the next something happened. In the days between seeing him and not seeing him the waiting was too long but there was nothing I could do about it. I couldn't make time go faster or go back, and that's all I wanted—to go either backwards to the last time I'd had my beloved ether, or ahead to the time when I'd have it again. Everything between was waiting . . . and then Horror, Horror, Horror!!! oh God, and after, I was on a train and ahead was a tunnel and we were speeding into it—was that what happened?—and when I came out of the darkness I was at Channing begging to get out, not remembering I'd begged to get in, and when I did get out, it was still there—the hole—those apes hadn't been able to fill it up with their peanuts or anything else—so you can understand my dilemma, what I've been trying to tell you, don't you? I started talking to you so long ago and you've become not just a diary, but (silent though you may be) the only friend I can talk to, who's there whenever I need her, who listens and doesn't judge or make me feel guilty and hateful. What I'm trying to tell you is that someday I'll become worthy to meet a man who will be like you, though not silent, of course. I won't have to explain anything to him. He'll understand from the beginning and explain it to me—everything—and he'll forgive me, and when that happens I'll know for sure he loves me and I'll be saved. I'm going to say bye for now. I feel better having told you all this. I love you, Mem.

Starr

*L*ast night a crowd of us went to see the new show our queen of the nightclubs, Texas Guinan, is putting on at her Three Hundred Club on West 54th Street. Her showgirls have the longest legs in town and they shimmy like the devil to the music, but the *real* something to see last night was at a table next to ours . . . Aimee Semple McPherson. There she was sitting up very straight drinking a glass of water. I could have reached out and touched her. She's become oh so famous since that summer when she preached in a tent in Boston. Now she has her own Angelus Temple in Los Angeles. Remember her standing in front of her Gospel Car with JESUS IS COMING SOON on one side and WHERE WILL YOU SPEND ETERNITY? on the other? And the white uniform and cape like Florence Nightingale and the long golden hair coiled in a braid around her head that the papers talked about and how I longed to follow her and be like her? Well, the cape etc. etc. are gone. Instead it's a satin evening gown and her hair's marcelled in tight curls done up in a peak. She wore tons of makeup, much more than I do, and looks like a movie star. But then the music stopped and Texas announced that Sister Aimee was going to speak and—suddenly, the room became quiet as she left her table and stood in the center of the dance floor. It was as tho' an angel had come into a place where noise and clatter had made things crazy, and by the angel's presence everything was made not only quiet, but *real*, yes—as if there existed a place somewhere that *was* real and she had come from there to tell us about it. I can't remember her words exactly but it was something like—behind these beautiful buildings, behind

THE MEMORY BOOK OF STARR FAITHFULL

these beautiful clothes, behind these good times, in the midst of shops and pleasures there is another life . . . something on the other side, and that with all our playing and getting and good times we should not forget we have a Lord and to take him into our hearts. Easier said than done, eh Mem? Anyway, she sure got into everyone's heart last night including yours truly. We'd come there for laughs, but after she spoke all I wanted to do was go home.

$\mathcal{D}$arling, darling Mem, I'm just this minute back home from a Bon Voyage party on the S.S. *Franconia*—I must try to be calm and sane so I can tell you what's happened, but the words jump into my mind, one on top of the other like popcorn on a hot stove. I'm so dizzy I have to take deep breaths to keep from choking . . . Someone extraordinary—I've met someone—his godlike face spoke to me though silently—worship me, love me, adore me—all he needed to do was look into my eyes to find the answer for I can be his slave for the rest of my life. I tremble as I write, as you can well surmise by this quaky handwriting. If you could see him you'd know right away that he's somebody, and even tho' I'm nobody he hasn't found it out yet and never will, I vow. He's tall (6 ft.) and handsome with sandy hair and a bit of grey at the temples—44 years old, I'm told, but you'd never guess, because despite the wee bit of grey he looks much younger. And his eyes—brown and piercing—I knew right away I'd captured his eye even tho' there were hundreds of Bon Voyage merrymakers around us and he was the center of attention. He looked straight at me and put his hand out, touched my arm—a moment, a gesture only, but it connected us with a wire of steel. Later on the deck we leaned over the railing for a minute talking, and it was then I knew I'd met destiny, knew that he will need only me to worship him, adore him, love him for the rest of our lives and that I'll need only him to give me reason that I'm worthy of walking on this earth. No longer will I be bad, sinful, unworthy, for I shall be made whole by his love. He's the rock I'll hold to, the stream of crystal water rushing over me cleansing me of sin. Scientist and world traveler, he's the ship's surgeon on the *Franconia*—oh, I tremble as I write his name—Dr. George Jameson-Carr. Ah yes, Mem—I for this and this for me (read that somewhere—now I know what it means).

*G*eorge Jameson-Carr and Starr Faithfull. Yes. It is to be. Now I know why Clive Brook is married. Fate meant it to be so, for how else could I be free and ready for Dr. George Jameson-Carr? I forgot to tell you—he also smokes a pipe. Yes, everything does happen for the best. Thank you, God.

*L*ike some besotted schoolgirl I write his name over and over again. Dr. George Jameson-Carr—Dr. George Jameson-Carr—Dr. George Jameson-Carr—but the more I think about it the more it comes to me that George doesn't suit him. But what does? How about Bill? Yes—definitely—he's a Bill. That's what he's to be from now on. I always fit a name to its face and his face is not a George face, it's a Bill face. Don't ask me to explain how I know this, but I do. Yes, in our intimate moments I'll call him Bill, but that's only for us. The *us* of Bill and Starr. How thrilling it is to say aloud, how thrilling to write, for eternity, on this page! Yes—for informal occasions it will be Starr and George Jameson-Carr—and for the formal ones we will be known as Dr. and Mrs. George Jameson-Carr—Starr and George Jameson-Carr, Dr. and Mrs. George Jameson-Carr, Starr and George Jameson-Carr—oh, I could go on writing it a million times over but I'm getting a cramp in my fingers and have to stop. Does he have a middle name? I must find out—then the first initial of it will go after the George. Ah, to think that initial is drifting around somewhere in the alphabet and I don't know yet which one it is.

I keep expecting to hear from him every day. But it's been one long wait and one long hope and I can't understand why, after the looks between us, the thrilling touch of his hand on my arm, the seriousness of our conversation as we leaned on the railing looking down into the sea at the waves lap lapping against the ship. What were they lapping about and when it comes down to it what were we lapping about? Porpoises—yes, that's what it was. He was telling me about seeing them off the coast of—some place, I forget where. Anyway, beneath the lap lapping of the waves and the telling of flip flapping porpoises there were definite signs and portents in the looks we exchanged—silent vows never to be forgotten. But let's get back to—now. Not only the now, but the days that have gone by—weeks—with not a word from him—nothing. Not even a postcard. I'd told him I collect them and he said he'd send me some. Some?—not a one's arrived. He did say this, didn't he?

*T*he days slip by without a word. What can be wrong? Something terrible must have happened. I'm praying constantly, but what good has it done? He's so fine, responsible in every way, even in life's little details I'm sure—so if he said he'd send a post-card there is no question that he'd keep his word. I've been lying low, turning down parties, hibernating, becoming clearer in body and spirit so I'll be ready when he does show up for us to start our life together. He will, won't he? Show up, I mean. He can't just drop off the face of the earth or dive down into the sea like one of those porpoises we were lapping on about—can he? Dive down into the sea out of sight and never surface again? Oh God, Mem, a man and a woman who love each other should be transparent to each other so that they merge into one crystal—am I a fool?

*W*hat the hell, I got fed up waiting around the house for post-cards that never arrived and started going out again, out with all those stupid Jays and Rollos, Stubbys and Petes, not to mention other Vanity Fair clowns whose names elude me at the moment due to my horrendous headache. Now I'll have to atone, which will take weeks, months, years maybe.

*F*at lot of good it does me. This going out on the town is only stepping onto a train—careening through a tunnel—there are no lights—only laughter, but it's not laughter, it's the sound of bones hitting against other bones as we speed through darkness . . .

*A*ll hope lost, and then—a postcard . . . a picture of the Taj Mahal. What can it mean? What the hell was Bill doing in India?

The card's postmarked Le Havre—and if he was there, why wasn't I with him? I look for hidden meanings but can't make sense of it. I read the fact that he's arriving sometime in the future, which tells me nothing. Could I be getting a run-around? Deem me worthy, please, that this may not be so. I hate to have to mention this and I wasn't going to, but—well—the postcard says "Having a wonderful time, wish you were here." Banal, eh. But then he may have meant it to be humorous—you know, satirical. He's so clever, that must be it. But then again maybe not. Maybe he doesn't give a damn about me. But then, why send the postcard?

Went to May Lark's opening at the Klaw Theatre—a swell musical, *Merry-Go-Round*. She's in the chorus. After, went to El Fey (sort of named after Larry Fay otherwise k.a. Public Enemy #3). Most expensive place in town. Bootleg champagne $30 a bottle and a pitcher of water $2. Thought I saw Bill in the crowd. But what would he be doing in a place like that? Oh, Mem, I can't forget him. I love him. I love him.

I'm exhausted, bewildered, oh God—put me to sleep. He turned up totally unexpectedly two weeks after I got the damn postcard from India. Soon after it arrived I'd been hot-cha-chaing around town, out every night and so busy I can't even remember now where I went or what I did, except that yesterday morning I found myself waking up in the St. George Hotel in Brooklyn with that clown Jay Sparks. He said we'd finally done IT, but who knows?—I'd been turning him down for months and can't stand his paunch but we woke up in bed together and he said we had, so maybe we did. Still, I told him he was pipe dreaming and that I only do IT with serious persons and to shut up, and out I ran taking one of the hotel's towels with me because it had George on it. (George for you know who.) When I got home there it was— a message from Bill asking me to meet him under the clock at the Biltmore in two hrs. I threw myself together as best I could, hot-footed over and just made it. Well—now I've spent the afternoon with him and I'm in a stew because I've no way of knowing how he really feels about me or if he feels about me at all. He doesn't seem to realize yet the course our destiny is inevitably to take. The gist of it (as it now stands) is that he'd like us to get together now and then. This sounds to me more of the way of acquaintances than the way of one and onlys. Doesn't it appear so to you? I didn't want to appear too eager or rattled so I rattled on about food—because I'm most interested in people's likes and dislikes and so do extensive research on the subject—God— what a food—fool, I mean. If I hadn't been so frazzled after my night with Jay I would've managed better. Anyway, this is what my research dug up. Bill likes corn, Brussels sprouts, lima beans, potatoes—mashed, baked, or in jackets—parsnips, beets (pick- led), artichokes (sometimes), cauliflower, peas, rice, smoked trout, steak, meat loaf, chicken, squabs, and he loves baked beans (*loves* baked beans—oh goody goody, yummy!), with a poached egg on top + toast. He doesn't like carrots, spinach, asparagus, broccoli, turnips—I forgot to ask about tomatoes, but that'll come up next time. Oh yes—we'll have a lot to talk about. So— for whatever it's worth, I now have this important information engraved indelibly on my brain forever. You know, in profile he does look like Clive Brook. Really. By the time we parted I was more my old self, flirting outrageously, smiling a lot, asking him if he minded if I called him Bill instead of George, as Bill's my fa- vorite name and I think he's pretty swell. He was mildly amused and told me I was pretty swell too, and that's when he said let's get together again sometime. I've got to rest and think this out, over and out as they say. Out with Jay and Rollo and the others and over to Bill. Yes! Bill Bill Bill Bill—

*M*y second date with Bill has taken place, sooner than ex- pected. But at least I have had time to rest up and so looked my best, whatever that means. It's confusing because I still have no clue as to who he'd like me to be so played it safe, stalling for time until I find out. Now, looking back on it tho', I played it all wrong—talked too much instead of too little, made up things about myself—told him I'd had a short story published in a liter- ary magazine, using a nom de plume because it was a risqué story and my mother was old-fashioned. And what is your nom de plume? he asked. Naturally, I couldn't think of a one, not even my own, so I blurted out—Elsie Dinsmore. Sounds familiar, he said. Good God. No wonder it does, I said, it's the name of a boring character in the most boring babyish book I've ever read, and I was only saying it to pull your leg—my real nom de plume is Mary Lennox. Well, Starry-eyes—you haven't fooled me, he said. I have heard of her, she's the girl in *The Secret Garden*, my niece's favorite book. Then he said he'd love to read my story no matter what name it was under and what was the title? "The Day We Met"—sounds more like a song, doesn't it, but it's not, sir, I can tell you . . . it has a dark side. He said he couldn't imagine me having a dark side, so I laughed and said, oh, it's only a silly story. He looked at me in a contemplative way and for a moment I wanted to tell him I'd been lying about the story, lying about everything. All I wanted was to have him hold me while I told him everything, everything from the beginning. I started to cry and he couldn't understand why and asked if he'd done something to offend me. Oh God. What a mess—that's when I said I love you I love you and I always will, but it was a dreadful horrible awful mistake to say that. It startled him and pushed him away instead of bringing him closer. He kidded me for talking like that—we hardly know each other (which from his point of view is true) and his saying that made me pull myself together as best I could and tell him how impulsive I always am and it came out for no reason, meant to be a joke so forget about it. He was all for that and suggested we get a sandwich. In my eagerness I poured too much ketchup on mine but I smiled a lot and told him lots of ketchup was one of my little failings. When he walked me to my door I invited him up to meet my old-fashioned mother (they were all out that night) but when we got upstairs they'd had a change of plans and there they were. It gave me quite a shock. I wasn't ready for it, had no time to get it set in my head, for my plan was that they should meet him after. After what? you may ask. Good question. Anyway, there they were in wrappers (Stanley's flannel with the hole) and Ma in scuffs, Tooka wandering out in a flimsy whatever, clasping a pink novelette to her bosom in a most provocative way. Ma wouldn't stop chattering, Congo wouldn't stop sniffing his shoes, Stanley wouldn't stop pressing his good gin on Bill, Bill wouldn't stop saying thanks but it's getting late . . . and I wouldn't have been able to stand it another mo. if he hadn't left. I did get a parting kiss on the cheek, and, brotherly though that may be, it's not to be sneered at and he did turn to me as he went down the stairs and said, "You're a peach." So—reassessing it over again for the millionth time, maybe I played it better than I thought. Then again, maybe not. I can't make up my mind about any of it. What do you think?

*A*fter having met him, my loving family is most impressed with Dr. Jameson-Carr. Ma laps up the gossip columns and has read about him, which impresses her even more. He's a close friend of the William Durants and dozens of Long Island people, like the Clarks and Phippses, and Ma's always reading about parties where they all have the time of their lives. Forget about the columns, says Stanley—in his opinion Bill's a fine man and would be a good influence on any friends be they Phippses or Clarks. That remark irked me, it's his way of telling me he doesn't approve of my other friends. Still it's also his way of saying he loves me and worries about me. As for Ma—well, Mamacita's not going to change. She thinks her Favorita's perfect—ha ha. I'm dying to confide in her that Dr. Jameson-Carr is the man I'm going to marry, but restrain myself. She might—might?—*would* be sure to say something to Bill the next time she sees him and why not? After all I am her daughter. But until things are more set I don't want anything coming up that might put him off. Of course it's inevitable that people will start suspecting, because we'll be going around town together as a couple (practically engaged), house parties at Old Westbury and you know what gossips people are, they'll put two and two together. Then, when he entertains (which he does quite frequently, I hear), I'll be by his side playing the role of gracious hostess. I hope to be worthy of this honor. Surely I am so within my heart, for that is my true intent and "as a man thinketh in his heart—so is he" (right, Mem?). That counts for a lot, doesn't it? Who said those words anyway?

*T*onight's to be the night (I know in my bones). I'm never wrong when I listen to my instincts—trouble is, I don't listen often enough. Dinner? Yes, yes, yes. A little dinner by candlelight—the Waldorf. A corsage—gardenia. My nose touches the petals. Must stop or they'll turn brown. Oh, I can't wait for the corsage to arrive, orchid perhaps instead of gardenia? The entire day's to be spent with Ponds cream on my face while I make lists of topics to talk to him about. Does he know, for example, that Leviathan was the Hebrew name of the great serpent god called Lotan in northern Canaan? Ladon in Greece and Sata or Apep in Egypt? Or that much ancient literature suggests that the boat, like other vessels, was often chosen to represent the cradle rediscovered and the mother's womb? That surely will interest him, since he's surgeon on a ship. I'm full of such info, if only I can remember it, or even some of it, for to impress him with my erudition is what I earnestly desire. Later in the day I'll steam my face over the tea kettle (before my bath) to make it dewy. I'm going to wear the sleeveless georgette with pleated collar which even Tucker admits I look nice in. They're going out, Ma and Stanley, so I'll have the house to myself to make my preparations. I must be perfect for him tonight, beautiful and intelligent in every way. Not only tonight, dear Mem, but always.

I'm going over it in my mind's eye as I tell you about it. At the Waldorf we sat on a banquette. I could see in his eyes that I was v. beautiful. There were white roses on the table in a silver bowl and shaded lamps glowing. He took charge ordering the dinner— Beef Wellington with Crabmeat something or other to start. And oh, Mem, when I spoke he was more than attentive, listening to my every word about Lotan, but when I got to Apep and Egypt he became so ardent (or bored) I never did get around to mentioning that in the Middle Ages, green was considered to be the color of the Holy Spirit, of life, procreation and resurrection—a color of a kind of life-spirit or world-soul which pervaded everything. If he questioned me about this I was fully prepared to tell him my source. That might have caught his interest, loving nature as he does (at least I think he does—especially porpoises, n'est-ce pas?), so I was kind of disappointed after the effort I'd gone to, but we'll have a lifetime to have interesting discussions, won't we? So, after the crab and the beef, marrons glacés were in the offing, but because he wanted it I wanted it too (not the marrons, silly, but to go to bed), we skipped the dessert and went up to Rm. 526 (a shrine in my memory). I sound like a foolish schoolgirl in the way I'm telling you this, but I am newborn, happy, so happy happy happy—yes that's the word for it, isn't it? I've been putting off telling you certain things (which you already know anyway) about me—maybe that's why I've been putting it off, hoping so much time would go by that I wouldn't have to go into it at all. But I'm going to—and now. Actually, talking to you about it may help me to clarify my thoughts. My head's not on quite straight since my night with Bill—it's awful to have to say, but you know how it is with me when it comes to making love— it was only really pleasurable with AJP at the beginning, when he gave me the little green bottle and made me creamy dreamy with his finger—making my body do what no one has been able to do since—It wasn't until later—but forget that—I'm talking about the beginning—that's what I miss. But I want it sane and real with someone I can trust and love without the little green bottle. Yes, I want that with Bill and I thought it would be—oh yes, I was sure it would be like that, only I have to tell you it wasn't. I'm not being disloyal to Bill in telling this, because I know that the first time it often isn't. May Lark says it took ages for her to feel safe with Arnie and nothing happened until she came to trust him. Of course I trust Bill, but I was overly apprehensive with wanting to be so perfect for him that I couldn't think of anything else. Then once we got up to the room, it happened faster, much faster than I expected and altho' I did my best to pretend, I don't know how convincing I was. As for me, it was more thrilling (much) before it happened than during. And now after (as I go over it moment by moment), I can tell you this confidently because the next time it will happen for sure, I know it will, and you and I will be looking back to that first time, puzzling over how I could have been making such an issue of it. One thing, tho', I may not have made clear to you. The best thing about it was the pleasure I gave him. He was so ardent and crazy to have me and his excitement gave me everything I could wish for. So I don't know why I sound as tho' I'm complaining, that is if I do. What I'm trying to say is that his passion for me is all I could ever ask for, and will always make me the happiest girl in the world, no matter what it's like next time or ever. One moment of great significance came when he asked me to give him my wisp of lace with its wedge of charmeuse to cover my most secret place. It had alighted like a butterfly on top of my dress where I'd thrown everything any which way on the floor even tho' I'm usually tidy and fold things just so. This particular wisp had been bought for the occasion—the lace isn't scratchy—I can't stand scratchy lace when it's combined with creamy charmeuse, an insensitive combination you so often come across when looking for undies. But I digress—He said he was sailing for England soon, and would bring them back to me covered with him. I was thrilled at this—it meant he'd be faithful to me, lying in his cabin or in a hotel room somewhere after the ship docked, using them to make love to me in reverie even tho' we were parted. That is what it meant, isn't it? And *so* significant, his saying he'll bring them back—means he isn't leaving forever and never returning—it means I'll see him again. But then he asked if that embarrassed me. I swooped the butterfly up from the floor and lay back beside him pressing the softness inside me and then I placed it on his mouth (a souvenir tendre). "Thanks, Starry eyes"—and he got up and started dressing—then he rolled it up into a wad and stuffed it into the pocket of his jacket. That's when I was sure he was going to say he loved me but all he said was, "Well, you're a swell girl, but I'd better be off—Ship ahoy." What do you think, Mem? Maybe I'm not telling it to you right.

*E*ven tho we aren't together now I have to talk to him as if he's here or I'll burst with the happiness of our having been together last night. Oh my darling Bill, I'll never fail you or let you down in any way—ever. I love everything about you—your body, your soul, which I am now a part of as you are part of mine. I woke this morning looking forward because you are my first thought and I hear your voice calling me "Sweetness." How happy we will be in the day-to-day closeness of a life together, bringing out the best in each other—for you do bring out the best in me. You inspire me to be the best I can be so I can be there for you and give my best to you. Oh darling, you are my great love and all I long for and hope for is to make you happy. Not only in fleeting moments like those we have had so far but in the life we have ahead of us to share. I love you so much. I want us to be together for the rest of our lives. It's going to be the best for both of us, isn't it?

*I*t helps to go over things, run them across my mind and tell you about them after they happen. Once I have, it's like they really did. Happen. Otherwise, I might lose track of them. I've been shuffling things around in my head, this way and that way, since the night at the Waldorf, but not coming up with any answers, not coming up with anything at all, if you really want to know. I look at the clock and it points to 11:00 a.m. precisely—so I've come up with something, haven't I, as I sit here imagining what he's up to right now. Bill, I mean. Not Daddy. Come to think of it, what is Daddy Lincoln up to right now? That would be of great interest to me. Yes, it would. Anyway, to get back to Bill—his ship's sailing later today and I can't make up my mind whether to go down there or not. As he didn't invite me or even give a hint suggesting it—I hesitate. On the other hand—why not? I go to Bon Voyage parties all the time. Still, it does seem odd that he didn't invite me after that night. Too much on his mind probably. All those last-minute details he's responsible for. Yes, that's it.

*O*rchids arrived with a letter.

Dear Starr,
   It's off on the bounding main in a few hours, and I didn't want to sail away without saying goodbye and telling you how much I enjoyed your company at dinner. I hope you had a good time too. You're hard to read sometimes, little girl, but you sure make up for it by being pretty. Just a joke of course, but coming from an old salt like me you can be certain of its sincerity. After we land I'll be going on leave to take care of some family matters in Liverpool, and then it's on to London or Paris on holiday. So who knows when we shall meet again? You be good now and if you can't be good, be careful.

Your friend,
George
alias
Bill

Well—that settles that. No need to hotfoot it down to the S.S. *Franconia* for Bon Voyage or anything else. What does he mean by "family matters in Liverpool"? And "London or Paris on holiday"—that's the one I don't like the sound of. Surely I haven't been fooled about his not being married. I must look into this immediately before I go a step further. Not a step out of this room, much less out of this house, until I know for a fact he's not one of the M.M.'s. I must stay put, stay right here where I am and go over his letter more carefully, read between the lines. Surely there's more there than meets the eye. Actually, I'm going to tear it up.

I couldn't bring myself to do that. Or throw the orchids out either. Instead I'm pressing both between pages of my *Sonnets from the Portuguese*—ah yes—*How do I love thee?*—*let me count the ways.*

*M*ade myself go with Rollo and others to the Cotton Club to hear Duke Ellington—So packed we could hardly move. Rollo and I jigged opposite each other in a double-time Charleston. But did it take my mind off Bill? Even stuffing myself after at the Yeah Man with pigs' feet and black-eyed peas didn't help. Nor did the reefers passed around. Can't remember how I got home.

I need—must—get away from New York. Come to think of it, a holiday's not a bad idea—in ye merrye olde—why not? I've always longed to go here, there and everywhere—so why not there? After all I have money, a lot of it—and it's mine really, isn't it, even tho' Ma takes care of it for me. Why shouldn't I spend it as I choose? As of right now I feel somewhat of a fool regarding Dr. George Jameson-Carr and if this doesn't take my mind off him nothing will. If I run into him in London I shall hold my head high, you can bet on that, so don't worry about me.

I've checked every source and he is not married, at least we know that, and never has been, so maybe I've been unfair to him. He might be taking time off to slowly make up his mind. Having waited this long to find the right girl he must certainly want to be certain, absolutely certain that at last in me he's found her. I shouldn't be so impatient, but it's always been one of my worst failings, as we well know. A little vacation would be perfect for you and me right now.

*M*a's not a bit averse to my suggestion. She needs a vacation too, so does Tooka. And what better place than England, where we'll meet friends of our friends here in New York? She's asking them to write ahead saying we're on our way. Stanley's to stay here with Congo and keep the home fires burning. Mamacita and Papacita haven't been getting along too well lately so perhaps it's best this way—a vacation from each other might do them both good. Stanley doesn't seem to mind. I can't wait to get moving. All I think about is Bill and that I'll be seeing him soon.

The more I go over recent events the clearer I see things. There is no reason to feel I've made a fool of myself over Dr. George Jameson-Carr. He sent orchids, didn't he, with a letter, not necessarily a love letter but a love-ly letter, and I'm the one at fault for rushing things. The future of Bill and Starr is a much too serious matter for me to be my usual impulsive and impatient self. After all, his dependability is one of the qualities I most cherish and admire. So hold on, Starr girl, and make your plans accordingly. If I miss him in London—it will be on to Liverpool. He may be there with his Mother, who I hear has been ill. A trip to Liverpool might be fun—run into him by chance—what could be more romantic, more suitable, more everything in every way? Yes, definitely. That's what I'll do.

On the morrow we sail on the *Majestic.* I can't wait!! This time I'll not be an imposter at a Bon Voyage party—I'll *be* the party— and after the ship's passed the Statue of Liberty and I'm on my way to Bill, I shall believe firmly and forever in God, fairies, Elsie Dinsmore and Santa Claus.

Oh, Mem, the tugboats guided our giant into the safe deep, and—that moment I'd been waiting for—the Statue of Liberty standing in the harbor came to me full plain, torch held high, signaling that I was on my way to Bill at last.

Woke sobbing—why?—can't remember.

Tooka's seasick and so is Ma. They stayed in the cabin moaning and groaning as did many of the other passengers. I walked the ship exploring every nook and cranny—free to fly with the wind as it buffeted me around the deck. Later they put metal borders around the edges of the dining tables to prevent dishes from scooting off onto the floor.

*I*t was colder today and, chilled, I went into the bar and found myself ordering a double old-fashioned to warm up. Until then I hadn't talked to anyone—not that I haven't had the chance, as there are plenty of fellows on the ship waiting for a glance from me, but I've been veiled and had no intention of revealing myself until face to face with Bill. It's been fun being a Mysterious Passenger, keeping to myself, but sitting next to me at the bar was a tall Englishman who quite intrigued me, and I decided to open up a little. He introduced himself as Chauncey Plowright (no kidding) and we got to talking about one thing and another which finally led to sex. I told him the only fun parts are the preliminaries leading up to the main event. Can't think why I got into all this—must have been the second round, which we were well into by the time the subject came up—and I heard myself saying, Oh, you English, all you really like is spanking. "Tell me more" (he was most interested). "Is that what you enjoy?" I laughed and didn't answer. "I have a jolly hairbrush in my cabin, smooth and flat as a paddle," he said, ordering more cocktails. "You're a beautiful girl, surely not just a tease, are you? You sound English, but I'm not sure. Where are you from?" The land of dreams, I told him—honest, I never fib about anything. "Not even a teeny bit, once in a while?" Absolutely not—never. "Well, then, answer my question." What question? "Oh, you *are* a tease, you know you like it." Like what? "What we were talking about before." Before what? I'm only interested in art and psychology—ethics, things like that. He grabbed my hand and pulled me off the bar stool, whispering to come off it, he knew what I'd like, he could tell by the way I wiggled around, up and around the deck—he'd had his eye on me ever since the first day we boarded the ship. Don't, don't, I begged him, but he wouldn't stop. I got scared and started crying, making a spectacle of myself. The bar wasn't that full but someone near us said leave her alone and he did, he scurried out, leaving me there while someone else ran out and came back with a Steward who took me down to our cabin and had to put me to bed. Ma and Tooka were asleep and woke up when we came in.

They groaned and turned over and went back to sleep. How did I get myself in such a mess? Well, it won't happen again.

*N*eed a new powder puff, but loath to get one. I've become most attached to the worn down velour of this one. Slightly grey-red from the powder and rouge and the fierce pats I sometimes give my face.

A sunny day and as I stretched out on a deck chair bowls of chicken soup with rice and saltines were being served. Not for me, I told the Steward, bring me two beers, one for me and one for my friend who's appearing any minute. The very thing for my head-ache, n'est-ce pas, but of course I didn't go into that with him. My friend never did show up so I finished the two and ordered more. My friend's been delayed. He's definitely expected. Then who should breeze around the corner but Chauncey Plow-Wrong (ha ha), sailing by as if he didn't know me. Beth and Betty Dodge are on the ship making flappers of themselves over him—they just passed by trying to catch up with him.

*T*hese headaches of mine won't go away. Can't imagine why. I now only go into the bar when it's practically empty, to enjoy my White Lady cocktails in peace. As Tooka and Ma stay in the cabin most of the time, everyone still thinks I'm traveling alone—well, let them. Who cares? As for me—Bill—Bill—Bill—that's all I care about.

*T*onight's the Ship's Ball. Maybe I'll go, maybe not. Maybe I'll jump overboard—when it gets dark—into the dark cold sea.

I don't know what got into me but I was determined to go to the Ship's Ball in an officer's uniform. It was a hassle getting one but after all else failed I finally succeeded by bribing one of the offi-cers. Pleased with myself I made my entrance into the smoking room when it was most crowded with revelers. It caused quite a stir, I'm happy to say—at least that's what I thought at the time.

Now as I tell you about it I'm not happy one bit and wish to hell I'd never taken such a notion into my head. Why did I? Also wish to hell I'd kept my mouth shut but no. I announced that I was on my way to London to marry a merchant marine surgeon. There was much clapping, with Ma and Tooka simpering around as they mingled with one and all accepting congratulations. They were more than an embarrassment to me in their Baby Peggy get-ups, but what the hell, everyone else looked ridiculous too so why comment on my poor little Mamacita and Sistercita in this sarcastic way? Could it be because Ma kept following me around at the party harassing me with questions about when when??? and going on about how there must be an announcement in the newspapers—yes, quickly—and Stanley (she left to radio him before I could stop her) and Bill—why hadn't Bill talked to them and where was he? And even tho' she didn't know, she sent a radiogram to him aboard the S.S. *Franconia* at the same time she sent the one to Stanley, saying how happy she is for us (oh God!) and contact her at the Savoy immediately to finalize wedding plans. After a while it got to me and I had to have more drinks and Chauncey Plowright kept bothering me, clapping his hands and lips together with a smacking sound, and I was sick of all of them and left the party and went up on deck where I fell asleep in one of the lifeboats. The whole ship was in an uproar looking for me. Ma had put out an alarm as she'd seen me leave the party and she and Tooka had been all over the ship looking for me. Anyway, the commotion of them running around searching woke me up and now I'm back in the cabin, still in this damn uniform. Ma and Tooka have gone back to the party. We land tomorrow.

1928

We're at the Savoy but so busy hardly time to unpack much less even think about a Birthday letter. You'll have to bear with me. You will, won't you?

Now, let's see—first thing I have to tell you is that the wedding plans have to be postponed for a while due to the state of Mrs. Jameson-Carr's health (his ma's, not mine—I just like to write the name Mrs. Jameson-Carr so I take every opportunity I can to do this). It is true, I'm sure, that his ma is not well. Otherwise why wouldn't I have heard from him? Also, there is the Mamacita to more than consider. She thinks (and she does have a point) that it's v. odd we haven't heard a word from him. I've had to restrain her every day from sending Stanley a cable to jump on the next ship and meet us in London—she keeps talking about "presenting a united front" when we get together with Bill's family to plan the wedding. Then there's the question of "the announcement." She goes on about that too—"a formal announcement to be put in the society pages of the New York and London newspapers." We don't want that, Mem, do we? No, definitely not—a bit premature at this point and might delay future developments. I calmed her down by telling her Bill had called me here at the Savoy the day after we arrived (she'd been out shopping at Harrods)—yes, a call came for me from Liverpool regarding Mrs. Jameson-Carr's illness. Luckily she's diverted by all the attention we're getting. Seems as if tout le monde in London has been waiting for our arrival—thanks to her forethought, tales of my beauty and wit reached here weeks before we did and so far I've hardly had a mo. to see the sights or do anything but look at myself in the mirror to make sure I'm really here.

*D*ozens and dozens of chaps are lined up waiting their turn to take me out. To name a few—there's Rudolph Montague and Wilfred Sheldon and Lester Witherspoon, a Wooley Roger, a Desmond, a Lonnie and so on. Desmond's cute and Wooley's quite intelligent, which is more than you can say for Lester. Rudolph has a mustache and got angry when I called him Rudi— "No—Rudolph, please," he said, bowing slightly and clicking his heels. I'm out every night with one or another—oh, there's a David too, and two Armandos. They take me dancing at the Cavendish Hotel and to pubs in Limehouse, and to the Café Royal and the Cheshire Cheese—they take me to all-night parties and parties on river barges and to the Eiffel Tower in Soho and Ma won't stop pestering me to take Tucker along. I do whenever I can, but does it make Ma happy? No, it's questions questions questions about each and every one of my Davids and Armandos. She's not worried about me, it's Tooka she wants introduced to Viscounts and Royal Highnesses and they not only have to be handsome but rich too.

I got fed up with Ma and Tooka and moved to the Winthrop Hotel. Ma was furious when I left them but what a relief to be free and not have her interfering with my ins and outs. I wouldn't tell her where I was going because if she knew it was a hotel she'd be sure to leave the Savoy and follow me here. It's not as nice as the Savoy, but I don't care as I'm out most of the time anyway.

*A*re you wondering why I haven't mentioned Bill? Do you think it's because of the Rudolphs and Wilfreds and so on? Has the attention I'm getting made me perfidious? Oh—how could you—how could you who know me so well know me so little as to have that even cross your mind? There are times, I must admit, when I'm not actually thinking of him in my head—but in my heart there he is thump thumping away with every beat. Yes, even when I'm out and forget him for a moment it's only to protect myself from staying in my hotel room with my heart thump thump thumping away as it pines for him. You wouldn't want me to do that, would you? No, I must be brave, have coraggio and press on, for he's sure to turn up any day now, I'm more than certain. And you know that even when I flirt a little it's only a wee bit little and no one takes it seriously. When Bill turns up it will be another story. But I need not reiterate that as you already know so well my true heart in this matter.

I got worried my little Mamacita would work herself into a state not knowing where I am so called her at the Savoy. She'd already heard I was at the Winthrop, but hadn't had time to call as Tucker's met a Hungarian Count—"so don't worry," she said. Then, as we were about to say goodbye, she mentioned she was short of money, but not to worry about that either, as she'd "sent a cable to that nice Mr. Rowley in Boston telling him there has to be an operation (!?) and to send $10,000 immediately" and that when it arrived she'd let me know.

*M*a and Tooka left London after some difficulty with the Hungarian Count and Ma's taking Tooka back to New York. Well, no need to worry about them. They should be able to make do on that $10,000 for a while—Ma kept all of it, but who cares?—I've enough for myself. If only Stanley had been along on this trip everything would've been easier. When he's around he soothes Ma with his passivity, calms her between those ups and downs, which got more frequent of late. She sounded frantic and didn't even mention Bill or press me about my plans or ask if and when I was coming home. I didn't see them before they left—apparently they went in a hurry.

*N*ow that they're gone I kind of miss them. Not that things aren't swell-o, simply swell-o—but where the hell-o is Bill-o? Don't think I've given up my plan of going to Liverpool to accidentally on purpose run into him, but every time I get set to leave something turns up, and before I know it it's too late to catch the train and I have to put it off to another day, then when that comes

round, something else comes around too and I—oh what the
hell—

Went dancing with Lonnie and we ended the night in a private
club. When we came out, the sun was blinding. It was breakfast
or maybe lunch time, but who cared. We went on across the street
to the Six Bells and hooked up with some of Lonnie's chums. Got
back to the Winthrop, God knows when, and woke up on the
floor without a stitch of clothes on. Now I'm staying put until I
feel better—may not go out tonight, but may change my mind. If
I didn't have you to talk to, I'd go batty. That's why I carry you
everywhere. When people ask what's that, I tell them I'm a jour-
nalist taking notes on an article for the *Manchester Guardian.*

What day is it? And what the hell am I doing at this hotel in
Camden Town? I don't remember how I got here or why my Innovation trunk is here by the bed. Why isn't it at the Winthrop
and why aren't I there too? Someone's shoe was squashed up in
the W.C.—when I pulled it out the dye on the leather ran all
over and now I've got blue hands and can't get the blue from
under my nails. Where the hell is Lonnie? It's certainly not his
shoe, and there's no sign of him, not even a note, and I can't find
my money. What about the others? There was a girl and another
man, or was it two? It may be the girl's shoe. But I don't think she
was wearing blue ones. Daphne—was that her name? Was the
other man AJP? No—I don't think so. He wasn't bald—or was
he? And the girl with him—who *was* she? It may have been the
second man's shoe, but then again no—couldn't have been.
Where is the other shoe, the one that goes with the one that got
squashed in the W.C.? I can't find it anywhere.

I've got to get myself out of this fleabag. I keep cabling home for
money, but no answer. Has something happened to them? Something terrible? Or did they take off for somewhere else instead of
going back to N.Y.? Now that I think of it, maybe Ma said she
and Tooka were going to Hungary with the Count, which is why
they left so suddenly. Mamacita has her eye on a coronet for
Tooka and won't give up easily—Countess Tooka. I like it, I like

it. Maybe they sent word to me at the Winthrop but I wasn't there to get the message. (I am out most of the time.) But Stanley'd be in N.Y. and get the cable, wouldn't he, so why haven't I heard from him? I'd cable Mr. Rowley direct but I'm scared to. Ma always communicates with him and I wouldn't know what to say.

No—I'm sure Ma didn't mention anything about going to Hungary. I cabled her again, "Are you mal—are you mad at me, dear? Sorry."

Lonnie turned up and we got into a row. The hotel asked us to leave, but he said his "wife" was coming out of a fever and hallucinating, which was what all the noise was about. He had them come up and see for themselves and pushed my head down on the pillow, shushing at me to lie there as if I was in a coma, and when they came in he said, "See, the fever's broken, the dear's resting now." The dear indeed! I went along with it only because getting off the bed, much less out of this place, is more than I can manage right now, tho' I'd be out in a shot, exhausted or not, if I had money to pay the bill, but he has none and no idea what happened to mine. He wants to leave our stuff here and skip out. Well, he can do that if he wants, but I haven't come to that yet. Where the hell is the key to my Innovation trunk? Lonnie had to break the lock to get it open. At least all my things are there. Nothing's been touched. Lonnie's angry because there's nothing in it to pawn. My jewelry is in the safe at the Winthrop except for the earrings and bangle bracelets I was wearing the night we went dancing. The rat's disappeared with those and lied to me about where they are—says he has no idea what happened to them and "are you sure you were wearing them?" I know he's lying. The earrings were the emerald-bead tassel ones AJP bought me at Tiffany that time in New York. I've worn them constantly since I've been in London. Oh God.

Back at the Winthrop but they've asked me to leave soon as poss. I told them it'll take me two more days at least to get my things together. I need time to gather not only my things but my thoughts. Where am I going from here? It's a week (I think) since I got out of hospital, where they had to give me strychnine to get me conscious and pumped my stomach out too. The doctors told me I took 24 tablets I'd gotten at the chemists, and that "it was enough to kill a normal person." They don't know me (ha, ha). Anyway, I'll take their word for it, because I don't remember a thing after Lonnie left me in that fleabag, that is, if he did leave. I was rushed to hospital and someone there got in touch with the Am. Consul who called Ma and she sent money so now I know they're in N.Y. and O.K. She sent me a cable saying they'd come back to London if I wanted them to but that's exactly what I *don't* want, so I immediately cabled that I'd gotten in touch with Duke Marbury and not to worry. Actually I hadn't yet. But Duke was going around saying mean, nasty things about his "Susie" (that's what he calls me), how he never wanted to see her again and had put up with her moods long enough and that she was "a spoiled American brat" and so on. I didn't care because I'd gotten mixed up with Lonnie again—or was it Colin—anyway it dawned on me lying there in hospital that if I could bring myself to be a sweetie-pie with him again he'd forgive me. In that stuffy British way he does mean well, and I should have phoned him when I got in the mess with Lonnie—he'd have been a pal and helped me out of it—but as you know I couldn't think straight. And still can't. I'm so mixed up—how could I ever have fallen so from grace as to be asked to leave that fleabag in Camden Town and now "requested" to get out of this common Winthrop?

The dear came to my rescue and got me out. Yes—Duke Marbury in his Bentley with two butlers, and I wish you could have seen their faces at the desk when he paid my bill and they had to turn over my jewelry, which they'd been hanging on to in the safe as if it belonged to them instead of me. It was a fine moment when bill paid and jewelry in hand, I asked that flat-faced manager to if-you-please kindly forward my mail and any messages to the Connaught (where I am now ensconced). Things are better, yes better times ahead. I've cabled my address to Ma and "letter follows." And it will once I get a grip on myself, yes definitely, and until then I shall lie low with cases of Evian water and books—lots of books—as my only companions. Right now by my side is *The Intelligent Woman's Guide to Socialism and Capitalism*, by

G. B. Shaw. It's recently come out here in London and neatly fits in with my take-it-easy-self-improvement plan. I am determined (more than determined) to be rested and fully informed in all areas in time for my meeting with Bill. Thank God I'm out of the mess I was in. Of course, if I'd met Bill before I got in the mess I got in I never would have gotten into it. I need time to become pretty again and lose weight—tons of it. No telling when I may run into Bill. Once I make up my mind to do something—well, you know me better than I do, Mem. I must say Duke is more than sweet and understanding. He received a shock, I could tell, when he saw me and is doing everything to cosset me and make me well again. Best of all he leaves me to myself. We talk every day on the phone and he sends flowers, caviar and other trifles to amuse me. I've told him I'm too tired to see him yet. I want to get pretty again before I do.

I feel much better. For one thing the rain has stopped. It's been pouring for days, adversely affecting me with dark thoughts which I shall overcome, for the shadow side must not take possession. I must lift my spirits to the sun.

*D*uke's persistence wore me down and I finally agreed to accompany him to a masked ball "on the largest floating ballroom in the world." It turned out to be none other than that ballroom we know so well—the one on the *Aquitania*, now docked at Southampton. It was a strange feeling being there again, but worth it because I kept seeing Bill every moment, yes—Bill instead of the Fou, Bill here, there, and everywhere in the crowds smiling the night away in their grotesque masks. I'd push toward him every time I spotted him. But of course I was the most grotesque of all, because I was only pretending.

I hardly know how to tell you or where to begin for THE MOST EXTRAORDINARY THING HAS HAPPENED. It started out with Duke showing up earlier than expected, knocking on my door as I was rushing around getting myself together, still in undies and mules—the red-gold kid with pom-poms (the ones he loves to play with). I'd thrown on my Japanese kimono to let him in, but soon after it slipped off as I sat down at the dressing table to put finishing touches on my toilette—Fix yourself a Cocktail, I told him, and then you may lie down on the bed and make goo-goo eyes at me from a respectable distance. I could tell he was dying to get hold of those pom-poms as I sat there crossing and uncrossing my legs. He started complaining that I'm the biggest tease he's ever known, so I told him he was being punished for all the rumpus he made last time when I couldn't get him to leave. He is so kind and sweet but can be persistent at times. I only put up with it because I'm passing the time until I hear from Bill—because I will. I will. I know I will. One of the fools from the Masked Ball, name of Lord Brendon, known as Boofy, is after me to go to Buda Pest (how the hell do you spell it?) and maybe I should accept his invitation, because Duke's been getting out of hand lately and all I seem to be doing here is fending him off, holding my breath waiting to see if Bill's going to show up in London. Until last night, when The Extraordinary Thing happened, all I'd thought about was—what shall I do do do do do do do, knowing I shouldn't be going around and about so much, but the alternative would have been to stay in my suite at the Connaught and brood. I found it hard to concentrate on anything but Bill—even my trips to the library had dwindled and try as I would *The Intelligent Woman's*—Whatever???—let's see, where was I? Oh yes—Boofy and the pom-poms—well— we were to meet Diana and Bordie at Claridge's but Duke was put out with me over the pom-poms and refused to go unless he had his way with me. I was sick of the sight of him and set on going out in my new Vionnet, so I hastily dressed and off I went, out the door on my own. That got him quickly over the sulks and he clattered after me in hot pursuit and together we were on our way. Diana and Bordie were having one of their set-tos by the time we got there, which in turn got Duke started, what with the champagne and all. It was getting pretty hectic when a crowd of ultra chics walked by our table—and with them—he stopped cold when he saw me—how could he not for we resembled each other as if we were twins, you'd be unable to tell boy from girl except by the way we dressed. Oh Mem, it was a stroke of lightning—those strange eyes of his—of mine—how I want them, close, so close, how I long for his angelic mouth to be on mine. I'd never be afraid to trust him, because it would simply be a turning loose, a letting go not to someone else, but into myself. I loathed his friends, giggling among themselves at private jokes—"buffy" (word for tight)—with names like Tootie and Baby, Cecil and Puffin, but it gave them pause I can tell you, the uncanny resemblance he and I have to each other. It put a halt, if only for a moment, to their idiotic shenanigans. Soon Duke was insisting we go on to the Embassy Club, but as we were leaving the maître d'hôtel slipped something into my hand—a match folder from one of the tables and inside the flap, the message—Stephen Tennant, Smith Street #5, Westminster, tomorrow 4 p.m.

*M*ark this day, for it is the day I went through the door of a flat on Smith Street in Westminster and found myself. Now I know there's one person in the world besides you that I'll never have to pretend with. This will give me strength while I wait for Bill. To know there's a person walking the earth that I can look at and talk to and know that all we want from each other is to know that the other exists. For if Stephen Tennant exists then so do I. Are we twins separated at birth by some mishap? I'll have to look into this further. Question Ma. Check hospital records in Evanston. Maybe Daddy could shed some light if only I can get ahold of him. Where the hell is he? Daddy Lincoln, I mean, not Bill—but now that his name comes up—where the hell is *he*? But what matter these details of why and how? There are other ways of looking at it—each of us has a double floating around somewhere tho' we may never meet. They say it's true, Mem. Who are "they"? you may ask. None other than those ancient Egyptians I got so caught up with—the Boston Public Library, remember? According to them, Stephen Tennant could be my ka (the shadow double), which is now reunited with his ba (the spiritual individuality) to become inseparable. Am I interpreting this correctly? I must delve further, but until then I'm on my knees thanking God that I've met my ka. Or it could be vice versa, couldn't it? I the ka and he the ba? How many of us in the world get this chance? Not many, that's for sure. With these new developments I'm beginning to understand more and more what it means to be born a star child and what a miracle it is that Stephen Tennant and I have found each other. I got no sleep last night holding the match cover in my tight little fist, knowing I'd see him today, praying until dawn it wasn't a dream I'd cooked up in my silly head as I sometimes tend to do. Well, it wasn't a dream and the match cover was still there in the morning to prove it even if the ink was all smudgy from the clutching so fiercely during the night. It was real all right, and I knew it more than ever when I walked into his flat, because there, once again, as I had last night, I came face to face with myself. And there were not only two of us, for his walls are papered with silver foil like smoky mirrors and reflected a myriad of—Starrs and Stephens—Stephens and Starrs—yes, there were kas and bas all over the place and they were moving to a silver brocaded bed where they lay for hours side by side (not touching), gazing into the mirror of each other's faces, and above the Starrs and Stephens a ceiling of sapphire blue, with silver stars, and below them a carpet of black velvet. Night or day?—they knew not until light filtered through the window and I realized it was dawn and I'd better get on my horse and get out of there. I'd had a row with Duke and left him distraught, having dumped him rather suddenly to keep my date with Stephen. Why, you may ask, did I have sudden qualms over this Duke dumping, letting it niggle into my newfound happiness? Well, I'm hard put to answer, but I suppose it's because I felt vague guilts about having left Duke sitting on the edge of the bed in the Connaught with his ding-dong up in the air. I do seem to excite him—all he has to do is lay eyes on me and up it goes. Still, I blamed myself for leaving him so. But there was no alternative, wild horses couldn't have kept me from Westminster and my 4 o'clock with Stephen Tennant. The dawn light, however, coming into that silvery room, kept getting brighter and giving an ugly glare to our paradise. Duke wasn't there when I got back to the Connaught. I'll have to make it up to him some other time as best I can.

I've neglected you, I know, but there's no time for anyone except Stephen, darling, darling, DARLING Stephen—his divine pursuits monopolize my every moment—there's a party every night—the circus party—the boat party—the white party—always a party going on and we hardly see the light of day except at dawn. I've become most friendly (intimate) you might say with his parrot, Gloria Swanson, for altho' I've done nothing to entice her she's completely bewitched by me and demands to be let out of her cage the moment she spots me coming through the door of his flat, calling out "Star-eee—sweetie-Starr—Star-eee—sweetie-Starr" (Stephen's taught her my name) and she keeps at it until she's let out to perch on my shoulder and nibble on my ear. But enough's enough and I put a stop to it. Stephen and I spend hours trying on each other's clothes—an enthralling fit. We had lunch at Cecil Beaton's flat yesterday. He served mauve cocktails with cream on top. And last night we went to the Café Royal for dinner and then on to the Eiffel Tower for sweet champagne, which put us in an exhilarating mood. Yes, quite buffy. Tonight it's Boulestin's for dinner, we're still not ready to exchange roles and are going as our real selves—girl and boy, but soon we're planning forays on the town impersonating a couple of swells dressed in his clothes. He's much more knowledgeable about maquillage than I, but I'm learning fast, discovering that the apricot shades are more becoming to our fair skins than the pinks. He's given me a jar of that gold dust he sprinkles through his hair. Oh, Mem, I can't stop looking at myself in the mirror.

Stephen has presented me with a book. One of his drawings is on each page, and opposite—a story by the Lady Pamela Grey (his Mum). It's titled *The Vein in the Marble* and was published in London in 1925—think of it, Mem, in 1925—we were in New York, driven by our passion for Clive, trying to devise ways of getting to London to meet him, while all along Stephen was there, too. No doubt they were passing each other on the street never realizing the bond they had—moi! Bit far-fetched, I guess, but why not? And picture too, Mem, while you're at it—unbeknownst to us this heavenly likeness of myself—Stephen Tennant—was drawing these illustrations for the Lady Pamela's stories. Had I but known my life would have been different (yours too, Mem). But destiny had other plans for us and we had to go thru three long years of whatever it was we were going through until the night of the fateful meeting at Claridge's when ka (the shadow double) and ba (the spiritual individuality) came face to face. I've left the book open on the table to a story called "The Woman of the Masks" and it tells of a woman who wore so many masks that she had one for every month in the year, and three over. Here is part of it, Mem—

She was a lovely creature; so sinuous there was hardly a keyhole she could not enter by, and so soft-footed you could never tell from which direction she came. . . . Sometimes she

reminded her friends of Ivy as she went on her way, oblitera-
ting and strangling all she touched. One day in a moment of
exasperation, someone called out:

"Can't you be yourself for once in a while?" And she
doffed her mask in the surprise of it. And then it was seen
that she had no face at all, no countenance. Only the mask
she had last worn, the one in her right hand, looked out
upon the world with eyes that seemed to find it hollow.

I didn't realize until now how these words chill me. Tell me, I beg
you, that this is not about me. It is *not* a story about me. So why
am I frightened? Not when I first read it, but now. Oh, help me,
Mem. Say something, please.

There's rather an impressive collection of engraved invitations
stuck in the frame of my mirror. Garden parties, balls and what
not. The one coming up next is an invitation to a Bath and Bottle
Party which is to take place tonight after the Ellesmere Ball.

Mrs Plunket Greene, Miss Ponsonby, Mr Edward Gathorne
Hardy and Mr Brian Howard request the pleasure of your
company at St George's Swimming Baths, Buckingham Pal-
ace Road, at 11 o'clock, p.m. on Friday 13th July, 1928. Please
wear a Bathing Suit and bring a Bath Towel and a Bottle.
Each guest is required to show his invitation on arrival.

Of course I'm going with Stephen. He's had his chum Charles
James design our costumes, which are to be identical—have no
idea what they'll be like, but the rumor is—trousers, blue and
diaphanous, a pink silk vest over whatever else he comes up with.

As it turned out what he came up with was nothing, so it was
trousers and vests over au naturel. Wish you could have seen our
entrance to the party as we stood in the doorway and paused for a
moment to present our identical selves to one and all before stepping forward into the gaping crowd. Wish I had a picture of
Cecil's face—twisted into jealousy as he saw us standing there, so
thin, so tall, so gorgeous, so divine—and what he couldn't stand
was seeing not only one gorgeous or one divine, but two gor-
geouses and two divines—well, you get the picture. Poor thing,
he couldn't come up with a mot, quite something considering his

glib and often accurate bitchiness. "Bathwater Cocktails" were being passed around on silver trays, so who was I to resist (God knows in hindsight wish I had). There were colored lights flickering over the pool and in it flowers floating among enormous inflated horses. Boofy Brendon and Elinor Wylie (?) were horsing around on one of the horses (sorry, Mem), while others horsed around elsewhere in one way or another. Cecil finally got his tongue back and kept after me to exchange costumes with him. Who wanted that? He was most effectively done up as Mistinguett, but was he satisfied? No. He was determined to exchange his getup for my pink vest and blue trousers, no doubt so he could get closer to Stephen, but when he saw I was on to him, he went after Stephen, who took his pink and blue off without a blink and gave it to him—made me mad as hell and I took my costume off and threw it in Stephen's face before I jumped into the pool. I was so angry with him—livid in fact—but once in the water I thought, what the hell, let bygones be bygones, and I spread my arms out and let the magnolia petals bob gently against my skin. Who cared what hullabaloo was going on around me as I floated there? I was almost in a trance when I felt hands sliding up and down my body in a most pleasurable way. Who could it be? I kept my eyes closed as my bosoms were pushed together and gently nibbled through the warm water. But good God—it was none other than Stephen. Naked, his body's oddly shaped, awkward almost (it doesn't fit with his head and the fine molding of his features—so exquisite). It was thrilling to excite him, however, and we wafted our way towards the edge of the pool. But as I said to Stephen's parrot, enough's enough (right, Mem?), and I had no intention of spoiling things by doing IT with him. I pushed him away and swam off, but he caught my ankle and pulled me back—so fast, yanking, pushing me against the steps of the pool. He's much stronger than I would have thought. Oh God, I pause now unable to continue, tears are starting and they'll fall on to you, blurring my ability to tell you about the betrayal— yes—for betrayal is the only word adequate for what happened. Stephen, my twin, my ka or ba (take your pick), my adored mirror image, betrayed me last night in the pool at that ridiculous party. Yes—yes—he pushed his damn ding-dong up inside me and from the back too. Oh, Mem, to think I'd trusted him, trusted that he was the other side of the coin, the missing piece of my jigsaw puzzle—but now I never want to see him again. You understand, don't you? Why I feel betrayed? I keep hoping maybe it didn't happen—but it did, it did—though right now the last thing I remember is suddenly seeing police there. A fight had started and for some reason I was in the middle of it even though it had nothing to do with me—at least I don't think it did. My costume had somehow got back on again (?) and was being torn off, and tufts of someone's hair (Stephen's?) were being held up as trophies. How did I get back to the Connaught—and with whom? But that's not the worst of it—there's no sign in my room anywhere of the pink vest and blue trousers. I've looked everywhere, even under the bed.

*H*ave to be alone for a while. Can't think, can't sleep, can't eat, can't concentrate on anything. Not a word from Stephen.

I've done more research on that ka and ba thing I was so intense about. Seems I got it all wrong, because what the Egyptians are saying is that you have to be dead before the body is transformed into an image of the collective unconscious and, in its aspect of oneness, into the Self—which means that the ka (shadow double) and the ba (spiritual individuality) of the dead person are united with this transfigured body, and together they become an inseparable unity. In a nutshell, you have to *die* to get that shadow double, which turns out to be you all along, because it's inside *yourself* and has nothing to do with meeting someone in the outside world and finding it there. How could I have paid so little attention to what I was reading that I deluded myself by turning it around to suit my own purposes after my meeting with Stephen?

I keep going over and over again a day when Stephen and I were walking along Bond Street looking at the shops and I'd turned to face him—don't think I told you about this but even if I did I've got to go over it again to make sure I remember it right. It was so clear to me then, I turned and looked at him and, without having to touch him, knew quite simply that if I did—I'd be touching myself. At that moment I knew who I really was. And now it's lost—gone. Stephen's like all the other Lonnies, Colins and Desmonds—he's killed the one thing I had to hold on to as I wait in this limbo for Bill. Mem, I'm not like Stephen's Puffins and Babas and Cecils. I'm a serious person trying to make myself worthy of the man I love—Bill. Why is he keeping me waiting so long—for while he does, things keep happening to me (instead of my making things happen), yes—things keep leading me astray, getting me into trouble, making me hate myself even more than I do already. If this keeps on—I'll never be worthy. The S.S. *Franconia* docked yesterday, but he must have been transferred to another ship—he's not on it. Maybe he's heard of my escapades in London—oh God—

Well, Mem, a lot can happen in seven days, n'est-ce pas? Here I am in Paris when only a week ago I lay abed with a splitting headache cursing the ringing doorbell, thinking what fresh hell is this? But instead of hell, it was a basket brimming with rainbow colors of sweet-peas and a crested card from Boofy, the Viscount Brendon. "Dear Little Girl—Have pity on me please for I miss you like the mischief. Put me out of my misery and come with me on a Bon Voyage of heart's desire, for I promise you the moon and the stars." No kidding, that's what it said. He must be a mind reader. I'd been at wit's end thinking up ways to get out of town, so I got myself together as fast as I could (my books take up an entire suitcase heavy as bricks to carry), checked out of the Connaught and off we went. We were late getting to Euston Station, with the express already sliding past the end of the platform, but the station master spotted Boofy and our entourage and had it whisked back again. Then, at Dover, the other passengers were ignored so that we could embark across a special gangway. I'm not pulling your leg and, Mem, believe me, it's the only way to travel. We took the Golden Arrow to Paris and are staying at the permanent suite Boofy keeps at Le Bristol. Oysters and champagne awaited us, muguet and white lilacs all over the place. We're an impressive entourage—Dawson (valet), Stringer (ladies' maid engaged for me) and others (I can't quite make out what these others are up to, but guess time will tell, as they say). Stringer is her last name. Don't know her first. In London ladies' maids and butlers are always called by their last names—formal, you know. Oh—and we have Boofy's Columbia portable gramophone with room in the lid for eight records! yes! The latest thing. So music surrounds us here, there, and everywhere—Josephine Baker and Mistinguett—oh how I become even more alive than I already am when I hear "Pa-ree, c'est u-ne blon-de." Yes, to hear Mistinguett makes me quite blonde myself, dancing around, uncontrollable. I don't have to lift a finger about anything, but I can't get used to Stringer hovering around—emptying my handbag every time I put it down, asking what frock will Miss be wearing next, so she can transfer things into the handbag I'll be carrying with the other frock. She expects to dress me, assisting me with my underwear even, and laying out stockings with the toes tucked inward ready to be slipped on. She made a list of what to declare at the Customs and speaks every foreign language known to man. I told her I'll be o.k. on my own, thank you very much. She wasn't pleased, and keeps herself occupied steaming my dresses, laying out my things on a chair, turning down the bed every night and leaving nightgown, slippers and robe just so. She makes certain my bath is the right temperature with a wood-backed thermometer. O.k., o.k.—it is nice, I must say, to drift down into water warmed just right and not have to think of a thing.

Boofy was crazy to have me in the tub while I was taking a bath getting ready to meet some Barons and Baronesses for dinner. He's turned into a different person—in London he'd been a limpo but in Paris he's a veritable satyr. I tried putting him off until after, but no luck and we ended up on the floor. It's the first time he or anyone gave it to me up my sit-upon, and I hated it. I'd had nothing but a few sips of champagne to relax a little so I'd be in the mood to titillate him with a bit of come hither. But he was more ardent than I expected (most unusual for him) and he chased me into the living room dripping wet (I'd only stepped out of the bath) and threw me over a cushiony chair. My hands were on the floor and my bosoms kept bobbing up and down on the carpet while my sit-upon, which was all he was interested in anyway, presented itself to him over the arm of the chair. In his hand he had some kind of cream as he started touching it and at first it felt good. Then he put his finger up me there and that wasn't bad either. But then he started with his big fat thumb and got crazed and spoiled it all and I told him to stop but he didn't and so I pleaded with him (hoping to get his mind elsewhere)— let's go into the bedroom please, but he would have none of that.

He was determined to have it right then and there. He's big and it really hurt. Now I'm sore and keeping my fingers crossed that he's not going to want it that way again but even if he does, he's not going to get it. I don't have to put up with anything I don't want to, so why is it so hard for me to say No? I'm beginning to realize it was a big mistake to come on this trip, not only for the reason I've mentioned—there are other reasons too, reasons you know well. I'm frightened—AJP's back in my head—haven't dared tell you, but he's here in Paris and he's never never alone—it's always Fou with a girl—a girl who looks like me. Oh God—I never should have come here, should've gone straight back to New York from London. Something's going to happen—

I have to get out of here. Soon as poss. Today, we were supposed to be on the night train to Venice, where one of Boofy's yachts is waiting to take us across the Adriatic and down the Dalmatian coast. Instead, Boofy's decided to stay on in Paris. He changes his mind constantly, and I have no say in the matter.

*W*e're still here, but I haven't caught sight of them in days—could they have died? Yes, that's it. Died and the bodies taken back to Boston on the *Franconia* for burial. Side by side they'll be, in the cold ground for all eternity. But no, Mem—not at all, because soon after having these thoughts I got another shock—yes, I saw him (alone without her) bouncing along the Rue Madeleine. I was in a taxi and from the distance he looked like a perfect ovoid person—Why had I never noticed this before? Then I got even more of shock because it wasn't AJP—it was Boofy. Oh God! Later, back at Le Bristol, when I saw him face to face and up close, it was clear to me that everything about Boofy has an ovoidness that was never apparent in London, not that it would have changed things but—Yes, Boofy's head is bald and smooth, egg-like, and it melts on down into the larger egg of his body, on into perfectly formed ovoid feet. Would his two-tone oxfords suit me? I wonder. Surely they'd fit, his feet are small. But would his shoes make me also appear ovoid? Or would the curvy part of me (I am curvy) counteract the effect? Now I puzzle constantly over this and over his face, so reminiscent of an ostrich egg—a hard-boiled one that's been peeled.

*E*ver since my new perception of Boofy as an Ovoid I've been nervous as a cat. Apparently he's more sensitive than I thought and senses my mood. He's calmed down considerably and today suggested we stroll in the Bois de Boulogne. It was peaceful there and we ended up in a rowboat on Lac Supérieur. His doughy hands clutched the oars like double-jointed flippers but he paddled much too fast and bumped into another boat. I could have screamed. "Be in a good mood, be in a good mood," he kept saying, which made me want to scream more than ever. Then I turned sulky and by the time we got back to the hotel he'd worked himself into a fit and had Dawson and Stringer hopping around fetching things to calm him (ice packs for head, hot water bottles for feet). What's gotten into him? Wasn't he a veritable dove in London? Any day now I'm going to tell him to go sit on a rock and tickle his cock and after that I'll hot-foot it out of here. Yes. Definitely.

*T*o put me in a better mood Boofy took me to a friend's house in Passy. It has a library, a circular room, wood-paneled (oak?)—no windows (to protect the bindings) but celestial light comes from a skylight above. Oh what a room, Mem. There was the sound of rain above, and surrounding me from floor to ceiling nothing but books with their scent of leather. The ladder made a whirring sound on the parquet as I positioned it to climb up and reach a book high above. In the center of the room a table covered with faded cloth and around the bottom of the damask, gold tassels brushing the floor. Nothing else in the room but that and two chairs—Gothic, with pillows—faded damask too and golden fringe. Boofy and his friend left me alone there for hours, and my spirit was restored. There were magazines on one of the shelves—interesting, especially one with an article by Carl Jung. And then I came upon a book on Buddha which intrigued me so much that Boofy's friend gave it to me. Now, I'm back at the hotel devouring it, making myself read s-l-o-w-l-y. It's about the Self, which as you know I desperately seek, but I'm having difficulty trying to make sense of this concept as presented by the

Buddha. Yes, as we've often said, Mem, it's what comes after that *but* in a sentence that reveals the truth of the matter—and I'm about ready to give up, go on to something else, eagerness drives me—can't stop myself from reading too fast (habit of mine)— too fast to absorb what it is I'm reading. But this time I'm determined to press on or rather press back, catch the lingo and when I do the concept will be made clear to me. Let me try to make sense of it by explaining some of it to you. Right now I've come to a part about a wordless sermon Buddha is said to have given, during which he presented a yellow flower to his disciples. No one understood him except this one pupil Kasyapa, who responded with a knowing smile. Ah, how well we know what is meant by those knowing smiles, eh Mem, even if we can't make out the rest of the damn thing. Anyway, there's this yellow flower used as a symbol for the man who, in the midst of a guilty, elusive, entangled life, nevertheless "lives in God," in the eternal light and life of Buddha . . . oh, I certainly understand being in the midst of a "guilty, elusive, entangled" life, but for god's sake, help me to understand the rest of it. Of course the problem is that I can't believe in God to begin with. If only I could believe in Him *or* Buddha—then no matter how stuck I am in my guilty, elusive, entangled life, I'd have a chance to live in one god or another and so expiate my sin. Isn't that it in a nutshell, Mem? But to absorb what's behind the Buddha's wordless sermon I must meditate and make every effort to understand it fully. Actually, forget about the fully—I'd be happy with even a little (understanding). Who the hell is this Kasyapa anyway? I'm getting fed up. Will have to do more research. Yes. Absolutely.

Clive Brook is playing in *Forgotten Faces* at the cinema on the Champs-Elysées and I insisted Boofy take me. Oh God, help me, Mem, my mania for Clive is returning, but on second thought it's only because he reminds me more than ever of Bill. His manner, his bearing, the way he lights a cigarette (so intimate) with his head bent over, the match flaring for a moment, his eyes gleam as he looks into mine. And then he turns and even the back of his neck reminds me of Bill and my heart twists itself into a terrible twist like a wet rag pulled tight by mad dogs in a tug of war. It's knotted, you see (the rag, I mean)—and my heart's in the middle and it hurts, Mem, oh how it hurts. Soon it will go pop! and there'll be nothing left of me. When we came out of the cinema, I couldn't stand to look at the ovoid, much less walk by his side, and I kept walking fast and faster so that he could hardly keep up with me. Who is he anyway? Who am I? And what the hell am I doing here?

Oh how I pine. Yes, pine like the pine in those pillows they used to sell in the General Store on Vinalhaven Island. I see it before me—a burlap pillow stuffed with pine needles, painted by hand with a drawing of a tree and it says—

Spruce up and come
I ball some

When I first saw those pillows I had no idea what the words really meant. Alas, now I do (only too well) so why do they leap into my mind in this way—so contrary to my mood? It's because they still hold for me the meaning they had when I first saw them. I really did think they meant "hasten, hasten, come to me because I miss you so much, oh how I pine and can't stop crying." That was the sentiment I thought had been shortened to fit on the pillow and rhyme as well. It's only now, grown-up, that the vulgar reality of the meaning sinks into my heart with a horrible thud. I can't stop tears from pouring down onto you, Mem. (Luckily we're alone.) How I long once again to be as I was. And I shall be I know, once Bill and I are together. Until then I am innocent in my tiny heart truly truly—you know that, don't you? Wish to God I had one of those stupid pillows with me right now. Yes, filled with pine needles—so fragrant, soothing. I could breathe deep—in and out and yes, yes, soon, yes, soon—I'd be asleep and then everything would be all right.

Now it's Boofy in a bad mood—says I don't pay enough attention to him and that I'm insensitive to his feelings. Look, I told him, I'm so sensitive I don't even need an egg timer to boil an egg—Get it? Of course he didn't and anyway it's only sometimes true—they usually end up hard boiled—like me (ha ha). Anyway, who cares, we're all but little grains of sand on the beach of time, n'est-ce pas?

. . .

This weird thing happened—yeah, a few days ago and I can't get it out of my mind. I've been putting off telling you about it, but now is as good a time as any. I'd taken a couple of hours off from Boofy to wander around the city, planning to end up in Montmartre in the Basilique du Sacré-Coeur. Light a candle for Bill—Bill—do something about Bill—anyway, light a candle. But instead, I found myself on a side street going nowhere in particular. There was not another soul in sight and I meandered on relieved at not having to pretend about anything or be somebody or something I'm not. Suddenly, behind me, I heard this sound— a shuffling shuffling. I slid my eyes sideways to see what it was, but got too scared and hurried on. The shuffling sound did too, and with it, another sound came at me like a hook and got hold of me, a hissing in German, "Grüss Gott, Grüss Gott"—and with the hissing, the sound of a lame foot dragging over the cobblestones. I hurried on but it kept after me until I was alone and it was midnight instead of morning and I dodged into an alleyway running running until I came upon a courtyard. There was no place to go from there, no way of getting out, except to go back the way I'd come—yes, I was in a cul-de-sac with houses around me, but the windows were closed except for one, high up. Curtains billowed in and out even though there was no breeze, for the air was sultry—heavy—pressing down upon the heart as it does before a summer rain. In and out, the curtains drifted in the breezeless silence, and sitting in the window was a woman with her back to me. Her hair rested on her head like a white serpent and in the serpent's mouth, something red—a poppy? No. Blood. I called up to her—Grüss Gott, but she didn't turn around or move. Was she a wax dummy? I ran back into the street even though I was more scared of what was out there than what was where I'd come from in the courtyard, if you know what I mean. The street was empty, though, and I was free, free as a bird is free, free to hurry on. But it was a joke, because behind me again came the lame shuffling sound and "Grüss Gott, Grüss Gott," and I knew it had been there all the time waiting. I kept falling as I ran on fast, until around a corner I stumbled to find myself on the hill of Montmartre with the Eiffel Tower, Notre-Dame and the Seine spread out far below, and I screamed and ran to meet them—Isn't it all too silly—silly old whatever it was—most of all silly old me to get the shiver-shakes spooking around like that and now I've told you, maybe it didn't happen, perhaps it was all a dream.

I'm glad I was able to tell you about that day. I thought for a while I couldn't. I may be leaving Paris soon, very soon, sooner than even you think, Mem, and when I leave a place my mind becomes an empty house about certain things, yes, vacated as if no one lived there or ever had. That's one of the reasons I keep talking to you, for there are some things I remember nothing about unless I tell you about them. A face passed in the street I might remember because it reminds me of someone, but this happens only sometimes, and—later, yes, I may remember it much later, but then again I may not. Anyway, I don't want to think anymore, not right now anyway.

*I*f I knew for sure Bill was in New York I'd hop on a ship and go back in a sec. I keep writing to the *Franconia* but he doesn't answer. I keep writing Stephen too, in London (surely he's there?), but someone is keeping my letters from him. What a fool I was to take off like that—I should have stayed on in London (never once saw the girl or AJP on any street or anywhere while I was there), should have tried to get back one way or another with Stephen, bided my time along those lines until I heard from Bill. Of course, at first all Stephen's chums were enthralled by the resemblance he and I have to each other (how could they not?) but soon jealousy took hold and they were conniving to come between us. Still, I was perfectly capable of rising above their petty intrigues and none of it would have mattered if I hadn't gone to that damn party at the St. George's Swimming Baths. That was our Waterloo, ha ha, but what happened that night in the pool would probably have happened sooner or later anyway so why am I making such a big thing of it? Speak up, Mem. The more I talk to you about it the more I'm convinced I'd better try to get Stephen back. Go to London as soon as poss., right now in fact. Face to face he won't be able to resist me. Why hasn't he answered my letters? I've even sent some to the Lady Pamela's house in Cap Ferrat on the chance he's visiting his Mum there. Oh to hell with it. By this time next week I'll be somewhere, if not London—

Bangkok. Why not? Might run into Bill there. Wherever, I'll be out of here—out of France—I swear it.

*L*ordy knows I hate farewells and am fresh out of ways to go through another one, which must be why I'm lingering on here in Paris, freezing—not with the cold, silly, but with lack of energy to get the hell out of here. Nothing can freeze if it's moving, can it?—so move—keep moving. Get on a train, stay on the track to get on a boat, move, move. One of these days I'll pack up and leave—move—go—disappear. They'll be sorry. Yeah, get on a train, sooner than yesterday.

*M*y reservation is made on the *Carpathia*. A secret one, under the name—Mrs. George Jameson-Carr. Don't you thrill, Mem, as you gaze at the ticket?

I fervently pray that at the hour of my departure the propitious moment presents itself so that I'll not run into Boofy and can evaporate into thin air without a fuss. My farewell note to him is about to be put to paper—something along the lines, Thanks for everything—you've been more than swell and I'm sorry we won't see the New Year in together, but duty calls and I must hasten home. I do have a home, you know, yes, a home—so, mon cher, it's goodbye, toodle-oo, adieu—in no matter what language, you get the gist of what I'm trying to convey, sensitive egg that you are (I really do mean it, Mem—au fond he *is* a good egg) so a thousand million mercis. No, that's too flippant—I'll do better— right now I can't sort my thoughts out.

*Y*es, Mrs. George Jameson-Carr has passage on the Cunard Line. Mrs. George Jameson-Carr has booked passage on the *Carpathia* of the Cunard Line. Mrs. George Jameson-Carr travels only on the Cunard Line as her husband Dr. George Jameson-Carr is chief surgeon on the Cunard Line's *Franconia*. The day approaches. Mrs. George Jameson-Carr is ready. Dr. Jameson-Carr awaits Mrs. Jameson-Carr's arrival and is ready. Congocita awaits

Mrs. Jameson-Carr as do Mamacita, Papacita and Tookacita not to mention countless other citas who are eager to welcome Mrs. George Jameson-Carr back to her native land. Ah yes, sweet Mem, the New Year will be the best one for us ever. You know how much I love you, don't you?

1929

*H*ere I am on the *Carpathia* hardly able to speak—feel as if I've been sipping champagne since New Year's Eve, even tho' I haven't had a drop and it's three days into 1929. Yes, at last here we are speeding towards Bill. Actually, my heart's speeding far faster than the ship, which is too slow for me. My head is hot, fevered as it races ahead, a motor out of control. I've tried taking deep breaths, but still can't get my breath.

*H*ave calmed down a bit. I'm sitting alone with you in the lounge looking directly out over the ocean. The string orchestra's playing Lehár medleys . . . I ask for another pot of tea while I ponder whether to have a cucumber sandwich or another slice of the Dundee cake—ah, yes, it's now that feelings from who knows where overcome me, float into me with the music, uninvited, as I settle back into the chair and the chair settles into me and I know once and for all that my best content would be to stay here forever . . . Why can't I live on a ship as I would on an island? Oh! to have this the home where I reside, never again search for another. Yes, to be at peace and free of pain—you could always reach me care of the S.S. Something or Other, but how stupid of me, Mem, for you'd be with me, of course.

*I*f only I could let what's inside out, find the way to do this. But no matter what I do or where I go, just when I think I have, it turns out to be a trick, and there I am—just as I'm getting out I'm getting further in. And what, you may ask, Mem, is this something inside that I want to let out? Perhaps you can tell me, if you'd only break your silence and speak up. Does it have something to do with that hole inside that I can't seem to fill? But no, because that would mean there was something *in* the hole to *let* out. And I'm not sure there is—sometimes I fear the hole is empty, and as much as I want to let what's inside out how can I do that if there's nothing there?

I wear no maquillage. I encourage no advances. I am veiled. I am as unattainable as the two nuns in the cabin next to mine. I keep to myself. The nuns play shuffleboard or walk side by side around the decks. We keep running across each other as we pass through the Palladian Lounge or more often on the Boat Deck under the glass dome atop the main staircase. Then this afternoon, when I was having my solitary early tea in the Winter Garden, in they came and sat at the next table.

*N*othing is demanded of me, nothing expected. I don't even take time out to read. I walk on deck, around and around, breathing deep breaths of the sea air to cleanse myself, for there's not much time left—I must be cleansed by the time we land. Yes, I must have answers to all the things that mix my head up. I must be clear as crystal, for soon I'll be seeing Bill.

*E*ach day I've been diligent in my task. Long hours circling the deck faster and faster, until I am about to drop from exhaustion—but I make myself keep moving, testing to see if my will can overcome body's fatigue, forcing will over body's endurance and in so doing I have come to realize that the deep breaths I take give me energy, propel me on. My shallow breathing in the past may be what's held me back. Yes, I haven't realized until now how little breath my body receives. That must be what's held me back. Yes, definitely.

*Y*ou at the Ritz—in Paris—standing naked in the bathroom—close to the basin—raising himself on tippy-toes so his ding-dong hangs over it—he turns the taps, tests the temperature . . . soaps his ding-dong, tenderly. How it annoys me. Why don't you use the bidet, it's right next to the basin—that's what a bidet's for, isn't it? He pays no attention.

The nuns—Sister Annunciata and Sister Paul (I think that's their names)—are sensitive to my reserve until last night, when they saw me entering my cabin as they were entering theirs next door. Was I crying? Anyway—they came to me, into my cabin. I clung to one of them (which?), not knowing who held me. I cried and cried, their arms around me; but then I came back from where I'd been to find myself ashamed and embarrassed that they'd seen me so. I told them to please leave me alone and fell into a deep sleep. Today they act differently towards me—as if they have the right not only to help me, but to be my savior. I'm furious at myself for getting in this spot, sick of having to fend off their efforts with politeness. They've followed close to me all day. I gave them the slip but at tea time there they were coming into the Winter Garden looking for me. They sat down at my table as if invited. I lost my wits and told them flat out I was a Jewish athe- ist, so it would be impossible for me to convert to Catholicism even if I wanted to. I jumped up, leaving my tea, ran out and left them sitting there, mouths agape.

Another day like this and the Sisters Annunciata and Paul will send me round the bend, off the wall, off the ship, off the track, into the sea. Good idea, why not? But I feel so guilty—how warm and sweet they are, truly concerned about me. Maybe their idea is a good idea. Maybe better than any I've had in a long time. It recalls my long-ago passion to become a nun. I was obsessed with it then—so why not now? Perhaps the time has come—timing is everything, n'est-ce pas? But Dominican, I will still settle for nothing less. Sister Starr—how does that sound to you?

Quite by chance overheard two men talking as they leaned against the rail looking out to sea—Stephen's mother, the Lady Pamela, is dead. She died while Stephen was touring Italy and now he's living at Wilsford Manor with Siegfried Sassoon. They said Stephen has tuberculosis, Mem. I loved him. I did. Oh God, Mem—but maybe none of it's true.

I apologized to the Sisters for my rude outburst. Still my mind's not made up. Instead of Dominicans perhaps I should be consulting this Carl Jung who's popped into the scheme of things again. When I left, everyone in Paris was talking about him and Sigmund Freud. Boofy thinks they're both crazy and make trouble in the world instead of making it better. But what does he know? Yes, something tells me I should have consulted Carl Jung. There certainly was no one like him among those apes at Channing. Should I be on my way to visit him in—Lucerne? (No, that's where Joyce is.) Basel maybe—anyway somewhere in Switzerland. Instead, here I am on the S.S. *Carpathia* going elsewhere.

*W*e land tomorrow. I forgo the Ship's Ball to be with you, Mem, as I see in my mind's eye that first sight of the Lady in the harbor. She'll be signaling that they'll be there to meet me—my little family and—and—dare I press on—I? Well—you know who. Perhaps—oh Mem, dare we hope? My pen fails and I cannot continue. Until tomorrow—must sleep, to look my best.

*I*t's taken me more than a while to gather my thoughts together—so many crowding in, or crowding out—but I'll try. First: The day we landed it was an eternity waiting at Customs under the big letter F in the Shed (why is the N.Y. Customs called the Shed when it's big as a football stadium?), for my heart was pounding and I was screaming inside Bill Bill Bill, hurry up, Customs, hurry up so I can get to Bill Bill Bill, but it was slow slow slow and cold cold cold standing on the cement floor and I sat on my streamer trunk accepting sips from a flask passed around by a man next to me. A lap robe was put over my shoulders from another who said he'd kept it out for just such a purpose. I smiled but didn't answer. Would Bill be with Ma and Stanley or separated by the crowds? I had my list ready to declare and hadn't left out a thing so why did I feel guilty?—gowns, handbags, silver fox jacket Boofy gave me—there they all were on the list. (Inadvertently forgot the sapphire brooch he got me at

Boucheron in Paris—only thought of it now.) Finally my turn came around to "open up." I'm a neat packer and into the oaf's hands went the tissue paper from my luggage—like two puppies playing with newspapers in a kennel—but I didn't mind, all I wanted was to have it over with so I could—and—oh, Mem—there they were—standing in the cold—waiting for me—my little mother, Stanley, Tooka and Congo (wearing a red and black sweater). I was so happy to see them. But no Bill. Since he couldn't be there, I kept expecting one of them to give me a letter. But there was no mention of him. Maybe, there would be a letter waiting for me, a letter with flowers to welcome me at home. For surely there was a good reason why he wasn't there to meet the ship. But then I couldn't stand it and asked about him. No—no news. They seemed surprised I'd asked. It was a setback—more than even you could know, Mem. But if *he* wasn't there to meet me, my family was and that counts for everything, so please don't think I'm complaining because I'm not. On the way home in the taxi I held Congo on my lap and it made me feel close to Bill, yes, sometimes I feel Bill near, so close we breathe together and that's how it was with Congo sitting in my lap as the taxi drove through the slushy streets on the way home but not to Grove—it was to St. Luke's Place. They'd moved while I was away. And oh, Mem, it's v. fine, yes it is. And everything else will be v. fine too from now on, now that we have this new home on the 2nd floor of a brownstone at Number 12. The houses on our street face south to James Walker Park designed by Stanford White. The park has walks with benches to sit under trees, and a bandstand for concerts in summer. Mayor and Mrs. Walker live at #6, a few houses down from us and it makes Ma somewhat conceited. And across the street right next to the entrance to the park there's a branch of the Public Library, so I can walk across the street, enter and find hundreds of friends waiting for me, silent though they may be. But Mem, the best friend we have was waiting for us when I walked in the door—Daddy's chest. There it was, locked safe and sound under my bed. So that's about it, Mem, as far as how we returned to our native land. Do not think I have lost heart. I am determined to have fortitude and patience so I can dwell in the Valleys of Faith and Virtue until Bill shows up, for he will, I know. All we have to do is wait.

*L*ast night—sobbing dream—pillow wet—can't remember.

I wasn't able to tell you about it until now but I can't keep it inside any longer. That first day home there was no letter or flowers or anything from Bill. All the way from the dock in the taxi I'd been thinking something might have come while they were at the dock to meet me, but if it did who would be there to receive it? Then when there wasn't anything that's what I kept telling myself had happened. I got myself in a stew over that, but held fast to our fickle friends *patience* and *waiting,* for surely something had happened to delay our plans and that would be explained when Bill and I were reunited. Anyway that's what I kept telling myself until now, but I can't hold it in any longer—Mem, I'm worried and frightened. It does seem odd, doesn't it. That we've heard nothing from him. Something must have happened. Something terrible. But what?

I'm trying to hold on by preoccupying myself—arranging books I found in Europe on the shelves, getting them acquainted with my old friends who were already waiting for me. It's preoccupying, too, getting used to sharing a room with baby sister again because she's dropped out of school (has plans she's not telling?)! Yes, that's what I'm doing even tho' it's only temporary until Bill shows up, because then I'll be moving out and into a real home—the home of Dr. and Mrs. George Jameson-Carr. This time sister and I each have our own beds (no bunks) and they face a window looking out over the park, which right now is lacy with frost of winter. I can also divert my thoughts by telling you about our large living room, which has the same view, and a marble fireplace, which Stanley keeps lit—so cozy. And our antique furniture, which fits in tho' a little crowded. Stanley and Ma's room is in the back (fireplace too). All the rooms have high ceilings with carved moldings, parquet floors—the only hitch is that to get to the bathroom and kitchen we have to go through Ma and Stanley's room. Sounds inconvenient, eh Mem? And it is. Still, other things more than make up for it—So despite the constant worry that Bill won't know where to find me since we've moved, I'm more than glad to be back in New York and was pleased indeed when the ship landed to see their funny faces looking for me on the pier—malgré tout. Yes, I have a lot to be grateful for. And I am. So I'm all right. Don't worry.

*N*o interest in seeing the old crowd and have stayed away from letting them even know I'm back. Haven't gone out at all. Keep arranging and rearranging my books (never did return *Salomé*). I try to read but can't concentrate. Need time to make my plans and in any event I'll no doubt hear from Bill before I need plan or do anything. He's to arrive any day now.

*O*h Mem. I wait and wait for a word from Bill, but find only signs and portents—from a bird perhaps who trills his name—but how can a bird trill Bill—well, a bird has a bill. Oh God—no—has it come to this?

*K*eep calling the Cunard Line but no luck—keep being referred to different departments and none of them have any info. regarding a Dr. George Jameson-Carr.

*S*aw May Lark. I'm in shock. She heard a rumor he's in Boston practically engaged to one of those beefy-legged girls. I had to drag it out of her—then when she saw how upset I was, she tried to calm me, saying it's only ridiculous gossip. I'm going to Boston. I must track this "ridiculous gossip" to the source. May Lark says that's not a good idea and wants me to go out with her tonight to Tonys on West 52nd St. The best new spot in town where all the literary and theatre people go and she can't wait to introduce me to tall, dark and handsome Tony Soma, the owner, who stands on his head like a Yogi while singing Puccini. He's introduced sometimes as Admiral Balbo, who's some fascist Italian aviator. What makes her think I'd even look at him? Oh, I was put out. Can't she see I'm veiled? A nun. Yes, definitely. And shall be so until I see Bill. Then look out, world. Sparks will fly.

*M*y plans are made. Ma and Stanley think I'm going with May Lark to Connecticut to visit friends she went to school with. When are you going? they ask. I smiled a lot and said today. Have a good time, Ma said.

I took off for Boston, but on the way to the station started shaking and told the driver to take me to the bus terminal. I got on the first bus I saw and ended up in Naples, Florida, which is where I am now. Don't worry, I'll be all right. Give me a little time to breathe in and out.

I feel better. My feet aren't cold anymore. It's hot even though it's March and was windy and cold when I left New York. On the bus coming here I sat next to a man who looked like AJP only he wasn't bald. He looked at the silver fox I was wearing and said, "You won't need that where we're going." It gave me a fright—that "we" along with his resemblance to Boofy—I mean AJP. He was the reason I hadn't gone to Boston as planned—He was why, in the taxi, I'd gotten scared, terrified if you really want to know, afraid I might run into him in Boston and if so my plans to find Bill would be thwarted. He'd see to that—make me do something I didn't want to do. Such as what?—oh shut up I can't think. Anyway, when the man on the bus said that to me I took the silver fox off and put it on my lap. I need time to think what to do, for if Bill is in Boston I'm further away from him here in Naples than I was in New York—I need time to gather my wits about me and make new plans.

*L*et's see, where was I—oh yes, it's hot here and there are houses painted the colors of Jordan almonds and I'm in a pink one right on a yellow beach. The house belongs to the man I sat next to on the bus, only he's not like AJP—no—how could I have been so fooled by first impressions? No, he's not like Fou at all—at least I don't think so—time will tell. Oh—and the roads are covered with shells instead of gravel and there are sandpipers on the beach. Yes, it's nice here, Mem, quiet and peaceful.

I sent Ma and Stanley a Western Union telling them May Lark and I had changed plans at the last minute and were on a beach and living in a pink house so not to worry. It was more than 10 words but what the hell—she'll like that. Ma loves pink. I covered myself by sending another telegram to May Lark telling her that if she ran into any of them (Tooka especially) to say she'd come back but I'd stayed on.

*L*ast night another sobbing dream. But when I woke—pillow dry.

*T*his man I'm staying with in the pink house is called Solly Winthrop. I asked him if he had anything to do with the Winthrop Hotel in London. Nope, he said. He doesn't talk much, which suits me fine. Even tho' I think about Bill, my decision is to make no decision so that's a decision, isn't it? I don't believe for one minute Bill's really in Boston, so it's as well I'm here in Naples instead of there.

*S*olly grills lobsters on the beach every night for our dinner. All the time he plays a record of Harry Richman singing "My Blue Heaven"—*A turn to the right, a little white light—will lead me to my blue heaven—a smiling face, a fireplace, a cozy room—a little nest just nestled where the roses bloom—just Molly and me and baby makes three will lead me to my blue heaven*—over and over again, but I don't mind. He doesn't seem to have any friends, which I don't mind either. Mentioned last night that he caught a 70-lb. amberjack but it was a long time ago. He didn't go into detail.

I really like his lime green Opel Reinette car and sometimes he drives me towards Jacksonville to see the sights—swampy swamps, palm forests and pelicans. I really like those pelicans. There's an island covered with pure white ones near Cabbage Key, wherever that is, but so far we haven't gone there. Oh well, no rush is there—no rush about anything. There were puffins on Vinalhaven Island, remember?—but they have nothing to do with pelicans and of course they weren't all white—

*S*olly lets me do whatever I want, which is to sleep when I'm not making my plans and talking to you. He never reads a book and I feel safe leaving you out and around anywhere. It's nice not to have to hide you, Mem, or worry someone's going to find you and take away the best friend I have.

I bought a bathing suit and two cotton dresses, which will be plenty enough for me. They're white. I haven't unpacked my suitcase. Why bother, as all the things in it were for windy cold Boston. Solly still hasn't asked me my name, calls me "kiddo."

*C*onversations from long ago drift in and out of my head. Francis Hamlin in particular. I'd cornered him at some party and couldn't stop talking about Bill and like a fool asked him if Bill had said anything about me. At that—in a rather pompous way—he said, "George Jameson-Carr is a real humanitarian, he's fond of you, I know, but more than anything he wants to help people, you can trust him, Starr, he's a fine doctor." Fine doctor. What the hell does that mean? Well, it's not hard to figure out, is it, Mem? and I told him off—I don't need help, Francis—what I need is George, not as a doctor but to stand by his side as his one and only true love. Of course I didn't actually say that. All I did say was, Why are you telling me this, did George put you up to it? "Oh no," he protested, "but you're a nice girl and I'd hate to see you get hurt—our friend George by now is a confirmed bachelor—44, you know—and dedicated to his work, which demands that he travel so much he really is in no position to have a home and family." This made me shaky at the time, shaky to say the least, and I put it out of my mind until now, when of course it makes me even shakier, spelling it out to you like this. Of course at the time I simply laughed and told Francis how little he knew me if he thought I could be setting my cap for the likes of Dr. Jameson-Carr, fine humanitarian tho' he may be, because I had other plans for myself, so please forget I brought up George's name and thanks so much for your concern but it's none of your business anyway. My face stings as I go over it—slapped—and my body trembles, the chill settling over me before the fever starts.

Would that I could lie naked in a cool stream, hold on to a rock, let the sun shine on my body, shine on my naked face—yes, hold on to the rock all day and through the night while the water rushed over me, through me, taking away the knowing that another dawn will come as this one has, and that I'll wake once more to face the void within, so vast, deep—so full of blood that flows, but never empties, drawing breath that never fills.

One day flows into the next. No one but you understands why I stay on here in this pink house on the beach with Silent Solly. At least I hope you understand because I don't. No, I don't know why except that it's easy and there's nothing to do but eat and sleep. The beach and the sea outside our door never go away—they're always there. We can depend on that, eh Mem? Anyway, it's all temporary—I'll let both go when Bill shows up.

I keep mentioning the pure white pelicans but he shrugs his shoulders. Maybe I'll go there alone without him—get on a bus—go to Corkscrew Camp Wildlife Sanctuary—that's where they are—yes, I'm v. interested in getting to that island covered with pure white pelicans. Who knows, they might think I'm one of them.

It's early morning and Solly's still asleep. There's not a soul on the beach except you and me and this seashell I hold in my left hand as I lie stretched out on the white sand talking to you. It's smooth as satin, empty and clean inside. A white butterfly just flew by and lit for a moment beside me. Now it's gone.

I'm on a bus going back to New York because Solly took me driving and it started getting dark and when it did something about him reminded me of AJP so I made him take me back to the pink house. I gotta go back to New York, I told him. Okey-doke, he said, and I packed fast. He drove me to the bus station. So long, kiddo, he said. So long, I said. By that time he'd stopped looking like Fou, but it was too late. The bus was moving away.

*W*hen I walked in back home the whole damn place smelled of Chypre. Ma'd dropped her perfume bottle on the bathroom floor—or so she said. Otherwise, everything was the same as when I left. Ma not v. pleased with my suntan—"Haven't I told you, Favorita—stay out of the sun—you never listen to me."

*N*o one's heard anything about Bill so May Lark must have been right—it was a ridiculous rumor, gossip, hateful gossip. But where the hell is he??

*W*ho is this Solly Winthrop?" Ma's curious. Just a friend I met on the bus. "Met on a bus!" she said. "This whole trip you've been on is beyond me—!?" I told her he has a lime green Opel Reinette and lives in a pink house (she'd forgotten the telegram) and that seemed to satisfy her, so his name hasn't come up again. No—nothing much has changed around here even tho' I feel we've been away for years instead of—how long? I do lose track of time. All I want to keep doing is to be able to breathe in and out—in and out until Bill shows up.

*W*hat do you think of this idea? Perhaps I really don't want to see Bill, which is the reason I haven't—yes, that's it—I don't want to find him. I want *him* to find *me.* Search me out till death do us part. As I said, keep breathing moment to moment—in and out—in and out—must keep reminding myself, otherwise I forget.

· · ·

THE MEMORY BOOK OF STARR FAITHFULL

Darling Mem, I am *reborn.* All has been made clear by dear darling Francis Hamlin who's back in town and told me why I haven't heard from Bill—Bill's mother is dying in Liverpool and he's with her so how could he possibly have time to think of anything else? I told Francis I'd be on the next boat to Liverpool, but he said that wasn't a good idea. Best stay here until I hear from him. Should I heed this advice or heed my heart and pay no attention to well-meaning friends? Oh, I'm torn this way and that—what shall I do?

The Church of St. Luke in the Fields on Hudson Street is just around the corner from us. Right next to it is a garden and a tree that reminds me of the one in our yard on Davis Street in Evanston. I like to go and sit under the tree in that garden and not have to think or do anything at all. By the church there's a stone with the date 1882 and poem—

> *Friend this village church*
> *open stands for thee,*
> *that thou might enter*
> *think kneel and pray,*
> *Remember hence thou art*
> *what must be,*
> *Thine end remember us*
> *and go thy way.*

These words are to be my talisman from now on. *Remember hence thou art what must be*—I say them as prayer, for it is carved in stone and gives me hope. This is a message to me that Bill and I *will* be together. Wait. Be patient.

Today for the first time I went inside the church. Often I've stood outside picturing in my mind's eye Bill and me coming down the steps . . . yes, so vivid, how it will happen and the way our wedding day will be. Now that I've been inside I'm more certain than ever that it's only a matter of time before Bill and I will be standing there at that altar . . . I holding a bouquet of white sweetheart roses and Queen Anne's lace, my dress white and pure as I am truly so in my heart, yes, you know I am, tho' sometimes (too often) I stumble and fall. And, oh Mem, how true and pure is the interior of the Church of Saint Luke in the Fields. I dipped my fingers in the marble font, crossed myself and sat down in the last pew in the back, on the right. How strong and simple everything is there. The white walls and arched windows, the altar framed with carvings of wood. I was happy alone there, but then I saw I wasn't alone, someone was kneeling in the front pew. She was kneeling, praying, giving herself to God in a way I've never been able to do, but it was so strange, Mem, because from the back she looked like me and I thought of Evanston—and singing in church—*Rock of ages cleft for me, let me hide myself in Thee*—Yes, carried away and out of myself merging—into some great thing, but then the music was over—the happiness vanished and it never came back. Who is God anyway? Nobody agrees, so how can anybody know? Maybe it's only someone in a story like Elsie Dinsmore who can be unwavering and live according to their beliefs—not like Ma and Daddy who would go to church but come home hating and doing terrible things to each other. I can't give myself to a faith people say they believe in but by their actions prove a lie. What isn't a lie is my faith in Bill, so that must mean that the only God I believe in is a man. I can only admit this to you. You'll understand and won't call me a wicked evil person. I keep thinking about that girl in church, when she got up and came up the aisle I got a good look at her and she didn't look anything like me. No, nothing like me at all.

*A*s you see, I'm staying home every night, taking Francis's advice, and practicing not to be my usual impetuous impulsive self, but gathering myself calmly together, serene as I breathe in and out so that I shall be a perfect person when Bill returns from Liverpool. For he will, sooner or later.

*G*ot restless—fevered with sooner or later, the waiting strain of it, and what the hell, I've started going out again—every night, I have to admit. Oh dear. You see, as I kept trying so hard to make myself into this perfect person things kept going around again and again in my head, barrel-organ music with Ma's voice weaving in and out, saying things I couldn't quite make out. Sometimes, Daddy's voice too, saying "Oh Hel, shut up, Hel, oh shut up, it's too late for that." I try to think clearly and if only Tucker'd shut up I could, but then I start screaming at her and she screams back and then Stanley says, Take it easy, Bambi— and I want to hit him too, but then he gives me a martini in one of those pretty glasses with a red enamel rooster on it (oh yes, the glass is important) and I calm down, sip, forget, close my eyes and loll in the tub ruminating about what fun it would be to go out instead of tormenting myself over Bill. And what shall I wear if I do go out? How will I look? And who might turn up?—who knows, it might even be Bill back suddenly, unexpectedly. He'd be the one finding me this time and when he does he'll understand—he'll love me as I love him and my life will change into something thrilling and wonderful. I'll be stripped clean—newborn, starting over from the beginning, as if AJP isn't somewhere in the world breathing in and out reminding me. Always.

Stanley doesn't want us to drink anything but the stuff he makes. He says what's in the speakies is still the same old reformed carbolic acid poison as it always was—no, nothing changed while I was away. Well, Stanley knows what he's talking about because he used to be a chemist. I always carry the flask he gave me, filled with the "healthy" (ha ha) stuff he makes. It's the Tiffany silver one with a star engraved on each side. Tooka took it upon herself to use my silver while I was in Europe. I had my leather-covered one for traveling. Some nerve. Anyway, after a rumpus I got it back but Stanley's had to promise her one from Tiffany with a T engraved on it—T for Tucker. Usually I come back with mine still full, but it's nice to know I have "healthy" handy, just in case. Stanley and Ma worry about me. Yes, they do.

Too many late last nights. It's 3:30 now (afternoon). Drink doesn't stay in me after 4 so soon the weight and pressure will lift, the nausea go—I'll slab Pond's over last night's makeup, nothing better to sluff off the old skin. Then I'll scrub my teeth to get the peanut butter off, but will I ever be able to get the peanut butter off my tongue—it's white peanut butter—ugh! Maybe I should stop talking to you, Mem. Close you up and never talk about anything again. Would that make it go away, ease, erase it all? I got up and looked at myself in the mirror just now but couldn't recognize the face. Who do those velvety eyes, that delicate turn of head and winsome smile belong to? Not me, for I am fat and ugly. How curious no one's found out yet, so who was that in the mirror looking back at me? And my feet—what's become of them?—I can't see them when I look down, but they must be there, for God they hurt from dancing. Ma and Stanley are in the living room playing Bezique. The radio is on. I can hear laughing. Tucker? Who else?

What to do, what to do. This waiting finally wears me down. Not that I'm complaining, because I'm not. The more time goes by the sooner it will be to the time when Bill gets back. That's the way I look at it. I just hope to God he doesn't hear vicious, malicious gossip about me that might be circulating among the speakies. People invent things about everybody. I hear gossip all the time about May Lark and know for a fact none of it is true.

I wonder about the elm in the yard outside our old house on Davis Street in Evanston. And the house—people must be living there, but who? I bet there's someone in my old room right now, biting her nails no doubt down to the quick, or maybe buffing them to a pearly sheen. Or has the house burnt down, with nothing left where the elm was—nothing but a big black hole. But my garden on Hudson Street is still here and so is the tree. I know because I'm sitting under it right now. It's v. early morning. I got home late last night, so late it was too late to sleep. I opened the door to my bedroom, but dawn was already there with that old familiar light that isn't light at all, but fog. Yes, fog coming in from the sea, drifting through the open window over my empty bed, over Tucker in the bed next to mine, lying there like a bag of cement, weakly snoring. I took you and turned away, ran out of the house back onto the street and around the corner to sit under my tree. No one knows I'm here. No one can find me. I like that. And as I sit here I feel that what we're living in, you and I, is a dream—Mamacita and Daddy, Stanley and Tooka, are all part of a dream we'll wake up from, and when we do we'll find ourselves in the real world and I'll understand everything—understand the nightmare part of the dream—AJP and what happened. And Bill—I'll understand that too, understand why he doesn't love me. What a relief to tell you this. I couldn't find the words until now, couldn't have found them unless I was here in my garden. Soon, alas, too soon, I'll get distracted. People will start walking by and the spell will break. What I've told you will elude me. I'll get restless and take my leave, and by the time I've turned the corner and climbed the steps back to our place I won't remember what I've told you or what I believed as we sat in the garden here under the tree. Yes—even now as I'm telling you, it's already a part of something from long ago and far away, yes, so long ago and far away it's almost forgotten.

*B*LACK THURSDAY. That's what they call it. Ma's crazy, along with everyone else. The Dow Jones fell to 261 and the stock market's crashed and it's v. terrible. I never understood what the market's all about, how it works, all I know is it's about money which everyone makes such a to-do over. Money's to spend— that's what money is. What's it but paper? Still, if you don't have it you're not free and if you do have it, you are. It's how you get it that bothers me, muddles my head thinking about it. Why Black Thursday happened no one seems to know. Some say the weather had something to do with it—Western cities covered with snow and sleet, communication with New York more difficult, but for- get about New York—Boston's all I keep hearing about. "When's the next train? Where's the timetable? Don't sit there, Stanley, get busy, get busy—*do* something—get the timetable. How about you, Starr, how do you feel, dear?" Fine, fine, I scream back at her. "I don't know, I don't know—" Well, I'm not going back to Snodgrass, I've said it to her 100 times. "No need to get upset, dear, no need for that, is there, Stanley? I don't even think the good doctor's in practice anymore—didn't he retire, Stanley? Speak up! No dear, no need for upsets—that's all in the past." Not upset, not upset, I yell. Stanley tries to calm me with a mar- tini, but I'll have none of it, already having had two and enough's enough.

*M*a keeps looking furtively around as if news will come any minute from God telling us that it's not the Day of Judgment, only one of her bad dreams. I would guess she's had more than one lately, and it's taken its toll. No more Beauty Parlor appointments for Mamacita and her manicure's chipping. She's usually so attentive to such things and has even let her pedicure go. Stanley keeps saying, "Don't distress yourself, Helen, don't distress yourself, dear," but his concern enrages instead of soothes and she bobs her head up and down, imitating him, "Don't distress yourself Helen, don't distress yourself Helen." She sounds exactly like Gloria Swanson (Stephen's parrot), obsessed with getting out of her cage to get at me.

*B*lack Thursday hasn't stopped anyone from going out on the town and I'm out every night which is why it's been days since I've talked to you, dear Mem—and now I can hardly get my thoughts together. It's about May Lark, who can't be alone for a minute. Her Arnie's been shot and is dying in hospital. She can't get near him because wee witch-wifey sits like a watchdog by his bed, not for love but for money. May Lark never should've gotten involved with someone like Arnie, but when love hits, what's to be done? Right? I'll try to tell you what happened from the beginning. There'd been a farewell party for Miriam Hopkins, who's leaving for Hollywood (to be in the movies), and I was all ruffled by the time I got there, delayed by a row with Tucker who'd gussied herself up like a toot-toot-tootsie to tag along with me to the party even though she hadn't been invited. Dammit. Why the hell should she? I was furious at her from the night before when we'd been at Club 21 and she'd told the whole table we were sitting at that I'd "be happier dead," that I'm "peevish all the time and dominate everyone." The bickering with her made me so late for the party it was almost over by the time I got there. I drifted around and settled by a group of God knows whos when a rich financier, A. C. Blumenthal, came up with that big producer Zukor, both quite taken with me (you can always tell). Call me Bloomie, A.C. kept urging. I hope I can remember all this and not leave anything out but my head's not on straight yet. About then May Lark arrived—without Arnie. People kept milling around, coming and going and leaving until suddenly, the room wasn't so crowded—you know how it is, and someone got a bright idea— come on, let's go to Joe Pani's. So a few strays attached themselves to each other and piled into Bloomie's Rolls-Royce. There were silver embossed bud vases filled with carnations and Bloomie held a carnation out to me and became most courtly, presenting it to his Carmencita. I was in no mood to be his or anybody else's Carmencita, but behind my ear it went and I was singing the "Habanera" with everyone joining in. Bloomie pressed a button and a wood panel slid open to reveal a bar stacked with Louis Roederer—pop pop it went and we were on our merry way, arriving at Pani's feeling no pain and finding ourselves sitting right next to Mayor Walker and Betty Compton. Vincent Lopez and his band were on a raised platform in the center of the room and he was jumping around leading the band in a song from Betty's new show and she was waving at him, singing along to the music. She's English—snooty, I bet, and has a squeaky voice. Guess you think I'm jealous, Mem, and I am. Anyway, the Mayor was nodding to me as if we'd met. Betty's tall and thin and smiles a lot. Gay too, like me when I'm at loose ends—but what the hell has she got to be at loose ends about? Everybody knows he's divorcing his wife to marry her. *She* doesn't stand alone. They seemed in one of those tiffs, the kind you get in for the fun of making up. But he looked tired and fed up with her—you'd never catch me sulking like that if Bill loved me, at least never without good reason—at lowest ebb, at low tide so to speak—oh, what the hell. She got up to leave, but the Mayor caught her and pulled her out onto the dance floor. She pushed him away and took off her white satin slippers, and ran up to the bandstand—"Vincent, Vincent—I'm Cinderella—sign my slippers!"—What a good idea and I pranced up too, holding up my slippers, and other women started running, holding up their slippers for him to sign. Everyone was laughing except the Mayor, who kept pulling Betty away from the bandstand, but not before I slipped him a scrap of paper on which I'd scribbled "Your friendly neighbor—Starr Faithfull—12 St. Luke's Place." I'd scribbled it down on a little note pad I always carry in my handbag the moment I spotted him—you know—just in case. It was right after this (at least I think it was) that Bloomie said he'd have to leave—fast, right away—but that we should stay. Fuzzy buffy by then, no one would hear of it, so off we went, piling back into the Rolls. Was May Lark with us? Can't remember. I think I was the last to be dropped off and that the chauffeur helped me out muttering about a shooting at the Park Central Hotel—and Arnie Rothstein. I don't remember how I got up to my room. The next thing I knew it was morning and here I am, Mem, trying to tell you about what happened before I forget. I'm too tired to move or undress or take a bath or scrape yesterday's makeup off or brush the peanut butter off my teeth. All that's sane are my white satin slippers with Vincent Lopez scrawled across them. They're placed neatly, side by side on the table by my bed. By whom?

*M*um went on a mysterious trip. Boston no doubt, but Stanley's mum about how, where, why? He sits around playing Solitaire. Every now and then he goes and stands in front of the mirror over the mantel where he's pasted the Oct. 29 clipping from *Variety*—WALL STREET LAYS AN EGG. He stares at the headline shaking his head. Ah me—speaking of eggs—haven't thought of Boofy in a long time. Yes, Boofy did love me, which is more than I can say about Bill, tough as it is for me finally to have to admit even to you, Mem. Still, I'd be a fool if I didn't finally question—if only a little bit—the sincerity of his intentions. Not even a postcard from him. At least he could find time for that, couldn't he? Or, maybe he's heard mean gossip about me and believes it. Oh God—

*T*he rumor is that Arnie was shot in a card game. It's being hushed up and nothing's been on the radio or in the papers because he has powerful friends. May Lark cries and cries, has lost pounds and won't eat. What can I do to help her—what can anyone do? I'd like to take her away somewhere—to Solly Winthrop's pink house on the beach or that island that floats around in my head—the one I never got to—yes, better still. She'd be soothed by the pure white pelicans. Me too. I'm sick of it here.

*A*rnie's dead. Murdered. May Lark's left town. No one knows where. But I do. I swore not to tell a soul but you don't count, Mem—she's at a convent in Vermont. One of the nuns there is her sister. She left with a toothbrush and a jar of Pond's in a brown paper bag, that's all. Money was behind it—the murder—Arnie bet more than a million on Al Smith's being defeated in the election. Well, at least she's out of it now. Maybe she'll become a nun. Maybe I'll become a nun. Then we'll be nuns together—walking in twos thru the green hills of Vermont. It's not such a bad idea. What do you think, Mem? Is that the answer?—if so, then all I'll need to do is remember what the question is.

Ma returned from Boston quite transformed into a sunny, sunny person. If we had to give a guess why, dare we suggest that sunny sunny sunny means money money money—and from whence it cometh? And where it goeth? Ah me—oh hell—I can pretend not to care but I hate her I hate her.

Oh Mem, a miracle has happened. You won't believe it—I must take deep breaths and try to tell you slowly one word at a time. Listen, listen—As I was coming down the steps of the Library on Fifth Avenue—there *he* was, about to pass me. I called out to him and he turned—Starr! He gave me a hug and as we walked along together he told me he'd arrived in town this very morning—from Liverpool where he'd been with his mother through her last illness. See, Francis was right—Oh God how could I have had so little faith? He was surprised of course to run into me so unexpectedly. How was I? Fine, just fine, more than fine, finest, I smiled and smiled. Then he said "What's the gossip?" Gossip? I was more than taken aback. I'm not interested in gossip. What did he mean? Oh God—if only I'd followed my instinct, taken the next boat as soon as I heard he was in Liverpool, then I would have been by his side to give solace as his mother was dying instead of jazzing around town thinking only of myself, imagining I hadn't heard from him because he'd heard about my goings-on in Europe. And by what he said I was more than certain he *has* heard vile rumor. All I could do, tho', was to keep smiling foolishly. Then he said, "Well, Beauty, have to turn off here." We were on 40th and Fifth. "Let's have dinner sometime—sometime soon." Yes, that's definitely what he said. I hurried home for I must rest up, not go out, stay in preparing myself for our next meeting. I must be at my best. Perfect in fact. Yes. That's definite. Oh Mem, that walk we had tho' only a block is held in my heart surrounding me with his love until we meet again. Soon—that's what he said.

*W*ell into my 2nd day of rest and beautifying with a new lime juice treatment I'll tell you about later—right now I want to tell you about an invitation from our neighbor—Mayor Walker— an invitation to dine at his penthouse on West 58th Street. It's a hideaway he leases from some grand dowager who's living abroad (wife's foot sets not there). Not so secret, however, are the parties he gives—caviar and partridge, vintage wines, staffed with an English butler, et cetera. Could he have broken up with Betty? Is that why he's inviting me? Did I tell you his pet name for her is "Monk"—no one knows why, but it's kinda cute, n'est-ce pas? Still—has a serious ring to it too. Of course, such invitations have no interest for the future Mrs. George Jameson-Carr. But can't wait till Ma gets back from shopping so I can show it to her. Quite a few days have gone by and no word yet. He must have a million important things to attend to having been away so long. And he's saving the most important for last. Me. Yes, the last shall be first.

*M*a says the Mayor hasn't broken up with Betty but urges me to accept the invitation. I never told her about the dippy thing I did slipping him that note (never thought for a sec he'd respond). Of course I sent my regrets—leaving for out of town—Boston family visit. Would I have accepted if Bill hadn't come back? Perhaps—perhaps, but only out of desperation and longing, imagining Bill didn't love me.

*F*inally—Gardenias and violets, a bouquet, a white rose in the center and a card "Dinner? Club 21? Please say yes!" Oh the darling—yes, yes, more than yes. I keep looking at myself in the mirror. Am I thin enough after more days than I care to count on the lime juice treatment I started telling you about—partaking of nothing but that over ice cubes? It's supposed to shrink the fat in some way, but oh so ughsome to get down. My mouth puckers mentioning it, much less partaking of it, straight (no sugar, of course). My stomach has shriveled, though—definite results, results, that's what counts—the scales prove it—I've lost 6 lbs. And my energy's high, more than high, feverish. Tomorrow's the day.

. . .

*I*t's freezing cold but I have insisted the rendezvous take place in the garden of the Church of St. Luke in the Fields. Have I mentioned to you (think I have but like going over it again) that my wedding is to take place there—not in the garden, silly Mem, but in the church. Still, maybe the garden's not such a silly idea—of course you're right. I'm the silly for not thinking of it first. Under the tree in the garden of St. Luke in the Fields is not only the fitting spot but the only spot. Yes, this is to be and so no matter what the season or climate I shall insist that the ceremony take place there in the garden under the tree. Bill will agree. But to get back to right now, it's too risky having him pick me up at my house with Ma and Stanley hovering around, not to mention Tucker behaving outlandishly. Lately she's taken to getting herself rigged up like Greta Garbo, cloche hats and reasonable facsimiles, slouching around drawing attention to herself. She's become a veritable Nosey Parker as well ever since she wasn't included in the Mayor's invitation to his penthouse party. She even went through my handbag and found Bill's postcard, which I always carry with me. I was so mad I hit her. We haven't spoken in days. And oh, my dear, would she like to get her hot little hands on you, dear Mem, but feel safe, friend, there's no way she can, short of taking an axe and giving Daddy's chest forty whacks. Yes, all my plans are coming to fruition. The waiting and longing are about to come to an end and life is to begin—yes, my darling, *after long long nights of waiting all my dreams will come true . . . tis the day when I'll be going down that long long trail with you.* What of the engagement ring? you ask. A heart-shaped diamond perhaps? But be it diamond or pebble picked up on the beach set in tin I shall be the happiest girl in the world (even a ring from a merry-go-round would suit me fine).

*O*h Mem—this time I've messed it up beyond all hope. I shake as I write, trying to tell you slowly and clearly from the beginning—oh God help me—you see I wanted to make my entrance into St. Luke's garden a few minutes late to find him waiting for me, but I couldn't restrain myself and got there way too early and then—instead of sensibly walking around the block to observe his arrival, then make my entrance, like a fool I hurried into the garden and sat down under the tree to wait for the fateful meeting. It was freezing cold, but I didn't care and I took the time to sort out some future plans I had in mind for Bill and me, and as I did something clicked into place (as it does sometimes after I've had a drink), and I knew it was imperative the minute I saw Bill to tell him—everything. All, hold back nothing. Once he knew, he'd forgive me because he'd understand, and from that time on, no matter where I went, or whatever happened, I'd be whole and centered in the crystal of myself without sin, because the whole of me would belong to him. I felt so free, knowing I'd never have to pretend about anything, ever again. Quelle fool. Oh Mem—there he was coming towards me, and I stood up in the white garden, my body crystal to receive him, calling out—Bill—pulling him down beside me—Bill—I've things to tell you, things I've been wanting to tell you for a long time. "What a peaceful spot," he said, looking around. Oh—it's much more than that, I said, but I couldn't find a way to explain why or how to tell him or even where to begin. I had to make him understand what had happened before I met him and once I did it would be Bill and Starr for the rest of our lives. But I couldn't get started, and he said, "Come on, it's freezing here and we're late now as it is. We're meeting Francis and Priscilla at 21." Francis and Priscilla! Nowhere in my plans had I foreseen or even imagined that our first night together after the long separation would be spent out on the town, fond as I am of dear Francis, forget about Priscilla. But he was eager to go and I shuffled my point of view around, maybe it was even better this way, would give us time to build up to my declaration—time too to be a little flirty with each other—he likes that, I know. But no—I changed my mind back to being *determined* that he would hear me out before we set foot out of that garden. He kept saying, "Come on, little lady, we're late," and he started to move away, but I pulled him back. Something was slipping away, water down down into a well, as I clutched at his hand. "Come on, Starr," he said, "I don't like to keep people waiting," and I was propelled out to the street and then there we were at 21 not only with Francis P. Hamlin and Priscilla Fairmont but others who kept joining our table, and as they did, I found myself falling, falling into my old ways. Words kept going around in my head as I chatted away, words of Bill's which Francis had repeated to me—"She has decided charm and is possessed of a vivacity which makes her attractive to most men, so no wonder they call her the Flame Girl, but being a professional man I guess I'm immune." When Francis told me this it shook me up so, I haven't been able to tell you about it until now. I knew telling you would somehow make it true but not telling you would mean it hadn't happened. I'm a serious person, Mem, and you know it better than anyone. Now that I have told you it won't be hard to guess my feelings as I looked across the table at Francis, reminded of the bitter memory. Not to mention those other clowns sitting with us who reminded me of other things best forgotten, things I'd vowed to entrust to Bill—and Bill himself taking that very moment to whisper in my ear, "Now what was it you had to tell me that's so important?" Forget it, I said—I'm having such a good time it's plum flown out of my head. "So—Miss Sugar Plum—plum flown out of that pretty little head, has it—well, we'll have to see about those plums later." Well, Dr. Jameson-Carr, you can take your plums and stuff them up your ass, and I jumped up and ran out, leaving him sitting there looking like I'd thrown bouillon in his face. Out on the street I ran and ran—what had I done?—oh God, what had I done? Then something grabbed me and I almost fell—it was Bill with my coat. I'd run out without it and he was holding it around me. "You'll freeze to death," he said, and he put my arm through a sleeve and bundled me up. "What's wrong—Bambi, what's wrong?" He kept saying it over and over—Bambi, Bambi—he'd never called me by that name, altho' I'd asked him to more times than I care to think of. Nothing, nothing, you don't understand, I kept saying. "No, I don't," he said, "I don't, but I will if you'll tell me." The intermittent light of the traffic flashed over his face, changing it from moment to moment into someone I didn't know, someone who frightened me. "Starr, let me help you," he said, and he took me from the curb to a quieter place against a building. I leaned back choking on my tears, and he put his arms up to shelter me from passersby. Yes he did. "Come," he said, "we can go to my place—how about that—a nice cup of hot coffee?" It turns out he has a pied-à-terre in a brownstone across the street from Club 21 so it wasn't far to go. His arm stayed around me as we walked up the stairs to his room on the 3rd floor. While he made the coffee I absorbed every detail of that room—his room. At least I thought it was his room, but now, as I'm trying to describe it to you, what I remember is a feeling of being in a hotel, for there was precious little of him anywhere around—not a photograph, a book or anything of his. Everything was brown on brown, brown rug and a brown chair (comfortable), a table, two chairs beside it, bureau and a bed set in an alcove. Of course I hadn't expected knickknacks—actually hadn't expected him to have a pied-à-terre in New York. I'd always pictured him living on shipboard when in port. Coffee was in a heavy white china cup and, on the saucer, a spoon—a spoon with an embossed cameo likeness, and inscribed under it "Marion Davies," and along the stem—her very own signature. I made an effort to focus on this. Interesting spoon—where did this come from? I asked. "Oh that." He was amused. "Just a little souvenir someone gave me." Ah yes, a souvenir—of what, pray tell? "Oh nothing in particular—a friend of mine collects these—ah—movie star spoons and she, ah, she has quite a few—prizes from a contest in one of the magazines—she has most of the stars, but knows I'm somewhat of a fan of Marion Davies so she gave this one to me." She must think highly of you, I said—very highly indeed to break up her treasured movie star coffee spoon collection. He smiled and offered me cream, sugar. Oh yes—both, tons if you please. I was cold, oh so cold as I held the cup of hot hot creamy, sugary coffee. The tick-tock-tick-tock of a Big Ben on a bedside table in the alcove pushed into me with a nasty sound, and I'd have given my soul to be back on the street, back in the joy I'd known on seeing him when he ran after me out of 21, instead of here with this stranger in this brown room with noisy brown silence pushing into my head. "Look, Starr," he said. "I only want to help you— be a pal—hadn't realized you were so sensitive, but I do now and hope that in future, should the occasion arise, I won't do anything to intrude on your sensitivity." Mem, though he did sound weary it was in a way a formal little declaration and there are different ways to interpret it, but none of them come out anyway near the way I'd like them to. First of all, I don't want to be his "pal." I want to be his love. Not only his love but *the* love. Then that sudden awareness of my "sensitivity" shows that I haven't been able to convey anything to him about my real self or the person I hope to be once I have his love to cherish and guide me. That sounds selfish on my part, but you know me well enough to know that it's not the way it sounds, for as I've tried to tell you before—in me he has met his destiny, for no one can make him as happy as I can. I know this to be a fact even though at this point I can't prove it. How can I after the mess I keep making of things? But give me time, for I will soon. Very soon I'll have positive proof and you'll be the first one to know, believe me. Anyway, you can see why what he said gave me a shock, but I willed myself to stir Marion Davies around in the empty cup, willed myself to keep my mouth shut and look peasant—I mean pleasant. Yes, pleasant. "Believe me, I don't want anything from you, Starr, but your friendship. So many courting you—should be a relief to have a pal like me, wot?" We're more than that, aren't we? He reached across the table and took my hand—"Sweetness, how could I forget the lovely time we had at the Waldorf—but—well, you know how unpredictable my life is—living at sea, never planning ahead the way most people do." I could feel my mouth shaping a hideous grin—yes, of course, who knows what the future will bring. "Words of wisdom." He nodded. "Ah yes, we never know what's in store for the morrow, but let's not talk of that now. Come on, Bambi, I'm curious, be a sport, what's that big secret you were going to tell me in that freezing garden before I whisked you away?" Okay, I'll tell you, if you'll tell me—tell me who parted with the spoon from her Marion Davies collection— I mean movie star collection—and off we went, flirty sallies back and forth, but I soon ran out of steam, my gay badinage changed into strident bitterness, shouting—Well, Dr. Jameson-Carr, if Marion Davies is your type, I hardly see why you're wasting time with me. He turned, repelled, desperate to get this crazy person out of his house. But did that make her stop, Mem? No, it made her louder than ever—I don't give a damn who gave it to you— you'll never know anything about me—never—never, and she threw the spoon at him and ran down the stairs, into the street, hating him, hating Marion Davies, hating everybody in the world, but most of all hating herself—shouting—Mer-ry Christmas—careening down the street until a policeman stopped her. Oh God, Mem—level with me, this is it, isn't it? He'll never want to see me again. It's really over.

*I*t's December 21st, the shortest day of the year. I hate these days of winter when the light goes early and darkness comes at 4, sometimes sooner. But I try to think of it this way—from this day on, the days become longer, light is a gift slowly given as the days move towards summer. It'll get better then, won't it, Mem? Better as the light stays longer. Better as the nights grow shorter—yes, the nights shorter, and as the days lengthen into light, he'll come back.

*I*t's the night before Christmas and all through the house not a creature is stirring, not even a mouse—no, not a stir in the house, only the stir in my gut swirling because I know once and for all that I'll never hear from him again. I know that as well as I'll ever know anything. I lie abed with Congo beside me and look out the window at the snow, which has started again. Soon everything will be white, whiter than ever before. I'll open the window and let the snow drift into my white room, over my white sheets— it'll be nice, won't it, Mem, so nice, so white, so clean.

*S*top feeling sorry for yourself, Starr. By the way, I found out that Carl Jung lives in Zurich—not Basel as I'd thought. I'm going to write to him. Why not? Take my mind off white sheets, white snow and other white things here in New York. Much better to dwell on the whiteness of Swiss Alps. Yes, let us see, dear Mem, what comes up when I take pen in hand to write Dr. Jung.

Dear Dr. Jung,

Please don't think me too forward in writing to you, but it's Christmas Day and my impulse to do so overcomes my shyness, which is extreme. (I am definitely an introvert and certain you would agree with this diagnosis.) It's been somewhere in the back of my head to write to you for a long time—ever since I first heard your name and that you could help people find out who they really are. I can't specify exactly who first informed me of your mission, but I assure you he exists, altho' I have for the moment forgotten his name. Now that I think about it, it may be that I read about you in some publication. I was sojourning in Paris at the time, visiting the friend of a friend, who has a library with copies of all the magazines. I was greatly tempted at the time to flee that city and come to you. Yes, Dr. Jung, I longed to throw myself on your doorstep begging for clemency. But it's a good thing I didn't because I was under the misapprehension that you lived in Basel or perhaps Geneva instead of Zurich, where I now know you to reside. I would have been rattling around in those other cities, hope dwindling with each rattle until finally, who knows? It would have been a death rattle and the trip all for naught. No matter, I don't want to take up more of your precious time and will press on to the reason for this letter. It's hard to do this because my feelings get in the way of my thoughts—heart versus head, let's say (why not?)—and I end up in a white place (I'm most partial to white)—this time it's a white expanse of snow that stretches far as the eye can see with not a blot of any-thing on it except the tracks of a bird (webbed feet), which zig-zag along quite crazily and lead nowhere. They must lead somewhere, you are thinking. You are thinking that, aren't you, Dr. Jung? Don't deny it. I'm somewhat psychic myself, which is how I know these things. Well, if you know those bird tracks are leading somewhere, pray tell me where? That's why I'm writing to you. See! I was able to pinpoint why despite the battle of heart versus head, so that's a victory of sorts, isn't it? Now perhaps the two will be *integrated* and I will have to thank *you*, Dr. Jung, for this. That article in the magazine, the one in Paris, said you helped people towards "the integration of the personality." This I ardently desire. While you're at it, tell me also what kind of bird the bird is whose tracks are in the snow? This perhaps will be even more helpful than knowing where the tracks lead. What are your thoughts on this, dear Carl? I hope I'm not presuming too much. I'd better stop now before it's too late. Too late for what? Good question. Perhaps you know the answer. I hope so because I sure don't and it's getting too late to see those zig-zaggings in the snow, the dark is coming fast, the shadow of it descending onto the snow, blacking it out—nothing will be left but empty dark-ness not to mention the cold of the snow on my bare feet, ha ha. Well, thanks anyway for listening. I don't really expect an answer because I know how busy you must be. Sorry to have bothered you, but I couldn't have stood it another mo. if I hadn't gotten some of this off my chest. Getting up courage to write you this letter is my Christmas present to myself.

Thanks, really,
Starr Faithfull

P.S. That shadow, by the way, comes from the wings of a bird, a really big one moving over the snow, but it has nothing to do with the bird who made the ziggy-zags over the snow—they're much too small, those feet-prints, to belong to anything but a small bird. Maybe not even a bird, maybe they're the imprints of a child's tiny hands—some children not only do handstands, but can actually walk for long distances on their hands so as to give their feet a rest. And they're not circus children—I mean their parents aren't performers in a traveling circus. Why, I myself had that facility up until age eleven, but then something happened and I fell on my feet and from then on lost the knack. Anyway, enough of that, eh? Thanks again for listening.

Starr

P.P.S. In one of your articles you speak of a mandala (Sanskrit for "circle"), informing me that you consider it an "archetype, a universally occurring pattern associated with the mythological representation of the Self." This interests me enormously. Pray, I beseech you, enlighten me further. I am picturing myself as a circle and through this circle I see a—well, the only way I can explain it is to show you like this:

See, the circle is myself, and through it is that ziggy-zag whatever. What the hell is it? Why is it there and is it good or bad? I have no way of knowing. Maybe it's the electricity bringing me to life or the opposite—electrocuting me. The more I look at it the more ambivalent I am about the whole damn thing. Well—so long again. Hope you're having a merry Christmas and that the new year—1930, isn't it?—will inspire you to take pen in hand so that I hear from you. Even a postcard would be most welcome. I collect them, you know. But of course you don't. How could you? Anyway, it's been nice talking to you. Ta ta.

1930

*D*ays go by and not a word from Carl. Sometimes I imagine he's sent one, not one but more, more than one, several in fact, a significant message only I would understand, such as . . . Dear Miss Faithfull—You interest me enormously—never has such an interesting case come to my attention. You must come to Zurich as soon as possible, for I have the answer, Miss Faithfull, the answer to your question, and once you hear it, your life will change—you will never be the same again—the pain you experience each day, each hour, will disappear and you will be one with yourself. Those curious footprints in the snow are indeed the handprints of a child. They too will vanish and in their place flowers will grow. Yes, I promise you faithfully, Miss Faithfull— so tarry no longer, come to me for salvation. Yours sincerely, Carl Jung. How's that, Mem? Well, more than several words indeed and too many to fit on a postcard (unless he writes smaller than small)—it'll be in a letter, better still, yes, a long letter from Dr. Jung—any day I expect it.

Sunday, January 26th

Dear Mem,

It's been a long time since I've written you a birthday letter, hasn't it? But don't despair, I still have high hopes that things will turn out all right. I just need more time to think so I can make a new plan. No, not one plan, but many plans, yes—many plans, for one of them will surely come to fruition. Not that this has anything to do with anything, but I read in the newspapers that Mr. and Mrs. Albert Einstein dined with Charlie Chaplin at his home on Jan. 14—12 days before my birthday. What were we doing, Mem, on the night of Jan. 14? Up to no good probably, but mercifully I can't remember and since I haven't had a really serious talk with you since Christmas Day—our activities the night of the 14th are lost to history. Ah me. Well, anyway, Stanley's gin does get better and better and there's always Naples and Silent Solly in that pink house on the yellow beach to turn to, not to mention the deep blue sea. I'm not v. good company these days, but I'm firm in my resolve to do better. Don't give up on me, please. Don't despair. Help is on the way. Maybe I'll meet Charlie Chaplin and he'll take us to Hollywood and make me a movie star. Maybe I should go to Hollywood on my own, run into him at the Brown Derby (hear he goes there frequently), and be discovered that way. Starr a star. How about that? You'd like that, wouldn't you, and be proud of me when I'm famous. Not that you aren't proud of me now, right now, because I know you are—no matter what happens I have you and you have me. We have each other. I love you, Mem, and as I said, don't despair. Our old pal Help from *Pilgrim's Progress* is on the way.

Always your
Starr

O̲ut till dawn and didn't bother to sleep. Instead went to meet the Twentieth Century Limited. Clara Bow was arriving from Hollywood at 8:45 a.m. and I wanted to get a look at her. Wouldn't have gone had I known there'd be such an enormous crowd—but worth it to see the It Girl. An endless line of redcaps had been positioned to keep the crowd back, and when the train pulled in, guess what? There was Harry Richman in a raccoon coat and slouch black hat—*A turn to the right, a little white light—will lead me to my blue heaven*—running along the platform from car to car, trying to find her. Then she appeared, wearing a brown fur coat and a little brown hat fitted close to her face, and everyone cheered. The hat was fringed with feathery somethings with her hair streaming out on either side. And oh Mem she was carrying a large limp doll. I really like that doll. Photographers were falling over each other snapping pics, and when they took her luggage off the train I counted forty pieces. You know I like the idea more and more of going to Hollywood. Not because of the 40 pieces of luggage but because of the attention I'd get with crowds and crowds loving me everywhere I went. After all, this is not exactly a new plan for us, is it, Mem—not an impulsive whim—we had this in our mind at one time or another. Then other things came around and it got lost by the wayside as they say. Yes—let's say, but don't say I told you so if I change my mind again. Still . . . Is it too late to revive? Not only revive but pursue? What thinkest thou?

*S*tarted a letter to Silent Solly

Dear . . .

but only got that far.

*W*hiling away the hours making lists of all the men I've been to bed with—trying to do it alphabetically, but the problem is there are so many whose names I don't remember—not to mention others whose faces I've forgotten. Also my mind wanders, I lose interest. Yes, names, faces forgotten—no, not forgotten—never known to begin with. Elsie was right—there's no such thing as a *little* sin. I can't bear to think of it, so why torment myself? To what purpose? I must put such thoughts out of my head permanently, for they make me feel I'm further away than I ever was from—what?—Home? Call it that for want of a better word.

I remember saying to my father when I was about eight, "Oh Daddy, wouldn't it be wonderful if it was just you and me, and Ma never came back?" (She was walking Puddin and Pie.) And he said, "You bet, old top. We understand each other, don't we, sweetheart?" Oh, Mem, however to replicate that golden moment?

*H*appy Memories are few. Oh Hell! I wish I were starving in Bramerton Street in Chelsea with the roof falling and the rain pouring in—anything but this. I wish I were having a nice long double whiskey with Lonnie at the Six Bells. Everything now seems so arid, blank, negative and futile that I wish some geological phenomenon would wipe the U.S. of A. off the map. I am bored with my native land. If I were a man, I would join the Foreign Legion and forget my past. Yesterday, I was completely overcome by depression. New York seemed like a huge graveyard. To think, Mem, I once believed it was going to be the Celestial City.

I'm sick of wallowing in the Slough of Despond and feeling sorry for myself. So unlike me, isn't it? To hell with Bill. I'm pulling myself out with Hopeful and Curiosity, and, much as I hate to have to tell you, Love of Flattery, which gives me the biggest boost of all—which is my way of telling you I'm open to being lured out on the town again. Ah, mercy me.

*T*his new fellow I met, Archie Truesdale, keeps after me but I put him off—I'm sick of everyone around town and so from this night on, staying in. May Lark's still secluded with the nuns in Vermont—God knows when she'll be back. She's butter-making and the churning soothes her nerves. Just what I need, but our place is crowded as it is—where could I find a spot for the churn? Without her around to liven things up I much prefer to stay home reading and studying books on Italian Renaissance painting, also the paintings of Erté. How I pine every time I look at his *De Choix d'un Coeur*—how I long for Paris. Ah yes, 'tis April there now—how divine it must be, but here we are, Mem, pining away in little old New York, which could be pretty nice too if only I could find surcease from whatever it is I need surcease from. Until then I shall put Erté aside and immerse myself in my books. Yes, I'm occupied, as you can see. Actually I'm scared to leave the house—every time I do I get into tangles I can't get out of, meet someone I don't want to see. Archie turned out to be another Lonnie. Knew he kept reminding me of someone but he seemed such a sincere person the resemblance didn't occur to me until that morning when I woke up and found myself in—oh hell, Mem—it's too involved to go into right now. It's such a bad feeling to do something I'm sorry for later. Or worse still—not be able to remember what it is I did—oh what the hell.

· · ·

*M*aking plans, new plans to venture forth—haven't been to Julius's speakie in ages.

I've met this girl who dresses like a man (sort of a he-she) and likes to be called Don. She's quite intelligent, drives a taxi and very independent. Maybe that's what I should do. I'd have to learn how to drive first, though. Don could teach me. Do you like that idea, Mem, or not?

*J*ay Stoner talked me into modeling again and I've been posing for him. He has nothing to do with the Jay I wound up with at the St. George in Brooklyn the day I got home exhausted and found a message from Bill to meet him under the clock at the Biltmore—no, this is another Jay, an artist. I'm posing for him wearing one of his shirts and nothing else. I nose around in his closet while he isn't looking every opportunity I get and yesterday came upon a pinstripe I took more than a fancy to. I put it on then and there and it fit me to a T. Jay almost dropped when he saw me, but soon recovered, and got so excited he started whizzing around doing charcoals of me. By that time I'd gotten hold of his grey fedora and was fooling around with that too—what a piece of swank! The sketches are intriguing and I begged him to let me borrow the suit—hat—everything, for a little mischief. He was curious to know what I had in mind and wouldn't let me have it until I'd told him. What the hell—told him about my new pal Don and how she dressed in men's clothes and that we go to Julius's sometimes, and I'd always thought it'd be fun to be dressed in men's clothes too. He's mesmerized by this and "crazy" to meet this Don. Sometimes she's Johnny instead, I told him—it all depends. Depends on what? he wanted to know. She's capricious, I told him. "More so than you?" He kept needling. I—capricious? Ridiculous. Anyway, Jay's really, really interested and I suggested we all go out together some time soon if—anyway, that's how I ended up getting the suit and fedora.

I did myself up in Jay's pinstripe, shirt and tie, excited by thoughts of the evening ahead. Jay had been put off with some excuse or other so it could be just me and Don. But now that I'm going into it I realize the preparation for my date was more fun than the date itself. I always like the girly preparations, getting ready for a night on the town, and this time it was even more fun, something different, you know, because they were—well, laddie preparations, maybe? Yes, laddie suits me fine. So did the pin-stripe, if you'll forgive a pun. But best of all was not having to wear makeup—I have good skin (inherited from my little Mamacita). Not that I'd go out without makeup under usual cir-cumstances. I definitely prefer the veil of powder, the curve of lipstick that defines the smile, the rouge, mascara and so on that help mask the face. But last night no mask was needed, for laddies don't have to wear masks. It would have been inappropriate, n'est-ce pas, Mem? So after a long soak in the tub and patting of soap on face—cleaning inside ears, hard scrub with cloth on back of neck—I rose like Botticelli's Venus, ready for anything. My face was flushed from the steamy water as I rubbed ice cubes over it and on the back of my neck. Jay's told me that my face without makeup may lack masklike definition, but it has the vulnerable openness of a child's, and that's how I appeared, I must say, as I pulled my hair back and slicked it down with pomade—only a smidgen. The effect not greasy at all and with the fedora at an angle, I could hardly tear myself away from the mirror. I'd filed my nails down, short and square, and I liked the effect they gave without the usual red laquer, but best of all was the feeling that they are meant to be used for something—not simply the allur-ing accoutrements they usually are. These hands had strength of character, yes. Hands meant to do something, but what? Take clay in hand, sculpt a bust perhaps. Of whom? Gandhi, maybe. Yes, but not only a bust—it would be Gandhi with a small group of his followers, on their protest march to the sea. And I would be part of the group—the one by his side of course. Yes, definitely. Or maybe even leading him. Better yet. Shoes were a problem— mine are high heeled—so I had to resort to sneaking a pair out of Stanley's closet and lo and behold they fit perfectly. My plan was to put them back before they were missed, along with the socks. Once put together I looked quite a toff, I will say, and it was easy to slip out while Ma and Stanley were doing God knows what in the bedroom. I'd told Don I'd pick her up around nine-ish and I was right on the dot. It was a real surprise to her, my being dressed so. Delighted? Well, actually, I thought she'd faint. She lives in a one-room walk-up on Christopher Street and when I knocked on her door and she saw me standing there she pulled me into the room saying let's not go out, let's stay in in in. I had no interest in shenanigans at the moment, but the more determined I was to *go*, the more determined she was to stay. Now you know me, Mem—I can't stand to be pushed this way and that, and I regret to report it all ended badly, with my telling her I never wanted to see her again, to leave me alone, and so on. I left her crying, but hardened my heart—something one just has to do from time to time. Ah me, more's the pity, but I had fun anyway. Hurried home and spent hours gazing at myself in the mirror before taking off my fine feathers. No, the evening wasn't a total loss by any means.

I'm running low on money and asked Ma to give me a couple of fives. "Money money money money," she muttered, jogging her head side to side ticktock ticktock. Put her on the mantel and she could be a clock. "You think I'm made of money honey money, don't you?" Look, Ma, I said, but she told me to shut up and this would have to do for now—$2. She ticktocked on about how we'll be in clover again any day now and how she can't fathom what's gotten into Andrew lately or *to* him more likely—so many envious, mean people who want for themselves what out of the kindness of his heart he gives to us. Then the ticktock winds down and it's—Maybe I'm being unfair to him such a fine important man so busy with important things on his mind time slips—yes, no doubt, Starr-baby, that's what it is—it'll all be cleared up soon—I have an appointment with that nice Mr. Rowley in Boston on Wednesday so put worries out of your head and let your little Mamacita carry the burden. But I can't put it out of my thoughts. Money tick tock money honey tick tock tick tock tock ticks around in my brain all day. Even listening to loud music doesn't help—makes it worse in fact, makes me think of Fou all the time, instead of only now and then, which I sometimes do, no matter how I try not to.

I went to the bus station and now I'm on one going guess where? Florida. Silent Solly'll be glad to see me, I know. How do I know? Oh, didn't I tell you, we have mental telepathy—Solly and I. Yes, we do. He's waiting for me in that pink house on the yellow beach by the blue sea.

*S*olly's not here. The pink house is. The yellow sand is. The blue sea is. But he isn't. I asked all over, everyplace. No one knows where he is, or where he went. I have a strong hunch he drove to Mexico in his lime green Opel Reinette. Maybe I should go there and visit Daddy Lincoln at his silver mine in Guanajuato. Don't leave, Mem.

*S*ent Ma a telegram not to worry. Found a room overlooking the sea. It has a balcony too and I snapped it up. I'm in this room right now. At least I think I am. The room has louvered doors opening on the balcony, and the hish hish of the sea comes to me muffled thru the heat. It's 95 in the shade the landlady informed me. I believe her. The room has wallpaper—fans and parasols, but so faded maybe it's really something else. I'm lying on the bed, which is narrow, and there's only 1 pillow. I'll have to ask for another. I sleep with 1 pillow but like 2 for reading. On the night table lamp is tea rose silk with beaded fringe (real beads). The best thing about this room is that no one knows I'm here. Oh, Ma will know when she gets the telegram, but she won't be able to picture me in this room because she'll have no idea of my address. The landlady thinks my name's Miranda Augustine and that I came from Chicago. That's what I told her. Call me Auntie Lil, she said, everyone does. Please don't shorten my name, I told her. I prefer to be called Miranda (no Manda or other improvisations). So far no one I've seen around here reminds me of anyone (always a good sign). Back to you later, Mem, must take a hot bath hotter than the heat outside (bathroom down the hall), then unpack, then go out, do something.

*T*orrents of rain. Lie abed and watch the fan above me. When it stops, I stop too—stop my heart from racing back, racing ahead, racing to nowhere at all. Must get a mosquito net to put over the bed. There's no switch to turn off the fan even if I wanted to.

· · ·

*M*em—shaking shaking—the drawer of the bureau in my room—the bottom one—hadn't used it until now—opened it—there's something written on one side—at the corner. I had to kneel down on the floor and lean in close to read it—*How are you?* It's AJP's handwriting.

I'm at the Western Union waiting for money I telegraphed Ma to send. Had to give my real name. Forgive shaky writing but can't stop. I'm going to sit here until the money comes.

*L*eft the rent money on the bed with a note. It was pouring rain, and oh the wind, a hurricane coming . . . Terrified I wouldn't get out before it hit. Ma sent more than enough to get out. I'm on the train now, going back. We make a lot of stops before we reach New York. May get off, spend some time somewhere. But then again may not. *How are you?*—that is what it said.

I'm scared, so scared. Towns go by and I'm still on the train glued to the seat.

*F*irst thing I did when I got home and could shake Ma and Stanley was to empty my bureau drawers. I stood at the window looking inside each one, searching to see if he'd written anything. I used Stanley's magnifying glass to do this and can swear to you that there is nothing—no *How are you?*—no anything but smooth pine wood. I put my things back in place oh so neat just the way I like them.

*N*o one's heard from George Jameson-Carr all summer. Ma has an opinion and it's that I'm too thin. Stanley doesn't say anything. Just looks at me. So I have no idea what his opinion is. Tooka's visiting friends in Blairstown, New Jersey. Congo gets in my lap whenever I sit down.

*H*ow are you?

*D*id I tell you a man on the train gave me a Voodoo doll? I didn't want to take it but he said it would bring me luck. Since I got back I've been reading about Voodoo in the library. It's a religion. But you knew that already, didn't you? Yes, a religion. Started on the Island of Saint-Dominique, as Haiti was known before 1804. The Fon (not the Fou) were natives and cast a spell over the island's slave communities. The Fon (repeat, not Fou) summoned spirits called Loa. To the Fon (*not*, I repeat again, the Fou) "vodun" means "god" or "protective spirit." It's more complicated than this but you know more about it than I do anyway. My doll is small. Just right. It has a pear-shaped head, no face except for 2 little eyes not level with each other. No hair. I haven't made up my mind if it's a girl or a boy. Its body is soft, and when I hold it in my fist the head sticks out over my hand and the eyes look at me. I look back and squeeze it—filled with beans, maybe? That's the kind of feel it has but I'm not sure. What I am sure is that I believe in it. It's not a doll, of course, it's something far more important, but we can't go into that right now. I don't want Ma or anyone else to see it. I keep it in Daddy's chest when it's not in my fist. No matter how hard I squeeze it doesn't break. Now you know what I'm talking about.

*T*he *Aquitania*'s sailing on Thursday. May go to the Bon Voyage party.

*G*ot all dressed to go then didn't. Too thin or is it too fat? No, it's because I'm afraid he'll get into my room while I'm out. There will be a message waiting for me when I get back.

*W*ent out for the first time since I got home. Yes, to the Church of St. Luke in the Fields. It's still there. Nothing's changed. Went to the mass on Sunday. Alone without telling them. The girl wasn't there, the one praying that day alone in the front pew. After, sat in the garden then walked around for a while instead of going home. Thought I saw Bill in front of me on Sullivan Street and ran towards him, but suddenly he turned and didn't look anything like him at all.

*S*earched bureau drawers soon as I got back. Nothing. Maybe he's dead. Maybe I'm safe.

I do like having the room to myself—lie abed looking at my books, knowing they're here, knowing they'll always be there no matter where I am. That's true, Mem, isn't it? Everyone's pressing me here to go out, word's gotten around that I'm back in town. Even Archie's surfaced again. And Rollo's especially persistent— oh well—why not.

A big snowfall. First of the season and before Thanksgiving too. What do you know? Went out to visit my garden. Walked and made a trail of footprints in the snow for Bill to find me.

*O*h Jesus God, Mem—you'll never guess what happened! Bill showed up without warning. I was lying abed in my terry robe having had a long soak in the tub when the doorbell rang and there he was, saying he hoped he wasn't disturbing me, but he'd been passing by our house and couldn't resist ringing our bell. It was as if a lifetime hadn't passed since we've seen each other. Haven't seen you in ages and ages, he said—Hope there are no hard feelings about that last meeting. I tried to look perplexed. Oh well, he said breezily, it was last year, wasn't it. No wonder you've forgotten—now how about bundling up and coming for a walk—see the park in the snow. I threw on woollies, grabbed mittens, and he took my hand and out we went into the clean cold white world. I held myself straight, proud, fine and dandy sugar candy, telling him how busy busy I've been traveling—Hollywood, busy busy writing stories and the magazines after me pestering for more. Oh god, Mem, it had been almost a year since that terrible Marion Davies night and I kept dreading the moment when he'd bring it up. But moments passed with no mention of spoons, so it was all for naught my steeling myself, wracking my brain for excuses to explain my unforgivable behavior in case he brought it up, which I was sure would happen. But he didn't and once I knew—I felt compelled to. About that night, Bill, I said, merr-ee Christmas and all that. Oh, forget it, Starr, it's way in the past, it was late and we were both tired. But I can't—how can I forget when I haven't heard a word from you since? I've written countless letters (well, I have in my head) apologizing to you but—Oh, come on, he interrupted, there's nothing to apologize for—forget it—I have. (He took my hand again.) I've been busy, that's why you hadn't heard from me. You're a fine young lady and you know I always wish you the very best. I squashy-squeezed his fingers, no doubt too hard for he pulled his hand away and looked at his watch. Wish we had more time, but I gotta go now. Yes, me too, gotta go, gotta go, Bill, gotta go too, I told him. I'm late, very late, later than you are, bye bye. There was a lot of waving as I ran up the steps, but at the door I hurried in without glancing back—yes, I got inside fast, as I said, without a look. Now—don't know what to think. But I'm full of hope again—"busy, busy," that's what he said. I believe that. He doesn't lie. He is a sincere person. There must have been good reason for his silence. He doesn't hate me. Quite the contrary. How could I have doubted?

*N*ot a word from him . . . waiting in the station for that train—waiting and waiting but it never arrives—

I go back over the walk in the snow and think in my eagerness to tell you about it I may have left some things out, may have forgotten to tell you that he did say he was off to sea again but he'd send a postcard, remembering I collected them. Oh! how sweet of you to remember I collect postcards—yes, my postcard collection is growing by the minute. Only yesterday I received one from Dr. Carl Jung from Zurich, Switzerland, we correspond you know, but I have only one from you, dear Bill—India, remember? So another would be nice from wherever you may happen to be— then I'll have two from you instead of one. That's when I tried biting my tongue off but it didn't work, and I was asking him, When will I see you again? "Not sure, may be leaving the *Franconia* and taking another position on a Greek cruise liner." My, my—

they're swell, I hear, and I told him I may be leaving for Greece myself any day to visit my dear friend Nicholas Zographos, so we might run into each other—who knows? "Good-o," he said, "but either way, let's keep in touch." Keep in touch—yes, touch is important. Congo and I do it all the time. Of course it was a fib about postcards from Carl. I haven't heard a word from him, but what the hell—tomorrow maybe. Or certainly by New Year's Eve. Yes, better late than never. Dr. Jung is full of surprises. All brilliant people are. But what do you think, Mem, about these new details about the walk on the snow?? I go over them constantly and the more I do the more I feel I may have put out too many tentacles?? Maybe that's been my problem with him all along? Strike me dead if that's true, Mem. Help me.

*T*he holidays loom closer—sometimes I can hardly breathe. Bill—this time last year.

I'd like to have one of those Marion Davies spoons in my hands right now—two would be even better. Oh God, I don't know. None of it matters. But come to think of it—if I did have those spoons, I could bend them, fold them over—yes, I've the strength of ten musketeers when I'm in a rage. I'd bend them in a circle to wear as bracelets around my wrist. I'll tell everyone they were a Xmas present from Bill. Now—how to get my hands on them?

A Christmas card's arrived from Bill!!! Looks hand painted. A sleigh on its way to a snow-covered house in the distance and in the sleigh a smiling couple, so we know they are happy, very happy. They're holding packages. They look like Bill and me (the couple, silly, not the packages)—well, sort of like Bill and me. "Merry Christmas to you and your lovely family, Sincerely, George Jameson-Carr." That's what it says inside, but it doesn't look like his handwriting. Do I imagine this? No, I do not. It is *not* his handwriting. I put it next to his postcard. But maybe this is his handwriting and the one on the postcard isn't???? Sincerely. What do you make of that?

Where is Bill tonight? Busy no doubt, yes busy busy, of course, because it's New Year's Eve. Congo and I are listening to the horns tooting outside. It's not that I have to be alone—I am alone by choice. I know tonight I won't have to try to please anyone or strain to be anyone or anything but myself. What a relief. Of course I'm not that alone. Congo is by my side. And that's the best because I don't have to do anything to please him or put out tentacles to sense if he loves me. All I have to do is be myself to know he does. Do you suppose if I stopped trying so hard to please Bill, he would love me too? That's why it was so nice with Silent Solly in that pink house on the beach. He expected nothing from me and I could do nothing all day, if that was what I wanted. Nothing except breathe in and out and be myself. Right now, here with you and Congo, I'm content. I'm taking *Pilgrim's Progress* and *Elsie Dinsmore* off the shelf—our two oldest friends— *Should old acquaintance be forgot and never brought to mind*—No—they shall not be forgotten by me, not on New Year's Eve or ever. I'll browse through each in turn as the New Year sweeps out the Old—and Happy New Year to you too, Mem. You love me, I know.

1931

Weeks have gone by and I've neglected you, I know. I'll do better. I have plans—can't reveal them yet, but soon—That's definite.

Sometimes I drink and drink until the pain is only as the softest rain, falling on softest snow, falling on softest cotton, falling, falling down into nothingness. Then—later pain returns as if it's salt water I've been drinking and I go about dying of thirst, but not for water—for Bill. Last night with three men. It meant nothing—nothing—nothing.

Sorry, Mem, no time, no time for a birthday letter. You'll have to excuse me. Pardonne moi, s'il te plaît. Too busy going out, too busy being happy, too too busy—later, but only perhaps—you understand, don't you, Mignonette?

How are you?

I know now what's gotten me feverish—it started weeks ago and gets worse. He's here in New York, but this time without the girl. I'm not telling Ma, Stanley or anyone. I'll find him and when I do I'm going to kill him. No one will know of course. Everyone else will think he's still alive but he'll be dead, my fine Fou Cousin Mr. Mayor of Boston.

I'm organizing it in my head secretly. No one is to know but you. Its success depends on no one knowing. If I fail it's the end of hope for us, Mem. I must succeed. I will succeed. I'm the master planner, planning each step even though I tremble to think of it, and when I tremble I forget what the plan is exactly and have to rest a bit until I can go back and start planning it over again.

*O*h God, *Dear as remember'd kisses after death, and sweet as those by hopeless fancy feign'd—on lips that are for others—deep as love, Deep as first love, and wild with all regret, O Death in Life, the days that are no more—* What the hell is that from? Tennyson. I hardly know what I'm saying. Now I remember—*Ah, sad and strange as in dark summer dawns—the earliest pipe of half-awaken'd birds—To dying ears, when unto dying eyes—The casement slowly grows a glimmering square*—Yes, that glimmering square is what I am seeking, for it is there that I shall find Bill ambling around feeding the birdies, killing time while he waits for me—but let's not digress. Forget about Tennyson. My plan is not to find Tennyson, stupid—it is to find Fou. And when I do, once I set eyes on him, once I've found him—well I'll know exactly what to do even if I can't think what it is right now. Determination will give me the strength I need, for this must be a work of art, a perfect scenario—a masterpiece. Oh God, if only I knew what I was tumbling on about. Still—I will not fail. If the girl's with him, I'll kill her too.

*W*ires of steel have woven themselves into the cells of my brain, which explains why my head's gone awry. It happened long ago and was a terrible mistake. There's a birthmark too on my face and a crack in my head, only they don't show. I'm flawed, there's no denying it. That's why I've got to find him. He's the only one that might be able to remove the birthmark, mend the crack. (I say might, for it remains doubtful.) There's a reason for this, but I've forgotten what it is. I beg you, help me remember. Once I do find him the wires of steel will dissolve and the cells in my brain will be freed. It will be as it was when I first met you, Mem (it wasn't there then), for the crack in my head will have also disappeared—no one will ever know it was there. Not even you. Now you understand the urgency to find him.

I'll never find him if I just keep sitting around talking to you about the plan—it's action that's needed—action and energy, and I've harnessed both to go out every night—yes, I go forth on the town making my rounds. Mori's, Pirates' Den, Lafayette's, Barney Gallant's—my mission takes me to every speakie in town. I don't drink. I'm saving my Allonal and won't use it again until my plan is in motion, maybe not even then. I take great care over how I look, more so than usual. Every night—a different lipstick. If I have no luck finding him here in New York I may have to go up to Boston and ferret him out there—but only if all else fails.

*L*ast night a crowd of us were walking in Sheridan Square on our way to the Greenwich Village Inn when I spotted him. As I surmised, the girl wasn't with him. Wherever she is it's not with him. I know for sure it was he, because soon as I ran after him I started choking—seeing that Fou head sent blood straight up from the gut into the throat, on up into the brain. I ran faster, but as he turned the corner I faltered—the blood had exploded into my eyes and when I came to, he had disappeared. At least we know now that it wasn't my imagination—he is here in New York, not only in this city but in our neighborhood. Now it's only a matter of time before we find each other.

*I*t's Valentine's Day and I am preoccupied more than ever with these matters, which at least give me some respite from torments over Bill, yes, solace if only intermittently, for I do not have to give a thought regarding sending a valentine to Jameson-Carr. But I'm weary, oh so weary, dear friend, for to tell the truth valentines are really all I think of and if I did send one to Bill, which valentine would it be? Handmade or store bought? I need—surcease. I'm going to take a few nights off, not look in the mirror or give a thought to valentines or what lipstick to wear or where I'll go when I do decide what lipstick to wear. No, I don't want to give a thought to anything at all but to scrub my body with soap and water, hot as it can stand, cover my face with a hot hot cloth and loll in the tub as long as I wish. After, I'll lie abed, sipping the bitter lime juice I punish myself with and for surcease from that reread *The Great Gatsby*.

*M*em—this is very important—what I'm about to tell you. You're the only one I can count on. You must see to it that this is put on my tombstone. It's from Stephen's book, *The Vein in the Marble*. It calms me even now as I'm telling you—knowing I can depend on you to have these words engraved on the stone, the stone that will rest on me even though I am elsewhere. Remember, too, Stephen must know of this. He particularly must know. These are my wishes: Starr Faithfull is to be engraved on the stone (white marble) and under it the date of my birth, January 26, 1906, and———, the date of my departure, and under this . . .

> Say not
> good-night
> But in some
> brighter clime bid
> me good-morning

You, Mem, will be placed under the stone with me of course. To have your name on the stone is redundant—for you and I are one and the same and we don't want to confuse Stephen, do we? (I never told him about you.) You'll see to it, friend, I know. I can trust, depend and count on you.

*T*rying to remember it as it happened. Sometimes my thoughts are so disconnected I can't put them together to tell you. I need days of rest to restore my confidence, but then—oh God if I'd only stayed put, lolling around, cleansing myself in the hot tub, purging myself with lime (no ice) a few days longer, things might now be different. But they're not and I'm sick with trying trying to remember what happened—how it happened—what went wrong. I want you to understand the events step by step. Perhaps the Allonal was a mistake and the drink even more of a mistake, but I wanted to do everything to please him—had to, so he wouldn't suspect I was leading him on to a totally different conclusion than anticipated—could I have refused the friendly stingers and not come under suspicion even tho' I was smiling a lot?

He was bald and not as tall as Fou, but no matter—if I'd waited until I found him again I might have waited forever, and Mem, you know patience isn't my strong suit. Anyway, I thought to hell with it, a substitute would be more than acceptable for my purposes, and he had Fou's affable fat Fou face. Yes, I knew the second I walked into the Blue Horse—this is it, he's the one—and I drew him like a magnet. He offered me a drink from his flask— oh god, those stinger cocktails—but I thought, why not? I hadn't had a drink in who knows—days, weeks, minutes. After the first sip my head was as clear as ice and I knew I was home free—what a fool!—

Stanley came in just now with a bowl of tomato soup for his Bambi. There's a blob of sweet whipped cream floating on top. He smiled at me so tenderly and when I thanked him I called him Daddy. It made him happy, I could tell. He's so good to me. He's so good to us all. I feel so bad making him sad. Sounds like a stupid poem, doesn't it, so good, so bad, let's add a so to the sad and we'll be all set, eh Mem? I'm going to stop now for a bit because I'm v. tired. Maybe after the soup I can sleep a little. I'll get back to you later . . .

Let's see—where was I—oh, yes—Stanley. I hate myself for having made Stanley so unhappy—I keep seeing his face, the way he looked when he came into my room at Flower Hospital to take me home. Yes, Mem, I've been in hospital. I want so much to tell him what happened and try to explain it, but I can't, I'm too ashamed, and anyway I don't even know myself, I'm still trying to piece it together—the speakie and the man's face, with the fat bald dome I wanted to crack open, but it was my head instead that cracked open as we left the Blue Horse and went in a taxi to a hotel—the St. Paul on West 60th St. He told them at the desk I was Marie Collins—his wife—and he was—?? Joseph Collins—yes—Joseph, because I remember saying we were like Mary and Joseph checking in at the Inn—but he said he was Catholic and not to say things like that. I was being jokey, but he didn't go along with it, and we got into an argument. I ended up telling him I was Catholic too, so not to try any monkey business. We were in the room by then and I said I'd be going on home.

Stay awhile, he said, and patted me nicely here and there. But I said, No no no I have no interest in anything like that. He took out a bottle and asked if I had any interest in *that*? It was gin, and he went into the bathroom and brought back a glass. Only one? I said. He smirked and said he thought I wasn't interested, so I went into the bathroom myself to get one, forgetting I'd had the stingers and that my mind usually goes blank after two drinks, so I shouldn't have anything more to do with gin or anything else for that matter. He poured gin into my glass and I let him put his hand on my bosoms, but when he tried to kiss me, I said no, I never went all the way—Catholics are virgin girls until they get married and so we'd better stop. He didn't like that one bit and roughed me around, making a racket, calling me names—cock tease, ball snipper—and I kept pushing him away. He got hold of me as I ran for the door and put his hand under my dress, up behind, and I turned around fast and pushed my foot hard, up between his legs. He let out a bloody yelp, but I don't remember much of anything after that. I was told later that a bellboy was called by someone next door because of "trouble in Room 206" and a clerk came up with him and they got in with a pass key. I was lying on the bed without anything on and Collins was sitting there in his B.V.D.'s in an awful state. They called an ambulance and took me to Flower Hospital. I don't remember much of that except they kept calling me Marie. I told them Marie wasn't my name, it was Starr Faithfull, but none of them would believe it. The nurses said I was making fun of them—the doctors too— and this was a serious matter so they put me in the psychopathic ward as an "amnesia victim." I was there all night trying to get out, begging them to call Stanley, but it wasn't until the next day that he came to rescue me. Ma wasn't with him. She was waiting at home, mad as a hornet. She'd learned who this Joseph Collins was, a war veteran discharged from the Army in Massachusetts, who had been a cook on a Clyde Liner out of Boston, and she was determined to learn how I'd met him—on one of your jaunts to the piers perhaps? She went on and on. This Collins man needed money—what did I think about that? And he'd gotten a loan at the Irving Trust Bank. I don't give a damn about that, I told her. Then she said I might give more of a damn if I knew Cousin Andrew might be back of it. That threw me, but when I asked her—pleaded with her to tell me why, she zippered up like a clam and wouldn't open her mouth except later to say to shut up because that was the end of it. I keep begging Stanley to tell me what she meant about Fou, but all he does is shake his head and look so sad I can't bear it.

I'm staying quiet—I never want to see anybody ever again. I'm so scared—quiet, I want to be quiet. Why is Ma hinting that Fou had something to do with it? How could she possibly know about my plan to find him? There's no way she could have gotten her hands on you, Mem—or is there? While I was in Flower, maybe? I'm sick with worry and confusion. Tell me, did she get at you? If she did, she knows all my secrets and I've nothing left.

*D*oes Ma mean that Fou is in some way connected with Collins?

*H*ow are you?

I pleaded with her to tell me and she finally broke down and said that things had been difficult lately and "dear Cousin Andrew" had not been behaving with his usual understanding of the situation. What situation? I asked her. "Well, dear," she said—"your health, you know." No, I don't, I shouted at her. Stanley came in—so unlike him, but he did. He came in and stood there while Ma blurted out that she feared for my safety, feared that he might harm me in some way so he wouldn't have me on his hands anymore as a responsibility. "Hasn't it occurred to either one of you that it's very strange, odd, peculiar, to say the least, that this Collins man was let go scot-free to leave the hotel, walk out without a care in the world, while you, Starr, were on a stretcher being taken in an ambulance to Flower Hospital as Marie Collins? Hasn't any of that dawned on either one of you?" Ma was looking at Stanley, then at me. "Hasn't it dawned on you that our dear Cousin Andrew might just be sick to death of the lot of us and not want to be responsible anymore?" I started crying that I didn't want to be his or anyone's responsibility. Bambi, Bambi, Stanley kept saying, we love you, we'll take care of you. I don't want you to take care of me—I can take care of myself—but I was crying so they couldn't understand what I was saying. "This Collins creature"—Ma raised her voice—"this Collins creature—Andrew may have hired him to"—"Shut up, Helen," Stanley shouted. "Can't you see the state the child's in?" I'm not a child, I cried out. "Stop it, stop it," Ma shrieked and kept at it, "stop it," and she whacked me on the head. "Stop it or I'll call Snodgrass." "Helen doesn't mean that—" Stanley was real mad and he pushed Ma out of the room and slammed the door as she tried to get back in. "Helen didn't mean it," he said again, and he put his arms around me and rocked me to and fro, to and fro, humming something or other until there were no more sobs in me and my arms and legs felt like they were falling, falling into a tingling tingling into a numbness until—until I couldn't move my arms or my hands or my legs or anything and that's all I remember until I woke up, who knows when, but it was dark and Congo was lying in the bed close to me and the house was quiet and still as they'd all gone out and no one was home.

There's been no more mention of Snodgrass since that night. Ma acts like none of it happened. So does Stanley. Tooka was out when the screaming was on. So she knows nothing. At least I think she doesn't.

This morning I woke up believing that this would be the day I'd hear from him—Bill—that everything would be all right—be as it was before. But before what?

I've been invited to a swell party. Better rest up and go—Bill might be there. But what if he isn't—what if Fou's there instead? Fou in costume to fool me—Cardinal's vermilion so I'd trust him. Little does he know my thoughts on religion these days—if he did he'd soon come up with something less colorful. Would it make a difference tho'?—he knows it's in my nature to be trusting, and seeing him costumed as a religious personage I'd be sure to hasten towards him eager to sink to my knees and confess my sins, seek absolution. Yes—he knows me well, knows that's exactly what I'd do. He'd be alone. The girl wouldn't be with him. She'd be going towards him.

*D*ecided not to go to the party—but you knew that already, didn't you, Mem.

*A*nother day of depression—Blue Monday. What can I expect? It will soon be light.

*T*he *Franconia* docked yesterday. No word from Bill—nothing.

I have experienced every sensation life holds and if he doesn't come to me soon, I have nothing to live for.

*T*he days slip by and I forget about things. I still hurt, but it's disconnected, has nothing to do with anything. No, it has to do with nothing. Maybe it does but I've forgotten.

*S*ometimes, I'll catch a glimpse of the stripes on a scarf worn by a passerby and I'll remember Bill had a tie with a pattern almost the same, and he falls into my gut whole, and I feel his body and his hands, so strong and clean when he took my head and held it as he did that first night, when he looked into my eyes and said he could help me and I believed him. Or was it the night after we made love—when he looked at me and said that? No—it was the first night. I'm sure of it. Because it was after that he went away and when I saw him again, in Room 526 at the Waldorf—after that everything changed and I'll never get it back.

*T*he only real pal I can count on is my dog (present company excluded). Congo, I say, you're a pal I can trust. He comes right over, jumps up onto my lap and looks at me so true. What a friend. I really love that dog, and forgive me for saying this, Mem, but it's nice to have a pal you can trust who's also able to respond to you, even if he can't talk.

*I*t's dawn, Mem, and guess where I am? Once again in my St. Luke's garden sitting under my tree. Not a soul in sight except Congo. He's curled up beside me on the bench. The light around us is flat like it could be a late summer's evening instead of an early spring dawn. So who knows which way is up or down, eh? Think of the times, Mem, when I pressed my lips against the windowpane to warm the falling snowflakes as they swirled against it. But the pane of glass was between us and I couldn't break through. I longed so to be part of everything, yes—for then I would be out of pain. Now—I am part of all that surrounds me for I have broken out of myself and—I'm free. Free of Bill, for he has faded into distant landscape, and AJP has become naught but the forgotten nightmare of a child. If only I can hold onto this when I leave the garden. It's so clear to me now, it always is when I am here because there's no one around to turn me into someone else. But already I'm changing as the light is changing. Changing as people start hurrying by on their way towards whatever it is they are hurrying to. Have to leave now. Someone just came into the garden—to tend something. Good morning, Miss, he says. I don't like the look of him, Mem—let's go.

A week later—Just reread what I told you in the garden— can't grasp any of it. We'll talk about it later. Have to rush now—meeting Rollo somewhere—late late late—

*H*e shoots in and out of my mind—Fou's bald head turning into Boofy's bald head mixing me up and I look at myself in the mirror and think what's going on—? What's going on?

I really miss May Lark. Had a postcard from her. She's still churning away in Vermont—may become a nun. No one even asks me about her anymore.

· · ·

*M*em, I can't believe this has happened. I must be dreaming. I'm going to see Bill. Just when all hope was lost a letter comes and he wants to see me—how about dinner some night when his ship's back in New York? Oh God—dinner? Forget about dinner, forget about lunch, forget about tea, forget about food. If only I can set eyes on him again.

I found out when the *Franconia* lands—oh God, I have to wait weeks. Well—two.

*S*pend hours arranging and rearranging my bureau drawers, putting sachet among undies and rearranging the books on my shelves. Everything must be perfect, I mean not only me but the room I set foot out of on my way to meet him—that is when he does arrive.

*I*t's TOMORROW.

I'm spinning like a top—I don't know what to think except now that I have hope I let my true feelings surface and know I'm more in love with him than ever before—could that be possible? Yes, yes, it could and it is. I had definitely decided before this dinner date that he'd respect me more if I didn't go to bed with him but waited till the next date, or maybe the next or the next, but once in his presence previous decisions, plans, everything flew out of my head. I'd go into detail but I'm so in a tizzy I can't seem to gather my thoughts together. I'll try to take it one step at a time . . . First—we went to Sherry's for dinner but all he talked about was the downfall of King Alfonso of Spain weeks ago and then he went on into Chiang Kai-shek and the fighting rebels on two fronts. I'm not much up on international politics and tried to come up with something, anything, to say, but finally decided (wisely, don't you think?) to keep silent and listen. I couldn't make sense of any of it, not having read up on these events, and in the middle of this it dawned on me that he might be rambling on so because my listening, adoring attitude was putting out tenta-

cles and making him nervous. So I adored less and stopped listening so intently. I concentrated on folding my napkin in a different
way on my lap. Something about my manner must have caught
his attention because he changed the subject to me and said he'd
been worried about me and "heard I hadn't been feeling well
lately." Not true at all, I told him most emphatically—why do
you say that?—do I look ill? No no, beauty, he hastened to say,
but it put me on edge—what had he heard? I couldn't stop from
interrupting him, even tho' I was trying to control my apprehen-
sion—I kept asking him if he'd listened to gossip about me and
if so from God knows who, pray tell? I could not compose myself
into the calm lovely person I wanted to be for him, but finally I
must have succeeded because things eased up and he took my
hand—how about coffee at my place? I'd like that, I said. Yes, I
very much liked the idea of going back to that room I'd behaved
so disastrously in over the Marion Davies spoon. I'd never
stopped worrying that the memory of that lingered in his mind as
it did in mine. I more than liked the idea of going back there to
redeem myself by having everything perfect so the other memory
would be erased as if it had never happened. As we left Sherry's I
fully intended to do that, Mem, fully intended we go back to
those rooms so that he'd make love to me on that bed in the alcove as the Big Ben clock tickey-tocked away. But it was not to be
because in the taxi on the way there, he'd gotten hard, unzipped
his trousers actually, and put my hand on his ding-dong. So I
grabbed it and ran my cupped hand up and down over it which
pleased him, I know, because he got quite crazy with excitement.
There we were, not giving a thought to the driver who was sitting
so close to us up in the front seat. Anyway, it happened in my
hand right there in the backseat, even though it certainly didn't
happen for me. How could it? Still, it did give me a thrill to excite
him so. I do do it like that rather well. May Lark told me long ago
never to touch a ding-dong like it was a stick of celery (some girls
make that mistake). A ding-dong must be approached with a firm
grip (you can't hurt it, she says), that's what a ding-dong likes,
you have to take charge, and she showed me how to do just that
using the Coke bottle (so handy for all kinds of things), but this
time she pretended it was a ding-dong as she showed me how to
do it right. So I've had a lot of practice one way or another and
would have put my mouth on him if it hadn't been for the driver
who kept looking at us in his rearview mirror, even tho' I'd put

my scarf over Bill's lap and who was to know what was really going on except Bill and me. By the time we climbed the steps and got to Bill's room, he seemed tired and yawned while he was making the coffee. I was so happy I'd pleased him in the taxi and didn't want to press my luck so I took a few sips and said it was time to go home as I had an early modeling appointment in the morning. He took me back in a taxi and here I am, Mem. It's midnight. Everything's going to be all right, isn't it?

*F*lowers arrived—red roses and a card. On it—*Bill*—nothing else.

*N*ot a word since the roses. I keep going over the last time I saw him, trying to figure out what I did wrong?? Spring is almost over and I seem to have no more breath to hold inside much less breathe out.

*A*JP has erased himself from my mind. Why I was so obsessed with finding him I can't fathom. I only think of Bill now. Think about Bill or think about not thinking about him—devising ways to cut him out of my heart. Cut him out so the hole I have inside me starts to bleed, blood runs so fast through my veins they'll burst. The blood tinting my skin . . . tinting red—changing into someone else—someone to draw his attention, please him. How about a star tattooed on my forehead in the custom of a Hindu princess and then I'll dance for him by moonlight. But to what music? Can't decide—keep hearing it in my head but have no tune for it, comes as muffled sounds from under wet blankets like the ones they smothered me in at Channing.

*J*ay Stoner took me dancing and longs to take me riding in his plane—a Savoia-Marchetti 80 HP amphibian. He keeps it at the Port Washington airport near his Sands Point house. Yes, I've been out a lot lately with this one and that one. Between this one and that one I read up on international affairs so I'll be more informed the next time I see Bill (for I will see him again I know). Here's one interesting bit of news. In Rome Mussolini's started some purge of the Catholics. If May Lark and I were nuns we'd be among them. Of course we'd have to be in Rome for that to happen but I'm here and she's in Vermont. My this ones and that ones aren't interested in any of this but maybe it's because I don't get the facts straight. When I was telling Jay about the Catholics, biffyness had us enthralled, and all Jay wanted to do was get me back to his studio so I could dance naked for him wearing his fedora. He really likes that hat on me.

I'm going to sit right here in this house until I hear from Bill. I wouldn't go out anyway, it's too hot.

I keep hearing the phone ring—but we haven't got one and I've given up trying to make Ma and Stanley get one. If we did have a phone the ringing I hear would be Bill calling me. There's got to be some answer to this—forget about the phone, I mean an answer to what's happening to my insides, because they're filling up again with tangles. Sometimes one of the tangles loosens, but as that happens another one knots itself over it and pulls even tighter. This knitting started in my head and now it's in my stomach. All day and all night it goes on, even when I'm asleep. Still, there are times when I wake and think okay, it's going to be okay. But most times I wake knowing another piece has been knitted knotted knitted during the night. It's all part of a big sweater started a long time ago, all neat and nice and pretty, oh yes—so pretty. Some days I forget about it but back it comes, that old familiar whatever—knitting away when I'm asleep, getting all mixed up in a bowl—spaghetti covered with glue—that's what it's like—only you can't see it.

*I*t's more hotsy-totsy outside as the days pass and the heat comes up from the pavement, blankets of it float right up under the awning, through the open window into my room, and settle down over me on the bed where I'm lying naked. These hot blankets pile themselves up over me, one by one, which is why I'm so hot and why it keeps getting hotter. Hot as my forehead, which burns my hand when I touch it. Ouch! Maybe I have a fever. Maybe something really is wrong with me, something so terrible I can't talk to anyone about it—even you. If only we had a phone I'd send a radiogram to—

Doctor George Jameson-Carr
S.S. *Franconia*
  Urgent you call me now. I'm a serious person. Starr

That's ten words exactly, including the signature. That's just what I'd say to him. If I could do that he'd come to me, here in my room even though it's so hot you can hardly breathe. He'd understand right away. I know he would. But to get back to those ghoulish dreams—I did mention them, didn't I? Maybe not. Anyway—they've come back lately. Every night, one after the other. Then I'll wake up between them for a bit, press my head against the bedpost—it's a smooth polished wood, but the heat's eaten into it so what good is it to me? None at all.

*H*ow do people live so long? There's this Mother Jones person—I read somewhere she lived to be 100—others whose names slip my mind right now. How do they get through all those years doing this and that? They must know something I don't. Maybe if I live long enough, I'll know too. But I don't want to get old. If I was Mrs. Jameson-Carr and Bill was by my side I wouldn't mind because he'd be old too. We'd look at each other and I'd say Hey, Bill Old Thing, we made it, and he'd smile back and say—oh something. Something perfect and wonderful like *"grow old along with me—the best is yet to be,"* and I'd be happy even though I'd be old and going to die soon.

*T*hose dreams keep coming back. Last night Camilla Foldes showed up most unexpectedly, wearing a Panama hat of all things and smiling a weird smile, like she was older and I was younger and she knew something I didn't. What could it be? And what's she up to these days? I wonder. Now that I think of it, the hat was the one in Marjorie White's Ma's cedar closet, where we had our meetings of The Ten Musketeers Club. That fur animal with beady eyes and greedy smile was snaking around trying to get at me with its horrid little paws. It hung there between the ermine and sable, remember?

*H*ere goes with another letter to Bill. Maybe this one will be good enough to send.

Dear Bill,

You don't mind if I keep calling you that, do you? I hope not, because as I once told you, you're much more Bill than George (to my mind at least). Not that I don't adore George, because I do, and it's certainly most appropriate for formal and professional occasions, but writing as I am now, informally from my room on the second floor where we live, it seems a cozy way of addressing you, n'est-ce pas?

It's hot today, very hot, but I'm cool as can be as I look out across the street at Walker Park which is filled with green leaves and think about you with sea breezes all around you no doubt. Remember the day we walked there—in the park, I mean—it had been snowing, but the snow had stopped and unexpectedly you showed up at my door, merrily taking me for a walk. I re-member it simply because I lost a mitten, yes, that was the day I lost my best mitten—you might even say my favorite of favorite mittens. That's why I remember the day so well. I have a lot, you know—of mittens I mean, not memories. It wasn't the angora one, but the handknit—oh well, who cares. I don't want to bore you with details of my wardrobe. Anyway, it was the day I lost a mitten. You'd taken my hand and I didn't want a silly mitten be-tween us so I took one off and it fell in the snow. It was near the bandstand. I didn't mention it at the time. Later, the next morn-ing, I went to look for it, but more snow had fallen during the night, so—no luck. Even our footprints were covered over, but what matter. I knew we'd been there and I still have one mitten to prove it.

There was quite a racket outside in the park just now, shouts and so on. I didn't pay any attention, since I didn't want to inter-rupt our little tête-à-tête. But Ma and Stanley were in the living room and stuck their heads out the window and saw crowds in the distance behaving in an unruly manner and thought possibly it was a hunger march of park bums organized by the Commu-nists. They scurried down to see what was up, but it turned out only to be NYU freshmen starting a snake dance. How about that! And on this hot hot day. Imagine! Ma still thinks the Com-munists are back of it—oh well.

What's new on the S.S. *Franconia*? How jolly it would have been to have sailed with you. I'm planning another trip to England, soon, very soon. All my friends there keep writing and asking when I'm coming back and I'm always so happy there, so why not?

Well, until later, cher ami, now it's back to D.H. Lawrence and *Women in Love*. I took a break to dash this off to you. If we don't run into each other in London, let me know when you get back. Hope I'll be here, but I may accept another friend's invitation to visit him in Paris. In any event,

A bientôt!
Starr

P.S. Would love to talk to you some day about the D.H. book. It's about the consequences of trying to deny man's union with nature. Most provocative!

*R*emember, Mem, that first day I met him—that Day of Days on the S.S. *Franconia* at a Bon Voyage party. Later when he called me "sweetness" it was like getting a piece of chocolate. Then there are times when he'd be formal, cold, almost like we were hardly acquainted. Still—in spite of himself he was intrigued by me, I could tell. After all, he is the ship's surgeon and had to be professional, I told myself as we walked along the deck of the *Franconia* the day we met. There's lots of time, I kept telling myself, but it didn't help. I couldn't wait to get him off that ship. Alone somewhere—the two of us. I go over it again and again.

*H*e's back again—AJP. But this time the garlicky rabbit is with him. I'm certain Patsy Pierce still has it. She really liked that rabbit. I'm going to look her up and get it back one way or another even if I have to steal it. I've got to get it to Fou some way. They belong together. I'll go up to Boston. No problem about getting to him there once I have rabbit in hand. But what if I can't find Patsy? Don't worry about that now, only when the time comes if I can't find her. I'll have to plan it out carefully—especially what to wear when I see him—he always loved me in pêche—said it was my best color.

I'm—going over things, trying to figure out what I did wrong. I always only wanted one thing and that was to be worthy of Bill, but none of it ever came out right, which made me keep on pretending more and more, only I never found out the right person to pretend to be so as to please him—except that night in the taxi. Maybe? Somebody help me please . . . to find the knack. What a relief it would be not to have to pretend anymore, but "Needs must when the devil drives," as my Ma's often said and God knows I'm one big need, but every time I see him I get weak in the knees, so desperate to attract him I can't stop myself from becoming the giddy creature he already believes me to be with nothing but prettiness to commend her (he hasn't found out yet that's pretense too). If I'd stopped pretending he'd have found out what I'm really like and would never have wanted to see me again—maybe he's already found out and that's why I don't hear from him. If I could merge into him I'd never be afraid again. But he doesn't let me. He thinks I'm just a foxy girl like all the others after him, but the only good that's done me is to get him into bed and now something I've done must be pushing him away, *is* pushing him away— HAS pushed him away. At least I've some pride left. I can hide things (nothing shows on my face) if I want to. I'm good at that—so far I've put up a good front—except for that ghastly night over the Marion Davies spoon when I ran into the street—no, Mem, we can't forget that—nor does he, I'm sure. Oh God. If only I could have another chance, I beg for one more chance to see him again—I know I could make him know how much I love him and then everything will be all right.

*B*ill doesn't even suspect the words don't exist to describe how I feel, or if they do they're in Zulu or some language I'll never master. So what's the use even of telling you when the only thing that'll stop my pain is to get out of my skin and into his? If he'd let me do that I'd never want anything in the world again. I want so much to be good. I do try, honest I do, Mem, I really do, but things happen that keep killing me and even though it's my fault I can't seem to put it right because I can't get back to the beginning

THE MEMORY BOOK OF STARR FAITHFULL

and start over. Maybe I'll have to die first. Don't ask me why—it doesn't make sense, but that's how it is.

*H*eard by chance that Bill's sailing back to England tonight on the *Franconia*—I've got to see him. I'll die if I don't. Yes, Mem, I'm going—you can't stop me, I'll get myself together as best I can—hurry to the ship to wish him Bon Voyage, look my best, be gay and happy . . . happy happy . . .

*O*h God—what a fool—what a fool—what a fool—now I've really done it. Bill will never speak to me again. Forget about the Marion Davies night—that was a curtain raiser—this the finale. Oh I looked ginger peachy all right, in a new outfit, even the hat swell-o, and got myself in the best mood ever to hasten to the S.S. *Franconia*. Everything was going fine until I saw Bill with that girl hanging on his arm, she'd caught his interest I could tell, and I couldn't stop myself, I forged through the crowds, yanked her away, demanded to speak to him urgently right away—had to see him alone. Later, later, he kept saying, I'll come to see you later—we'll talk later but not now—can't you see I'm busy with the passengers? I don't give a fuck about the passengers, I shrieked—I can't remember what happened next, but he must have hustled me away because I remember coming to my senses in his cabin and begging him to love me, telling him that he'd never find another who'd love him as I did. Give me a chance, I pleaded, but the more I begged the angrier he became. Can't you see I'm busy?—oh, he was mad, shaking me—listen to me, woman, how dare you come here like this? Oh Mem, my heart burst with happiness to have him call me woman, because I knew then that he really did love me. I was his woman, am, and always will be and for a moment I thought it was going to be all right and I held him so tight I couldn't breathe—but then a voice—his—shouted—get out of here, woman, I want nothing to do with you. Oh God yes, he hadn't meant it the way I thought—and it set me off on a roller coaster, careening on into a place I know only too well, and he kept saying Go, go!—go! But there was no chance of go for I held tighter as he tried to thrust me away—pried my arms away as they clung, yes, but I didn't care—kept clinging and pleading with him when suddenly the ship started moving and he ran out, as evil faces rushed in through the door, staring at me askance, mumbling among themselves and giving suggestions as to how to get her off the ship. Throw me overboard, throw me overboard, I kept screaming—kill me! What's the use of going on living? He doesn't want me. He hasn't any more use for me. I want to die. If only they'd done that—thrown me overboard. Instead they carried me up on deck and put me in a rope sling and lowered me over the side into a tugboat as I kicked and screamed while crowds gathered along the rails of the ship to watch me being escorted (ha ha) ashore. When they left me off at Pier 56 I got into a taxi and told the driver to take me to a speakie, no matter which, but I changed my mind on the way and told him to take me back to the pier. When I got there I demanded to know when the next boat sailed for Europe, determined to be on it. Not until next week, said the men standing around on the pier. It was a Friday so maybe it was true. Still, I was sure, because of the nuisance I was making, that they were lying to get rid of me. There was a cop lurking around during all this and he gave me a lemon—how the hell did he come up with that? Suck on it, he said, best thing for what ails you. That's a new one on me. He must've been putting me on—Who's loony now? I laughed in his face—Oh, to Hell with the lemon—if only they had thrown me overboard I wouldn't be here now, wouldn't be having to tell you about lemons, wouldn't have to be telling you about humiliation seeping into me telling me there's no hope left, for now I'm truly nothing.

I'm sending him this letter. Yes, I have my plans.

May 31, 1931

Dear Bill,

I am going (definitely now—I've been thinking of it for a long time) to end my worthless, disorderly bore of an existence—before I ruin anyone else's life as well. I certainly have made a sordid, futureless mess of it all. I am dead, dead sick of it. It is no one's fault but my own—I hate everything so—life is horrible. Being a sane person, you may not understand—I take dope to forget and drink to try and like people, but it is of no use.

I am mad and insane over you. I hold my breath to try to stand it—take Allonal in the hope of waking happier, but that home-sick feeling never leaves me. I have, strangely enough, more of a feeling of peace, or whatever you call it, now that I know it will soon be over. The half hour before I die will, I imagine, be quite blissful.

You promised to come to see me. I realize absolutely that it will be the one and only time. There is no earthly reason why you should come. If you do, it will be what I call an act of marvelous generosity and kindness. What I did yesterday was very horrible, although I don't see how you could lose your job, as it must have been clearly seen what a nuisance you thought me.

If I don't see you again—goodbye. Sorry to so lose all sense of humor, but I am suffering so that all I want is to have it over with. It's become such a hell as I couldn't have imagined.

If you come to see me when you are in this time, you will be a sport—you are assured by this letter of no more bother from me.

My dear—

Starr

*A*nother letter must go off right now too, a separate letter that he can show the S.S. *Franconia* people saying it was all my fault and that he in no way should be held responsible for my behavior. Everybody's saying he'll lose his job because of me. Fools.

June 2, 1931

Dr. George Jameson-Carr
c/o Cunard Co.
Liverpool, England

I want to apologize and to tell you how deeply I regret my conduct on the *Franconia* last Friday. I had come down hoping to renew our acquaintance, but I fear I only made a fool of myself and that it was very disagreeable for you. I had brought some drinks on the boat with me and drank them too fast. I become intensely irrational when I drink and I want you to know how deeply sorry I am for the embarrassment I must have caused you.

Very sincerely,
Starr Faithfull

June 4, 1931

Hello, Bill, Old Thing:

It's all up with me now. This is something I am going to put through. The only thing that bothers me about it—the only thing I dread—is being outwitted and prevented from doing this, which is the only possible thing for me to do. If one wants to get away with murder one has to jolly well keep one's wits about one. It's the same way with suicide. If I don't watch out and accomplish my end this time. No ether, Allonal, or window jumping. I don't want to be maimed. I want oblivion. If there is an afterlife it would be a dirty trick—but I am sure fifty million priests are wrong. That is one of those things one *knows.*

Nothing makes any difference now. I love to eat and can have one delicious meal with no worry over gaining. I adore music and am going to hear some good music. I believe I love music more than anything else. I am going to enjoy my last cigarettes. I won't worry because men flirt with me in the streets—I shall encourage them—I don't care who they are. I'm afraid I've always been a rotten "sleeper"; it's the preliminaries that count with me. It doesn't matter, though.

It's a great life when one has twenty-four hours to live. I can be rude to people. I can tell them they are too fat or that I don't like their clothes, and I don't have to dread being a lonely old woman, or poverty, obscurity, or boredom. I don't have to dread living on without ever seeing you, or hearing rumors such as "the women all fall for him" and "he entertains charmingly." Why in hell shouldn't you! But it's more than I can cope with—this feeling I have for you. I have tried to pose as clever and intellectual, thereby to attract you, but it was not successful, and I couldn't go on.

I don't have to worry, because there are no words in which to describe this feeling I have for you. The words love, adore, worship have become meaningless. There is nothing I can do but what I am going to do. I shall never see you again. That is extraordinary. Although I can't comprehend it any more than I can comprehend the words always or time. They produce a merciful numbness.

Starr

. . .

With this final letter sent I set a seal upon my heart. I think about it now all the time. Different and varied scenarios play themselves out, project themselves like movies on a silver screen. Sometimes I put the projector on rewind—play them backwards—or torment myself that none of them will work and I'll have to live the rest of my life without ever seeing him again.

Went to Lord & Taylor and found the dress—silk, the yellow of jonquils. So smooth it slips over my body like minnows from the pail in the fairy tale when the Princess poured them over the naked boy's head—fanciful, Mem, but true. Yes, this is the dress I shall wear on my last day. I had a soda at Schrafft's on the way back. The cold ice cream going down my throat was the only thing that was real. It was a hot day.

Today I went to St. Luke's garden with the intent of sitting for a while under my tree, looking around before saying final farewell. But when I got there and looked through the gate it was exactly as I'd remembered so I didn't go in. No, there was no need to. I'd already said goodbye.

What do I want to do on my last day? It shall only be what *I* want, what *I* choose. My choice, yes, no one else's. Mine. There shall be no one to please but myself. And where will this last perfect day end? Perhaps a hotel—one I've never been to before. I'll check in, go up to a room and put the Do Not Disturb sign on the door.

I haven't slept and it's now the hour before dawn. Mysterious things happen then or so I've heard said. Sea creatures on beaches return to their habitat—birds wake in nests—call to each other across empty spaces of dark sky. How do they know the dawn is coming, what signal tells them that day is soon?—I can only say that in this hour I too have heard that signal and with it has come another answer. It's a risk of course, but then the idea of Russian roulette has always appealed to me. It is a risk because plans can go awry—and if mine do I'll be back where I started and that must not be. Mem, listen and I'll explain what I'm going to do. I'll take the train to Long Beach—it's only an hour away—and it's by the sea—it must take place by the sea. I almost went to Long Beach one summer—remember, with Rollo, but at the last minute he changed his mind, said he needed a restful evening and it was too frequented, too much the popular place to be on weekends with the world and his wife there for sunny days on the balcony of the Bathing Pavilion and later dining and dancing at Healey's or the Lido by the Sea. I also remember seeing that stretch of beach from the railing of the *Aquitania* with AJP on our way to Europe. The boardwalk too and the Lido—I see these now in my mind's eye in the distance as I did then a fata morgana. But soon it will not be illusion—soon it will be real—for I shall be on the beach looking out at ships sailing by, yes, seeing them this time from a different point of view. It occurs to me as I'm telling you this that I'll never again have to hear the "All Ashore Who's Going Ashore"—that sinking knell I used to dread, telling me the Bon Voyage party was over and I must leave, go to shore to watch the crowds sail away as I am left behind—but I digress—what I'm trying to tell you is that I have chosen the death I deserve. Ah!—no fear of flirts that day as I carry out my plan, no not at all, I'll encourage them, in fact, lead them on. I'll let myself be picked up by a stranger, but oh how I'll flirt with others first—in my yellow dress strolling along the boardwalk, the silkiness swinging around my legs promising heaven underneath. I'll be choosy, though, turning them away until Mr. Right comes along—oh I'll know you all right, Mr. Right, when you catch my eye—my smile beckons you, promises you the stars of starry eyes, the moon. And once we've met, the preliminaries will last as long as I decree—we'll have dinner in some nice place—the Lido, where there's music—for there must be music, yes, and a long dinner with one or two sweets for dessert, maybe three to linger over until the moment comes when I choose to leave. Then we'll drift down to the beach, to the sea. I'll take off shoes, stockings, to feel the waves over my feet as we walk in the hot summer night, footprints erased by the waves as we move on. When he touches me I'll pull away, teasing, but only a little (nothing impulsive this time, no moving too fast—nothing to tip my hand). And soon—so persuasive is his wooing—I'll cleave to him, let his manly arm support me as we move along the beach whispering sweet things to each other. I'll wave to a passing ocean liner, confiding to him about friends on board no doubt already missing me, but since this chance encounter I miss them not at all. He'll touch me oh so tenderly, and beneath the yellow silk my bosoms rise to meet his hand—ah yes, and yes . . . *moment of peril, perilous sweet* . . . (I read that somewhere) . . . *when woman joins herself to man.* I'll not be shy, as a snake sheds skin I'll let my dress slip upon the sand and then—then, Mem, I'll laugh, I'll laugh, Mem—NO! And laugh again, provoking him to strike, and in the killing I shall be punished for my guilt and in turn pass guilt onto him . . . Is it true that when you're drowning your whole life passes before you to live over again? Yes, of course. As I hit the sand he'll hold my head under water—salt sea will be my breath—ah yes—I'll breathe deep, once more so deep—oh God—to be forced to live it over again from the beginning.

Good-bye, Mem

Soon after Starr Faithfull's death in June 1931 her diary, which she called her *Memory Book*, was found by the police as they rummaged through her library of treasured books at 12 St. Luke's Place, where she had lived with her family.

According to the tabloids, the "love diary" had been turned over to District Attorney Elvin H. Edwards. Edwards announced, "Starr Faithfull's diary will never be made public. I have made an agreement with the family to burn the diary as soon as we are through with it, without showing it to any person not officially connected with the investigation into her death. I intend to keep that agreement. No reporter has seen any part of it and none will see it."

And none did. But the diary was not burned. It was returned to Starr's mother, Helen, and her stepfather, Stanley Faithfull, who, through lawyers, turned it over to A. J. Peters in acceptance of a final settlement.

And there the matter was thought to rest until the diary, which was assumed to have been destroyed by AJP, turned up quite by chance during renovation by new owners of the Peters' family house in Jamaica Plain in Boston. It was discovered in a lockbox hidden behind paneling of the library, and with it a diverse collection of items—a linen napkin from the Narragansett Hotel, a velvet jewel box from Shreve, Crump & Lowe, empty, six loose pearl beads, mother-of-pearl opera glasses, and a valentine, made by a child, upon which was written—

XYFWW   QTAJX   FSIWJB

Afterword

The Memory Book of Starr Faithfull is a work of fiction based on a true story. Starr Faithfull, her mother, her father, her stepfather, and her sister were real people. So were Andrew J. Peters, who was Starr's cousin and was mayor of Boston from 1918 to 1922, and his wife, Martha Phillips Peters (although the Peterses had five sons and no daughters). There really was a Memory Book, and whatever it was the police read in it sent them to Boston to question Andrew J. Peters after Starr's death. Despite the District Attorney's promise that the diary would "never be made public," some revelations in it found their way to the press: that Starr's intimate relationship with "AJP," as she referred to him, had begun when she was eleven and he forty-five and about to announce his candidacy for mayor; that he had read to his young cousin from Havelock Ellis's *Studies in the Psychology of Sex;* that he had taught her to sniff ether; that Starr had accompanied him on several trips, including one to Europe; that after two nights of "Horror, Horror, Horror!!!" with AJP, Starr wrote, "Mr. Peters would be very relieved to find me dead." There are certain other known facts: that Starr had had a nervous breakdown not long after moving to New York with her family, and that Andrew J. Peters subsequently paid considerable sums of money to Starr's mother and stepfather, who apparently had no other means of support. A few entries in my version of Starr's Memory Book are "real" — quoted from the newspapers of the time — as are her last letters, to Dr. George Jameson-Carr, a ship's surgeon with the Cunard Line; these led the jurors at the inquest into Starr's death to reach a verdict of suicide.

Those are the facts as we know them. The rest — including what was said, as well as what happened (except as noted above) when AJP and Starr were alone together; what went on within the Wyman and Peters households and, later, when Starr was living with her family in New York; the discovery of certain objects in the Peters house after AJP's death—is all fiction: the way I imagine it to have happened.

A Note on the Type

The text of this book was set in Centaur, the only typeface designed by Bruce Rogers (1870–1957), the well-known American book designer. A celebrated penman, Rogers based his design on the roman face cut by Nicolas Jenson in 1470 for his Eusebius. Jenson's roman surpassed all of its forerunners and even today, in modern recuttings, remains one of the most popular and attractive of all typefaces.

The italic used to accompany Centaur is Arrighi, designed by another American, Frederic Warde, and based on the Chancery face used by Lodovico degli Arrighi in 1524.

Composed by ComCom, a division of Haddon Craftsmen, Allentown, Pennsylvania. Printed and bound by The Haddon Craftsmen, Scranton, Pennsylvania

Heart map by Madeline Sorel
Designed by Anthea Lingeman